# In the Absence of a Body

## A Frankie Wilson Story Volume 2

By K. Britt-Badman

This book is the sequel to In the strictest Confidence.

# Chapter 1

*I WARNED YOU BITCH!*

My eyes were transfixed by the words daubed in red paint on my solid oak front door. I could see the words, read the words, and yet I couldn't make sense of them. I was aware that there was a part of me that understood the ramifications of the words that gripped me. And yet, the remaining part refused to acknowledge it. Then, as if my mind decided I could handle it, the meaning hit me with the force of a sledgehammer. I lost control of my body. My knees buckled, and I slid to the floor. I was conscious of the fact that I was shaking quite violently, but I couldn't control it.

First there was Verity's death and now this. They were connected. It all made sense now. He'd killed her! She hadn't committed suicide; these words proved it. He'd killed her!

Was he threatening me? Was I next? Or, was he simply letting me know that he considered me responsible for her death? Perhaps he was right!

I grasped the wooden doorframe and hauled myself to my feet. Using my hand to shield my eyes from the glare of the midday sun, I frantically scanned the street for any sign of him.

Was he watching me? He had rung the doorbell only moments ago to alert me to the message he had left for me, so he couldn't have gone far. The paint was still wet. I was sure it hadn't been there when I'd returned from my monthly supervision meeting with Rachel only a few minutes ago.

Out of the corner of my eye, I saw a movement from behind a parked car halfway up the street. Was it him? I was sure he would want to see my reaction to his handiwork. He would want to see my fear; to enjoy it even.

Come on Frankie, my brain was screaming at my body. MOVE NOW! Don't let yourself be a victim. Don't give him the satisfaction. As if by my command, I felt the adrenalin surge through my limbs. My body had suddenly been freed from its invisible restraints, and my legs propelled me into the house.

As I slammed my front door, I just had time to see the back of the person who had been obscured by the parked car walking up the street. It was a woman. I felt myself relax a little. I had been wrong. He wasn't watching me. I shut my eyes. With my back against my front door I allowed it to support me for a moment as I gathered the strength to locate my mobile phone and call PC Acton.

Where had I put my mobile phone? I had only just put it down. So, why couldn't I remember where I had put it? Opening my eyes and pushing myself away from the front door, I propelled myself forward with intent. But it was short-lived as I came to a blinding halt a matter of nanoseconds later.

I was staring straight into the eyes of Glenn Froom. He was standing in my kitchen with his mobile phone in his hand. I knew the instant I looked into his eyes; I had the answer to my earlier question: he meant to kill me.

Strangely, I felt completely calm. My body felt light as if I were floating.

I noticed how smartly dressed Glenn was. He was dressed far too smartly to be painting graffiti on front doors. I found myself wondering if he had got any paint on himself. I always changed into my old tracksuit when I did any painting.

He seemed to be saying something to me. His mouth was moving, but I wasn't aware of the words. He was saying it again.

"I said, you're scared, Frankie, aren't you? I could hear the fear in your voice a moment ago on the telephone, and I can see it for myself now." He was grinning, revelling in what he perceived as my fear.

He'd been the silent caller. I was considering his question. Was I scared? I wasn't sure. I didn't seem to be feeling much of anything. I was numb. Perhaps I was in shock I reasoned sensibly. Yes, that must be it.

I noticed his watch; I remembered admiring it when he came to meet Verity from a session one day. It was a very expensive Tag Heuer. He followed my gaze and lifted his wrist as if to offer me a closer look.

"It's a Tag Heuer," he commented.

I nodded. "Yes, I know," I muttered.

"I have to say, Frankie, this is not how I imagined this scenario would play out. I imagined you would try to run or fall in a screaming, crying heap. I have to give you ten out of ten for unpredictability. Never in my wildest dreams, did I imagine we'd be discussing my watch in the moments before I kill you." He took a slow step toward me.

I imagined the purpose of his long, lingering step was to both prolong my agony and his enjoyment. He was enjoying himself; I was sure of it. This man was a sadist. He was going to enjoy watching me suffer as I imagined he had enjoyed watching Verity suffer. The thought of Verity seemed to galvanize me into action. She was dead! He'd killed her!

"Why did you do it?" I asked with more force than I'd expected considering the situation I found myself in.

"Do what? Buy the watch? Break in to your house? Kill Verity? Let's face it, Frankie, that question could have so many different answers. You really do need to be more specific."

While he'd been speaking, he'd taken another step toward me. I instinctively took a step backwards, which brought a wry smile to his face.

"There is no escape, Frankie," he said, while pulling a silk scarf from his pocket.

I must have appeared confused because he seemed compelled to explain the presence of the scarf.

"This is one of Verity's scarves." He held it up for my inspection. "You should recognise it. I chose it because I knew you would recognise it; what with you being so clever." He paused, and I realised he was giving me time to look at it. So I looked.

My brain was unable to comprehend anything beyond my current situation. It was so preoccupied with survival that it was struggling, unsurprisingly, to focus on a nondescript silk scarf. Did I recognise it? It was black, silk and exceptionally plain. Verity had worn black clothing a lot. Now I come to think of it, I was sure I had seen her wearing a black scarf. He frowned. His impatience for my recognition of the scarf was evident as he held it at arm's length and waggled it in front of me.

I nodded slowly. "Yes, I recognise it. Verity wore it during our sessions together."

A large grin spread across his face. "You see, I knew you wouldn't have forgotten." He started to wrap one end of the scarf around his left hand and then the other around his right. He moved his hands apart pulling the delicate material taut as he did so.

Menacingly, he took another step toward me; his intentions were obvious. I took another step backwards, and found my back was once again against the front door. Only this time, it wasn't protecting me from the outside world; it was my barrier to it.

I decided in that instant that if this was it, and I was going to die; I was at least going to get some answers to some of my questions. Before I could ask my original question again, but this time more specifically, Glenn cut across my thoughts with questions of his own.

"So, have you worked out why I'm going to kill you with Verity's scarf yet?"

Shaking my head, I remained mute.

"Are you sure? You're such a clever lady. Always going around telling people what's best for them. How they should live their lives. Who they should live their lives with," he said pointedly.

I could see his muscles trembling with an all-consuming rage; a fine sweat had broken out on his face. He was ready to wrap that scarf around my neck, and watch the life drain out of me. If I was to buy myself some time, I needed to start talking right now. Not that I knew if that time was going to prove useful, or if I was going to end up dead anyway.

Quietly, I mumbled, "Are you using Verity's scarf because you think I'm responsible for her death?"

"You see, I knew you'd understand. I don't THINK you're responsible for her death. I KNOW you are. She'd still be alive now if she had never walked into those counselling sessions. You filled her head with all that nonsense. What was it she called it?" I could see he was trying to recollect something Verity had said. "That's it – 'empowerment'." He had virtually spat his last word out such was his animosity toward me.

"So, how did her feelings of empowerment result in her death?" I asked.

This simple question appeared to enrage him further.

"You know how it resulted in her death. Don't insult my intelligence. You made her feel that she could leave me. She would never have even attempted to deceive me before she met you. Suddenly, my quiet, acquiescent wife is lying to me, and sneaking off to see you even though she promised me she wouldn't."

"How did you find out she attended her final counselling session?"

"Oh, it was easy. After I rang you to see if she was going to show up, and you said she had cancelled, I decided to give her a call at her desk. She wasn't there. Her colleague had said she would be away from her desk for the next hour. It was obvious that she had gone to see you. I decided to bide my time. Wait until I got back from my business trip before I punished her for her defiance."

Based on what he'd just said he hadn't intended to kill her at that point, just punish her. Although, I had to consider that his definition of punishment may have meant death. It was time to get an answer to my original non-specific question.

"Did you kill Verity?" I asked. And desperately wanted to add, is that specific enough for you? But now was not the time to inflame the situation.

"You killed her, the minute you gave her that card for a women's refuge."

He was refusing to take any responsibility for Verity's death. I needed to be even more specific it would seem. "Did you push Verity off of the multi-storey car park today?" I asked bluntly.

"Yes, I did. But you see you are responsible for both her and your own impending death. I made sure the only identification she had on her was the card you gave her. I wanted to make sure the police rang you first. I hoped I would be able to watch your face as you took that call. To watch as you realised it was because of you she was dead."

Had he been watching me when I heard the news about Verity? I had answered my mobile when I pulled up outside, and had let myself in and walked through to the kitchen.

He was watching me intently and followed my gaze toward the wide-open back door. "I watched you through your kitchen window. I had wanted to see guilt on your face at the news, but instead you just looked grief-stricken."

"I am grief-stricken. I liked Verity. I had thought you loved her, and yet you've killed her. Why?"

"Because of you," he exploded. "You encouraged her to leave me. You gave her that card; even put your own mobile phone number on it. Why was that? Did you want her to ring you when she'd left me so you could be sure you'd succeeded?"

I was shaking my head as he spoke. "No, it wasn't like that at all. I was just providing her with information. I was offering her options."

"She didn't need options. She was my wife, and that was the only option she needed."

"How did you come across the card anyway? I had thought she was going to destroy it."

"You're so curious, aren't you? You want to know every detail. It's OK. I'll answer your questions, but only because I don't want you to die thinking you've outsmarted me at any stage." He was shaking his head with a smug smile on his face. "I found the card under the trays on her desk at work. She didn't realise I knew, but she would slide things under those trays that she didn't want me to see. She thought it was a safe place."

She must have intended destroying the card later when she had a chance. Perhaps she got distracted when she got back to her desk and just forgot about it. Somehow, I wasn't entirely comfortable with that explanation. She had been so careful, so aware of Glenn's wrath should he find it. Still, for whatever reason and I would probably never know, she had not destroyed the card. And now she was dead because of it. She was dead because I had given her that card.

"Starting to feel guilty yet?" Glenn asked, keenly observing my facial expressions as he spoke.

"Yes," I said honestly. "I am."

"Good," he said smugly. "All of this could have been avoided. If you'd just done as you were told in the first place."

I was puzzled, and it must have shown as he went on to explain.

"The graffiti told you to back off. Oh and by the way, you really shouldn't walk alone after dark. It really isn't safe you know."

It had been him. He had followed me back from the takeaway that night and painted the graffiti on my door. I hadn't realised at the time that the graffiti referred to Verity.

"Earlier, you said my questioning wasn't specific enough for you. Well I'm afraid your graffiti isn't specific enough for me. I had no idea that it was you following me that night, or what the graffiti referred to."

"You mean that you interfere in so many lives it could have been any number of people. Somehow, I'm not surprised."

"I'm just trying to help people."

"Well, you helped Verity. You helped her meet her maker sooner than planned."

This was hopeless. What was the point of anything? I had tried to help, and Verity had ended up dead. I was next.

"I followed you home from work that day. You stopped at some school first; I sat there watching you as you walked back to the car with your kid. Then you drove home, and I sat and waited. When you left the house, and

I realised you were walking somewhere alone. I couldn't resist. I had to follow you. I wanted to have a little fun at your expense. I could tell you were scared. But you weren't sure what to do, were you?"

"I wasn't sure whether I was being followed or whether I was being paranoid."

He laughed out loud taking pleasure in my discomfort.

"I wanted to shake you up a little, so that when you saw the graffiti you took the threat more seriously."

"Oh, I did take it seriously. I just thought it concerned something else."

"Well that was a mistake with serious consequences, wouldn't you say?"

"I would," I said gravely.

"You, so clearly, didn't heed my advice; you continued to see Verity. You were having a profound effect on her. She was changing and getting stronger somehow. Of course, she tried to hide it from me, but I could tell. She even stood up to her supervisor, Maria. She would never have done that before."

"She told you about that?" I was surprised that she would have told him about successfully tackling her supervisor.

He shook his head. "No, but I have my ways of finding things out," he said.

I could remember Verity saying pretty much the same thing to me when she had asked me to lie should anyone enquire about her attending her final session. I remembered the way she had darted into the room and closed the door quickly for fear of being observed. It couldn't have been Glenn she was concerned about at the time because he was away on business.

"I decided, as she grew stronger, you were more of a threat than I had first thought. And that frightening you wasn't enough as you weren't backing off. In fact, I suspected she had been talking to you about things she shouldn't." He was staring at me intensely.

I gave nothing away. I was terrified, and he knew it. I hadn't been able to save Verity. The least I could do was keep my promise of confidentiality.

He seemed to decide I wasn't going to confirm or deny his suspicions. "No matter," he said shrugging. "I'm sure she did, or you wouldn't have given her the card for the refuge, now would you?"

I remained mute. It didn't seem to matter to him as he continued.

"I saw my opportunity to get rid of you, once and for all, when you were leaving that block of flats that day. I had been following you, deciding when and where to kill you."

I shuddered at the matter-of-factness of his tone.

He continued seemingly unaware or disinterested in the effect his words were having upon me, "It was relatively quiet, not many witnesses. There was a young guy walking down the street, but I figured he probably wouldn't want to get involved. I thought it would be easy to just hit you and leave you for dead in the street, but somehow you managed to evade me."

It had been him behind the wheel of that car. It now made sense that the witness hadn't identified Lee Mason, James Simons or Andy Brooks as the driver.

"Verity thought I was away on business that week and the following week. I was, for the most part, but not the whole time. A man needs some time to himself, don't you think, Frankie?" The question was rhetorical; he didn't pause for a response. "It was time for a little fun."

What did he mean by that? I wondered. It wasn't unusual for very jealous, controlling men or women to have affairs. They seemed to behave in exactly the way they feared their partners would.

"Verity was lovely. Well, she was before you started influencing her, but she wasn't any fun any more."

Not fun, I thought. That was hardly surprising given the beatings he was giving her, and the complete control he had over her every move. Not for the first time, I considered the irony of someone being attracted to a person for their lively, gregarious personality only to extinguish it in them, for fear of losing them to someone else who would find those qualities equally attractive. Then to go on to vilify them for not being the person they first met.

"You've got to have some fun in your life, haven't you, Frankie? She's a good girl. She understands the situation, or perhaps I should say understood as things have changed."

So, he was having an affair. He pulled the silk scarf taut and advanced upon me with renewed intent.

I needed to keep him talking. "Why today?" I blurted out. "Why did you kill her today?" My last session with Verity had been last Wednesday. Today was Thursday, so it had been over a week since he'd learned that she had defied him by coming to our session.

He hesitated, his resolve to finish me in the next few seconds wavering. He seemed keen to let me know every detail before he made sure of my demise.

"Today was my only free day. My only window of opportunity you might say."

I gasped at his coolness. He had planned to kill both of us on his day off. Was he planning to go back to work tomorrow as if nothing had happened? Was he completely mad?

"After I found the card, I decided killing you wouldn't be enough; Verity needed to go too. I couldn't have her leave me. No one leaves me! I planned a trip into town on our day off. I suggested I buy her some brighter clothes.

You should have seen her eyes light up at the prospect. Of course, I never intended to buy them. No wife of mine is going to dress like a whore."

I could imagine Verity's excitement at the thought of new clothes. We had discussed her changing her image. She hadn't been keen, but she had explained that had only been because Glenn didn't approve.

Tears stung my eyes. I supposed I could take some little comfort in the knowledge she had been excited about her shopping trip.

"We drove to the shopping centre and parked on the top floor of the multi-storey car park. She asked me why I was driving to the top even though there were spaces on the lower floors. I told her there was a lovely view of Bristol I wanted her to see. I can remember the smile on her face."

I shuddered. I didn't know if I wanted to hear any further details. But hear them I would. He had a faraway look in his eyes as he continued to describe what happened next.

"She looked beautiful again. She was the Verity I met that night in Bristol all those years ago. She'd been with her friends and had fallen over drunk. I had swooped in and picked her up and taken care of her," he was smiling fondly.

He didn't realise it, but I already knew the story having been told by Verity.

"She was smiling up at me as I opened the passenger door and held out my hand to help her out of the car. Her face glowed with excitement at the prospect of buying new clothes. Her hand was warm with anticipation as it held mine," he said gently. His tone changed rapidly, hardening suddenly, as he said, "She was excited to be buying cheap, slutty clothes that she could wear to attract men when she had left me."

I recoiled at the maniacal expression on his face as he went on, "At that moment, I knew she had to die for her disloyalty. Her expression changed to horror as I gripped her hands tightly. Pulling her from the car I propelled her with such force to the side of the car park that her feet only barely skimmed the floor. She felt like a rag doll. Holding her face tightly in one hand I forced her to take in the beautiful view. After all, I had promised her that. She didn't seem to appreciate it.

"I took her handbag off of her arm, and I checked her pockets. She kept asking me what she'd done wrong. As I took the card from my pocket and showed it to her, she fell silent. There was a resignation in her eyes. She knew what was coming next. I could see she had accepted her fate; that she deserved it for what she'd done.

"She didn't struggle as I lifted her; she didn't say a word. As I let go of her and watched her fall, I felt regret at what she'd made me do. I heard the thud of her body hitting the pavement, and I knew it was time to punish you. I think that's enough chatting, don't you? I just wanted you to fully understand your part in Verity's death before you see her again." He looked upward as if he believed in heaven.

I felt hot, very, very hot. My cheeks were burning and perspiration trickled down my back between my shoulder blades. I wasn't sure if I could keep control of my bladder as he advanced toward me. Oh please don't let me wet myself in front of this monster. I couldn't give him the satisfaction of witnessing my final indignity.

I focused on the silk scarf. It was coming closer and closer. Odd thoughts were skipping around my mind. I couldn't concentrate on any one of them as they jumped and bobbed around: I could see my boys laughing; my mum and sisters smiling at me, and then a rational thought that told me I wasn't surprised he was going to strangle me.

Strangulation was an act of passion. The killer wanted to be up close and personal. Glenn blamed me for Verity's death, and he wanted to watch the life drain from me.

Suddenly, I realised he was telling me to shut up. I didn't understand why until I became aware of screaming. Who was screaming? I wondered. All of a sudden, I realised my mouth was wide open. I was screaming. I couldn't ever remember screaming like this before. It sounded alien even to my ears.

He was so close to me now that his face was only inches from mine. I could feel his hot breath on my face. His eyes were searing into mine. Instinctively, I turned my head away. Grabbing my jaw with his hand he snapped my head back to face him. His, was going to be the last face I was ever going to see. He was smiling at me as he looped the scarf around my neck and pulled it tight with both hands.

No, my every instinct was demanding that I fight. I lashed out with every ounce of force I had. I was kicking out at him while trying to loosen the scarf. He pulled it tighter around my throat. I was struggling to breathe. I couldn't remember ever feeling so utterly terrified.

The pain was excruciating. I was desperately clawing at the silk in an attempt to pull it away from my neck. I didn't know how long I could last. I didn't know if my mind was playing tricks on me, but I thought someone was banging on my door. Everything was getting darker, and I felt my body start to sag. I was sure I could hear banging and shouting before I wasn't aware of anything any more.

# Chapter 2

My eyes flickered open. I was attempting to focus. Was I dead? I didn't feel dead. But then, what did dead feel like? My face was on a cold, hard surface. Come to think of it, so was the rest of me. My throat was dry; I couldn't stop coughing. I realised I was in my hallway as I stared at the picture I had of my children on the sideboard. Why wasn't I dead? And more importantly, where was Glenn?

I could hear voices. They sounded panicked.

"Quick, she's in here!"

I could hear feet approaching. I looked up from my prone position into the eyes of a young policeman.

"Hello, you must be Ms Wilson. I'm PC Travis. Don't worry; we're in pursuit of the man who did this to you. The paramedics are en route. They won't be long. Please don't try to move. I'll find out what's happening."

PC Travis was walking away from me, and the sound of his footsteps reverberated through the floor and into my ears. Instinctively, I lifted my head, and ignoring the young policeman's advice I attempted to sit up.

I could hear him talking into his radio. He was updating someone on my condition. I could hear a male voice coming from the radio saying they were in pursuit of the suspect. It was hard to hear what he was saying above the background noise of the police car's sirens and the roar of a car engine being driven at speed.

PC Travis was interrupted by the arrival of the paramedics. They had entered my house via the back door. That seemed odd. But then I realised I was blocking the front door. The door would have hit me had they tried to come in that way. A paramedic approached me.

"I'm going to take a look at you. OK?"

I didn't know why he was asking me. I wasn't in a position to say no.

The paramedic knelt down beside me and started to remove the silk scarf from my neck.

"Are you experiencing any breathing problems?" he asked.

I shook my head.

"Officer," he called, as he held up the silk scarf in his gloved hand. "I imagine you'll want to bag this as evidence?"

PC Travis approached holding a clear plastic bag, and the paramedic dropped the scarf into it. Turning his attention back to me, he asked, "Can you speak, Ms Wilson?"

"Yes," I said, but I was surprised at how weak and croaky my voice sounded.

He must have registered my distress as he reassured me, "Don't worry, it's perfectly normal for someone who's been strangled to experience temporary hoarseness. How is your vision? Is there any blurriness?"

"No," I croaked.

He was looking closely at my eyes, face and neck.

"What's wrong?" I asked.

"There's nothing wrong. I've noticed areas of petechiae on your face and in your eyes."

As my eyes widened in alarm, he sought to comfort me. "All it means is that as a result of the strangulation small blood vessels in your face and eyes have burst. It's just a medical term for a red rash, and it should clear up in a few days. However, although all the signs are positive, I would like to take you to the hospital just to get you checked over properly."

"Better safe than sorry," I murmured.

"My thoughts exactly. Do you think you'll be able to walk to the ambulance?" he asked.

"Let's see, shall we," I croaked as I took his hand. I was feeling shaky, but I managed to walk to the ambulance. "Have they caught him?" I asked the paramedic.

"I don't know. My job is to worry about you. I'm sure the police will update you as soon as they can."

I nodded. I suddenly realised no one knew about what had happened, and I had to pick Henry up from school later.

"My son needs to be collected from school."

"Don't worry. Is there anyone we can contact?"

"Yes, my mum."

"Great," he leaned out of the ambulance and shouted, "Constable, Ms Wilson needs you to contact her mum."

After a brief discussion, PC Travis managed to find the mobile phone I had been looking for earlier, and I was able to give him my mum's telephone number.

As the ambulance took me to the hospital, I imagined the panic she would feel as she answered the telephone to a police officer. I should have spoken to her myself. I wondered how the police had arrived so promptly. I vaguely remembered shouting coming from outside as I was passing out. It must have been the police. I shuddered as I realised just how lucky I had been. If only Verity had been so lucky. Tears welled up in my eyes as the friendly paramedic sought to distract me from the bleakness of my thoughts by talking about the British weather.

"It's a nice day out there," he said as he sat beside me.

Why do the British do that? I wondered. We were always so distracted by the weather. It was our favourite topic of conversation. If in doubt, talk about the weather. And if at all possible, offer a nice cup of tea.

"When will I be able to talk to the police?"

"We need to check you over first," he said reassuringly. "I'm sure they are as keen to speak to you as you are to speak to them," he said gravely. "We're here," he said as I felt the ambulance come to a halt. As the ambulance doors opened, I could see someone waiting with a wheelchair.

"No need to walk if you don't need to," the paramedic joked.

I managed to step down from the ambulance, and was surprised at how wobbly I felt. I sat down on the chair and was wheeled into the Accident and Emergency department.

"I just need to update my colleagues on your condition and the circumstances, and then I'll leave you in their capable hands," he said.

"Thank you for your help."

He smiled at me briefly before turning away and hurrying down the hospital corridor in search of assistance.

I sat there watching a mixture of doctors, nurses and orderlies rush from one cubicle to another, and the reality of my situation hit me like a freight train. A mad man had just tried to kill me. He had tried to kill me before and failed. He had failed to kill me twice now. What was that expression? Was it third time lucky? Silent tears were streaming down my face.

A kind voice seemed to come from nowhere. "That will be the effects of shock; it's nothing to worry about. You've had quite the ordeal, I understand. I'm going to wheel you into this cubicle over here; a triage nurse will arrive shortly to check you over."

I nodded my acceptance as she took control of my chair and wheeled me toward the cubicle. She turned, and was closing the curtains as she said, "If you're given the all clear to drink, we can arrange for a nice cup of tea soon."

I had no idea how long I was sitting there. After what seemed like an age, a man entered the cubicle. He introduced himself as Dr Howell. He explained that he would be assessing my condition. He glanced at my hospital notes and gave me a gentle smile.

"I understand you've been through an ordeal this afternoon."

He had kind eyes. They were a muddy brown colour. No, on further inspection and thinking more charitably, they were the colour of milk chocolate.

Tears welled up in my eyes once again. I was powerless over my emotions at the moment. "I'm sorry, I find myself unable to control the tears at present."

"That is completely understandable and perfectly normal . . . ," he hesitated as if looking for my name on my notes, and having found it added, "Ms Wilson."

I smiled my thanks.

"From what I've been told, you were the victim of an attempted strangulation. Is that correct?"

I nodded my confirmation.

"A ligature was used: a silk scarf," he added by way of explanation. In case I hadn't understood what a ligature was I imagined.

"That's right," I confirmed.

"I know you will have been asked this already, but are you experiencing any problems breathing?"

I shook my head.

He examined my neck closely.

"You have some red marks on your neck, as you might expect, from the scarf. The marks should fade quite quickly. There are also some scratch marks. You also have petechiae on your face and eyes; it should fade in a day or two. You may experience some outward signs of bruising on your neck. Please open your mouth. I just want to check your tongue."

I did as I was asked.

He seemed happy with what he saw and confirmed this fact. "Good, there are no signs of swelling. Have you been sick or felt nauseous at all?"

"I haven't been sick. I do feel sick, but I think that might be related to the situation I find myself in," I answered honestly.

"Yes, yes I can imagine. I'm assuming, please tell me if I'm wrong, that you didn't urinate or defecate as a result of the strangulation."

"No, I didn't," I said and felt my cheeks flush.

"I can assure you it wouldn't have been through choice if you had. It would have been an involuntary reaction to the strangulation. Are you experiencing any light-headedness?"

"No."

"It's my understanding that you were unconscious only briefly. That's a good thing. It implies you weren't strangled for long.

"Ligature strangulation results in the incomplete occlusion of the carotid artery. Basically, that means pressure is put upon the carotid artery in your neck blocking blood flow. It can render you unconscious within ten to fifteen seconds. If the person strangling you stops at this point, you have a good chance of recovering consciousness within ten seconds and not having any long-term effects. However, if the person continues to exert pressure after unconsciousness for approximately fifty seconds or more, then unfortunately . . ."

I shuddered. He didn't need to finish his sentence. I knew it meant death.

"How do you know I wasn't unconscious for long?"

"The officer on scene told the paramedic he was approaching your front door when he heard your screams. He said he was with you within seconds of you going silent, and that you regained consciousness quickly."

"I don't understand? How did he get in? Where was Glenn?"

"Glenn?" he asked.

"He's the man who attacked me."

He shook his head, "I don't know any other details. I've only been informed of the facts that directly affect your health. I don't know anything else. I'm reasonably happy that you shouldn't experience any long-term effects, but I would just like to keep you in overnight just to be sure. Sometimes the effects of strangulation aren't immediately obvious. We can't be sure the carotid artery hasn't been bruised; sometimes it can swell several hours after the event."

My hand flew protectively to my throat and my eyes widened.

"It's just to be on the safe side," he reassured. "I'll arrange for you to be transferred to a ward."

"Thank you, doctor."

"There are a couple of policemen waiting to talk to you. Now I've checked you over, I'm happy to let them see you. Is that OK with you, Ms Wilson?"

"Yes, thank you. I'd like to know what's going on."

"Hmm, I'm sure," he said as he left.

A few moments later, I heard someone clear their throat on the other side of the curtain that was affording me some semblance of privacy.

"Erm, excuse me, Ms Wilson?"

"Yes?"

"It's PC Travis and DC Smithers. Can we come in?" PC Travis asked.

"Yes, please do."

The curtain was pulled back, and both men filed into the confined space. I recognised PC Travis. I was able to take more note of his appearance than I had the last time we met. He was around my age, mid-thirties, I guessed.

He was tall, at least six feet four inches. He was what I would describe as pleasant looking. He was neither overly good-looking nor plain. He was just right. I sounded like Goldilocks picking the type of porridge I preferred. Under different circumstances, that thought might have made me laugh out loud, but it wasn't a different circumstance.

He extended his hand to shake mine and announced, "PC Travis. We met at your house earlier, and before that we spoke on the phone."

"Yes, I remember. We spoke about Verity."

"Yes," his tone was sombre to match the seriousness of the situation. "This is Detective Constable Smithers," he added.

I eyed the other man in the room. Aside from the very obvious difference in the two men's heights they were dressed differently. PC Travis was in his police uniform as expected, but DC Smithers wasn't. He was obviously a plain-clothes officer as I observed his grubby jeans and very tired-looking t-shirt. A pair of dirty old trainers completed the ensemble.

DC Smithers was significantly shorter than PC Travis. He wasn't much taller than me, I surmised. He was older, perhaps mid-forties. I noticed a few resilient black hairs peaking through DC Smithers' predominantly grey hair. I wondered quite inanely if those few black hairs, reminders of his former youth, comforted him or depressed him. As if on cue, he stepped forward proffering his hand.

"I'm part of CID: Criminal Investigation Department," he added by way of explanation.

I'd heard of CID. What self-respecting, television-watching person of the twenty-first century hadn't? I just didn't imagine I would have to deal with the real-life CID. I had been more than happy restricting my knowledge to the reality TV version.

I needed answers I decided, and I needed them now.

"Have you caught him?" I asked.

They exchanged a knowing look with one another. What exactly did that mean? I wondered. Were they going to include me in their circle of knowledge? It soon became evident they weren't, at least, not immediately.

"Before we get on to that, we would like to know exactly what happened in your home earlier today." DC Smithers enquired. He seemed to be the one in charge.

"Well, shortly after I spoke to PC Travis on the telephone someone knocked on my door."

"That would be approximately 12.23 p.m.," he said knowingly.

"Would it? I'll take your word for it. That does sound about right. I left my appointment at around noon and it takes approximately fifteen minutes to get home."

"Go on," DC Smithers encouraged.

I went on to describe the events of the afternoon: the discovery of the graffiti, Glenn's confession to Verity's murder, and his subsequent attempt on my life.

"I'm very grateful to you PC Travis. If you hadn't turned up when you did . . ." I left the sentence unfinished. We all knew it would have all been over for me if he hadn't shown up when he did.

"When I rang you, I wasn't planning on coming straight round to see you. However, after having spoken to you, I got the distinct impression you didn't think it was suicide. I was intrigued, and decided if there was a possibility it was a suspicious death, then it was better I get as much detail about the victim as I could. When I arrived at your home and approached your door, I could hear voices. And then, of course, I heard your screams."

"So, it was you I heard banging on the door. At the time, I wasn't sure if I was imagining it."

"That was me. When you fell silent, I knew I had to take action. I tried to peer through your letterbox; when it wouldn't budge, I suspected you were against the door. I gained entry to your property via your living room window. I had to smash it with my baton, I'm afraid."

"You saw Glenn?"

"He must have heard the glass smash. As I entered the hallway, he was exiting your house via the back door. I started to give chase on foot, but by the time I'd gotten to your back door he had made it to his car. I took a note of his registration, and then let my colleagues know I needed back up. I returned to you in the hallway; you were just regaining consciousness."

"Well, what happened next? I demanded. Did you catch him?"

"My colleagues were told to be on the lookout for the vehicle. We ran a check on his number plate, and we quickly established the registered owner was a Glenn Froom. We couldn't be sure he was driving the vehicle. But it seemed likely.

"I was able to let my colleagues know the direction he took off in, and they started examining the traffic camera footage in the area. We located his vehicle on the M32 motorway heading out of Bristol.

"The last I heard, my colleagues were involved in a high-speed pursuit with the vehicle on the M5 Southbound after a police car had tried to flag the driver down, and he'd taken off at speed."

DC Smithers' mobile phone started ringing. Was he allowed to have it switched on in here? I wondered. But then he was a police officer, so perhaps the rules were allowed to be bent a little where they were concerned. However, I soon realised that was not the case when I spotted the outraged look on the face of one of the nurses as he left the cubicle to answer the call.

I reached up to touch my neck. As soon as my fingers made contact with my skin, I winced. With a feather-light touch, my fingertips gently traced the sticky, sore lines of raised skin they found. I was confused. Why did I have scratches on my neck? Glenn hadn't scratched me, and the scarf was made of the softest silk. I glanced down at my nails and could see dried blood under them. I had done it to myself. It was only then that I remembered clawing at the scarf in my attempts to loosen it as he pulled it ever tighter. The image of his face, only inches from mine in those moments, flooded my mind.

"Do you mind if we stop now?" I asked PC Travis. "I don't feel too good; I could do with a rest."

He was studying my face intently as I spoke, and he shook his head. "I just need to take some photographs of your injuries as evidence." He produced a small camera and continued to speak to me as he took the photos. "I'll take photographs of your neck first, and then I'll take close-up shots of your face and eyes."

I grimaced. I didn't like the idea of close-up photographs. Quite irrationally I thought, but I look dreadful and then realised that was rather the point. He announced he'd finished in no time, and I was thankful that he worked quickly. I was impressed; when I took photographs, it took me forever to get the right shot. But then, he wasn't concerned with the aesthetics of the scene.

"We've got what we need for now. You're a brave lady. You've been through quite an ordeal. Get some rest; we'll talk later."

"You'll let me know when you manage to arrest Glenn, won't you?" I asked.

"Yes, of course. We will be keeping an eye on you until he's apprehended. Try not to worry."

People always said that in times of extreme stress. I knew they were only trying to help, but it was a completely useless comment. Of course I was going to worry. A man who had just tried to kill me was still out there. Still, I knew PC Travis's words were well-intentioned. I made an attempt at what I knew was a weak smile. Seemingly satisfied with my response, he turned and left.

Moments later, a hospital porter appeared, and announced he was moving me to a ward. Luckily, I was given a side room on the ward all to myself. I lay on the hospital bed. My brain was racing in its effort to make sense of everything that happened to me today. My body on the contrary had given up. Every part of me felt extremely heavy. Gradually my brain decided to follow suit as temporary oblivion descended.

# Chapter 3

A dark figure loomed large over my bed. His arms outstretched toward me. He was saying something. I wasn't sure what it was.

"This time I won't fail," he said, while his hands reached for my neck.

No! It was Glenn. He'd found me. This time he was going to kill me. I had to run. I had to get away. I tried to get off of the bed, but my limbs wouldn't move. I tried to scream, but no sound would come out of my mouth. What was happening? Someone help me. Please.

"She's having a nightmare," said a familiar male voice somewhere in the distance.

I was confused. Who was that? Why didn't they stop him?

"Mum, are you OK?" asked another familiar male voice.

I could hear fear in his voice, and it stirred something in me; I jerked awake. Bleary-eyed I looked around me. It took me a few seconds to work out where I was. Then recent events crashed into my consciousness like an open door slamming on a windy day. The fear I felt bubbled up from my stomach and got stuck in my chest making it hard to breathe. I was trying to take a deep breath as I had told my children to do so often when they were feeling scared. I was fighting a battle with my physical reaction to what had happened to me.

I caught sight of my children standing by my bed. They appeared younger than they had this morning when I had waved them off to school. They seemed more vulnerable somehow. They had both been crying. I could tell by the puffiness of their eyes and incessant sniffing. If I'd told them once, I had told them a million times not to sniff. They were to blow their noses with a handkerchief, and definitely not to use the sleeves of their jumpers.

As if on cue, Henry raised his arm to wipe his nose on his sleeve.

"No, you don't!" I commanded. My tone of voice had caught me by surprise. It had sounded much harsher than I had intended.

Henry's eyes began to fill with tears and involuntarily mine followed suit. I held out my arms in silent request, and both boys rushed into my embrace. The tears flowed unchecked down my face. I hugged them to me; I never wanted to let them go. Both boys hugged me as if their lives depended upon it. They clearly felt exactly the same as I did.

Eventually, I raised my head from their embrace, and I saw my mum standing there watching us. She, in comparison to my sons, actually looked older than she had the last time I had seen her, which was only yesterday. The fear and worry she must have felt for me had deepened every line on her face. My mum wasn't one for crying, but I could see the tears silently coursing down her face, and knew that what had happened to me had taken its toll on her.

She was hanging back as if waiting for an invitation to join the hug.

"Come on, Mum, there's room for a little one," I said attempting to widen my arms still further.

She gave a little chuckle and moved toward the three of us. She placed her hand on the top of my head and started to smooth my hair in the same way as she had done when I was a little girl seeking comfort. In that moment, I would have given anything to be that carefree little girl again.

We stayed in the same untidy, sweaty, sobbing huddle until a knock on the door disturbed our embrace.

"Come in," I said as I extricated myself from three pairs of limpet-like arms.

DC Smithers stuck his head round the door as if checking it was safe to enter. He took in the scene before him, and it seemed to terrify him. Perhaps it was the clear evidence of heightened emotion in the room that made him appear pale and nervous.

"Come in," I reiterated in as reassuring a tone as I could muster.

He hesitated as he entered. "I wonder if I could have a private word with you, Ms Wilson. There have been significant developments."

Every nerve ending in my body had suddenly returned to high alert. "Yes, of course." I turned to Mum and asked, "Could you take the boys to find a vending machine or the restaurant?"

"Yes, absolutely," she said, her usual cooperative self. She busily shooed the boys from the room happy to have something to distract her from the events of today, if only for a short while.

I smiled as I heard Alex ask for a big piece of cake as he was leaving followed by Henry asking for some chocolate. It was comforting to know their stomachs at least hadn't been affected by the day's events.

DC Smithers took a seat beside the bed. "I thought it best if I told you what's been happening over the last few hours."

It suddenly occurred to me that I didn't know what time it was. How long had I been asleep?

"What time is it?" I asked.

He looked at his watch. "It's 7.30 p.m."

I was surprised that I had managed to sleep for so long in the circumstances. He cleared his throat as if to get my attention.

"You were saying . . ." I encouraged, attempting to reassure him I was listening.

"Yes, so as you know, the last time we spoke we were in pursuit of the suspect, Glenn Froom."

I nodded. "Did you catch him?" I asked eagerly.

He was avoiding eye contact, and I knew the answer to my question before he uttered it.

"No, the call I took as I was leaving you earlier was to inform me they were abandoning the pursuit in the interests of the general public. He was driving at very high speed. He left the M5 motorway at junction 20 and proceeded toward Clevedon. It was decided the risk to the general public was too great should they continue the chase."

My rational self knew it was the sensible decision, but I wasn't ready to be rational. What about me? What about the risk to ME? Wasn't I part of the general public? My internal rant was cut short, as he continued.

"However, it wasn't the end of the matter. During the chase we didn't have time to get the helicopter mobilised. We had wanted to continue following the suspect from the air, but it wasn't possible."

"So, effectively, you lost him!" I blurted out.

"Yes. But approximately two hours ago we received a call from the general public telling us they had found the clothing of a man together with a note at Brean Down Fort in Somerset."

I was perplexed. What was he trying to tell me, exactly?

"When a PC arrived at the scene, he quickly identified the clothing as belonging to Glenn Froom."

"And the note?" I asked.

"We need our handwriting experts to look at the note and confirm it's Glenn's handwriting, but on first inspection it appears to have been written by him."

"What did it say?"

"I'm afraid I can't tell you word for word as it's officially evidence. But I can tell you that it appears to be a suicide note."

I was surprised and enormously relieved all at once. The relief was swiftly followed by guilt that I should feel relieved at someone having taken their own life. Still, perhaps I could forgive myself considering that same someone had tried to kill me a few hours ago. I found myself asking, "Have you found his body?"

"No. Not yet, but we do have both a search and rescue helicopter and RNLI lifeboat trying to locate him around Brean Down coastline."

"I have to say that I'm surprised he has chosen to kill himself. To do so implies feelings of guilt and remorse that he clearly didn't have. When he was speaking to me earlier, he made it clear that he thought I was responsible for Verity's death. He took no responsibility for her demise, whatsoever, despite having confessed to throwing her off of the top of the multi-storey car park. Why, then, kill himself?"

DC Smithers was studying his shoes intently. He was avoiding eye contact, and his brow was deeply furrowed. He was clearly a man with a dilemma. He sighed as he looked up to meet my gaze. He had plainly come to a decision. "Can I trust you?" he asked meaningfully.

"Of course. Do you know what I do for a living?" I retorted a tad too sharply.

He nodded and relaxed a little. "This is completely off the record, and I'm relying on you not to breathe a word of this." As he spoke, his eyes searched my face for visual reassurance of my dependability and sincerity. He must have been satisfied with what he saw because he continued. "I've seen the note. He blames you for everything, including his own suicide."

I took a deep breath as I digested what he had just said. His blaming me for everything was much more in keeping with my understanding of him.

"He basically ranted on about how the events of today were all the result of your interference in his marriage. How Verity would still be alive if you hadn't meddled, and how you had left him no choice but to kill her. He went on to say how he couldn't bear to be incarcerated for something that was effectively your fault. He thought he'd killed you by the way."

"What?" I asked bemused by his last comment.

"He thought he'd killed you when he fled the scene. He wasn't there to see you regain consciousness. So, to all intents and purposes, he thought you were dead."

"A fact I'm sure he was proud of."

"It would seem so," he said deadpan.

I winced in reaction to his thoughtless words.

His tactlessness registering as he said "Sorry, I wasn't thinking."

"It's OK. It's just one thing to think something, and another to have it confirmed."

"Yes, I can imagine," he said, nodding his understanding.

As he hesitated, I urged him to continue, "Go on, you may as well tell me what he wrote on the subject."

His eyes once again downcast he said quietly, "If I remember rightly, he said he was master of his own destiny. That he chose to take his own life rather than have it taken from him by going to prison. He took comfort in the knowledge that he gave you, 'that bitch' as he put it, no choice in your destiny."

I shuddered at the intensity of Glenn's evident hatred. His words gave credence to his suicide. Initially, I had been surprised that such a man would take his own life, but now his reasons for doing so made sense. He had been a very controlling person. So it made perfect sense that someone who had controlled others would insist on complete control of their own life, which included their death. Still I wanted proof he was dead. I wanted to know they had found his body. Only then, would I begin to feel safe.

# Chapter 4

**1 year later**

***Session ten - Richard Sullivan 5.30 p.m. - 6.30 p.m.***

Today was Richard's last counselling session. I found myself sitting in a comfortable silence as Richard appeared to be deep in thought. He was in a pensive mood today, I observed.

I glanced covertly at my watch, only a few minutes until the end of the session. I was happy not to disrupt the silence that was enveloping him. We had said everything that needed to be said and now all that was left to say was goodbye.

His eyes were fixed firmly upon the floor, but I knew his mind was not filled with thoughts of the carpet. He was somewhere else at the moment, not in this room with me, but elsewhere. I was content to leave him to his introspection as I figured I'd done more than enough probing into his life over the last ten weeks; it was time for me to stop. Instead, I marvelled, once again, at how good he looked for his age.

When I'd met Richard Sullivan, ten weeks ago, I had taken him for a man in his late forties perhaps early fifties. I was surprised to find out he was in his mid-sixties. He was marvellously well preserved for his age. When he told me how old he was, he took great pride in my shocked expression. He had informed me with glee that he was well used to people assuming he was younger and never tired of being told so.

He was a tall man, approximately six feet, and was always dressed impeccably for our counselling sessions. He had told me during our first meeting that he would be attending our sessions straight after work, which was why he always turned up in a suit. I initially wondered if he was approaching retirement, but dismissed that idea as he informed me he owned the company and had no intention of ever voluntarily retiring.

Looking at his auburn hair, I wondered if he dyed it. I couldn't picture him wearing plastic gloves and applying a bottle of Just For Men in his bathroom. I couldn't picture him in a hairdresser's chair having his roots dyed either. No, it just wasn't something I thought he'd do. He was one very lucky guy not to have grey hair at his age. As if he sensed my looking at it, he brushed his hand through his hair. He wore a troubled expression, and I sensed he was in the grip of a dilemma.

"Frankie," he said breaking the silence. He appeared to have wrestled free of his earlier introspection, "I have a little something for you." He reached into his pocket and pulled out a box.

Being a woman with a penchant for jewellery, I could identify the box and take an educated guess as to its contents.

The box had a jeweller's name on it: Masons Freemantle. I happened to know they were exclusive jewellers based in Clifton. This knowledge came from many happy hours spent gazing longingly at the contents of the shop window.

The shape of the box indicated it was either a bracelet or a watch. Richard had observed my Gucci watch at our first session together. He had commented that he, too, loved watches. My guess was that knowing how we shared a passion for watches he had bought me one.

"I just wanted to thank you properly for all your help. I'm so very grateful," he said earnestly.

"Richard, it's a lovely thought, but . . ."

"Don't say no until you've at least looked at it," he interjected.

Oh this was going to be torture. I absolutely adored watches; especially the kind I couldn't afford. I knew before I even opened the box that it was going to be expensive and gorgeous. He knew it too by the way he was smiling. He fully intended on making this very difficult for me to turn down, but turn it down I must.

I picked up the box and opened it. My stomach did an excited flip, and I groaned inwardly as I beheld the most beautiful Gucci watch I had ever seen. I was right. This was torture. I hoped it wasn't obvious to him how much I liked the watch as my eyes took in its every detail.

The watch band was stainless steel; which I had always preferred to a leather strap. The watch face was pearlescent and there was a circle of diamonds around its rim. I tilted the box, so that the diamonds would catch the light, and I found their shimmer mesmerising.

Had the situation been different, I knew I wouldn't have been able to resist the temptation to count just how many diamonds there were. It was heavenly. And had I been able to afford it; I would have picked it myself. He had incredibly good taste.

He had been watching my expression as I opened the box, and even though I had tried hard to remain impassive, it was obvious I had let some of my excitement show. He was grinning from ear to ear.

"I knew you'd love it," he said.

I decided to be honest. "I do, it is quite simply beautiful. But I have a policy of not accepting gifts from clients. The agreed fee for my services is sufficient recompense."

As I finished speaking, I closed the box and handed it back to him. I had to fight hard to control the watch-loving side of me, which was demanding that I put that watch on my wrist right now. Just try it on, my inner voice wheedled. What's the harm in that?

Richard's grin faded at my words. The triumph I'd heard in his voice, only moments ago, was replaced with disappointment and dismay.

"While I applaud your professionalism, I cannot deny my disappointment. I picked the watch because I suspected you'd love it.

"As you know, I'm a wealthy man. The cost is nothing to me. I can buy what I want, but what you've given me money can't buy. I wanted you to know just how much you've helped me."

"Richard, I'm truly touched by the gesture. But believe me when I say that your thanks are enough. My reward for doing this job is to see the change I help facilitate in my clients. You're the one who has done all of the hard work. I have just helped along the way."

"I understand what you're saying, but please don't underestimate your contribution. I really wanted to express my thanks by giving you a nice present. But, if that isn't to be, then so be it. You're a woman who knows her own mind, and I must respect that."

We both stood and shook hands.

"Thank you, Richard. It's been a pleasure. Should you need my services in the future, please get in touch. Good luck with Relate."

"Huh?"

"We discussed the fact that you would contact Relate for couple's counselling," I said as a reminder.

"Oh yes, that's right. Don't worry, Frankie, I know what I need to do next," he said, and placed the jewellery box back into his jacket pocket as he left.

I returned to my seat and my trusty notebook. We covered his overall journey in today's session—where he'd been at the beginning and where he was now. I decided to read over the previous weeks' notes before embarking on writing up this week's.

Sometimes I enjoyed reading over the notes in solitude and enjoying the successes. It wasn't like that for all clients. It always depended on just how much effort a client was willing to put into counselling in order to get the outcome they wanted.

Richard had faced some difficult truths about his life during counselling; he had been brave.

I recalled how Richard had telephoned me, initially, as all my prospective clients now did. I no longer worked for ASF Technologies; the managing director had asked me to continue to counsel its staff for one day a week, but I decided the experience had been too traumatic to repeat. I recommended a few counsellor friends who might like to fill the vacancy and politely took my leave.

Interestingly, though, it would seem not all ties with ASF Technologies had been severed; when Richard first contacted me, he explained that its CEO and former client of mine, Michael Graham, had recommended me to him.

I sourced my clients via various routes these days. Some came to me through word of mouth like Richard; others saw my advert in the local newspaper and decided to give me a call. I'd decided long ago I didn't want to counsel people in my own home. The idea of having strangers in my home made me feel vulnerable. Especially in light of what had happened to me last year.

Memories of my old home came flooding back. I had loved that house. A sigh escaped me as I thought of the hours I'd spent lovingly sanding the floorboards in my bedroom. And all the effort I had put into decorating every inch of each room. But, after that day . . . the day everything changed. I couldn't stand to be there again. I couldn't stand in the hallway without reliving every second of it over and over again.

I could feel the familiar panic rising in me at the thought of it. Time to practise what you preach Frankie, I said to myself. I pinged the elastic band around my wrist. Ow! I felt a slight pain as it slapped the skin on my wrist. I repeated the now familiar mantra silently to myself: he cannot hurt you any more; you are safe. My process was to repeat this twice more. I knew it had worked, as it always did, when I felt the familiar overwhelming anxiety start to lose its grip upon my body.

I'd been advising people for years about the simple benefits of the 'wristband' technique. In the early years, I had used it mainly with drug addicts and alcoholics. It was effective in momentarily distracting an addict from their overwhelming desire to use drugs or drink alcohol.

The moment of pain inflicted by the wristband was useful in distracting the brain from its current obsessive train of thought. The disruption in thought pattern could be used to replace the thoughts with more positive ones that were of the person's choosing.

More recently, I used the technique for anxiety sufferers including myself. It worked in much the same way as for those with addictions. But in the case of anxiety sufferers, it momentarily stopped the thoughts that were fuelling the anxiety; giving the sufferer the opportunity to consciously replace them with positive ones. In my case, I reminded myself that I was no longer at risk, and that Glenn Froom couldn't hurt me.

Having successfully calmed myself, I returned to my notes. Richard's reason for attending counselling, or what I called his presenting problem, was that he was drinking more than usual. He recognised it had gone beyond drinking to be sociable. He said that he knew he had a problem when he got behind the wheel of his car and drove drunk. Something he prided himself on never having done before.

During our first four sessions together, we had talked about his drinking. The specifics of his drinking: how many, how often, and where. We had identified that his drinking started to escalate over the last twelve months. He explained his business to me and his role within the organisation. He owned a software company selling software to the National Health Service (NHS).

It was during a meeting with the North Bristol NHS Trust that Richard met Michael Graham. Richard described how they hit it off immediately and were now firm friends. As he talked about his company, and the work they did, it was clear he still had a hands-on role, which he clearly relished.

I wondered if the pressure of work was contributing to his increased drinking, but it was obvious from our sessions that he enjoyed work and had been coping successfully with the pressure of it for years.

Richard talked about his wife, Margie, with great fondness. He explained that they met and married when they were both twenty years old. Their relationship sounded like the traditional marriage of yesteryear. He worked; she took care of him, and that suited both of them very well indeed. His business became successful, and they both enjoyed the trappings of unexpected wealth.

Unfortunately, Margie developed breast cancer four years ago, and despite a double mastectomy they discovered the cancer had already spread to her lungs. He cried when he explained to me that the doctors had given her a life expectancy of two years, but she, in fact, only lasted nine months. We discussed the possibility of the drinking being a delayed reaction to the loss of his much loved wife, but I wasn't convinced.

The breakthrough came in session five when I asked him how drinking made him feel. He said it made him feel free. I inferred from that that he felt trapped by something or someone. When I voiced this sentiment to him, he looked like a man surrendering to the enemy. After having taken a deep breath, he explained he had a second wife, Abigail.

Up until that point, Richard led me to believe that he had only one wife, and she was dead. In fact, he went on to explain he had been married to Abigail, his second wife, for the last two years.

I wondered at the fact that this was session five, and he was only just admitting to having a wife. Why? It was usually second nature for people to inadvertently mention their spouse, should they have one, when talking about their everyday life. Why, then, hadn't he?

After having admitted Abigail's existence, he looked like a man in the dentist's chair facing a painful tooth extraction. This man did not want to talk about his wife, which was exactly why I thought it might prove enlightening if he did.

Over the next four weeks, Richard experienced the equivalent of a full-mouth tooth extraction. Or at least that was how it seemed. It was evident that he found it extremely painful to discuss his current relationship, and to admit to the issues they had, not least of which being her violence toward him.

Abigail's aggression toward him, which manifested itself in physical violence, both baffled and shamed him. He constantly compared her to his first wife who had been placid and easy-going.

Abigail, from Richard's description, appeared to be her polar opposite. Where Margie had been a supportive wife and homemaker, Abigail did little to support Richard. Abigail wanted all of Richard's attention, and she wasn't used to housework.

It was all I could do not to laugh out loud when Richard sat upright in his chair, pushed out his chest, held out his hands and waggled his nails in front of my face as he quoted Abigail, 'Housework? I don't DO housework!

With these nails, darling! Please be realistic!' The way he portrayed his wife spoke volumes about his attitude toward her. He didn't respect her.

Richard explained to me how he had gone from a low-maintenance relationship with Margie to a high-maintenance relationship with Abigail, and the difference shocked him. Once he allowed himself to talk about his relationship with Abigail, I watched his shoulders droop in relief.

I got the feeling he hadn't wanted to admit to being married to Abigail because then he knew he would have to tell me about her, and that would lead him to admitting the truth to himself as much as to me. Although not openly articulating it, I could see from his demeanour that he felt he'd made a mistake in marrying her.

He explained that after his wife died, he found solace in his work. He was working even longer hours than he had in the early days when he had been building the business. Occasionally, he would allow himself the odd round of golf with prospective clients. It was during one such occasion that he met Abigail at the 'nineteenth hole' as he put it.

"From the moment I saw her, I felt a connection, Frankie," he said. "She was standing beside me at the bar when I was waiting to order a round of drinks. Being a gentleman, I insisted she be served before me even though it had been my turn.

"She smiled at me. Her smile was like a ray of light in a pitch-black room. Suddenly, for the first time since my wife's death, I felt a glimmer of hope that life might in fact still be worth living.

"We struck up a conversation. She was so different to any other woman I'd ever met. She was exciting, vivacious and outgoing. I was flattered by the fact she wanted to talk to me that first night when there were so many attractive younger men in the clubhouse that evening.

"She was younger than me, but not too young. She had just turned forty, and I got the impression that rather depressed her. So, I flattered her by telling her she didn't look a day over thirty."

It was at that point he got out his wallet and showed me a picture of her. The picture had been taken by a professional. She was posing in a studio type style. The camera lens focus had definitely been softened so as to present her in the most flattering, youthful style possible. She was an attractive woman, and I believed would still have been equally as attractive without the photographer's trickery.

She had long blonde hair, green eyes and fuller than usual lips; the words trout pout sprang to mind, which I quickly dismissed. As if he read my mind, Richard announced that she regularly had her 'lips done'. I nodded. He went on to explain the many enhancements she had had to her face and body since that photograph had been taken, and that he paid for. It was quite an exhaustive list. I was left wondering if there was any of the original Abigail left. Perhaps that was her intention.

They dated for a little less than a year and during that time resided in their respective homes. Richard was old-fashioned and believed that you should only live together when married. Their 'courtship', as he called it, had been idyllic. They travelled extensively, and he enjoyed wining and dining her. She was the life and soul of every party, and he was happy that she should be so.

The cracks started to appear six months into their marriage when, it seemed, the honeymoon period was over. Abigail had never been married before, so Richard informed me, and had not lived with anyone either. She was unused to sharing her personal space.

He, on the other hand, had previously been in a forty-year marriage. He wanted what he had before: to be looked after. He didn't bargain on the fact that was precisely what Abigail wanted as well. They each wanted the other to look after them. The result being that neither of them was getting what they wanted.

Richard expected his tea on the table when he came home from a busy day at work. Abigail expected to be wined and dined at the best restaurants as she had been when they were dating.

As it became clear to each of them that their marriage was not what they expected, rather than modify their expectations and find some middle ground as some couples do, they argued—a lot.

It was during one such argument that Abigail first became violent. It sounded like the violence was borne out of frustration as it so often is. Abigail wanted to dress up and go out for the evening, but Richard was tired. They argued, and she picked up an ornament and hurled it at him. It would seem that she was a good shot because it hit Richard on the arm and left quite a nasty bruise he informed me. Although she was horrified by her behaviour, it soon became a common occurrence until she progressed to punching and slapping him.

During our latter sessions, we established that his increased drinking coincided with the start of the physical violence.

Richard's drinking was a side effect of the powerlessness he felt. He was using alcohol as an anaesthetic to numb the pain of a dysfunctional relationship and his inability to deal with the problem.

Richard had been brought up never to raise a hand to a woman, ever. He talked about how if a man hit him, he would think nothing of returning blows to defend himself, but he couldn't defend himself against Abigail. He felt constantly conflicted.

He tried to hold her off, but she was like a mad woman when in one of her rages. He was frightened that if he gripped her too hard it would leave marks; she had already threatened that if that happened she would tell everyone he was beating her. He looked like a defeated man when he told me that.

I could see the predicament that he was in. It's more generally accepted that the man beats the woman in an abusive relationship, not the other way round. He had the added dimension of feeling ashamed of the situation that he found himself in. He was a man; a successful, rich, well-respected man, and he was being beaten by his wife.

Richard accepted that if the relationship were to survive, they needed some professional help. We discussed the possibility of couple's counselling. He was keen on the idea of my counselling them. I explained that I didn't provide couple's counselling and that perhaps Relate would be a better fit.

He wasn't entirely comfortable with 'airing his dirty washing in public' as he put it. He felt that I was more suitable for the role because he had already confided in me. I pointed out that it was precisely because I had already counselled him and heard his perspective on the marriage that it wouldn't be fair on Abigail. He reluctantly concurred and was going to talk to Abigail about the idea.

Richard and I had agreed that couple's counselling was the next step. I was fairly confident that sorting out his marriage would see a marked reduction in his drinking.

I turned the page of my notebook. I'd come to the end of my session notes on Richard Sullivan. I had to write up today's session. I turned to a blank page and wrote:

*Session ten . . .*

# Chapter 5

I checked my watch. It was six-fifty. My stomach rumbled, as if on cue, reminding me it was dinner time. I put my notes in my trusty briefcase, and I scanned the room for anything else I needed to take with me. It didn't take long as it was a small office.

There was nothing on the small modern oak coffee table except for my briefcase. Both brown leather chairs were empty as they should be. I liked to check the chairs just in case a client had inadvertently left something behind. Men so often liked to put things in their back trouser pockets and when seated they could so easily be dislodged. I had recently found a wallet tucked in the crease of one of the chairs.

I picked my jacket up from the coat stand, and giving one final glance around the room, I turned and left. I locked the office door behind me.

I shared the room, all nine feet by ten feet of it, with my counsellor colleague, Rebecca. We obviously didn't use the room at the same time as it clearly could only accommodate one counsellor and one client comfortably at any one time.

Rebecca and I both had a key to the room and an agreement on which days we used it. We divided the rent for the room between us according to how much we had each used it that month.

I used the room on Tuesdays, and Rebecca used it on Wednesdays and Thursdays. If, or when, I got more clients, I would use the room more. It suited my needs at the moment as my appointment book was quite empty. All of my current clients seemed to have finished counselling at the same time, which was unusual.

I had two new clients coming next week who I had sourced through my advertisement in the Portishead

Times. I hoped business picked up soon because if I didn't get more clients imminently, I was going to have to consider a part-time job to supplement my income.

As I walked along the corridor heading for the exit, I reflected, not for the first time, on how fortuitous it had been bumping into Rebecca after so long.

I'd initially met Rebecca years ago at college. We were both on the same course and had endured the trials and tribulations of being a trainee counsellor together. We had liked each other enormously, but had not kept in touch after we qualified. We had the best of intentions to do so, but life happens and our friendship fizzled.

I'd been out shopping one day nearly ten months ago and was admiring a rather nice dress in a little boutique shop called Glam. I was in the process of balking at the price tag when I sensed someone looking over my shoulder. I gripped the dress that little bit tighter as I thought I had one of those competitive women who only seem to be interested in the item of clothing another woman is looking at.

My instincts told me that if I put the dress down, she would snatch it up within a nanosecond, and it would be lost to me forever. Still, I did the mature thing and put the dress back on the rail. I couldn't afford it anyway.

I expected a hand to dart out from behind me and grab it, but it didn't. Instead, a hand gently tapped me on the shoulder. I jumped three feet in the air and whirled around.

"Whoah! Steady on, Frankie. It's me, Rebecca. Long time no see."

"Oh my God!" I exclaimed. "You frightened me to death," I said, starting to laugh.

After a quick embrace, we agreed a coffee was in order. We chatted and that conversation led to several more. We had soon discovered we were both self-employed counsellors who needed an office but were unable to afford it alone. The obvious conclusion we had reached was to share office space.

Ten months later, here we were, renting an office together in a building called Marina Offices. I smiled and waved at the receptionist, Theresa, as I left. She waved back, but couldn't speak as she was talking into her headset at the same time.

The building was modern; having been built, like so much of Portishead Marina, within the last ten years. Its location was convenient for both Rebecca and I as we both lived in the vicinity. In fact, my new home, of the last nine months, was a few minutes' drive from here. There were no more lengthy commutes for me into central Bristol. I especially liked the fact the building had its own car park, and I didn't have the hassle of trying to find a parking space every day.

As I placed my briefcase into the boot of my car, I could feel my mobile phone vibrating in my handbag. I hadn't turned my ringtone back on yet. I always turned my mobile phone on to vibrate during my counselling sessions. In fairness, I really should turn my phone off completely because I asked my clients to switch their phones off. However, in my defence, I kept my mobile phone on because I needed to be contactable at all times for the children.

I always had this great sense of urgency to answer a ringing phone or, in this case, a vibrating one. At least, I knew it wasn't a client trying to contact me because I never gave my mobile phone number out to clients.

My usually deft fingers had taken on a life of their own as I fumbled with the zip of my handbag. My brain was giving clear and direct instruction to my fingers in a timely manner, but somehow my fingers were not responding. The zip, which in other circumstances usually opened with one smooth action, now chose to get stuck on the handbag's inner lining. No amount of brute force was going to open it any time soon.

I knew from experience this was a delicate operation that required time and patience. Otherwise, my bag would be ruined. There was just enough of a gap for me to thrust my hand in and root around in the cavernous depths for my phone.

After what felt like an age, after having blindly located my purse, my lipstick, my keys and every other blessed thing apart from my phone, I finally had the familiar vibrating piece of technology in my hand. As I withdrew it carefully from the barely sufficient gap in my bag, it stopped vibrating. Of course it did. Isn't that what always happens in these circumstances.

I glanced at my phone as I got into my driver's seat. Maria had been ringing me. I felt myself relax. It wouldn't be anything urgent; she rang me regularly. She would probably just want to have a chat.

I looked at my handbag; I hoped I could free the lining from the zip without any damage to either. Mobile phones are both a blessing and a curse all at once. I could see that she'd left me a message. I pressed the necessary button, and her voice suddenly filled the car.

"Hi, it's me, Maria. I just called for a quick chat. I wanted to put a date in our diaries for a get together. Call me back when you've consulted with your babysitters, aka your mum and Rob." She giggled as she finished talking.

I'd been right. She had wanted to talk. I'd call her later. Starting the engine I drove out of the car park and turned right. I was thinking about her as I drove my usual route home.

I'd first met Maria at Verity's funeral, a year ago. It had been a sombre affair, which in view of the circumstances surrounding her untimely demise was unsurprising.

Verity's funeral was not a celebration of her life, as I had hoped it would be, but more a public outpouring of grief and outrage at the way she had died.

There were reporters and cameras outside of the church during the service, and I felt sure they would have filmed the ceremony itself had they had permission. What should have been a private affair for her family and friends was turned into a media circus.

I lost count of the times I saw coverage of the funeral reported on both the regional and national news that day. Each news bulletin showing a picture of Glenn and Verity's wedding photograph. 'The couple in happier times,' the reporter would state before going on to talk at length about Verity's murder, and Glenn's subsequent suicide following a police chase.

It seemed to me that Glenn always appeared to be the main focus of the news reports; it was as if the media were fascinated by him. I was outraged that Glenn overshadowed Verity even in death. However, I was pleased that Glenn's newsworthiness was greater than my own. Thankfully, the press had paid little attention to his attempt on my life choosing to concentrate on what they saw as the bigger story: his killing his wife.

From the beginning, I hadn't been cooperative with reporters who camped outside my home hoping for a story. I refused to answer my telephone, or answer the door and kept my curtains firmly closed.

It didn't make for thrilling viewing when on the Six O'Clock News a rather overexcited female reporter announced that somewhere in the ordinary terraced house behind her, in an ordinary street in Bristol, something horrible had happened to a lady called Francesca Wilson. Unfortunately, Ms Wilson was unavailable for comment.

Needless to say, Verity and Glenn were a much better story. Glenn's former colleagues were lining up to give the press a candid account of their encounters with Glenn in exchange for their five minutes of fame; the reality being more like thirty seconds.

The same overexcited reporter, who had reported from outside my home, was ready to harass me on the day of Verity's funeral as I walked from my car to the church. I now knew her name to be Louise Summers.

I could see Louise and her cameraman had me in their sights, and they were making a beeline for me. It was precisely at the moment Louise was about to step in front of me, thereby cutting off my route into the church, that a lady came from nowhere.

"Frankie, there you are," the lady said from behind me. As I started to turn, I felt a hand on my elbow. Somehow, she steered me, like the rudder of a ship, around the reporter and cameraman with astounding speed and agility. At the same time as performing this amazing manoeuvre, she was talking to me as if she'd known me her entire life. "How are you doing? Were you able to find the church without too many difficulties?"

As soon as we were safely inside, she let go of my elbow.

"Sorry about that," she said. "I could see what was about to happen. I hope you don't think it presumptuous of me, but I assumed you wouldn't want to talk to them."

"You're right. Thank you for that. I'm afraid you have me at a disadvantage: you know my name, but I don't know yours."

"Maria," she said extending her hand. "I was Verity's supervisor."

So, this was Maria. This was the lady who Verity had wanted to stand up to at work. It was rare that I got to put a face to a name of a person a client had spoken about; so rare that I couldn't recall it ever happening before.

I remembered the look of triumph on Verity's face the day she'd come into the counselling session after having successfully tackled Maria about her workload. She had felt empowered.

The memory evoked a depth of emotion that threatened to overwhelm me. I could feel it rising up within me, like a tidal wave, and I attempted to swallow the feelings back down. I was battling to keep the emotion within, so that only I was aware of it and not the whole congregation.

I was on the verge of losing all self-control. The last thing I wanted was to draw attention to myself. I just wanted to stand at the back of the church unobserved and silently say goodbye to Verity.

"You look uncomfortable," she said as she once again gripped my elbow. "I tell you what, why don't you sit with me at the back. No one will notice us there. Is that OK with you?"

I smiled my capitulation and thanks. I didn't trust that my voice wouldn't crack if I tried to talk.

She steered me toward the rear of the church, and we took our seats in silence. We remained in silence for the next forty-five minutes as first the vicar and then Verity's friends and family paid tribute to her. It was a moving ceremony. I had been particularly affected by her mother's tearful last words: 'a parent should never have to bury their child'. I didn't think there was a parent alive who wouldn't agree.

Maria and I waited for the church to empty before we followed our fellow mourners to the graveside. As we left the church, I glanced at her sideways. She looked my age perhaps a little younger. She was tall and willowy; with a natural grace as she walked. Short-cropped, naturally-blonde hair framed an oval face. I determined she was a natural blonde because her skin was pale and delicate.

Still, I could be wrong; hairdressers could do wonders these days.

Maria was dressed all in black; the colour did not suit her as it sapped her already pale skin of any colour it might naturally have. In fact, as you might expect at a funeral, everyone was dressed in black. And yet, I had heard of some funerals where people were encouraged to wear bright colours; sometimes the deceased's favourite colour.

"Do you know if Verity had a favourite colour?" I asked.

"Yes, it was purple," she replied while pulling a light purple silk scarf from her handbag. "Funnily enough, I found that out on the last day I saw her.

"She'd popped into town in her lunch hour, which was unheard of for her. She'd come back looking so happy, and I'd asked her why. She pulled this scarf from a carrier bag and commented on how pretty it was; how she couldn't resist it as purple was her favourite colour. She put it in her drawer.

"When I asked why she wasn't taking the scarf home, she said she wasn't ready yet. I found that odd at the time, but what with everything that's happened it now makes perfect sense."

As she spoke, my eyes were locked on to the silk scarf. It was only a few weeks before that Glenn had attempted to strangle me with one of Verity's scarves. The fear I'd felt then was once again gripping my body even though my rational self knew I was in no danger.

I could see Glenn's face as he stood in my hallway. The scarf pulled taut in his hands as he advanced toward me. The fear I felt was all-consuming, devouring me as he came ever closer. He was going to kill me. Time skipped a beat, and I could feel the scarf around my neck getting tighter and tighter. I couldn't breathe; I was battling to get air into my lungs, but I couldn't quite manage it. I had to stop him. I had to loosen the scarf.

"Frankie, are you all right?"

I heard a voice, but it didn't sound like Glenn's. It sounded like a woman's voice, but there was no woman here. I heard it again somewhere in the distance.

"Frankie, you're scaring me. Do you need a doctor? Are you OK?"

I was confused by the concern I heard in the voice. Glenn wouldn't say that.

Finally, my eyes let the real world come back into focus. Maria was standing before me with her eyes wide. She was twisting her ring round and round the middle finger of her right hand.

"I'm OK!" I muttered.

"Oh, thank God, you're back with us. I don't know where you were, but you weren't here. You really freaked me out there for a while. You looked awful, like you'd seen a ghost." She stopped talking abruptly as if something had suddenly occurred to her. "You didn't, did you?" she said looking left and then right.

"No. No ghosts. It's the scarf you're holding. It brought back some bad memories."

"Oh God! How utterly stupid of me," she said, hurriedly stuffing the scarf back into her handbag. "I'm so sorry; I'm mortified."

"You have nothing to apologise for. After all, you couldn't have known how the sight of that scarf would affect me," I said. I felt utterly exhausted and wanted to beat a hasty retreat. "I'm going to leave now," I announced.

"Oh, that's my fault, isn't it?" she exclaimed. "I'm so thoughtless."

"No, not at all," I assured her.

"I feel so bad. I brought the scarf because it was the last thing Verity bought, and she'd seemed so happy. I was going to give it to her parents at the wake." She shook her head. "I really am so incredibly stupid not to have realised what it would do to you."

"Really, it's OK. I'm OK now," I said attempting to reassure her. "I wanted to come to the funeral and now I have. I never intended to go to the wake. I don't want to intrude on the family's grief."

She hesitated. "Well, if you're sure. But I insist on checking up on you later. I feel responsible even though you say I'm not. Let me have your mobile number, and I'll call you later."

"OK, if it'll make you feel better, but you really don't have to."

"I know, but I want to."

That had been the beginning of our friendship. She had rung me that evening and pretty much every week since.

I was jolted out of my reverie by the car in front of me slamming on his brakes. I wasn't far from home now. An elderly gentleman with a walking stick was slowly and carefully negotiating the crossing on High Street in Portishead, bringing the traffic to a standstill.

I glanced around me at the shop windows as I waited. It was good to see that a variety of new, little independent shops had sprung up. I was tired of the multinational chains dominating our high streets. It was great to go into a shop and be able to purchase unique one-off items rather than the mass-produced items millions of other people were buying.

I realised the traffic must be moving again as a car went past me going in the opposite direction. I glanced at the driver as he passed. I recognised him immediately: it was Glenn; I was sure of it.

My heart flip-flopped within my rib cage. The meagre contents of my stomach rose within me with such speed it was all I could do not to be sick over the steering wheel. I'd broken out in a sweat that made all of my clothes feel damp; I desperately needed air. My finger was blindly trying to find the button to lower the window. I needed some air; I couldn't breathe.

I could hear a car horn blasting out. Looking ahead, I realised the cars in front of me had already moved on. Glancing in my rear-view mirror I could see the driver behind me gesticulating that I should move. I automatically raised my left hand in the air signalling an apology, and somehow put the car into gear and drove away. Not far now, the voice in my head was screaming. Not far to go. Within minutes, I was pulling up outside my home.

With shaking hands, I managed to get out of the car and let myself in. Shutting the door behind me, I stood there for a few seconds trying to calm myself.

"Frankie, you're back. Good day?" my mum said as she walked into the hallway to greet me, her face changing from happiness to see me, to concern. "What's wrong? Did it happen again?"

"Yes, but this time, Mum, I'm sure it was him."

Calmly and reassuringly, she took my hand in hers. "Love, we've been over this. Haven't we?"

"Yes," I nodded.

"Glenn is dead."

"No. I saw him. He was in a car on High Street. What if he knows where I live, Mum?" My voice was unnaturally high as I spoke. I was aware of how panicked I sounded.

Mum was patting my hand while leading me into the living room. "Let's sit down. Now," she spoke as one might seeking to comfort a small child, "Andrew explained to us, didn't he?"

My head was bowed, and my mum was bent low in front of me looking up into my face trying to see if she was managing to calm me.

"Yes," I muttered. She was referring to DC Andrew Smithers. He had been great throughout the investigation. Despite an extensive search and rescue operation, they had been unable to find Glenn Froom's body. He had explained early on that even though Glenn had drowned in the Bristol Channel his body could well have subsequently been swept into the North Atlantic Ocean. There was a possibility the body could be found in the weeks following, but equally that it would never be found.

At first, Andrew had agreed with my scepticism surrounding Glenn's death. He had explained to me that although it looked like a murder-suicide, without Glenn's body they weren't going to rule out the possibility that Glenn may have faked his suicide in order to evade capture.

The police decided to use specialist sniffer dogs to check the route Glenn had taken that day on Brean Down. An item of Glenn's clothing left at the scene had proved useful in supplying the dogs with his scent. They wanted to ensure he had only taken one route from his car to the proposed scene of his suicide and hadn't then left the scene via another route and subsequently escaped by other means.

The dog handlers confirmed that the dogs found Glenn's scent leading from his car to the point where he was meant to have entered the water and there the trail ended.

As far as I was concerned, all that meant was that Glenn had entered the water; it didn't mean he had died. He could have swum ashore. Again, Andrew agreed. He informed me they had searched the home Glenn and Verity had shared and had found his laptop computer together with his banking and financial details. They had already located Glenn's mobile phone in the pocket of his trousers, which he'd left at Brean Down Fort.

Once they had time to thoroughly examine Glenn's phone records and laptop, Andrew had confirmed that they had found nothing out of the ordinary. Using the banking details they had found on his laptop, they checked with Glenn's bank to see if he'd made any large withdrawals of cash just before the suicide. Obviously, if he had, it would indicate he had planned the whole thing. However, the bank confirmed that he hadn't strayed from his usual pattern of spending in the weeks before his suicide.

Glenn hadn't had any insurance policies, other than a joint life assurance policy payable in the event of either of their deaths. No one had attempted to claim on the policy since Verity's death.

Andrew had an agreement with Glenn's bank that should anyone attempt to take cash from Glenn's accounts that the police should be notified immediately. To date, Glenn's bank accounts sat untouched. I knew this because I regularly checked in with Andrew.

One night, unable to sleep, I had a brainwave: had the police checked Glenn's work computer for any incriminating evidence? I had rung Andrew's mobile and left a rambling message about how I couldn't sleep, and I wondered if they had checked his work's computer?

Andrew had returned my call the next day, and patiently explained they had indeed checked both his work computer and phone shortly after his disappearance. Once again, he uttered the words I had come to hate: 'they hadn't discovered anything out of the ordinary'. I didn't want benign reassurances. I wanted details. I wanted to know exactly what they had found and decide for myself if it was out of the ordinary or not. But, of course, that wasn't to be. The police didn't share details of a case with the public, especially a member of the public who was both a victim and a witness in the case. I was lucky Andrew had shared as much as he had with me.

There had been two occasions during the last year when my hopes had been raised by the discovery of a body: once by fishermen in the North Atlantic Ocean and once by birdwatchers on Brean Down. I felt ashamed that the discovery of a body should inspire such feelings in me, but I desperately needed closure. I needed to know I was no longer in danger; without a body I was never going to be sure. I had been informed on separate occasions that both dead bodies had been in the water for some time and were only identifiable by dental records. Both times, Andrew had called me to tell me it wasn't Glenn.

The absence of a body meant I was unable to accept Glenn was actually dead. My rational, logical self knew the absence of a body didn't mean he wasn't dead. But my fear of him was so great that I needed the discovery of his cadaver to be reassured. Andrew, having exhausted every avenue of investigation now believed Glenn Froom was in fact dead. He had on several occasions over the last six months attempted to convince me of this, to no avail.

"I know what Andrew told us, Mum. But I also know that I just saw Glenn Froom in a car on the High Street." I watched as the frown on my mum's face deepened, and her shoulders sagged in defeat.

"Go ahead and ring him then if you must. That'll only be the third time this month," she muttered under her breath as I watched her retreat into the kitchen.

I dug my mobile phone out of my bag and pressed number one. Needless to say, I had DC Smithers on speed dial.

# Chapter 6

The nerve of the man, I thought, as I inhaled deeply trying to calm myself. My hands were shaking with rage. How dare he dismiss me as if I had a screw loose. He had been talking to me as if I were a child. He was a condescending ass. Hoisting myself up from the bottom stair in the hallway, I went in search of my mum—to vent.

"Mum, you won't believe what DC Smithers just said to me."

"No need to shout, love. I'm only in the kitchen."

I stormed in banging into the working surface in my haste.

"Ow," I said as I gripped my side. My frustration was reaching boiling point as was my temper. Angry tears stung my eyes.

"Are you all right, Frankie? That must have hurt. Lift your top and let me see."

"I'm not a child," I spat.

I watched my mum visibly recoil at the ferocity of my tone, and I immediately felt guilty. She was just being Mum: trying to take care of me as always. My shoulders sagged with the weight of the guilt I now felt on top of the anger, frustration and physical pain.

"I'm sorry, Mum. You didn't deserve that. I'm just really angry that's all. Do you have any idea what DC smart-ass Smithers just said to me?"

"I know you're upset, Frankie, but language," she chastised.

Suddenly transported back to my childhood by my mum's rebuke, I once again felt compelled to apologise. "I'm sorry, Mum." And then adding as if an afterthought, "AGAIN," I said with feeling.

"OK, we'll start again then, shall we? What did Andrew say that has raised your ire so?"

My refusal to call him by his first name on this occasion was, I felt, testament to the depth of my feelings. Today, after that conversation, there was no familiarity, no friendliness; it was definitely all business from now on.

"DC Smithers did not take my sighting of Glenn Froom seriously. He pointed out it was my third sighting of him this month, and that was on top of the twenty possibly sightings I'd reported in the last year. What's more . . . ," and I paused for effect and attempted to root my mum to the spot with my glare, "he had the audacity to suggest that I see a counsellor. ME!" I raised my hands and shoulders to the heavens as I finished speaking as if to demonstrate the lunacy of his suggestion.

I heard my mum's sharp intake of breath. I took that to be her complete agreement with my outrage. As I watched her face closely for her reaction, I could see the lines around her eyes and mouth crinkle; her eyes were starting to water. She was biting her lip and trying to stifle something in her throat. I was confused for a moment, was she choking? Then it hit me like a thunderbolt. She was going to laugh. She was actually going to laugh. I was incredulous, and my mouth gaped as I stared at her. How could she? I felt betrayed.

She couldn't contain her mirth a second longer and, like a dam breaking its banks, loud raucous laughter erupted from her. It was deep belly laughter. She was holding her stomach and had clamped a hand over her mouth as if somehow that would contain, or at the very least muffle, the sound. The more I gaped at her in disgust the more she laughed. She tried to look away from me, but each time her eyes were drawn back to me like a moth to a flame, and upon seeing my face she would start again.

Finally, she was able to speak and in between gasps for air she managed to say, "Surely, the irony can't be completely lost upon you?" before she dissolved into more fits of laughter.

Her words started to permeate my anger. I, begrudgingly, began to see that it might be quite funny that someone might suggest to a counsellor that they needed counselling. My initial reaction to his suggestion was to be offended as I felt it meant he didn't believe me, and that was still my opinion. But my sense of humour was starting to break through my annoyance, and my mum's laughter was infectious.

Despite myself, I felt the corners of my mouth start to twitch, and my rib cage start to vibrate. My eyes were watering, and before I knew it I was holding my sides and rocking with laughter with her.

My mum and I were like a tag team in our efforts to stop laughing. I tried first as my sides felt like they were literally splitting. I found myself panting as I did during labour trying to quell the onslaught. I had it under control until one glance at my mum laughing caused an uncontrollable giggle to erupt from deep in my belly. My mum tried to stop next; she almost had it licked until I said brokenly between laughs, "Need counselling . . ." Upon which she exploded into raucous laughter once again. This went on for some ten minutes until Henry wandered into the kitchen wondering what all the fuss was about.

"Mum!" he shouted to make himself heard. "What's up? When you came in, you sounded upset, so I stayed in my room. What are you laughing about?"

Mum and I made eye contact and although the mirth was very much still there we fought to regain our composure. Mum managed to say that she was going into the living room to calm down and swiftly took herself off in that direction. I started to take lots of deep breaths trying to pacify the stitch I now had in my sides.

Eventually, the feelings subsided, and I wiped the tears from my eyes.

"I can't tell you why we were laughing, Henry. At least not at the moment, for fear it will start me off again."

He nodded."I get it. You OK? Aside from the laughter, I mean."

"Yes, yes I'm fine. Don't worry about me. How was your day?"

"Yeah, fine. Can I have something to eat?"

Here we go again, I thought. These boys were bottomless pits. Not for the first time in recent months, I considered changing their nickname. They were currently affectionately known as the Pant Bros because of their penchant for lounging around the house in only their pants. However, just recently their food consumption had increased to such a degree that Pit Bros might be a more suitable nickname.

"Haven't you had your dinner?" I asked already knowing that they had.

"Yeah."

"Have you had pudding?" Again a question I knew the answer to.

"Yeah."

"Then . . . ?"

"But, Mum, I'm hungry," he moaned.

I studied him. He'd grown a good two inches in the last year. Thankfully, that was in height and not width. He was ten, and still very much above average height for his age. As a growing lad, he clearly needed his calorific intake, but I was more concerned about what he was scoffing rather than the quantity.

"OK, you can have something to eat."

His eyes lit up.

"There's plenty of fruit in the bowl," I said, nodding in the bowl's direction.

The light in his eyes dimmed; his shoulders drooped. "Oh, Mum, can't I have a biscuit?" he wheedled.

"How many have you had so far today?" This was a familiar line of questioning. One we seemed to repeat on a daily basis.

"Hmm, let me see," and he stood there appearing to try and add up how many biscuits he'd had that day. Having decided upon a number he said, "One."

I laughed. "That was an awful lot of thinking and counting to arrive at a grand total of one. Are you sure?" I asked fixing him with one of my, 'I'm your mother and I know everything,' looks.

He looked down at his feet and shuffled uncomfortably as he mumbled, "Two."

"Honest answer, please."

Sighing, once again defeated, he sneaked a peek at my face in an attempt to gauge my mood before fixing his eyes once again on his feet. He appeared to decide honesty was the best policy and said, "Six."

"How many?" I erupted in mock disapproval.

Looking up with a worried expression on his face he said, "Grams let me. It's not my fault."

"What's this?" Mum said as she walked back into the kitchen having successfully regained control of her emotions.

Henry looked from one to the other of us, guilt etched into every inch of his face. Like a rabbit in the headlights, I thought.

Mum must have thought the same as she said, "Come on, Henry. Spit it out. What did I let you do?"

"Have six biscuits," he mumbled.

"What was that? Speak up," she said slowly and deliberately, not letting him off of the hook for a second. I almost felt sorry for him having experienced my mum's interrogation technique innumerable times.

"Have six biscuits," he said louder, his eyes still fixed firmly on the ground. I suspected he was willing it to open up and swallow him whole.

"Did I, now?" said Mum, with that tone of voice I knew and had come to fear as a child, and that still sent a chill through me. I hoped for Henry's sake he confessed and quickly. My mum was the loveliest person I knew, but you didn't lie to her or about her. She wouldn't stand for it.

Henry's body was visibly sagging, and I could hear the emotion in his voice as he said, "No, Grams. I took them out of the biscuit barrel without asking." His confession complete he looked up; his eyes beseeching us for leniency.

I wanted to laugh because anyone would think he was going to the gallows for what he had done such was the extent of his fear.

Mum and I regarded each other seriously and nodded our agreement.

Turning to Henry I shook my head. "So, you've taken biscuits and lied about it."

His expression was grave as he nodded.

"What do you think your punishment should be?"

"A ban from the laptop for the night," he suggested, wincing at the thought.

He loved playing on the laptop. It was a serious punishment to be banned from it for any length of time. He obviously thought what he had done was serious to think it warranted a ban from his beloved laptop.

"I'm inclined to agree with you and, in addition, apologise to Grams please."

"Sorry, Grams," he said and started to sob.

Mum held out her arms to him, and he shot into them relieved by this signal from her that he was forgiven.

"Don't do it again," I heard her mutter into his ear.

"I won't," he said seriously.

Taking pity on him I said, "Good, now that's over. Always remember, Henry, tomorrow is another day." I was never one to dwell on bad behaviour.

"But, Mum . . ."

"Yes."

"I'm still hungry."

All three of us descended into laughter once again.

"Grab a couple of breadsticks. What's your brother doing?"

"He's on the computer. I can hear him chatting to his friends."

Of course he is, I thought. It was a stupid question really. Both Alex and Henry loved computers. It was a battle to get them to do anything else these days.

"Now I'm banned from the laptop, is it OK if I play on the Wii?" Henry asked hopefully.

"Go on then," I succumbed.

His face lighting up, he said, "Great! Thanks, Mum." He'd already grabbed the breadsticks and had rammed one in his mouth as he left the kitchen. No wonder my house was always strewn with crumbs, I thought.

"Cuppa?" My mum offered as she held the kettle aloft in front of me.

"Yep, that would be lovely," I said as I flopped on to a kitchen stool.

I surveyed my new kitchen. It wasn't a brand new kitchen, but it was new to me. I'd been living in this, my new home, for the last nine months. It still didn't feel entirely like home yet. I missed my old house, but I didn't miss the bad memories that were inextricably linked to it thanks to Glenn Froom.

This kitchen didn't really compare to my old kitchen. In fact, nothing about this house with the exception of the garden compared favourably to my old home. Except for the fact that it was a fresh start, and what I could afford in this part of Bristol. My new kitchen was small and modern with a breakfast bar and tall chrome stools that I sometimes struggled to sit on. Luckily, the room could also accommodate a small table in the corner.

Everything about this house was the opposite of my old house, and that was why I had chosen it. Well, that and the fact that it was the only house for sale at the time that I could afford.

It was a modern house with small, characterless square rooms, and walls that you couldn't hammer a picture hook into for fear of them falling down. While my previous home had been characterful and charming, it had also been a money pit. I was always having something renewed or repaired. The advantage of a modern home was there was nothing to renew or repair, and I didn't anticipate having to do anything for the next ten years, at least.

I glanced out of the kitchen window at the garden while my mum busied herself with tea making. I did like the garden, though; that was one thing I did like. It was longer than the average garden, and the previous owner, a retired school teacher, had been an amateur but enthusiastic horticulturalist. Since living here, I'd been constantly enchanted by the differing plants that would flower with each changing season. I didn't know an allium from an anemone, but I could admire their beauty nevertheless.

I had absolutely no gardening skills and, as a result, was apprehensive about necessary tasks such as weeding. The last time I'd attempted that particular task I'd enlisted my mum's help and expertise. I was now completely confident that, not only didn't I know one type of flower from another, but I also didn't know the difference between a flower and a weed. There had been a few near misses. On one occasion, my mum had drolly informed me that the weed I was pulling out was a marigold. The next occasion it was a cornflower and the next an iris.

I'd got to the point where I either needed to seriously swat up on flowers, or leave it the heck alone and trust the experts, aka my mum, to deal with it. I clearly chose the latter; it was more convenient and less time-consuming. Luckily for me, Mum enjoyed gardening.

Mum placed a large mug of tea in front of me before attempting to settle on the stool beside me. A smug smile played at the corners of my mouth as I watched her multiple attempts to hoist her petite five foot frame onto the high stool. Deciding to take pity on her, I reached out an arm and hoisted her onto the stool.

"Thanks, Frankie, I'm still getting used to them."

"Do I need to buy you a footstool so you can get on them when I'm not here?"

She playfully thumped my arm. "OK, cheeky, I'm not that short."

I simply raised my eyebrows in reply.

"Hmm, OK, I am that short."

Changing the subject I asked, "How were the boys when they came home from school?"

She hesitated slightly, "They were OK."

"Mum, what aren't you saying?"

She let out a sigh, "I'm worried about Alex. He's too quiet. I ask him about his day, and he just shrugs. He can't wait to get on his computer and talk to his friends. I suspect they're his old friends from his previous school. He doesn't mention any new friends from Portishead Secondary."

It was my turn to sigh. This wasn't anything new but nevertheless still worrying. The move, however necessary, had affected Alex deeply. I suspected he was attempting to protect me by trying to shield me from his difficulties.

Glenn's attempt to kill me and everything I had found myself embroiled in at ASF Technologies hadn't just affected my life but everyone's around me.

Alex and Henry had clung to me for weeks after the attempt on my life, and in truth I had clung to them in equal measure. When I had explained to them that we would need to move away and they would need to change schools, they had been surprisingly compliant. I suspected at the time, and it was subsequently confirmed by my mum, they hadn't complained not because they were OK with it, but because they couldn't bear to worry me.

Alex had confided in my mum shortly after the Glenn incident that he figured I'd been through enough. He didn't want me to worry about him and Henry on top of what I was going through. I applauded his thoughtfulness, and was relieved, truth be told, that they weren't making the whole transition even more difficult than it already was. I figured that although they were worried about the move and everything it entailed it was a natural worry and one that would soon be allayed. They would soon settle in, make friends and everything would be fine.

While everything had worked out just as I had hoped for Henry, who loved his new primary school and new friends, it had not worked out thus far for Alex. He didn't say much about his new school, Portishead Secondary, which incidentally was just around the corner from our new house, or any of his fellow students. In truth, this worried me more than if he had ranted that he hated the school and everyone in it. He seemed to be internalising his feelings; burying everything deep within him. I was concerned that I didn't know the true extent of his unhappiness. It would seem from my mum's comment that she felt the same.

"What do you think I should do? I've tried getting him to open up, but he's resisted me so far by saying he's fine."

"I've got an idea that will hopefully kill two birds with one stone. I hope you don't get offended, Frankie, but it's obvious you could do with some 'ME' time. Have a weekend away with a friend and have some fun. Can you remember what that is?"

I smiled ruefully. "If I concentrate really hard, I think I can remember. But how is that going to help Alex?" I asked.

"Well, and please don't get upset, I think Alex won't open up to you because he feels responsible for your happiness. Since the . . ." she hesitated as she always did when trying to discuss what had almost happened to me. "Since what happened last year," she continued, "he has taken on the self-imposed role of your protector, and I think he feels he has to be strong for your sake. Part of not telling you what is going on for him is so that you won't worry about him. I think Alex and Henry should stay with Rob, Lucy and the twins while you're away."

Rob was my ex-husband and the Pant Bros' dad. Since our divorce, he had married Lucy and they had fourteen-month-old twin girls.

"If we tell Rob our suspicions, he can encourage Alex to tell him what's going on. I think Alex is more likely to open up to Rob. He doesn't feel responsible for Rob's happiness the way he feels responsible for yours. Not that it's your fault," she added hurriedly. "Sorry, Frankie, I don't want to upset you," she said while searching my face for just such evidence that she had done so.

I experienced conflicting emotions while Mum was speaking. Initially, I had wanted to tell her she was wrong. I could feel the anger welling up inside me; it was warring with the sensible, rational side of me that insisted I actually consider what my mum was saying before reacting. The counsellor in me quickly saw my mum was right in what she said, but the mother in me completely rejected the idea.

If I were to accept my mum's explanation of Alex's behaviour, would that make me a bad mother? My psyche immediately dismissed the idea simply because I didn't like how it made me feel; it made me feel guilty. I didn't like it. Still my rational voice asked, if this were happening to another family who had experienced the same things, what would I be saying? The answer: the same thing as my mum just did.

"God, I hate it when you're right. I mean really hate it," I said, and stamped my foot, much like a child would, for good measure.

"I know you do. Well, what you actually 'hate' is my pointing out what your subconscious has been trying to ignore."

She was right on the money, as usual. I'd known what was happening on some level, but my consciousness didn't want to acknowledge it because then I would have to deal with it.

"You're good. Ever thought of being a counsellor?" I asked with a twinkle in my eye.

"Funnily enough . . ." she started to say and then stopped herself. She took a deep breath and said, "No, that's my daughter's job and very good she is at it too."

"Ha! Thanks, Mum. I'll ring Rob first and see when he can have the boys, and then I'll see if Rebecca is up for a weekend away."

"Great," said Mum.

I could hear the relief in her voice. Reaching for my mobile phone, I speed-dialled Rob.

# Chapter 7

I got out of bed quietly and tiptoed downstairs. I didn't know why I tried to be so quiet each morning as, in reality, the Pant Bros could sleep through a full-scale riot and not lose one second of precious sleep. I clicked the kettle on in the kitchen, and realised I hadn't checked to see if I had any answer machine messages from the previous day.

After the silent calls I'd received last year leading up to Verity's death, I no longer answered my landline telephone. I used the answer machine very much as a boss used their personal assistant to screen their calls. I figured any new clients would assume I was busy and leave a message.

I had received a few silent answer machine messages over the last year. Each time I'd been convinced it was Glenn letting me know he was still alive. But no one else believed me. DC Smithers was of the opinion that because my landline number was the number I used in my advertisements in the local paper that it was probably just kids calling to cause mischief; their idea of a silly prank. I knew what he said made sense, but still . . .

You never know, ten new clients could have called yesterday wanting to book a session.

"And pigs can fly," I muttered aloud.

I had three new messages. Not quite the ten clients I'd hoped for. But if the messages were all from prospective clients, then I'd be more than happy with three. I pressed the play button and waited.

"You have three new messages," the familiar pre-recorded voice announced. "Message one: . . ."

The air around me was filled with silence. My heart started to pound. It wasn't the brief silence you expect when someone realises they've dialled the wrong number. It stretched on and on. It was him! I knew it was him. I didn't even want to touch the machine to skip to the next message; it was as if to do so would somehow mean I was coming into contact with him.

My finger shot out and pressed the button and then recoiled as if it had touched fire. I couldn't breathe. Please let me hear a friendly voice. Again no one spoke, but this time I could hear him breathing. Each breath seemed to be taunting me. It was his way of saying I'm here; I'm alive; I'm coming for you!

The familiar feelings of anxiety were building in me, and I reached automatically for the elastic band around my wrist. Damn! I had forgotten to put it on when I woke up. I considered going back upstairs to retrieve it, but decided I'd endure the final message.

I looked down at my shaking hands, and gathering my courage I skipped to the final message. I was hoping to hear a voice, but in my heart of hearts I knew it would be the same as the other two calls—silent. I was right! My knees startled to buckle from beneath me.

Would this ever end? It was Glenn. I knew it was. I would go through the motions of trying to find out the telephone number of the last person that had called. But even before I reached for the telephone, I knew it was hopeless as it had been on each of the previous occasions. I blindly dialled 1471.

"We do not have the caller's number to return this call," said the automated voice on the other end of the phone.

"Of course you don't! You never bloody do!" I said out loud knowing I was free to swear as there was no one on the other end to offend.

In a moment of pure frustration and anger, I jabbed the message delete button repeatedly and with unnecessary force. I'd succeeded in deleting the messages. If only I could delete Glenn Froom from my life so easily. I fleetingly considered telling Mum about the messages. I certainly wasn't going to tell DC Smithers after our last encounter. What was the point! No, I'd keep this to myself. It was time for breakfast and a calming cup of tea.

*****

I stood at my kitchen window and gazed at my garden as I often did of late. Its beauty usually soothed me, and I was hoping it would now. I took deep, slow breaths in an effort to calm myself. After a minute or so, I could feel my breathing return to normal. My heart was once again beating a steady tattoo.

Thankfully, the boys were still asleep in their respective rooms. I didn't want them picking up on my heightened emotions. I really needed a weekend away, and it looked as if it was going to happen sooner than I'd expected.

I'd called Rob last night. He'd consulted Lucy, and they were happy to have the boys for a weekend. In fact, they said next weekend would be perfect if I could organise my weekend away at such short notice. Could I! I'd texted Rebecca, immediately, to ask if she wanted to accompany me on a girls' weekend away.

I was quite excited about the idea now. Coincidentally, my phone pinged and looking down I could see she'd responded. It simply said:

*HELL YES!*

Chuckling at her blatant enthusiasm, I texted back:

*I'll call you later. We'd better book something pronto.*

I held my warm cup of tea between both hands and returned my gaze to the flowers in my garden. I watched the bees flit busily from one blossom to another. I marvelled at their internal navigation system: never once crashing into one another, instead gliding around each other. I wondered if they ever fought over the same flower. It's my nectar. No, it's my nectar. Hey dude, I saw the flower first. A smile spread across my face at the ridiculousness of my thoughts. You're cracking up, Frankie.

Out of the corner of my eye, I saw something dart across the garden. My eyes, like radar tracking a ballistic missile, homed in on the area of detected movement. What was that? Oh no, not a rat, I thought. I stood stock-still, watching and waiting for it to make another appearance.

There was a beautiful little robin that visited my garden often around this time in the morning. In fact, I could see the bird on the grass attempting to pull a juicy worm from the ground. I assumed it was the same robin, but in reality it could have been a different one each day. I had as much knowledge of birds as I did of plants: pretty much zero. Still, that didn't stop me appreciating both in equal measure.

Suddenly, a cat leapt from underneath a bush in my garden and launched itself at the bird. The bird was too quick for it and seemed to mock it slightly as it flew up just outside of its reach. It hovered momentarily before flying to higher, safer ground.

"Yes!" I said out loud as I punched the air in triumph. "Good for you! If I were in the same situation, I might have been tempted to say 'nah, nah, nah, nah' myself. I might have pooped on his head too for good measure. But only if I were you, of course." I added for clarification, as if it were needed, which of course it wasn't. I was talking to a bird.

The cat was still standing in the middle of my garden. It started to claw at the ground; I suspected it was preparing the ground before it did its business. Now the bird I could tolerate, but the cat pooping in my garden?

No. My garden was not its litter tray. I opened the back door and ran outside.

"No you don't! Scoot cat. Go back to your own toilet." I said perhaps a tad too loudly.

The cat shot out of my garden as if a bomb had gone off.

"Excuse me," I heard a female say in a tetchy tone of voice. I wasn't sure where her voice was coming from. I turned my head from side to side to see which neighbour was trying to get my attention. It had to be a neighbour as no one else could possibly be in the vicinity. All of the gardens backed on to each other. I was surrounded by neighbours' gardens.

"Excuse me," she repeated deliberately and loudly.

Her voice was loud enough for me to determine it was my neighbour to the left of me. Which made sense as that was the direction from which the offending cat had come.

"Yes?"I said, aware I was in the garden in my dressing gown. Pulling the belt of my dressing gown ever tighter, I walked over to the fence that divided us and peered over it.

"Did you just scare my cat?" said a confrontational octogenarian.

I knew she was in her eighties because I'd popped round when we had first moved in to introduce myself. She'd informed me her name was Peggy. She'd told me she'd lived there for three years and had moved to Portishead to be near her son and his family. She went on to tell me that he was a great source of disappointment to her as he never visited. She blamed his wife, whom she felt was the main culprit in keeping her son from her.

If only I had a pound for every time the wife got blamed for the son's inattention, I'd be rich. Didn't women raise sons with a mind and will of their own? I had made a mental note after that conversation: if my sons didn't visit me when they were grown-up, it was because they didn't want to, and not because their wife didn't let them.

"Good morning, Peggy," I said, a smile pasted on my face.

"Morning," she said huffily.

I could see my greeting had reminded her of her manners, and she wasn't best pleased by it. "How are you today?" I persisted.

"Did you just scare my cat?" she repeated, her eyes narrowing in an accusatory fashion and her finger jabbing toward me.

I sighed. I could see that she was determined to make an issue out of this. The counsellor in me wondered how best to defuse the situation; the neighbour in me wanted to tell her to let her cat crap in her own back garden. However, she was an old lady, and I didn't want to upset her. I certainly didn't want her keeling over and dying on me, so tact and diplomacy was the order of the day.

"I may have, Peggy. I didn't mean to frighten it, but it was just about to do its business in my garden. Needless to say, I didn't want it to, so I encouraged it to go home."

"Hmm! Well Tibbles shot into my kitchen as if she'd been shot. I had my windows open you know. I heard you shout at her."

"My voice may have been a tad louder than I had intended, I'll grant you. I'm sorry Tibbles was frightened. She had just, however, tried to catch a beautiful little robin that visits my garden daily." My point being that Tibbles wasn't the only animal that had been frightened.

"She's a cat! What do you expect her to do? Cats catch birds," she said with her chest puffed out indignantly, and an expression on her face that indicated she thought I may be mentally challenged.

I could see that where Tibbles was concerned she wasn't to be reasoned with.

"Yes, I know that, Peggy." I needed to close this situation down before it escalated as I could feel my temperature rising. I was starting to get irritated, and I needed to walk away before I said something I would regret.

"Then you'll also know I can't stop it pooing where it wants to." Her voice was rising; her face was turning a deeper shade of red with every word.

I found myself hoping she didn't suffer from high blood pressure. I needed her to calm down for her own sake but knew better than to say it. I mean, who actually calmed down when told to do so. If anything, those two words only ever exacerbated a situation.

She was in full flow now as she continued, "I suppose you're worried about your precious flowers. Not that you do anything to make them so lovely. I see your poor mother working in your garden every week. What do you do? Nothing. Typical. You get your mother to do the hard work, and you take all the glory."

Even though she was talking about my mum and me, I felt she was actually referring to her relationship with her son. She thought what she saw going on between my mother and I reflected her own experience of motherhood. Her words, when applied to her own relationship, implied that she felt she had done a lot for her son, and that somehow he hadn't acknowledged her contribution.

I understood why she had said what she had, but it didn't mean I liked it. I could have retaliated. And believe me, the dutiful daughter in me wanted to say something extremely cutting, and shut her vicious diatribe down in seconds. But did I really want to hurt an old lady who appeared to be unhappy?

So, swallowing down a stinging retort, I merely said, "The arrangement I have with my mother is my business, and no one else's." I ended with a friendly smile, one which I wasn't particularly feeling. I started to walk away from her back into my house and quickly tossed in, "I hope Tibbles is feeling better." It was almost certainly disingenuous of me because right now I'd quite like to throttle its tiny neck. No, I chided myself, that wasn't true. She was just a cat; she didn't know her owner was going to be so protective.

I clicked the kettle on and prepared to make another cup of tea. As a result of that little debacle, my tea had got cold. A niggling thought crept into my consciousness: was Peggy right? Was I taking advantage of my mum's generous spirit? I determined to ask her later. Not that she would say I was, even if it were true, but I'd watch her closely and discern if I had any cause for concern.

I still had half an hour before the Pant Bros needed to get up for school. I switched on my iPad and googled the Portishead Times. I found the announcements section and searched for celebration notifications. They had a section called 'All Wedding Bells'; that was the section I wanted. I checked this week's wedding messages; I scrolled down to the surnames beginning with 'S'. Someone called Harry Sanderson got married this week as well as a Larry Scrivens. Right, I had it, the 'Sh' surnames. I held my breath, as I searched for his name, and exhaled slowly as I couldn't see the name Shaw. This had become a weekly ritual of mine.

For the last six months, I'd placed a regular advertisement in the very same newspaper I was now scanning avidly.

Five months ago, I'd been checking to see if my ad was online as promised by the newspaper. It was, and I had been checking that the details had been printed correctly when somehow I inadvertently touched an area of the screen I didn't intend to. The screen changed, and I found myself staring at the engagement announcements.

One announcement, in particular, caught my eye and I read it. It didn't end there: I ended up reading all the messages of congratulations; thinking how nice it was to read about good news for a change. As I scrolled through, I happened upon an announcement of the engagement of a Sarah Flattery to a David Shaw.

Just seeing David Shaw's name in print sent shivers down my spine. My mind automatically shied away from recollecting any detail of our last counselling session together. It couldn't be the same David Shaw, could it? After all, it was a common name, and at that point it had been less than a year since his wife died.

I'd almost convinced myself it wasn't the same David Shaw, when looking through the local news articles; I found a local interest piece on the engagement of a local couple and the details of the unusual proposal. There was a picture of the happy couple, and smiling up from the page as if mocking me was the handsome, narcissistic face of David Shaw.

It was a light-hearted article on how Sarah Flattery, a well-known local girl, had been whisked off her feet, quite literally, by David Shaw. He'd arrived at Flattery's Haulage, where she worked, on a horse, dressed in knight's armour and carrying roses. My gag reflex was working overtime as I read. I thought I might actually vomit, and it wasn't just because the whole thing was so corny.

The article explained that Sarah was the daughter of local entrepreneur, Mike Flattery. He owned the very successful Flattery Haulage, and it alluded to his wealth by showing a picture of the happy couple posing at his home in Cadbury Camp Lane, Clapton-in-Gordano. That particular private road was known locally as millionaires' row. Only the very rich could afford to live there.

So, David was doing it again. He was targeting a rich girl for her money. I could be wrong; he might actually love her, but I doubted it. What concerned me more than his gold-digging ways were his murderous ways. Was she going to experience the same fate as his first wife if the money dried up? I had to do something.

I considered going to the police and telling them everything I suspected. I knew it may jeopardise my professional reputation, but I was less concerned about that and more concerned about Sarah Flattery's safety. However, when I reread the notes I'd made on David's last session, even I could see that I had absolutely no evidence a crime had been committed; he never actually admitted killing her.

I could explain to the police that in my professional opinion he was admitting to killing her, but he could just as easily explain away his words as those of a guilt-ridden, grieving husband. Guilt-ridden, not because he had killed her, but because she had been shopping for his birthday present the day she got knocked down and killed. After all, I had believed exactly that when he first insisted he was responsible for her death.

I had to find a way of stopping him marrying Sarah Flattery. I thought back to the night I'd been having dinner with Mum and had seen him in Mizzi's with a young lady. The girl, on that occasion, was not Sarah.

Now, here we were, only six months or so later, and he was engaged to Sarah Flattery. The fact they were engaged implied they had been dating for a while. I considered the very real possibility that he had been or was still seeing both girls at the same time.

I found myself wondering if David was a creature of habit. If he was, and if he was still seeing the other girl, then it might be worth me staking out Mizzi's. If I could get an incriminating photo of him with her, then I could send it to Mike Flattery. I wouldn't send it to Sarah. She may not believe it, or she may allow David to explain it away. Daddy would be another story. No man likes his daughter being made a fool of especially a rich and powerful one. I felt sure he wouldn't fall for any of David's sob stories. Or at least I hoped he wouldn't.

I had no idea whether or not my plan would work, and I didn't have any real backup plan. The last time I had seen David Shaw at Mizzi's had been on a Friday evening. So, I determined to become a regular Friday night patron of Mizzi's. There was no sign of him on my first two Friday visits. I was beginning to think it was an incredibly stupid idea when on the third visit, there he was.

He was sitting at the bar, and the same girl I had seen him with last time was draped over him like a blanket. Her arms were wrapped around his neck, and she was looking lovingly up into his face as he ordered drinks. I scrabbled for my phone, and prayed the quality of the photo would be good enough in this lighting. I needed something more intimate, more incriminating. He could explain her away as some over-friendly colleague in the pose they were currently striking. Then it came, the money shot: she pulled his face around to hers and almost devoured his face with her mouth.

Adjusting the focus on my camera phone, I watched as their faces filled all of the available space on the screen. It was as close up as I could achieve. Seizing the moment before it passed, I took the photograph. The camera decided it needed more light. The flash went off. It must have caught David's eye because he broke away from the kiss and turned in my direction.

I was in the back corner of the restaurant. I was sat in the same seat I was in the last time. This time, I thanked God it was a dark corner. I grabbed the rather oversized menu and stuck it in front of my face. Please God, let him think it was just another person taking a selfie. Let's face it, everywhere you go these days someone is smiling inanely at their camera phone.

I gave it a few minutes and slowly lowered my menu. I was safe; they were chatting and drinking. Phew! I wasn't going to risk another photograph. I inspected the picture I'd taken. I didn't feel proud of myself.

Sarah Flattery was going to be hurt when she saw this photograph. But I decided, better emotionally hurt than dead. When they left twenty minutes later, I paid the bill and left. I was quite relieved that my plan had worked, and that I didn't need to visit next Friday. My mum was beginning to suspect I had a secret boyfriend because I was going out so regularly of late.

On the Saturday morning, I printed out the photograph and wrote a note that said:

*Last Friday at Mizzi's in central Bristol. Is this the kind of man you want your daughter to marry?*

I slid the photograph and note into an envelope. I had a prick of conscience as I was about to seal it. It was an underhanded thing I was about to do, but it was for the greater good, I decided. It had been easy to find Flattery Haulage's address online. I had addressed it to Mike Flattery, for his attention only, private and confidential. I had posted the envelope later that afternoon.

There was no way of my knowing the outcome of my interference. But, since that day, four and a half months ago, I had checked the wedding announcements every week. So far, so good, their wedding had not appeared. I sincerely hoped my plan had worked, and that they were no longer engaged. My mind turned to the next young lady he would meet. I shook my head as if to empty it of its contents. I couldn't be responsible for the fate of every young woman he met. Could I?

# Chapter 8

***Session one - Tom Ferris 10.00 a.m. - 11.00 a.m.***

"I feel anxious all the time," he said, his head in his hands. "It's become intolerable. It's gotten so some days I don't want to leave the house." He looked up at me, desperation carved into his facial muscles. His eyes were imploring me to help him, as he ran a hand through his already tousled hair. The action left his brown hair sticking up in strangely angled tufts. He reminded me fleetingly of a mad professor.

I would try to help him. But I needed to know more, much more, before I could help him in any meaningful way. Tom was the first of the two new clients I was seeing today. He'd rung me after seeing my advert in the local newspaper. He'd explained on the phone that he was experiencing anxiety. He had seen a doctor several times in the last few months, and they had recommended that he see a counsellor.

"The doctor recommended a combination of both tablets and counselling to help me. But, I'm not keen on taking tablets. I never have been. I don't even like taking an aspirin when I've got a headache."

I nodded, understanding completely where he was coming from. I didn't like taking tablets either, but sometimes they were necessary.

He continued, "What was it he called them?" clearly asking the question of himself. "Setralin . . . ? No, Sertraline," he corrected. The doctor explained they were some kind of SSRI. Whatever that is?"

I hadn't heard of 'Sertraline', but I had heard of SSRIs. SSRI stood for selective serotonin reuptake inhibitor.

"They are a type of antidepressant. They work by increasing serotonin levels in the brain," I answered in response to his unasked question.

"Oh, I see."

I could have gone on to explain that seratonin is a chemical that carries signals between nerve cells in the brain, and that it is thought to have a good influence on mood, emotion, and sleep. An increased level of seratonin is believed to improve symptoms in people suffering from depression and anxiety. I could have, but I didn't. Instead, I asked, "How long have you been suffering with extreme anxiety?"

He was giving my question some thought. I absently observed that his hair was no longer standing up on end; it would seem that gravity had done its job. He was younger than me. I would have put him at around thirty years old. He was dressed casually in jeans and a long-sleeved t-shirt. His trainers were well-worn and grubby, but one of the more expensive brands, nevertheless.

When he had greeted me, not more than five minutes ago, I had noted that he wasn't particularly tall, approximately five feet eight or nine. Now, as I watched him, I could almost see his brain calculating the duration of this unpleasant malaise.

"I'd say the last nine months or so." He paused as if to check his math and then nodded. "Yes, nine months." He eyed me nervously, as if considering whether he could trust me with what he was about to say next. His eyes searched my face for whatever reassurance his mind sought and seemingly found it as he said, "It's not just anxiety. I'm losing my temper. I'm getting really angry, and I don't know where it's coming from." His eyes were downcast as if ashamed of his admission.

Reflecting what he had said back to him I repeated, "For the past nine months you've been experiencing extreme anxiety and bouts of anger."

"Yes. Listen," he said, and put both his hands out in front of him in a back off gesture. "I need you to help me cope with it. I'm not interested in the touchy-feely side of counselling. I don't want to talk about my life history. I want practical help for anxiety . . . and the anger of course," he added.

I wasn't offended by his outburst. I understood his desperation for some kind of quick fix and the fact he didn't want to spend weeks talking about his feelings in case it didn't help. However, I needed to understand what type or types of anxiety he was experiencing before I could offer any kind of coping strategies. He clearly wasn't ready to talk, if in fact he ever would be, but what I could offer him were some cognitive behavioural techniques for coping with anxiety.

"I hear you," I said.

He seemed to relax a little, clearly relieved that I wasn't going to make him talk.

"But . . ." I added.

I could see him flinch at the word, and his shoulders stiffen once again. I decided I had better let him know what I needed from him quickly as the unknown seemed to be fuelling his anxiety. "I need to know what types of anxiety you are experiencing."

He shook his head and shrugged.

I'd expected that reaction. I persevered, "People experience the effects of anxiety differently. I need to understand what you are thinking and feeling when you are particularly anxious."

He was looking at me as if I should know this already. "Well, I'm feeling anxious. You know how that feels, surely?"

Actually, I did, but it wouldn't do for me to apply my feelings of anxiety to his experience. I didn't want to lead him into an answer, but it was clear I was going to have to give him some examples.

"When I feel anxious, my heart starts to race," and I paused. I'd given him his starter for ten.

He nodded. "Yes, my heart races too. Sometimes, it feels like it will burst. I worry I'm going to have a heart attack. My chest constricts; I find it hard to breathe." He was on a roll now. "I start to feel hot all over, and I break out in a sweat. My hands shake, and then the rest of my body follows suit. It's uncontrollable."

"I know it can feel that way. But it is controllable. We can talk about some strategies you could use to help you with some of the symptoms you are experiencing. When you start to feel stressed, do you notice anything about the way you are breathing?"

He frowned at me, once again indicating he thought it was a stupid question. I wasn't offended. He would get used to me and my questions. He would come to trust that there was always a point to them.

"Umm . . . in and out," he said glibly.

I persevered. "I find that when anxious my breathing pattern changes from relaxed to rapid, shallow breaths."

His eyes widened, "Yes. That's exactly it. My breathing quickens. To the extent that it feels as if I'm fighting to fill my lungs with air, but I can't ever seem to get enough air into them."

I smiled and nodded. "It's a perfectly normal response to stress; it's called hyperventilation. Should you tend to breathe in this way often, it can lead to some really unpleasant physical side effects."

He sat forward in his chair, and for the first time since arriving I could see he was interested in what I had to say.

He was starting to believe that I could help him, which meant I'd won half the battle.

"Like what?" he asked.

I held up my right hand with my five fingers spread wide, and I touched each finger in turn with the index finger of my left hand as I checked off the symptoms. "Chest and stomach pain, tiredness, tingling in your face, hands or limbs, dizziness, and visual problems. That isn't an exhaustive list, but you get the point."

He wore a relieved expression as I finished speaking.

"That's good to know. As I said to you earlier, I've thought I was going to have a heart attack on several occasions. I've also felt a tingling sensation in my face. I thought I was having a stroke."

I nodded gently as I spoke. "That's a perfectly reasonable conclusion to jump to considering the symptoms you're experiencing. However, once you know the side effects of persistent shallow breathing you can start to rationalise the symptoms in a different way."

"Yes, I see what you mean."

"There is a technique called controlled breathing. I can show you the technique today, and you can practise using it next time your breathing becomes shallow. Is that OK?"

"Yes, yes, definitely. It's exactly what I want: some practical help."

*****

We were coming to the end of the first session, and Tom had enthusiastically embraced the controlled breathing technique. I had shown him what to do, and then we had practised together.

"OK, so your homework . . ."

He grimaced at the word 'homework'. Almost everyone did, and who could blame them, because it inevitably reminded them of school.

I smiled. "Your homework is to practise your controlled breathing, especially, if you feel your anxiety increasing. In addition, I want you to keep an anxiety diary." And I produced a piece of paper from my briefcase. Putting it on the coffee table, so we could both see it, I proceeded to explain what I wanted him to do.

"At the top of the piece of paper is a scale from one to ten. This is to measure the level of anxiety you are feeling: one being the lowest level of anxiety and ten being the highest. This diary is only to be used to record bouts of anxiety.

"You'll see there are columns to be completed. The first column is the date and time; the second is where are you and what are you doing when the anxiety occurs and the third is to rate your anxiety levels. In the fourth column, I'd like you to describe what it was about the situation you were in that made you anxious. There are a fifth and sixth column that covers what you did to cope and the revised anxiety rating afterward. You needn't complete the fifth and sixth column for now. I'd like you to focus on the first four columns for this week."

He frowned, and I sensed his unwillingness to complete the anxiety diary.

"It's only by completing this diary that we'll fully understand the type of anxiety you're experiencing and its possible triggers. It's only then that I can teach you the right type of techniques to combat it."

"But you've already taught me the breathing technique," he retorted.

"Yes, that's to combat the physical effects you're experiencing. But your anxiety is being triggered by your thoughts. We need to understand what those thoughts are, and in what circumstances they occur, in order to change them."

"Hmm," he said and reluctantly picked up his homework.

He was reticent to do as I asked. I wondered if he would return next week.

"I'll see you at the same time next week. If you can't make it for any reason, please let me know. And remember your breathing technique."

"I will," he said as he was leaving. He stopped, turned and said, "I was sceptical that counselling could help me, to be honest I still am, but less so than when I came in an hour ago."

"I appreciate your candour. Let's see if we can reduce your scepticism still further next week."

He smiled, nodded in agreement and left. I picked up my notebook and made my customary notes as I did after every client's session.

# Chapter 9

*Session one - Susan Mackintosh 11.30 a.m. - 12.30 p.m.*

The sun was shining through the windows and raising the temperature of the already adequately warm room. It was a small office, so any increase in temperature was quickly apparent. I shrugged off my cardigan and reached for my glass of water. I was already beginning to debate whether or not I should turn on the small desk fan when the phone in the office rang.

"Hello."

"Hi, Frankie, I've got a Susan Mackintosh in reception for you."

"Thanks, Theresa. I'll be right there."

Decision made; I clicked the desk fan on. I could always switch it off again when we returned to the room. At least it would have a minute or two to lower the ambient temperature. I cast a cursory glance around the room to make sure everything was as it should be. Once satisfied that it was, I left the room.

As I descended the single flight of stairs between my office and reception, I caught a glimpse of the lone female waiting patiently for me. She was attractive, and I would have guessed was in her early forties. She was tall and slim with auburn hair and pale skin. She wore a grey trouser suit, which I surmised by the cut and quality of the material had not been purchased in the stores I frequented. It fit her to perfection. I caught a glimpse of her manicured nails, and as I approached her caught a whiff of expensive perfume. Everything about her seemed to scream wealth.

Smiling as I held out my hand, I said, "Hello, you must be Susan."

"Yes, and you must be Francesca," she said, while shaking my hand.

"You can call me Frankie. Would you like to follow me," I said as I led the way back to my office.

We didn't talk while we walked as was often my way with clients. I didn't encourage conversation outside of the confidentiality of the counselling room. As we entered the room, I was glad to see the desk fan had done its job; the temperature had cooled to a comfortable level once again. Clicking off the fan, I asked Susan to take a seat.

*****

I'd delivered the obligatory housekeeping: the part of the first session where I explain the rules around punctuality and then cover confidentiality et cetera. I continued, "So . . . I've been speaking for long enough. It's over to you. What's brought you here today?"

She took a deep breath. I wasn't sure whether its purpose was to bolster her confidence or was in anticipation of a great deal to say. Her eyes were already brimming with tears before having uttered a word. I could see this was difficult for her. A single tear trickled slowly down her cheek. She hurriedly reached for her handbag.

Assuming she was searching for a tissue, I handed her the box on the table. She was clearly relieved, and plucking a tissue delicately from the box she dabbed at her cheeks.

I was surprised at how much damage the single tear had wreaked upon her, up until this point in proceedings, perfectly applied foundation and mascara. I made a mental note to suggest she pay a visit to the ladies' room before she left. I got the impression from the way she dressed that her image mattered to her. I couldn't let her leave the building with streaked make-up and panda eyes.

She sniffed a little and laughed. The type of laughter that resulted from embarrassment, I observed.

"Oh dear, I promised myself I wouldn't cry. It didn't last long, did it?"

I smiled. "Tears are a perfectly normal expression of one's feelings. That's why I always have a box of tissues on my table."

She seemed relieved, which indicated she had feared my disapproval.

"Umm. . ." she continued, "well . . . it's . . ." During her attempts to speak, she had tried to look me in the eye. Now her eyes were firmly fixed on the wall behind me. She didn't want to make eye contact. Perhaps she felt it might be easier for her to speak if she didn't look at me.

"Take your time." I reassured.

"Thank you. This is difficult for me."

"I understand."

"It's my husband . . ."

I waited for her to continue.

"He . . ."

My mind had already skipped ahead. I was dreading what she was going to say next. She wasn't another Verity, was she? I didn't know if I could cope with it.

Since counselling Verity, I had been trying to avoid domestic abuse cases. When I spoke to prospective clients on the telephone, I tried to get a handle on their issue. This was so I could decide in advance whether or not I could help them.

I scanned the notes I had made about our telephone conversation. What had she said? Here it is. She had said she was experiencing 'relationship issues'. I couldn't understand why I hadn't delved any deeper. Then my notes stated that she had started to cry. Agh! Now I remembered. I thought it best to agree to see her, and then decide if I could help.

I looked up from my notes. I was briefly taken aback; she was staring straight at me, and she appeared . . . I couldn't put my finger on it. Had she been annoyed? No, surely not. Whatever it was, it had been fleeting. She was, once again, the picture of unease as she attempted to explain.

"He's . . . ," and taking a deep breath as if for courage she blurted, "he's difficult to . . . live with."

"In what way?" I probed gently.

She looked up at me from beneath lowered eyelids and falteringly she continued. "Well, it's hard to explain really." Her face had the expression of someone pleading with me to understand her plight, which of course was exactly what I wanted to do, but I needed more information.

"Don't think about how best to explain it to me. Just blurt it all out. Say the first thing that comes into your head about him."

"He neglects me. He's either working or holed up in his study on the computer, sometimes into the early hours. He just doesn't have any time for me any more." She was visibly wilting. She reminded me of a once-beautiful flower that had lost its bloom, its petals drooping and about to fall to the ground.

"I get the feeling it wasn't always like this?" A questioning tone to my voice to check my understanding of the situation was correct.

She was nodding her head vehemently, and her eyes met mine as she continued. "Oh no, it hasn't always been like this. In the beginning, he couldn't get enough of me." She appeared a little embarrassed by her last words.

I smiled and waited for her to continue.

"It was love at first sight. You know the kind of thing . . ."

I was always fascinated by the number of people who assumed other people had experienced the proverbial lightning bolt as they had. The reality was, in my experience, few people actually felt the searing heat of instant burning desire, and more the slow burn of building attraction.

"Why don't you tell me about it," I invited her.

I could see my invitation had transported her to happier times as her memory searched its archives and started to sieve and sort its recollections into a meaningful order.

"We met in a bar. He was so lovely, such a gentleman. He offered to buy me a drink and was so complimentary. He said I was, 'the most beautiful creature he'd ever seen.' " She sighed as if she didn't think he thought that any longer. "We used to talk for hours; we had a connection . . . you know?" Her eyes searched my face for evidence of my understanding.

"You were very close; you had a deep understanding of one another," I reflected.

"Yes, that's it. We understood each other. But, now . . . he's so distant. I think he's having an affair," she blurted out. She had the 'there, I've said it' expression on her face.

"So, you feel the only explanation for his emotional distance is an affair?"

"Well, what other reason could there be?"

"I don't know. Do you have any ideas?"

Her eyes said she did, but her mouth said, "No."

"No ideas at all?" I gently questioned.

"He's unreasonable now. He never used to be. When we do speak, and that isn't often, he's aggressive toward me. He shouts a lot. Did I mention he's always on his computer? Surfing the net." She gave a little contemptuous laugh.

I noted that she'd deliberately ignored my question. She wanted to talk about her husband. I had yet to work out how I was going to help her. If her problem was the breakdown of her marriage, I wasn't sure what I could do. However, caution was the best way to proceed. It wouldn't be the first time that someone had come to counselling about one issue, and it had turned out to be another underlying issue altogether.

Following her lead, I asked, "I get the impression you're bothered by the amount of time he spends 'surfing the net'. Is that correct?"

"Yes, aside from the obvious reason that while he's on the computer he isn't paying me any attention. I'm dubious about what he's actually doing on there." She gave me a knowing look as if she had her suspicions.

"What do you suspect?"

"What any woman would suspect, of course. He's talking to other women. It's obvious. He's lost interest in me. When we do communicate, it's shouting not talking. I think his interest lies elsewhere."

"You feel the reason for his recent inattention and hostility is an affair with another woman."

"Yes, I do. It's too easy to meet another woman these days. At least in the past your husband had to actually go out to meet another woman unless they met them at work of course. I'm perfectly aware of the number of men that end up having an affair with their secretary. I was wise to that, though. My husband works for a small firm of solicitors. I made sure I met his secretary at the beginning of our relationship, and I have no concerns regarding her intentions."

"You don't?" I asked.

"No, Pearl prefers me. If you know what I mean."

I nodded to confirm that I did indeed understand.

She continued, "It's a process of elimination really: he can't be having an affair with his secretary because she's gay. He can't be having an affair with anyone else at work because they are all male. And he can't be having an affair with anyone he's met while out socialising because he doesn't socialise. So, he has to have met someone while on that bloody computer. I've tried logging on to it when he's at work." As if from nowhere, she fired, "Are you shocked?" Her eyes met mine as she awaited my response.

"No," I replied, shaking my head. There was little that shocked me about human behaviour any more, but I didn't say that aloud.

Seemingly satisfied with the genuineness of my answer, she continued. "I wanted to look at his search history. I wanted to know what he's doing in his study for hours, and what he's looking at."

"I think it's perfectly normal to want to know. Have you tried asking him?" I said in as neutral a tone as I could muster. I didn't want to sound judgemental of her investigatory methods in any way.

"Yes, I have," she said with no hint of defensiveness in her reply.

I had expected her to elaborate, but she seemed to have drifted away from me into her own little world.

"You weren't satisfied with his explanation?" I probed.

She gave a mirthless laugh. "He got angry with me. The question started a row."

"Did he answer the question?"

"No. He got so angry. I thought he was going to . . ." She shook her head. "He frightened me. I decided not to broach the subject again, and that's why I've turned amateur detective."

"I can understand why."

"You can?" she asked appearing relieved.

"Yes, of course."

"I can't talk to my friends about this. I'm . . . too embarrassed."

"Embarrassed?"

"Yes, embarrassed," she said. Her eyes were downcast and there was a defeated slump to her shoulders as she continued. "This isn't the first time this has happened to me."

"This isn't the first time this has happened with your husband?"

"No. I mean this isn't the first time I've had a relationship go wrong like this." She gave a heartfelt sigh. "Every relationship I've ever had has ended like this."

"This relationship hasn't ended."

"No, not yet, but it will. I know it will. I can't tell my friends about another failed relationship. They've been there for me over the years. I've lost count of the number of hour-long phone calls where I've poured my heart out over the man of the moment. I've had two failed long-term relationships and one divorce already. I can't tell them about another; I just can't. Why do men keep doing this to me, Frankie? That's why I'm here. I can't talk to my friends about it. Not again. You need to help me understand why men keep doing this to me."

I could see the hurt and desperation in her eyes, and felt the pull of her need to make sense of it all.

"I'm afraid I can't explain other people's behaviour. What I can do is to help you explore your own behaviour and decisions and how they may have influenced the outcome."

She frowned. "It isn't my fault that men keep doing this to me. Are you saying it's my fault?" Her voice rising steadily with each word she said, so that by the end it was nothing more than a screech.

Inwardly I winced. This first step was always so difficult. So many people wanted to blame others for everything that went wrong in their lives. They didn't yet have the self-awareness to realise they made the choices that led to the outcomes. It was as this point that those who wanted to blame others for their life's shortcomings rather than examine their own contribution chose not to return to counselling.

The people who genuinely wanted change were brave enough to face the fact that they needed to take responsibility for their own life and their own choices. To at least examine their choices and more importantly what may have led them to make the choices they did.

I was shaking my head gently in response. "No, I'm not saying it's your fault. I'm not apportioning blame. I would go so far as to say, I don't see the failure of your relationships as anyone's fault."

"Humph!" She fidgeted in her seat and folded her arms.

Taking a deep breath, I pressed on. "It is my belief that we make choices based on our past experiences. Sometimes, we choose a partner based on a set of criteria that isn't right for us and subsequently that relationship doesn't work. Instead of thinking about why it didn't work and revising our criteria; we keep repeating the pattern."

She stared at me wearing a blank expression.

"I'll give you an example: a young girl picks her first boyfriend on looks alone. He's gorgeous, and she's flattered he has asked her out."

Susan smiled and nodded her head.

"But it soon becomes apparent that they have nothing in common. They sit in silence throughout their first date, but she sees him again because her friends are all envious of her gorgeous new boyfriend. They stay together for a few months, but eventually he finishes with her. She's devastated, not because she liked him that much, but because her pride has been hurt.

"Some women would reflect upon that relationship and decide that next time compatibility, and not looks, was a more important factor. Other women would not reflect upon the relationship; they would go out with the next good-looking guy that asked them and hope for the best. Thereby establishing a pattern of behaviour related specifically to relationships. This applies to men as well, of course."

"I'm beginning to understand what you mean. I think."

"Good. We're coming to the end of the session. You asked why men keep doing this to you. I would like you to think about the men you have had relationships with and whether they share any common traits."

"They all looked completely different."

"OK. But were they similar in other ways? We don't have time to discuss it now, but if you could think about it over the next week."

She was staring off into the distance. I could tell she had already started to give it some thought.

"Same time, same place next week," I stated.

She nodded.

I wasn't sure whether she would return next week, but then I never was.

"Before I show you out, might I suggest a visit to the ladies' room to touch up your make-up? We ladies know how tears can impact upon our carefully applied mascara, even when the label describes it as waterproof," I said as I got to my feet.

"Oh . . . yes, thank you for letting me know," she said as she touched her face self-consciously.

"It's just down the corridor. I'll wait for you here."

"Thanks, Frankie. I won't be long," she said as she hurried from the room.

True to her word, she reappeared five minutes later looking her immaculate self once again.

As we approached reception, I could see a big bouquet of flowers on the desk. I was admiring the blooms' depth of colour when the flowers' sweet, pungent smell hit my nostrils. They really were beautiful.

Susan remarked, "Someone's a lucky girl."

I detected a note of envy in her voice. "Indeed," I replied.

Theresa glanced up from the desk. "Frankie, I'm glad I've seen you. I knew you had a meeting, which is why I didn't ring when they arrived."

"When what arrived?" I asked. "I'm not expecting anything."

"The flowers," she said, sweeping her hand across the bouquet to reinforce her words.

"Are they for me?" I questioned, not able to keep the astonishment from my voice. Susan was watching me with a quizzical expression on her face.

I felt the colour rise in my cheeks as I reached out to touch some of the flowers. They were breathtakingly beautiful. I could easily identify roses, and what I thought were irises. There were at least seven different types of flowers in the bouquet causing a riot of colour, and the smell they emitted was heavenly.

"It would seem you're the lucky girl, Frankie. Who are they from?"

"I don't know."

She raised her eyebrows; her scepticism obvious for all to see. "You don't know? Is there a card?"

That was a good idea. I was so shocked by the flowers that I hadn't yet thought about checking the card. I scanned the front of the bouquet; there was a small piece of paper stapled to the cellophane that had my name on it but nothing else.

"That's odd. There doesn't appear to be a card or note. Did you speak to the person who delivered the flowers?" I asked.

"I didn't. I had just gone to make a cup of tea and was walking back with it when I saw a gentleman leaving. I only caught a glimpse of the back of him. When I saw the flowers, I assumed he had delivered them."

The piece of paper on the bouquet was blank, no customary flower shop logo. "I don't suppose you saw the flower shop's van?" I asked.

"No, sorry, I didn't. It's quite the mystery, isn't it?"

"Hmm," I agreed. I wasn't comfortable with this.

"Do you have any idea who might have sent them, Frankie?" Susan asked looking intrigued.

"No. I'll see you next week, Susan." I said, trying not to sound dismissive, but wanting to give my full attention to the mysterious flowers and their sender.

"Uh, yes, see you next week."

I picked the flowers up and walked back to my room. Placing them on the table, I examined every inch of the cellophane. There was nothing to give me any clue about who had sent them. I had an uneasy feeling in the pit of my stomach.

Could Glenn have sent me these flowers? If so, why? Was he goading me? If he had sent them, he'd want to see my reaction to them.

I jumped up and ran to the window as it occurred to me that he could have been watching me in reception from the car park. A car was just leaving. I could see its right indicator blinking on and off. Was it the same car as the one I thought I'd seen Glenn in last week? I put my head in my hands. I wasn't sure. Was I losing my mind? There could be an innocent explanation for the flowers.

Mum was right. I needed a break. It was a good job I was going away this weekend. Trying to push my anxiety to the back of my mind, I returned to my seat and picked up my notebook.

# Chapter 10

"Right then, I think I'm ready," I said inspecting the neatly folded contents of my weekend bag.

Henry was standing there with my handwritten checklist in one hand and a pencil in the other.

"Shall we check you have everything, Mum? Just to be sure," he added.

"Absolutely, Henry, I don't want to arrive and realise I've forgotten my knickers, now do I?"

He started to laugh. "Oh, Mum, you are silly."

"Not to mention embarrassing," Alex commented as he walked past us in the hallway on his way back up to his man cave aka his room.

Both Henry and I shared a conspiratorial look before both poking our tongues out silently at his retreating teenage back. It made us both laugh. I could hear Alex tut in disgust at the sound as he walked up the stairs, which made us laugh all the more.

"Come on then. Let's get to it. Your dad will be here soon to pick you both up. What's first on the list?"

"Toiletries."

I peered into my bag. "Yep."

"Check," he said as he ticked it off of the list. "Underwear," he continued.

"Yep," I confirmed.

We continued until Henry had ticked everything off of the list.

"Great. I don't appear to have forgotten anything. I'd better zip my bag up now and wait for your dad to arrive." I glanced at my watch. "He'd better get a move on. Rebecca is arriving in thirty minutes." As I finished speaking, I heard a tap on the door. "That will be him now." I turned to open the door, and, sure enough, Rob was standing there grinning.

"Looking forward to your weekend away?" he asked.

"I am actually. Thanks for having the kids. Thank Lucy for me too."

"I will. We're looking forward to it."

"Henry, go upstairs and get your bag. Tell Alex to do the same." I said.

"Will do, Mum."

He shot up the stairs. I could hear him telling Alex to get a move on.

It was seconds before Henry came bounding down clutching his bag. Alex was slower to descend the staircase. They reminded me of the Hare and the Tortoise in Aesop's fables. I looked at Alex's face; he didn't look particularly happy. I wondered if he was unhappy about staying at his dad's house.

"You OK, Alex?" I asked.

He appeared not to have heard me as he fiddled with a stray strand of cotton hanging from his trouser pocket. His head lowered, he intently examined the cotton as if it were the most interesting thing in the world.

I knew my son, and I knew he didn't find cotton that captivating. "Out with it. What's wrong?" I demanded.

His shoulders slumped; he eyed me nervously. "I was hoping I wouldn't have to tell you until you came back from your weekend away."

"Tell me what?"

"I've lost my PE kit," he said barely above a whisper.

"WHAT? AGAIN?" I could feel my blood pressure rising. It was the second time this had happened since we'd moved here. The kit cost a fortune as it had the school logo on it and had to be bought from a specific shop on the High St.

"I've searched everywhere, Mum, honest I have."

"Oh, Alex, you know it cost a fortune. I can't afford to replace it again."

"Sorry," he mumbled.

To be fair, he did look the picture of misery. There was no doubt that he meant it when he said he was sorry, but an apology wasn't going to pay for his kit.

"Right, let's not worry your mum with this now. We want her to have a nice weekend, don't we?" Rob said.

Both boys nodded.

"I didn't want to tell her. I was going to wait until she came home, but she did ask," Alex said.

"Yes, I did ask. I should know better."

"Don't worry, Frankie. Leave it with me. I can sort his kit out this weekend."

Alex visibly brightened, and I relaxed.

"That would be great. Thanks, Rob."

"No worries. Now go and enjoy yourself."

I opened my arms for an embrace. Both boys hugged me before picking up their respective bags and following their dad out to the car. I watched them drive off down the road before going back in to add a few optional extras to my weekend bag. These items hadn't been on my checklist: "One bottle of Vodka. Check. One large bottle of Prosecco. Check," I said out loud.

I heard a car horn toot and assumed it was Rebecca. I opened the front door and peered out. Sure enough, it was her. She got out of the car to help me with my things.

As she teetered toward me, I took note of her red stilettos. She wore skinny blue jeans and a figure-hugging red t-shirt. Her blonde hair was tied up in a ponytail. The shade of her lipstick matched her shoes. Not for the first time, I marvelled at how fabulous she looked for a woman of forty-two. I looked down at my flat pumps, relaxed fit jeans and comfy sweatshirt and wondered if I should change.

"You look wonderful," she said guessing what I was thinking. Are you ready for an adventure?" she asked.

"Sure am."

"Let's get on our way. I'm looking forward to a nice glass of wine."

"Me too. Did you have any luck arranging some accommodation?" I asked.

"Yes. It wasn't easy. It was short notice, and they've got some sort of rally going on in Bournemouth at the moment, so a lot of the hotel rooms were already booked. But I found a hotel a little ways out that had a room. They mentioned something about a refurbishment."

"Oh well, anything will do as long as it's clean."

"That's what I thought. Come on, let's go party."

I chuckled. "Yes, let's." I settled myself in the passenger's seat and, for the first time in ages, started to relax.

*****

We made good time and were pulling up outside the hotel two and a half hours later.

The hotel was at the top of Westcliff Road. It would be a good fifteen-minute walk to the bars and restaurants, but we didn't mind. The hotel was a large old white building. It was impressive; I imagined it had been a stately home in its distant past. A large sign announced the fact that it was now called the Jubilee Hotel.

"It looks nice, Rebecca."

"Hmm, it does. Let's get inside and crack open that bottle of Prosecco."

I laughed. "Lead on."

I followed her in carrying my weekend bag. The reception area was impressive. There was an old-fashioned revolving door with gleaming brass handles. The floor was covered in a plush burgundy and gold carpet. I could smell fresh paint. Everything about the place screamed wealth and opulence. I looked around taking in the big sash windows and the comfortable sofas.

Rebecca and I looked at each other and smiled. We silently agreed it was beautiful.

"The girl done good," I whispered in her ear as we approached reception.

"I got it cheap too," she whispered back before addressing the receptionist. "I've booked a twin room in the name of Rebecca Booth."

The receptionist glanced at the screen in front of her before smiling and handing over an ornate brass key.

No nasty plastic swipe cards in this establishment, I thought with satisfaction and approval.

"You're in room three hundred and one. If you take the elevator to the third floor and turn to your left, it's the first room on the left. You have been told that the hotel is undergoing a programme of refurbishment at the moment." It was more of a statement than a question.

"Yes. It looks lovely," said Rebecca taking the key. We walked toward the elevator and Rebecca said, "What a bargain. It only cost thirty pounds a night."

"You're joking. That is a bargain. Well done you."

We pressed the button for the elevator and waited. The elevator doors slid open, and we walked inside. A feeling of unease started to creep in as I noticed the threadbare carpet in the lift. It was at complete odds with the luxurious carpet I'd just been standing on in reception. I remarked upon it to Rebecca.

"Hmm, well maybe they haven't refurbished the lifts yet," she offered by way of explanation.

"Hmm, maybe."

The elevator stopped on the third floor with a loud clunk. The doors opened to reveal the corridor beyond. I could see before even stepping out of the elevator that the refurbishment had not reached the third floor. It would appear Rebecca could too as we exchanged an anxious look. The wallpaper that I assumed was once grand was now dated and peeling at every available edge. The paintwork was chipped; the carpet so threadbare I could see the lining beneath.

My excitement had been replaced with trepidation as we walked toward room three hundred and one. We didn't have far to go as it was the room next to the elevator.

"Shall I do the honours?" Rebecca asked as she brandished the key.

"Please do. The anticipation is killing me."

She inserted the key in the lock, and with a look that said brace yourself she swung the door wide. We peered inside.

"Well . . . it looks clean," said Rebecca.

"Hmm, yes, it's fine. We won't be in the room much anyway."

We stood in the doorway taking in our surroundings. The room barely accommodated the twin beds. They were so close together it could actually have been a double bed. We had to enter the room in single file as there wasn't enough space between the end of the bed and the wall for both of us to stand side by side.

"There's an en suite. That's good," Rebecca remarked.

"Yes." Even I was aware that my voice lacked enthusiasm.

"I need the loo. I'm desperate after that long journey." Rebecca rushed into the en suite and shut the door. Well she tried to. The door had obviously warped over the years, and the result was that she had to kick it to fully close it.

Good luck with opening it again, I thought. I sat on the bed I was claiming, which was next to the window, and had some empathy for a hamster in its cage.

The room wasn't just small; it was dark and dingy. The decoration had seen better days. I could hear the flush and the flow of water from the faucet into the sink. Rebecca would be out in a minute. I needed to school my features into a more positive expression. I didn't want her to feel responsible because she had been the one that had booked the room.

Rebecca was attempting to open the door from the inside of the en suite. I could hear her tugging at the door handle. The door was creaking as she struggled to free it from its snug doorframe.

It was strange though because I could still hear the water gushing into the sink from the faucet. The water sounded unnaturally loud; as if she had turned the tap on to its full extent. Why would she do that? I wondered. And why hadn't she turned it off.

"Oh bugger . . . , Frankie . . . , can you push the door from your side? I can't get the door open," she said, her voice rising with panic.

"OK, OK don't worry. I'll get you out of there. Stand back from the door. I may need to give it quite a shove."

"OK, go ahead," she shouted.

I pushed the door; it didn't budge. I decided I would have to use my body as extra leverage. I turned to my side and shoulder first I barged into the door. It flew open and hit the bath. I saw a torrent of water flowing from the tap and shooting up in all directions from the sink. It had sprayed the mirror and the floor.

Rebecca was standing there; her red t-shirt now several shades darker in those areas the water had managed to saturate. The crotch of her jeans was so sodden; she looked as if she had wet herself. Her hair was hanging in damp tendrils around her face, and she was holding something in each hand. She silently held the items aloft, so I could see what they were. She had the door handle in one hand

and a tap handle in the other; the part you need to turn the tap on and off.

"I don't suppose you packed a wrench?" she asked with a straight face.

The humorous side of the situation hit us both at the same time. A giggle started to bubble up from somewhere deep within me. Before I knew what had hit me, I was absolutely hysterical with laughter. I stood there pointing at Rebecca's clothes and then at the broken tap because I was unable to speak. Rebecca was also incoherent with laughter.

"It's a . . . good . . . job, I had a wee before all that happened. Otherwise, I think I may have wet myself as a result of all that laughing," she blurted out on one breath. Tears of laughter were streaming down her face.

My sides ached with the sheer exertion of it all.

"You look as if you have anyway," I said pointing to the strategically placed wet patch on her jeans. After several more minutes of abandoned laughter, I calmed myself sufficiently to fumble around inside my weekend bag and locate the bottle of Prosecco. "Let's get drunk!" I announced.

"I'm with you there. Let's ring reception first." And she pointed in the direction of the free-flowing tap and the door.

Smirking, I nodded, unable to trust myself to speak.

*****

"A little dickybird told me you got some flowers last week. A mahoosive bouquet, I hear. Come on, spill," Rebecca said as we were standing at the bar of the Slug and Lettuce pub trying to order our second cocktail.

The pub was packed to capacity; it was obviously a popular choice of venue for those living and holidaying in

Bournemouth. We'd had to queue outside to get in; it had the effect of sobering us up a little. No bad thing, I decided. We'd drunk my bottle of Prosecco and then started on the vodka while still in the hotel room. Rebecca had popped to the local Spar for a bottle of lemonade to accompany the vodka.

We'd giggled like teenagers when the hotel's handyman had turned up wrench in hand. He'd gone into the bathroom, and we could hear a lot of banging and clunking. Eventually, the torrent of water had subsided. He asked if we could use the taps in the bath to wash our hands from now on. The tap in the basin would need replacing, and he would sort it out after we'd checked out. He'd managed to replace the door handle. He said that it happened all the time and that the full refurbishment of the hotel couldn't come soon enough. We felt sorry for him and offered him a glass of vodka, but he declined.

We hadn't eaten anything, which I knew to be a mistake. A mistake I was sure I'd only come to fully appreciate in the morning. The plan was to grab some chips at the end of the evening on the way back to the room.

I wasn't immediately able to respond to Rebecca's enquiry regarding the mysterious bouquet because I was trying to get the attention of the barman. Any distraction would result in our having to wait longer for a drink. I had my ten pound note in my hand, and I was waving it around. Should I swap it for a twenty pound note? Perhaps that would get more attention. It made sense in my drunken head.

I was being jostled and shoved continuously by the sheer number of people all standing at the bar trying to get a drink.

"What would you like?" a hassled-looking barman asked.

"Two Sex on the Beach cocktails, please."

"It's happy hour: two for one."

"Even better," I beamed. At least that meant we wouldn't have to stand at the bar again for a while. He came back with four glasses of the reddish-orange drink. He eyed my ten pound note with amusement.

"That'll be fourteen pounds, please."

"I don't get out much," I said by way of explanation as I fumbled in my purse for the extra four pounds.

He gave a polite smile that never reached his eyes and was gone; off to serve the next customer.

Rebecca grabbed her two cocktails; I grabbed the other two from the bar, and we turned to face the masses. We had to get through the crowd without spilling our drinks. It was a daunting task. Rebecca led the way; I simply followed in her wake. We managed to find a table at the back of the pub; it was strewn with glasses with varying amounts of alcohol left in each. One pint glass was filled to the brim with a cloudy yellowy-orange liquid. I hoped it was cider, but I suspected it might be something quite different.

Rob had once told me a story about how when he was younger he'd been on a night out in Bristol with his friends. There had been a large group of them, and they noticed that each time they put their half-finished pint down in the nightclub the glass would be empty when they returned to it. Someone was stealing their drinks. So they urinated in a pint glass and left it on the side. They figured whoever drank it got what they deserved. I shuddered at the thought.

We moved the glasses to the back of the table to make room for our cocktails and settled down for a chat.

"So . . . ?" Rebecca questioned with no small amount of curiosity.

"I don't know who they are from," I said guessing she was still talking about the flowers.

"Hmm," she said with purpose, as if it was a mystery she was going to get to the bottom of.

I didn't want to say that I thought they might be from Glenn because it only made me sound crazy. This weekend was about me having a break, some fun and trying to get Glenn out of my head. I had to accept he was dead, everyone else had.

Rebecca's phone dinged and she looked at the screen. I should have said phones were banned tonight as she was particularly addicted to hers. I didn't want to be competing with her phone for attention all night. She started to laugh. My curiosity got the better of me.

"What is it?" I asked.

"Look at this, and tell me what you think," she said showing me what had just appeared on her phone.

I glanced at the screen and then did a double-take. My mouth fell open in utter shock. My reaction seemed to fuel her amusement.

"Is that what I think it is?" I asked.

"Yep," she said through her raucous laughter.

"But . . . who does it belong to?"

"Just some guy. They all do it. I've joined this dating website, for a bit of fun really and this," she said pointing at her phone, "is the type of picture they send these days."

"What happened to a nice head shot?"

Tears of laughter welled up in her eyes at my last comment and she said, "Well it is a head shot of sorts."

My initial shock was replaced with amusement as I started to laugh with her.

"Only a man would think a woman would want a close-up picture of his penis," I commented.

"I haven't even met him, and believe me I won't be after this," she said.

"Give me your phone; I want another look."

She handed over the phone. After a few moments, I passed the phone back to her.

"Do you think it's real? I mean, it's massive," I said.

"Who knows? Did you notice that we can see his penis and his physique, but his face isn't included in the shot?"

"Oh yes, you're right. His body is amazing."

"Yes, well forgive me for being cynical, but I've seen quite a lot of these types of photos now. They seem to be all the rage, believe me. I think they're pictures of male models found on the Internet. I've got another one here I want to show you."

She passed the phone to me once again. There was a picture of a man's body complete with fully erect penis. In the background was an open window complete with a fluttering lace curtain. In order to capture that level of detail, it had to have been taken by a professional photographer.

"It's definitely not a selfie, is it?" Rebecca asked.

"No. But I don't understand. These men are trying to get dates based on the size of their bits. What do they think will happen when the lady in question turns up and discovers they're short, bald and fifty?"

"Exactly. Interesting you should mention fifty-year-olds. I thought when I signed up to this website that the majority of men who would be interested in me would be around fifty. But I was wrong."

"Oh right. Are they older?"

"Well that's the thing. They are younger, substantially younger," she said, grinning from ear to ear.

"You're joking!"

"I'm not. It would seem men in their twenties like women in their forties."

"No way." I knew my mouth was hanging open in shock.

"Yes, way. I'm meeting one next week as a matter of fact."

"What?" I said, my tone of voice registering my concern.

"Oh, Frankie, he seems so nice. Before you ask, he didn't send me a picture of his penis. He's different. He's interested in me. We just seemed to click; we talk for hours."

"You've spoken to him?"

"No, I mean online."

The expression on my face must have appeared disapproving because she went on, "I know what you think. You think I'm crazy to be meeting someone I don't know, but I'm not stupid. You know I'm not. We've arranged to meet in a pub. We are arriving separately. He doesn't know where I live. So if it doesn't work out, I will leave the pub and never see him again."

"Well, if you're sure," I said, my voice loaded with doubt.

She sighed. "Look, you know my history with men. It's abysmal. I just want to have some fun. He seems like a nice guy. OK, he's too young for me. But, hey, I'm not searching for my next husband. He's gorgeous, twenty-eight years old and wants to take me out. Allow a girl to be flattered for a little while at least."

I decided to lighten up. She was right. As long as she wasn't pinning all her hopes on this guy being 'the one', which she wasn't, then I was cool with it.

"What's his name?"I asked.

"Sam."

"Have you got a picture I could see?"

"Hang on; I'll show his profile picture on the dating site . . . Oh, he isn't here any more. Hmm, he said he was going to come off of the site because he'd met me, and we'd arranged a date for next week. But I didn't actually believe he would."

"I'm impressed. He would appear to have standards," I said.

She smiled. "Yes, I'm impressed too. I think I had better follow suit and end my membership."

I nodded in agreement.

"I don't know how I'm going to survive without my daily fix of penis photographs: short ones, long-ones, thin-ones, thick-ones and even bent-ones," she said straight-faced.

I nearly spat out my mouthful of cocktail.

# Chapter 11

I woke with a jolt as Rebecca knocked the end of my bed on her way to the bathroom. A searing pain ripped through my skull. Ow! I turned slowly toward the closed curtains to try to ascertain whether it was the middle of the night or morning. I could see bright light coming through the thin material. I winced as the light hit the back of my eyes, and made my brain hurt still further. My tongue felt as if I'd been licking the carpet, and no matter how much I swallowed I couldn't seem to generate any saliva.

Please God, let me have put a glass of water by my bed last night in anticipation of this moment. I reached an arm out from under the duvet. Tentatively, I ran my fingers across the carpet hoping to make contact with a glass. Bingo! Lifting it carefully I struggled to look at its contents. Great, it was water. I took a big gulp. I was so thirsty.

I realised too late, as the clear liquid hit the back of my throat, it wasn't water; it was vodka. I had taken a large gulp believing it was water, and now the liquid was burning its way down my throat. I started coughing, and with each movement, pain was shooting through my brain. It even hurt to breathe right now. I desperately needed water.

"Rebecca, are you going to be in there long?" I gasped.

"Uh-huh."

"I need a glass of water," I persevered. Total silence ensued. Was she asleep? Then I heard a noise coming from the bathroom. "Sorry, what was that?" I asked feeling confused. There it was again. Understanding crept, ever so slowly, through my alcohol-soaked brain. She was being sick, and violently so, from the sounds of it. I tried to get out of the bed to see if I could be of any assistance, but the minute I tried, the pain in my brain ramped up to alarming levels.

"Aaagh!" I said, wincing as I inched my way across the bed. "Are you OK, Rebecca?"

I could hear the toilet flushing. The bathroom door opened; she was standing there with one side of her face against the wall.

"What are you doing?" I asked in alarm.

"I need to keep my head against the wall because if I don't everything starts spinning."

"How are you going to get back into bed?"

She said nothing in response. She simply put the top of her head against the wall and started to slide her head down the wall lowering her body at the same time. She ended up in a kneeling position on the floor with her head still firmly against the wall.

I watched as she slid her head down the remainder of the wall until she could transfer it to the floor. She then started to shuffle along the floor on all fours with her head firmly fixed to the carpet. I couldn't recall ever having seen a funnier sight. But I knew with absolute clarity that to laugh at this precise moment would set a million grenades off in my brain.

I managed to stumble to the bathroom to replace the vodka in my glass with water. Each step was a master class in mind over matter. You can do it, Frankie! You can make it! I gulped down the cool, clear water. Nothing had ever tasted so good. I refilled my glass and drank it. I repeated the process several times before I felt able to return to my bed.

I fumbled around in my handbag for a few minutes trying to find my painkillers. Having eventually found them, I popped two pills in my mouth.

"Shall we have a quiet day?" I asked Rebecca.

"Hmm," she said as she turned over.

I suspected we wouldn't be doing much today, and that suited me just fine. I felt bloody awful. I got a whiff of the fried breakfasts they must have been serving in the restaurant downstairs and immediately felt sick. Please don't let me be sick. I hated being sick. I shut my eyes and willed myself to go back to sleep and not to wake up until I felt better.

*****

"Come on, sleepyhead. It's time to wake up."

"Huh! What?" I mumbled.

"It's two-thirty in the afternoon. It's time to shake a tail feather," Rebecca said.

The sleep fog was lifting. I opened my eyes gingerly. I was waiting for the pain to shoot through my brain but nothing happened. Phew! It had gone. I lifted myself up into a sitting position and squinted at Rebecca. She looked great. How was this possible? Had I imagined this morning when she was throwing up in the bathroom and unable to walk back to bed unassisted by the wall and floor?

"I've had a shower and got myself ready, so the bathroom's all yours."

"Great," I said with little to no enthusiasm.

"Come on. I thought we'd go and get some food. Then, afterwards, we'd take a little look at the shops. We'll give alcohol a miss for tonight. What do you think?"

"Yes," I said relieved. "I could murder a bacon sandwich."

"Me too. Come on, the sooner you're ready, the sooner we can eat."

I hoisted myself from the bed and into the bathroom. I was ready to leave within twenty minutes.

We walked into the centre of Bournemouth shopping centre and found a little cafe. We were both starving and tucked into our cooked breakfasts with gusto. We didn't say a word while eating; our complete focus was on the food. Boy, did it feel good to be shovelling copious amounts of fatty, salty heart attack-inducing food into my mouth.

"That hit the spot," I said, sitting back in my seat. My stomach had expanded so much that I contemplated undoing the top button of my jeans.

"Yeah, lovely," Rebecca agreed.

"Last night was quite a night. It was so good that I can't remember most of it. Can you fill in the blanks?"

"Hmm . . . I'm not sure. What is the last thing you can remember?" she said before taking a gulp of her tea.

"Penises," I said, deadpan.

Tea sprayed from Rebecca's mouth in all directions as she burst into uncontrollable laughter.

"Did I say something funny?" I asked all innocence.

Spluttering and dabbing at the front of her top in a vain attempt to dry the tea stains, she said, "Frankie Wilson, you know damn well what you said and how funny it sounded."

I grinned. "The last thing I remember was you showing me pictures of random guys' penises. Oh, and then you saying you were meeting a guy next week that you met online."

She nodded. "Sam," she said by way of explanation.

"Yes, Sam. I don't mind admitting that I think online dating is a risky business."

"I know you do," she said with meaning.

I cocked my eyebrow by way of a silent question.

Taking the hint she said, "You expressed your concerns several hundred times last night. The only time you stopped was when you passed out on your bed."

"Oops, sorry!"

She reached out and patted me on the arm. "It's OK. We were both drunk. To be honest, it's nice to have someone care enough about me to be concerned."

I put my fingers across my closed mouth in a zip like action and then mimed my turning a lock with a key and throwing it away.

"Yeah right, how long will that last?"

"Until about . . . now, I reckon."

Rebecca laughed. "Seriously though, I understand your concerns, Frankie. But you know my history with guys. It isn't good, is it? I have met guys the traditional way; they've turned out to be, pardon my French," and she lowered her voice as she said, "shits."

That was true. Rebecca had been married for sixteen years when she found out her husband was cheating on her with one of her friends. It turned out that he had cheated on her with pretty much all of her friends. This had all come to light four years ago before Rebecca and I had become reacquainted.

Rebecca had since explained to me that the realisation that her romantic, ever-so-attentive husband of sixteen years was, in fact, a serial womaniser had dealt a serious blow to her psyche. She was a counsellor for God's sake. She was meant to understand people; to see beneath the facade they presented to the world. Not only hadn't she seen what her husband was up to, but she hadn't seen her friends' duplicity either.

She threw her husband out, and she stopped talking to all of her friends. She didn't think he had slept with all of them, but she couldn't be sure. She no longer trusted her judgement. So the only thing she could do, for her sanity's sake, was to leave every single one of them behind and move on.

I was part of her new life. I hadn't known her husband, so she could be sure I hadn't betrayed her. Since the break-up of her marriage, she had dated a string of guys; each one more disastrous than the last. Either they cheated on her, sponged off of her, or hit her. Rebecca had questionable taste in men, and that was why I was worried about this guy, Sam. I wasn't buying this whole, 'he's different routine'.

I cared about Rebecca. She was my friend, and I didn't want to see her hurt again. The Pant Bros loved her too. She was great with them. When she came round to the house, she would treat them like friends rather than like children, and they loved her for it. She'd play with Alex on the PlayStation, which immediately gave her cool status in his eyes, and watch Henry's TV programmes with him. She was marvellous with my kids, and I knew she loved them too.

One day, six or so months ago, I'd commented on how great she was with children; she was such a natural. She told me how she loved children but she wasn't able to have one of her own. I didn't pursue the subject, at the time, because I saw the raw pain in her eyes. She clearly hadn't come to terms with it; I wondered if she ever would.

I was brought back to the here and now by a sudden vibrating sensation on my lap. Looking down I realised it was my bag, or more specifically it must be my phone vibrating from within my bag. My reaction speed was seriously impaired by my hangover. By the time I'd extricated my phone from my bag, it had stopped ringing. I had six missed calls.

My heart did a little tap dance as I realised I hadn't checked my phone since yesterday afternoon. God! What if something had happened and Rob couldn't get hold of me? My default panic mode was immediately activated.

I scrabbled to see who had called me six times. Hmm, No Caller ID times six. For a moment, I allowed myself to relax. At least that meant there was no emergency. If something had been wrong, then either Rob or my mum would have called me.

"I can tell by your facial expression that something's up. What's wrong?" Rebecca asked.

"I have six missed calls, and I panicked. But I've just checked to see who they are from, and there isn't a Caller ID for any of them. It's odd!"

My phone started to vibrate in my hand.

*No Caller ID* appeared on the screen.

I had to answer it. It might be an emergency. "Hello?"

Silence.

"Hello?" I repeated, my voice rising slightly with the first prickle of anxiety. The silence at the other end stretched on. "If you don't speak, I'm hanging up," I warned.

The silence continued.

I disconnected the call and sat back in my chair. It was Glenn. I was sure of it. But how did he know my mobile phone number? After Verity's death, I'd changed my number, and I was very careful who I shared my new number with.

I could feel the familiar physical effects of anxiety start to sweep over my body egged on by my thoughts. My lungs felt like they were being squeezed tightly, and I was fighting to get air into them. A wave of heat enveloped me; I felt overwhelmed by it.

"Frankie, Frankie, can you hear me? It's OK, you are OK. Remember to breathe. Let's focus on your breathing. Listen to my voice, only my voice. Look at me, Frankie, and focus on me and what I'm saying."

I could hear Rebecca, but I was struggling to focus on what she was saying. I was battling with my thoughts: you were right. He's still alive. The phone calls are his way of letting you know he's coming for you. He's going to kill you.

I couldn't breathe. My body felt like it was on fire; I was so hot. I was tugging at the collar of my t-shirt; it was too close to my neck. It was strangling me. It felt like the scarf was around my neck again. I was tugging at it. I needed to get it away from my neck. I was suddenly aware of a pair of hands on my shoulders. It was him! It was Glenn. He was here to kill me. No! I had to run. I had to escape. In my blinding panic, I cast my gaze around the room looking for the exit.

I could hear someone speaking. What were they saying? The words sounded familiar.

"He cannot hurt you any more; you are safe."

I'd heard that before. Someone was saying it over and over again. It was a woman; her tone was calm and gentle. She kept saying it.

"He cannot hurt you any more; you are safe."

I liked her voice. I trusted it. Who was it? I wondered. My eyes found their focus. There was a woman sitting on her knees in front of me; she was staring intensely into my face. I knew her. It was Rebecca. Yes, it was Rebecca.

"You're back. Thank God!"

"Sorry," I stammered. "I don't know what came over me."

"Yes, you do, and so do I. It was that bloody silent call. It's understandable after what you went through last year. But, Frankie . . . ," she waited until she was sure she had my full attention. "He's dead. Glenn is dead."

"I just wish they would find his body. Then I could be sure."

"I understand. But, all the evidence points to the fact that he is dead."

"My rational self knows that. But my irrational self just won't accept it," I sighed.

Rebecca took my phone from me. After a few minutes of tapping and swiping, she said, "The calls started at around 3.00 a.m."

I tensed.

"Relax, I have a rational explanation."

"Go on."

"Well, you don't appear to remember, but we got chatting to a couple of guys last night."

As she spoke, I vaguely recollected talking to a man outside of a chip shop.

"Did we buy chips last night?" I asked.

"Yes, we did. These guys came with us to the chip shop, and we chatted while we all ate."

I nodded. "I vaguely remember that."

"Great. Well, we met them in the club. We were dancing with them for most of the night. They were nice guys. If I weren't meeting Sam next week, then I might have considered calling mine. But I am, so I won't bother. You seemed to really like yours."

"Did I?" I asked. I couldn't even remember what he looked like.

"Yes, you did," she laughed. "You liked him enough to give him your mobile number." She looked at me intently, and waited for the implications of what she had said to sink in.

"Oh . . . you mean it could be him ringing me?"

She nodded. "He was keen on you. Extremely keen, I would say. He was singing Sister Sledge's, 'Frankie, do you remember me?' at the top of his voice at 2.30 a.m. this morning while walking up Westcliff Road."

I giggled as a hazy memory of the afore-mentioned guy came into my mind. He was indeed singing. I watched him zigzag his way down the road away from us.

"Did they walk us home?" I asked.

"You remember."

"Vaguely." I put my head in my hands. "I feel like such a fool now. Talk about overreact. I'm so sorry, Rebecca."

She put her hand on mine. "Don't be silly. You have nothing to be sorry about. The fact that you have a meltdown in a small local cafe in Bournemouth and that all the customers leave because they think you are a nutter doesn't mean you should feel sorry at all," she said and then promptly winked at me.

"Oh, very funny! Was I that bad?"

"No, not at all," she reassured. Leaning in close to me, she said poker-faced, "Let's pay up and leave; you aren't good for business." Immediately after she'd finished talking, she burst out laughing. "You should see your face. It's a picture. I'm joking. Come on, I know I said we wouldn't drink today, but . . ."

"What the hell. I'm up for it."

We walked out of the cafe and straight into the pub next door. I found a vacant table while Rebecca went to the bar. As I sat down, I heard my phone ping. I had received a text message.

Pull yourself together, Frankie. It's just a text message; you've had lots of them before. Before my anxiety-fuelled thoughts had time to do their worst, I looked at who'd sent the text. I exhaled deeply. It was from Maria.

*Are you OK? Judging by your text messages last night, I think you were very drunk. I waited until now to reply, so I could be sure you'd sobered up. Lol! Meet up this Thursday for a meal and a catch up? I'll pick you up at eight. xx*

I had better check the messages that I sent her last night. I couldn't even remember sending them. Perhaps I shouldn't have another drink. Oops, too late. Rebecca was coming back from the bar with two glasses of Pinot Grigio.

"What are you looking so sheepish about?" she asked, as she set the glasses down on the table.

"I've just had a text from Maria. Apparently, I was drunk texting her last night."

"Have you had a look at what you said?"

"I was just about to."

"You carry on. I'll sit here and people-watch while sipping my Pinot."

I returned my attention to my phone, and scrolled back through the one, two, three . . . , numerous text messages I had sent Maria last night. How embarrassing. I was never drinking again I told myself as I reached out my hand for my glass of wine and took a sip. The messages were long and rambling. The name of the guy I had met last night was John, so I discovered by reading what I'd told Maria. He was thirty-one, younger than me, and I kept referring to him as my toy boy. I said that I thought he was cute, and that he had a terrible singing voice. That last comment made me laugh out loud. Rebecca gave me a curious look.

"I'll tell you later," I said, before returning my attention to the ramblings of last night. I'd told her I'd given John my number, which tied in with what Rebecca had said. I couldn't quite believe that I had given my mobile phone number out to a complete stranger. Duh! Frankie. Still, I had been extremely drunk. Finally, I'd gotten around to explaining that I had listened to the voice message she'd left me the other day and was texting to arrange a night out. That made sense of her reply. I text her back:

*I'll explain on Thursday. I was very drunk. Sorry! See you at eight. xx*

"His name was John," I said.

"Eh?"

"The guy from last night," I explained.

"Oh, are you going to see him again?"

"No chance. I can't even remember what he looks like."

"Do you want me to describe him to you?"

"No, don't bother."

Rebecca sighed. "Seriously, though, when are you going to give a guy a chance?"

I shrugged. I knew what she meant. I hadn't dated anyone for a long time. It wasn't that I didn't want to. It was just . . . I was scared. I was scared of the emotional investment. What if it went wrong, like my marriage had? I wasn't only worried for my own emotional wellbeing but my children's as well.

"It's been a long time. I'm not sure I know what to do any more," I laughed.

"It's like riding a bike. Whatever happened to the policeman that was sniffing around you a few months back?"

"Beautifully put, Rebecca."

"Oh, you know what I mean."

I smiled. "Yes, I do. You mean Leo: PC Leo Acton."

"That's the one. He was really keen on you as I recall."

"Hmm, he was and still is keen on me. He asked me out again only last week."

"Why don't you give the poor guy a chance? At least you know you can trust him—he's a policeman."

I laughed. I did trust him but not because he was a policeman.

Since the kidnap and the attempt on my life, Leo had been a great support. He'd regularly been in touch, in a professional capacity, regarding the trial of Lee Mason, David Simons, and Andy Brooks.

The three men were remanded into custody at the time of their arrest. They were refused bail because they were considered flight risks. They pleaded guilty to the charges of two counts of kidnap, attempted fraud and burglary. Their guilty plea meant there wasn't a need for a trial.

Neither Isabelle nor I had to stand in the court and give evidence.

Lee and David each received a sentence of seventeen years; Andy received fifteen years. The judge explained that the kidnap charges alone can carry a sentence of life in prison, which is fifteen years minimum. However, because they pleaded guilty he reduced their total custodial sentence appropriately.

Andy's sentence was two years less than the other two because he showed remorse by returning my jewellery and cooperating with the police from the moment of his capture.

The court case was four months ago. I didn't attend court for the sentencing. Instead choosing to stay at home and wait for Leo to call me to inform me of the outcome. He called and let me know the news, and then he surprised me by asking me out. Apparently, he had been waiting for the trial to end before 'trying his luck' as he put it. I had to admit that I wasn't surprised. He had been remarkably attentive during the last twelve months.

From the beginning, he kept me up to date on every little detail of the case. I often wondered whether every victim/witness got this level of attention from the police. He would drop by at least once a fortnight because he 'just happened to be in the area'. I would make him a cuppa, and we'd sit and chat for the time it took him to drink it.

In the early days, after everything that had happened, I found it comforting; he made me feel safe. Then as time went on, I began to look forward to his visits. I'd got to know him quite well.

"How would you feel if he gave up on you and started dating some other woman?" Rebecca asked, breaking through my ruminations.

I felt a sudden stab of emotion at the thought. Was it jealousy? Yes, it was. It was an unpleasant feeling, and not one I was used to.

"Well?" she persisted.

I grimaced. "OK, you win. I wouldn't like it, not one bit."

"What are you going to do about it?"

I shrugged. "I dunno. Perhaps I'll say yes next time he asks." If I were to be honest with myself, he was probably the only man I would even consider dating right now.

"Wrong! There may not be a next time. You're going to text him now, while I watch, and suggest a night out."

"I am?" Suddenly, I felt like I was fourteen again and completely out of my depth.

"You are!" Rebecca said. The rigidity in both her tone and demeanour would brook no argument.

"I am!" I repeated with more certainty. I found the last text message from Leo on my phone, and I typed in reply:

*I've been thinking . . . you know that you suggested we might go out for a drink some time. Well, yes, OK then. I'd like that.*

I peeked up at Rebecca and winced with apprehension, my finger hovering over the send button.

"Send it, NOW!" she said firmly.

My finger descended and hit send. With the realisation that I'd actually sent the message came the physical aftermath: my heart began to pound in my chest; the palms of my hands began to sweat. This was ridiculous! I was thirty-six years old for heaven's sake. I lifted my glass of Pinot to my lips. It was empty! How had that happened?

"Do you fancy another?" I asked Rebecca.

"Oh yes. Arranging dates is thirsty work," she said as she held out her empty glass.

As I was walking to the bar, my phone pinged. It was Leo. Wow, that was fast.

*Great! How about next week? I'll pick you up. I'll text you tomorrow with possible day and time.*

My legs were feeling like jelly. This was now real. I was going on a date next week, and I was terrified.

"What can I get you?" the barman asked.

"I'd like a pint of Dutch courage, please," I said with a cheeky grin.

"He smiled, "Like that, is it?"

"You have no idea," I said. It was time for the big guns even though it was only late afternoon. "Two double vodka and cokes, please."

Moments later he was handing me the drinks, and I took a healthy swig from one of them.

*****

I couldn't believe it was Monday already, and we were on our way home. What a weekend! Rebecca pulled up outside my house at 1.00 p.m. precisely. We looked at each other and grinned conspiratorially.

"What happens on tour stays on tour," she said.

"Agreed," I nodded.

"Do you need any help with your things?" she asked.

"No. I'll be fine. It's been a blast. Thanks ever so much for organising it."

She grimaced. "Frankie, I don't deserve to be thanked for organising that hotel. It was a dive."

"It was being refurbished. You weren't to know it would be like staying at Fawlty Towers. And to be honest, I don't think I've laughed so much in my whole life."

"Hmm, I suppose it was entertaining," she smirked. "Let me know how your date goes with PC Acton," she added.

I blushed. "I will. See you soon."

I waved as she sped off down the road.

First things first, I thought as I opened my front door, where were the painkillers? My head was banging. We'd carried on drinking yesterday afternoon and on into the evening. We stopped drinking at around eleven. That was an early night for us. I sat at the kitchen table recalling the previous night's events.

The two men from the previous night had shown up in the pub we were in. Rebecca had recognised them. I hadn't. We proceeded to dodge them all night. It seemed every time we went to another pub, so they would turn up shortly after us.

In the end, we gave up and went back to the hotel. We were giggling like teenagers when we got back to the room. My phone rang two or three times last night, each time No Caller ID. We agreed it must be, John, the guy I had met the previous night. At one point, while covertly watching John and his friend at a distance we saw him making a call and my mobile rang. He had to have been trying to call me.

Thinking about John reminded me to check my phone. Perhaps he'd given up because there were no missed calls today. Right then, I had two hours before I needed to pick up Henry. Time to get on with the washing and everything else I hadn't done this weekend.

*****

After having done two loads of washing, the vacuuming, dusting, and ironing, it was time to fetch Henry from school. I decided to walk. The fresh air would do me good.

I arrived at the school as the bell was ringing; Henry came dashing out.

"Mum, you're back. Did you have a nice time?"

"I did thanks. How about you? Did you have a good time at your dad's?"

"Yeah . . ."

He didn't sound sure.

"What's up?" I asked.

"Nothing. Yeah, it was good. Let's go home."

Hmm, I got the feeling I wasn't being told everything. I'd find out later.

As we walked into the house, I could hear Alex in the kitchen.

"Is that you, Alex?" I called.

"Yep." He walked out of the kitchen and gave me a hug.

It was his way of saying he'd missed me without actually having to embarrass himself by verbalising it. I hugged him back.

I hung my coat on the coat rack and placed my shoes in the shoe tidy underneath. Next to my shoes, I noticed a brand new pair of trainers. Rob had actually taken Alex shopping to get a new PE kit. I knew he'd said that he'd take care of it, but I hadn't actually believed he would. I picked up the new trainers to get a better look at them. They were a pair of Nike Performance Air Max trainers. I knew they cost over one hundred and fifty pounds a pair. What the hell was Rob thinking?

"They're cool, aren't they?" Alex commented.

"They are. And they're expensive. I can't quite believe your dad bought them to be honest."

"Nah! Me neither," he agreed.

Hmm, I would have a word with Rob later. My mobile phone pinged, and my heart skipped a beat. It was a text from Leo.

*Can you make Thursday evening? 8.00 p.m.?*

Oh damn, I had arranged to see Maria that night. Mum had agreed to babysit. I'd have to text back and suggest the following Thursday. I hoped he didn't think I was trying to put him off.

"Mum, is it OK if I go on my laptop a little early?" Henry asked. "I've got a new friend called Max. We're having lots of fun. He loves Minecraft as much as me," Henry gabbled.

"Hmm . . . that's nice dear." I was all fingers and thumbs as I texted Leo back with the alternative plan. I could feel butterflies in my stomach at the thought of our date.

"Mum, can I?"

"Uh, yes, until teatime."

"Great," he said as he went stomping upstairs to get his laptop.

My mobile phone pinged. That was quick. There was a message from Leo.

*That's fine. See you Thursday after next. Pick you up at 8.00 p.m. We'll go into town.*

I responded that I was looking forward to it. Should I have said that? Did I sound too keen? Oh my God! How old was I?

Henry was setting the laptop up on the kitchen table. This was the rule we had: if he was online, he had to be in a room where I was able to see what he was doing. Not that I had any real understanding of the games he played online. He smiled at me over the top of his laptop.

"Glad you're back, Mum."

"Me too."

# Chapter 12

*Session two - Tom Ferris 10.00 a.m. - 11.00 a.m.*

"OK, Tom. Did you have reason to put the controlled breathing technique into practice this week?"

"Yes, I did. Actually, it has helped me to understand the physical effects of shallow breathing. I've found that I've been able to rationalise the tingling in my face and the chest pain I experience. When I focus on my breathing and slow it down, the symptoms disappear." He smiled with relief.

"That's great. Did you manage to complete the anxiety diary?"

"Kind of . . ."

"Shall we take a look at what you've written?" I invited.

He didn't look keen, but he pulled a folded up piece of paper from his back pocket. He unfolded it slowly and deliberately. Something told me he was reluctant to examine in any detail what he had written. He passed me the piece of paper; I placed it on the coffee table.

"How did you find the process of completing the diary after each bout of anxiety?"

"It was OK . . ." He paused and then added, "Actually . . . it felt pretty pointless, if I'm honest. I don't really see how it's going to help."

I nodded. "Well, let's have a look at what you've written, and we'll see if it helps in any way."

I glanced at the diary. I could see a pattern emerging just from looking at the dates and times of the bouts of anxiety.

"So, you've felt anxious at some point everyday this week. You had several episodes of anxiety at the weekend and every evening this week. You don't appear to have any anxiety during weekdays. Where are you then?"

"I'm at work except for Tuesday mornings when I see you."

"Work doesn't appear to cause you any anxiety."

He shook his head.

I studied what he had written in column two, which represented where he was and what he was doing when he felt anxious: *At home, Out for a meal, At home, At home, Food shopping*. The corresponding anxiety levels were seven, ten, seven, seven, and nine. Column four, which asked him to identify what had made him feel anxious on this occasion, had been left blank.

"Well at least the diary has established that your work doesn't cause you anxiety."

"I knew that already."

"That's good. But last week you said you were feeling anxious all of the time. We can see from your diary that you are feeling anxious at certain points in the day, not all of the time."

"It feels like all of the time; it happens so frequently."

"I can imagine."

He hadn't completed column four, it was either because he didn't know what made him anxious or he didn't want to write it down.

I pressed on, "I notice the worst occasion of anxiety this week was when you were out for a meal. Can you tell me about it?"

"Umm . . . well it was a meal like any other. I had steak with mushrooms and chips," he said and seemed to want to leave it there.

"Sounds lovely," I said.

"It was," he nodded.

"The food didn't cause you any stress," I stated.

"No."

He crossed his arms and legs in a defensive pose.

"Were you alone?" I persisted.

He stiffened still further and pursed his lips. I was beginning to get somewhere.

"No."

He wasn't going to make it easy for me.

"Do you mind my asking who you were with?"

"My wife."

"You were with your wife." I reflected. This was the first time he'd mentioned being married.

"Yes, and . . . ," he paused.

I waited for him to complete his sentence.

"My baby son."

I smiled. "You have a baby son. How lovely. How old is he?"

I was watching his reaction to my questions. He didn't look like the typically proud parent who was happy to talk about their child the first opportunity they got.

"Uh yes, he's great. Jacob is nine months old. He's a daddy's boy."

His words lacked conviction. It was as if he was saying what he thought I wanted to hear.

"Babies are hard work," I stated matter-of-factly.

He nodded all the while staring at the ground. After a few moments, he looked up and straight into my eyes.

"I was so looking forward to being a father," he said.

I believed him. However, something about his tone implied fatherhood wasn't turning out to be everything he'd expected it to be.

"But . . . ," he faltered. Unable to maintain eye contact with me, his gaze wandered the room.

He seemed unwilling to verbalise what he was thinking.

"But?" I nudged, encouraging him to continue. I wasn't sure he would.

Sighing deeply and sitting back in his chair he said, "I don't want you to think badly of me."

"I won't. Part of what I do as a counsellor is not to judge other people's behaviour. "

"Well, I think badly of myself."

"Go on . . . ," I encouraged.

"I don't think I'm cut out to be a dad," he stated.

"And why is that?"

"He cries all of the time. He won't shut up. I can't stand it. It was Jacob who made me feel anxious during the meal. He was crying, and he wouldn't stop," he admitted.

I made a point of looking at the anxiety diary again; at the dates, times and places where he felt most anxious. "And the other times you felt anxious, at home and while out shopping?"

"Look, it's Jacob. He makes me feel anxious. I've known it all along but didn't want to admit it to anyone. That's why I wasn't keen on completing the anxiety diary. You can't do anything about it. He's my son. He isn't going anywhere. I just need to manage the symptoms. What kind of a dad does it make me to admit something like that?"

Rather than answer his question, I chose to offer some kind of explanation for his reaction to his son's tears.

"We're programmed to respond to a baby's cries. There have been studies that show the sound heightens the activity in the same part of the brain that controls our fight or flight instinct. With that in mind, it wouldn't be a stretch to assume that if you have a child who cries a lot, it can cause anxiety. Especially, when combined with a lack of sleep."

He shook his head. "Don't make excuses for me."

"I'm not. I assure you."

"I was the one who wanted a family. I thought it would make my life complete. I nagged my wife to have a baby.

She's five years younger than me, so she was happy to wait a while. She wanted to enjoy being a married couple: holidays abroad, romantic nights out and that kind of thing. I was the one who insisted on a big family, so we had better get on with it." He sat forward in his chair and put his head in his hands. After a while, he looked up and said, "So you can understand why I can't admit how he makes me feel."

"I can understand your feelings. Your wife must see how anxious you are lately. Do you talk about it?"

"No. She has tried to talk to me, but I just shut down. She was relieved when I agreed to go to counselling. She doesn't mind too much that I'm not talking to her as long as I am talking to someone."

"She sounds like an understanding person."

"She is."

"To recap—we've established Jacob makes you feel anxious. Do your feelings of anxiety only occur when he cries?"

"Yes. No. Oh, I don't know. It's worse when he cries, but I'm never relaxed around him."

"Are you able to tell me what you're thinking when he cries?" I wanted to establish whether his anxiety was fuelled by his inability to understand his son's reasons for crying or whether it was something else.

"I just want him to shut up. The noise bothers me. It especially bothers me when we're in public. People look at us. He has to be quiet. He's drawing attention to us."

"You aren't comfortable with other people's attention."

"Not that kind of attention."

"How would you classify 'that kind of attention'?"

"It's negative attention. They are looking at us because they are disapproving. I hear them tut and huff. I can hear them muttering under their breath, 'why don't they pick the poor mite up, all he wants is a cuddle.' Then I pick him up and he screams louder."

Suddenly, the words of a song filled the air around us. A familiar male voice belted out 'Like a bat out of hell I'll be gone when the morning comes. When the night is over, like a bat out of hell. I'll be gone, gone, gone'.

It took us both a few moments to realise it was Tom's mobile phone ringtone. I had thought, momentarily, that somehow Meatloaf had entered the building and was serenading us, as implausible as that seemed.

I watched Tom's cheeks redden as he reached into his trouser pocket for his phone.

"I'm so sorry, Frankie. I thought I'd switched my phone off before I came in."

He frowned as he checked to see who was calling him. I assumed he rejected the call as the music stopped abruptly.

"Nothing urgent, I hope."

"No, it was just my stepdad." A sound emanated from his phone signalling the arrival of a text message. He sighed and glanced at the message; the contents of which appeared to annoy him.

"Shall we continue?" I asked, attempting to recapture his attention.

"Yes, sorry."

"We've established that you're struggling with aspects of being a first-time dad. Jacob's crying, especially his crying in public, makes you feel anxious. The negative attention it attracts from people adds to your feelings of anxiety. You were saying that 'he has to be quiet'. Why is that?"

He shook his head. "What do you mean? Of course he has to be quiet. I don't understand the question."

"Babies cry," I stated. "We all know that. So, why do you feel it is unacceptable for him to cry?"

He sat and thought about the question. "I'm not sure. I just know that I feel anxious when he does. I'll think about it. I'll let you know next week if I come up with any ideas."

"That's great. The anxiety diary has helped me to understand when and where you feel most anxious, which in turn has helped me to identify what triggers your anxiety. Had you been unaware of your triggers, it would have helped you too. But as you say, you knew what was making you feel anxious. You just didn't feel comfortable admitting it."

"I'm still not comfortable, truth be told." His expression was grim.

"Because admitting it makes you feel like a bad dad?"

"Yes," he said with feeling.

"No one is given an instruction manual when a baby is born. We all have to find our way through it. Some struggle more than others, but that doesn't make them bad parents. You're tackling your issues by attending counselling. I would say that is the behaviour of a responsible parent. Wouldn't you?"

He sat looking at me for a while digesting what I'd said.

"Perhaps."

"This week's homework is an extension of last week's: I'd like you to continue to record your bouts of anxiety in columns one to four. But this time, I'd like to know what it is you do to cope with the anxiety. After having implemented your coping strategies, I'd like you to record your revised levels of anxiety. Basically, I want to see if your strategies for coping are working. I'd also like you to continue to use the controlled breathing techniques."

I was expecting him to ask me some questions about the completion of the anxiety diary, but he didn't. He rose from his chair to leave.

"See you next week, Frankie."
"Yes, see you next week, Tom."

# Chapter 13

***Session two - Susan Mackintosh 11.30 a.m. - 12.30 p.m.***

Susan swept into the room on a wave of expensive perfume and took a seat. The scent surrounded her, and I felt it soon surround me too. Luckily, the smell, although pungent, wasn't unpleasant.

Once again, Susan was dressed impeccably. She was wearing a black pair of trousers with a pink Ralph Lauren shirt. Whilst the look was casual, it was an expensive casual. She placed her Marc Jacobs handbag on the floor at her feet before placing both her hands in her lap. She stared directly at me and raised her eyebrows.

I took this to be my cue to start the session, "How was your week, Susan?" I asked.

"Ghastly, Frankie, simply ghastly," she replied.

"Oh dear, I'm sorry to hear that. Would you like to tell me about it?"

"Umm . . . no, I don't think so."

Hmm, interesting, why allude to something she had no intention of explaining?

"OK, that's fine." I pressed on, "Last week, we were talking about your relationship with your husband . . ."

"Yes," she interrupted. "He's still treating me terribly. I simply don't deserve it, Frankie." She pulled a tissue from the box on the table and dabbed at the corners of her eyes.

"I'm sorry to hear that."

She smiled briefly. She seemed comforted by my concern.

"Thank you. He's been on that blasted computer of his more than ever. If I walk into the room, he becomes shifty. As if he's been caught looking at things he shouldn't. Obviously, by the time I walk around the desk to see what he's looking at, the screen is blank. Although, I did catch a glimpse of something the other day; his evasive action wasn't quite fast enough."

She paused, and I felt it was for dramatic effect. She wanted me to prompt her to continue. Why? To prove I was interested? Well, of course I was.

"What did you see?" I prompted obligingly.

She smiled her satisfaction at my question. "Well, I saw the picture of a man. He was in his late twenties, maybe twenty-seven or twenty-eight. He was a handsome young man. There was a name on the screen. I caught a glimpse of it, but only for a second before my husband minimised the screen. His name began with an 'S'. That's it, I'm afraid."

"Your husband was looking at a website that happened to have a picture of a young man whose name began with an 'S'. What do you think it was about?"

She shrugged. "I don't know. I have to admit, I was expecting to see pictures of women. Perhaps catch him on one of those dating websites. I wasn't expecting to see him looking at pictures of men."

"Do you think he was looking at pictures of men? Or could it simply be that your husband was looking at a page on a website that had a picture of a man on it as you happened across him?"

She gave me the kind of half-smile that said she knew better and I was deluded.

Unperturbed, I pressed on, "Was the man naked?"

She took a sharp intake of breath. "Of course he wasn't naked! Don't you think I would have tackled him, there and then, if he had been?"

"I'm simply asking because I'm trying to establish why his looking at a picture of a man on the Internet would make you so suspicious."

"It's not the picture of the man that bothers me but his general behaviour surrounding it. It's his behaviour that makes it suspicious. If it were innocent, why minimise the website when I enter the room? Why not let me see what he's doing?

"He did something else suspicious this week. Well, several things really. Dickie, my husband, had his hair cut. Usually, I organise that for him. But this time, he booked it himself. Then he announces that he's going out on Thursday night. He never goes out."

"You said last week that you'd asked him what he was looking at on the Internet, and it caused a row."

"Yes, he just says he isn't doing anything, and that I should trust him. Huh, trust him. I've trusted men in the past and look where that got me."

"You also mentioned last week that your previous long-term partners had cheated on you."

"Yes, that's right."

"You referred to previous failed relationships, and I asked you to think about whether the men you had dated had shared any common traits."

"Yes, I remember. I did give it some thought. They do share one trait . . ."

"And that is?"

"They all cheated on me. I pick unfaithful men. So, it stands to reason my husband will cheat on me, if he hasn't already." She shrugged.

"Did they have anything else in common?" I asked.

"Hmm, well, let me see . . ." She thought for a moment or two and then said, "I suppose they were all wealthy. They had money. Not that money matters to me you understand."

My eyes betrayed me as I glanced at the Mark Jacobs bag at her feet and her Louis Vuitton shoes.

She must have noticed because she said, "Of course I like the finer things in life. What girl doesn't? But it's not the most important thing."

"What is the most important thing for you?" I asked.

"Love," she said dreamily. "I thought they loved me, but they didn't."

"Would you like to tell me about your previous relationships?" I invited.

"How exactly is that going to help me with my current relationship?"

"Sometimes, when we reflect on our past, it can give us insight into a pattern of behaviour that we can change once we are aware of it."

"There you go again. I told you last week. I am not responsible for the failure of my previous relationships. They all cheated on ME. I'm the victim," she said sniffing into her tissue.

"You don't have to tell me about your previous relationships if you don't want to. These are your sessions; we can discuss what you want to. However, you've identified that the previous men in your life have been rich, and they have all been unfaithful.

"By discussing it further, we may well identify other traits that they share. Should your current relationship end, as you suspect it will, then you may choose to avoid those traits in a man in future."

She raised one eyebrow and the corner of her mouth twitched. I wasn't sure whether she was going to tell me about her previous relationships or not. She gave an almost imperceptible nod of her head, took a deep breath and opened her mouth to speak.

"My first serious relationship started when I was seventeen. He was perfect. He was older than me, not difficult I suppose at seventeen. He was twenty-four and the son of one of Daddy's friends. Daddy liked him." Her eyes glowed as she spoke of her first love. "His name was Marcus; he was a stockbroker. Oh we had such fun. He would take me to casinos and the races: Ascot and

Cheltenham. I would dress up in fancy frocks and hats. He said I looked good on his arm." She smiled as she recollected her youth.

"It sounds fun," I said. "What else did you do together?"

"What do you mean?"

"Well, it can't have been all about dressing up and fancy days out. What kinds of things did you enjoy as a couple? Going for walks, watching films, talking?"

"Oh, um, I don't recall. I just remember the glitz and glamour. Our picture appeared in the society pages of one of the big newspapers once. I forget which one. I have the clipping somewhere."

"So, what happened with Marcus?"

"I told you. He cheated on me. We'd been together for two years. I couldn't understand it. I'd done everything he wanted. He'd preferred blondes; my natural hair colour is brown. She touched her auburn hair; this isn't natural in case you're wondering. It comes out of a very expensive bottle. As I was saying, he had said he preferred blondes early on in the relationship, so I dyed my hair blonde."

"And yet he'd asked you out when your hair was brown."

"Uh . . . yes, he asked me out eventually."

"It sounds as if it took him a while to pluck up the courage."

"Kind of . . . when we first met, he liked another girl. Funnily enough, she was a blonde; a natural blonde no less. I forget her name. He was quite smitten. But she wasn't the right type, if you know what I mean." She was looking at me as if I would understand what she meant. I had an idea but wanted to be sure.

"By 'right type', you mean . . . ?"

"I mean her daddy worked for Marcus's daddy. They weren't wealthy, or anything."

"I see, so her suitability to date Marcus was measured by her father's position and wealth."

"Yes, that's right." She smiled as if these dating criteria were the most natural thing in the world, and she was pleased I had got the point.

Hadn't she said that money didn't matter to her?

"What happened?" I asked.

"Well before Marcus asked me out, he went out with . . . I remember now, her name was Kerry. He went out with her for a while in secret. When Marcus's dad found out, he forced him to finish it. He threatened to disinherit him. Well as Marcus said, he liked her and all that, but she wasn't worth losing Daddy's millions over."

I thought it best to remain silent. Anything I could have said would have sounded judgemental. My thoughts were definitely judgemental. It would seem that money ruled, over and above anything else, in the circles she mixed in.

"Marcus, his dad, and mine, felt it prudent that he ask me out. We were far better suited."

"In what way were you better suited?"

"Our backgrounds, of course: both of our fathers belonged to the same clubs, played golf together et cetera."

This wasn't a world I was familiar with. I was used to a boy and a girl dating for no other reason than they liked each other.

"So as I was saying, I dyed my hair blonde. He preferred girls in dresses and high heels, so that's what I wore. I had many a blister, I can tell you." The memory made her wince and absentmindedly rub her ankle. "I never let him down; I was always immaculately turned out."

"You spoke of having fun together."

"Yes, as I said we were always going somewhere glamorous. Until, it all went wrong. I was expecting him to propose. Daddy was expecting him to propose. Everyone was expecting him to propose," she said with meaning. "It was my nineteenth birthday party. He'd bought me a ring for my birthday. It was all planned. He was to get down on one knee at midnight."

She had a faraway look in her eyes, and her lips were turned up at the edges.

"That sounds romantic," I commented.

"Yes, Daddy and I thought so."

Hmm, shouldn't that have been Marcus and I thought so?

"What happened?" I asked.

"He didn't show up. He sent his best friend with a note. I remember the words: 'Sorry, Susan! I can't do it.' That was it."

"You must have been devastated."

"Yes, I was. It ruined my party. I'd been planning that party for six months, and it had cost Daddy a small fortune."

"I meant that you must have been devastated that the man you loved had jilted you."

"Oh, yes, yes, of course. I found out the next day that he'd run off with Kerry. Apparently, he'd been seeing her the whole time we'd been dating. I was his cover story to keep his daddy happy. It would seem, when faced with marrying me, he preferred to do without Daddy's millions and marry Kerry."

"That must have hurt deeply."

"I was devastated. Imagine how it looked, everyone laughing at me."

"Your ego was dented understandably. But you had loved him, and he had betrayed you. That sort of thing takes time to recover from."

"Well, exactly. It took me . . . let me see . . . a whole month before I started dating James."

OK, I thought, some people bounced back quicker than others. She seemed to think a month was a long time to mourn her lost love. I'd be interested to know what her definition of love was. That was a conversation for another day.

"We're coming to the end of the session, Susan. So far, we've identified that the men you've been in long-term relationships with have all been rich and unfaithful. Perhaps, next week, we'll identify further similarities when you tell me about your other relationships."

She looked dubious.

"Tell me, Frankie, have you received any more bunches of flowers since last week?"

I'd forgotten that she'd been present last week when I'd received the mysterious bunch of flowers. I shuddered. I still didn't know who had sent them.

"No. I haven't."

"They were beautiful. Whoever sent them had good taste."

"Yes, they were. I'll walk you out," I said. The scent of her perfume followed us both from the room. I suspected that I would need a shower to remove its smell from my skin and hair.

As we approached reception, I turned to say goodbye and could see Theresa, the receptionist, out of the corner of my eye. She had something in her hand and seemed to be waiting to speak to me.

"Goodbye, Susan. I'll see you next week."

"Bye, Frankie," she said as she turned to walk through the revolving door.

I turned toward Theresa. "I got the feeling you wanted to speak to me."

"Yes, I have something for you. It isn't flowers this time."

I smiled. Rebecca had told me she had ordered something online and arranged for it to be delivered to the office, rather than her home. She was going to pop by later and pick it up.

"That'll be for Rebecca," I said.

Theresa frowned and checked the label for a second time. "No, it's addressed to you."

"Me?" I hadn't ordered anything that I could recall. I reached out my hand to take the small square package from her.

The box was black, and it had a silver ribbon wrapped around it. Underneath the ribbon was a small envelope. The label had been typed and was addressed to me. Perhaps Rebecca had bought me a present. Perhaps her saying she was having something delivered was a ruse.

"Maybe it's from your secret admirer," Theresa said beaming.

The smile froze on my lips. I'd been feeling better since my weekend away. I'd hardly thought of Glenn over the past few days. But now he was slamming headlong back into my thoughts. Calm down, Frankie, and read the note. There may be a perfectly reasonable explanation. Trembling, I reached for the small envelope.

"Ooh, isn't it exciting," Theresa said.

That was one way of looking at it, I thought. I was less excited and more terrified, which was ridiculous because it was a harmless black box. Fumbling with the envelope, I managed to open it and pull out a typed card from within:

*Thank you for everything. How can I ever repay you?*

Theresa was saying something, but I wasn't sure what.

"Excuse me?" I asked inviting her to repeat herself.

"What does it say? Who is it from?" she asked.

I wasn't really listening to her.

She must have taken my silence as a sign of my disapproval as she stammered, "Sorry, it isn't really any of my business." She turned away from me and carried on sifting through the piles of post on her desk.

There hadn't been a note with the flowers. At least this seemed like a grateful client, still I wasn't sure. I glanced up and noticed Susan standing by the doors watching me. I'd thought she'd left. I took the lid off of the box and touched the softest, smoothest black silk scarf I'd ever seen.

Time froze as I stared at the scarf in my hand; my brain refused point-blank to process what it saw. My body seemed to already know, as I felt the trembling start in my feet and rise up through my legs and torso. The shaking had reached my arm and then my hand; I could see the scarf fluttering in my grasp as a result. Still my brain wouldn't let me comprehend what was happening.

I was gazing at the scarf; it was black. It was as if the black of the scarf grew bigger and bigger until I had no peripheral vision left. My body was suddenly weightless and everything was black.

*****

There was a voice. I could hear it, but it felt far away.

"Frankie . . . , Frankie . . . , are you OK?" Theresa asked.

"Call an ambulance," Susan said.

I could hear them; I just couldn't move or open my eyes. I could feel the cold floor through my clothing. What on earth was I doing lying on the floor?

"She's fainted," Susan said.

Had I? Why? My eyes flickered open to see Theresa and Susan standing over me.

"Oh thank God." Theresa said. "Are you OK? You gave us such a fright. You stood there transfixed by that scarf. You were ashen, as if you'd seen a ghost."

"Do you think you could get Frankie a glass of water?" Susan asked Theresa.

"Oh yes, sure." She jumped up and rushed off to the break room.

"I guessed you could do without her chatter for a few minutes. How are you feeling? Do you think you can sit up?" she asked calmly.

"I . . . think so." My body felt heavy, but I managed to haul myself up and into a sitting position. The floor felt cold and hard through my trousers.

"Let's get you into a chair, shall we," said Susan. She moved one of the reception chairs closer to me, and she placed her hands under my arms. "I'm going to help you. On the count of three, I'll lift you."

"I can do it. I'll be OK," I said feeling embarrassed to say the least.

"Let me help you, Frankie. You've had a funny turn." And without further ado she said, "Right, one, two, and three."

I did my best to get up on my own, but there was no denying that Susan's strength had been needed. It was good to feel the soft cushioning of the chair beneath me.

"I think you should lean forward, and put your head between your knees. I'm sure I've heard somewhere that you need to let the blood flow to your brain when you feel faint."

"OK, Susan." I did as I was bid and leant forward.

Theresa came rushing back with the water.

"Don't sit up too quickly," Susan said. "We don't want you feeling faint again."

Once again, I did as I was told and brought my head back up slowly. I took the proffered water from Theresa.

"Whatever happened?" Theresa asked.

I didn't trust myself to talk about the black silk scarf and its accompanying note. It had to be from Glenn. On the surface, it appeared to be a thank-you note from a grateful client, but I knew it was a threat. 'How can I ever repay you?' it said, and then he gave me the very item he planned to repay me with and what he'd tried to kill me with the first time. He was still out there. I was sure of it. He was playing a game of cat and mouse, and it was a game he wanted only me to be aware of.

"Would you do me a favour, Theresa?" I asked.

"Yes, of course," she answered.

"Can you call Rebecca? Ask her to come to the office, please."

"Yes, of course."

"I'll be going now, Frankie. I hope you feel better soon," Susan said.

"Yes, thank you for your help. You've been great."

She looked pleased with herself and said, "See you next week."

I didn't have to sit there long before Rebecca came rushing into the building.

"Whatever's happened?" she asked hurrying to my side.

"I'll explain later. Can you take me home? I don't think I should drive at the moment."

"Of course, you can tell me all about it in the car."

I nodded, grateful I was going home.

"Don't forget your present," Theresa called out as we were leaving the building.

"Rebecca, would you get it for me please?"

She took one look at the scarf and silently mouthed the word 'oh'. The situation needed no further explanation.

"Come on, let's get you home."

# Chapter 14

Mum had just arrived to babysit the boys for the evening. Somehow, babysit seemed an inappropriate term; the Pant Bros were hardly babies any longer. Still, they weren't old enough to be left on their own for the evening.

"I haven't had a chance to ask you about your weekend. How did it go?" Mum asked.

"Yeah, good thanks, Mum. Can I tell you all about it later? Maria will be here in twenty minutes, and I still haven't had a shower and changed."

"Yes, of course. I also want to know if Alex and Rob had a heart to heart. You know, like we discussed."

I nodded, immediately feeling guilty. I'd been so wrapped up in myself; I'd forgotten I was hoping Alex might open up to his dad about how he was feeling lately. The last year had been really tough on him. I hadn't asked him recently if he'd made any new friends. God, I was a crap mother.

"Don't do that!"

"Excuse me?" I asked.

"I know what you're doing to yourself, Frankie. Now stop!"

"What?" I asked, pretending I had no idea what she was talking about.

"You're beating yourself up about something. I can tell. You're biting your lip and avoiding eye contact. What is it?"

Resistance was futile. My mum could make anyone crack; she was as sharp as a tack. "You got me! The game's up! I haven't had chance to speak to Rob yet." That reminded me; I wanted to talk to him about the trainers.

"Oh is that all. That's no biggie, as Alex would say."

I laughed. "I'll speak to him soon. It's just been so manic."

"You don't have to explain yourself to me and there's no need to feel guilty. You're a great mum."

I sometimes wondered if my mum was psychic such was her ability to know exactly what I was thinking and when I was thinking it. I walked up to her and put my arms around her, kissing the top of her head. Not for the first time, it struck me how diminutive she was at five foot tall.

"I learned from the master," I said as I turned to go and get ready. I glanced in at Henry sitting in the kitchen on the laptop.

"You OK? What are you playing?" I asked.

"Minecraft with Max," he beamed.

"Oh, Max, your new friend?"

"Yep."

Max must have joined the school recently. I hadn't noticed any new children in Henry's class, but then I hadn't really been looking. Was I neglecting my children? It sure felt like it. Familiar slivers of guilt started to creep throughout my consciousness. Stop it, Frankie, this is not useful. I needed to start focusing more on my children and less upon myself. Memories of the black scarf from the other day came unbidden to the forefront of my mind. I felt a shudder of fear go through me. STOP, just stop!

My mobile pinged; I looked at it just in case it was Maria changing the plans for tonight for some reason. It was a message from Rebecca. I'd forgotten, today was Thursday: it was her first date with Sam. It said:

*I'm scared. What if he's not like his picture?*

I was more concerned that he was a mad axe murderer, but now was not the time to share my fears. Thinking about murderers, David Shaw came into my thoughts. I'd forgotten to check the marriage announcements last weekend because I'd been away. I must do that when I got home this evening.

First things first, I replied to Rebecca's text:

*Have an exit strategy as we discussed. If he isn't what he portrayed online, then pretend to have a family emergency and leave. Are you still driving and meeting him at the pub?*

I ran upstairs. I only had fifteen minutes to get ready. Alex's bedroom door was closed, and I could hear voices. He was chatting to someone online. He sounded unusually cheerful. I didn't recognise the voice, perhaps it was a new friend. I opened the door, so I could improve my chances of hearing what was being said. The moment he saw me he muted his friend's voice with breathtaking speed and looked at me guiltily.

"What are you up to?" I asked immediately suspicious.

"Nothing!"

"Hmm, who were you talking to? You remember the rule: only talk to people that you know in person."

"I know, I know. Don't sweat it, Mum."

"I don't have time, right now, to get into this. But we will be having a discussion later."

"I can't wait," he said doing his best impression of a morose teenager.

"Kids!" I muttered under my breath as I catapulted myself into the bathroom. I had thirteen minutes, twenty seconds and counting.

*****

I'd just finished applying my mascara when I heard the familiar beep of Maria's car horn. I flew down the stairs and opened the front door. Holding my index finger in the air, I signalled to Maria that I would be one minute.

"Right then, Mum. I'll be back by eleven. You know the drill: Henry in bed, lights off at 9.00 p.m. and Alex by 9.30

p.m. They are to stop using all electronic devices an hour before bedtime."

"Yes, yes, I know. Now, go out and enjoy your evening," she said, ushering me out of the door.

"Thanks, Mum. See you later. Bye boys," I shouted. Not waiting for a reply, I ran out to Maria's car.

I got in the passenger seat and put on my seatbelt before turning to Maria.

"Hi, how are you?" I asked.

"I'm good. How are you?" she asked. She emphasised the word 'you'.

I wasn't quite sure what she was getting at. She couldn't have known about the scarf drama. Only Rebecca knew about that. I hadn't even told my mum yet.

"You had definitely had a skinful on Saturday night," she commented as she put the car in gear and pulled away.

Now I understood: she was referring to the weekend and my drunken texts. I winced with embarrassment. "I'll tell you about it once we're in the pub, and I have a glass of something alcoholic in my hand."

She laughed. "It sounded eventful."

"You could say that."

We travelled in relaxed silence for a few minutes and then I asked, "What's Gav doing tonight?"

Gav was Maria's boyfriend. They lived together and had been dating for a couple of years now. She'd shown me pictures of him, but I hadn't actually met him yet.

"Oh he's happy to stay in and catch up on his programmes. He lets me watch what I want when I'm at home."

"Oh he sounds so thoughtful, Maria."

"He is. I'm so lucky."

"Hmm, you sound it."

"Anyway, enough about me," she said as we pulled into the car park of the Posset Cup in Portishead. "Let's get inside; you can tell me all about your weekend."

We strolled in and found an empty booth. Maria took a seat, and I went to get the drinks. Maria was very strict about not drinking and driving. She wouldn't even have one alcoholic drink and drive, which I admired her for. However, I wasn't driving. I was free to choose whatever alcoholic beverage I fancied.

"Hmm . . . I think I'll have a large glass of Chardonnay, please."

The barman smiled and prepared a glass of Diet Coke for Maria and a large glass of Chardonnay for me. I carried the drinks carefully back to Maria so as not to spill the Coke that was threatening to run over the side of the overfilled glass.

"You OK there?" she asked. "You look like you're walking a tightrope."

"I'm just trying not to spill your drink," I said as I set both glasses down carefully on the table.

"OK, come on then. Tell me all about it. I want to know everything."

"Are you sitting comfortably? Then I shall begin."

I told her all about the weekend with Rebecca. Well the bits I could remember. She knew some of the details already gleaned from my drunken rambling texts, which I apologised for again. We drew a few curious looks from the other customers in the pub as we rocked with laughter as I regaled her with details of the hotel's decor and the broken tap situation.

"It's like a clip from Fawlty Towers," she commented when she had stopped laughing.

"Yes, it was so funny. Of course, there was a more serious side to the weekend," I said as I recalled the missed calls from an unknown caller, and the silent call I'd answered.

"Oh, what happened?" She asked, her tone losing the joviality of a few moments ago. "Actually, hold that thought. Do you want another drink before you tell me all about it?"

"Oh, go on then. You've twisted my arm."

"Same again?"

"That would be lovely."

At that precise moment, my phone pinged. It made me jump. I glanced down at the screen. Rebecca had replied to my earlier text:

*Yes, I'm driving. And yes, I'm meeting him at the pub. I've just spotted him and panic over. He looks just like his picture. Woohoo! Wish me luck! X*

Her text made me smile, and I forgot what I'd been talking about momentarily.

"Is everything OK?"Maria asked.

"Yes, a text from Rebecca. She's on a blind date."

Maria frowned rather like I had when Rebecca first told me.

I pre-empted what she was going to say. "Yep, don't say it. I know it's dodgy, but she wouldn't be dissuaded. So we settled on her driving herself and her meeting him in a public place. Actually, that reminds me. I haven't told you about my date with Leo," I said, unexpectedly feeling my cheeks flush with heat. I must be blushing. How embarrassing, I wasn't a teenager any more.

"Leo?" she asked.

"You know, PC Acton."

"Oh, yes," she said with eyes wide open in surprise.

"Well, Rebecca and I discussed it, and it seemed like a good idea at the time. I'm going out with him next week."

She frowned and turning her head away from me she studied the other people in the pub. She was silent. What was wrong? Perhaps she was feeling left out because I'd discussed it with Rebecca and not her before making the decision. I hoped not, as I hadn't intended to leave her out.

After a moment or two, she turned back to me, smiled and said, "Fair enough, I'll just get those drinks." She walked over to the bar.

I sat and pondered on Rebecca's date. At least the picture on the dating website had been a current photograph; from what I'd heard that wasn't always the case. According to Rebecca, you were lucky if the picture was a photograph of their younger self. Sometimes it wasn't their photograph at all. I shuddered. Thank God I didn't have to online date. Well, not yet anyway. I had my date with Leo to look forward to. I felt my stomach somersault with nerves at the thought.

Maria was back from the bar with the drinks; she smiled as she placed my wineglass on the table in front of me. I took a large gulp to settle my nerves.

"Right then, what was the more serious side to the weekend?" she asked.

Maria knew all about my fears regarding Glenn. Aside from Mum, she'd been my rock over the last year. I could tell her anything, and I did.

"I had a meltdown in a cafe. I'd noticed that I had multiple missed calls with No Caller ID."

"You thought it was Glenn," she interrupted.

I nodded. I knew she'd understand. "Yes. But then while I was in the cafe, just before you texted me to check I was OK, I got a silent call."

"Let me guess, it reminded you of the silent calls you got from Glenn last year."

I exhaled deeply. "Yes. You understand. I knew you would," and I reached across to squeeze her hand.

"Of course I understand. Your reaction makes perfect sense in view of what you've been through. But a more rational conclusion would be that it was that guy you met the night before. What was his name?"

"According to the text I sent you that night, his name was John. I don't actually remember."

"Yes, John. You gave him your number, didn't you?"

I shrugged, "Apparently. Rebecca agrees with you. She thinks it's John calling me. But, why doesn't he speak?"

"Have you considered that there might be a problem with your phone? Or with his?"

Come to think of it, I hadn't used my mobile to make phone calls for a while. I tended to use it mainly for text messages. "Hmm, you may have a point. But the week before I was sure I saw Glenn in a car on the High Street."

"How many times is that now?" she asked calmly.

"A few," I muttered, staring at the golden liquid in my wine glass. "OK, then how do you explain the gifts?"

"What gifts?" she asked.

"A bunch of flowers last week and then . . ." I shuddered as I recalled the scarf.

"And then?" Maria was watching me intently, waiting for my answer.

"A black silk scarf with a note that said, 'Thank you for everything. How can I ever repay you?' "

Maria grimaced. "In the circumstances, the scarf is a poor choice of gift. But on the other hand, if it's from a grateful client, who doesn't know your history, then it's a perfectly nice gift for a lady. Wouldn't you agree?"

I nodded. "Yes, I suppose you're right. But the note felt like a threat, and the scarf felt so symbolic of that threat."

"Yes, I see your point. But, similarly, the note could be exactly what it claims to be: a thank you from a grateful client. The same goes for the flowers."

"Have you ever considered training to be a counsellor? I think you'd be great," I commented.

She laughed. "No, I don't think so. Anyway, you know I've got my sabbatical all arranged with ASF Technologies. Gav and I are off on our travels soon. I can't wait." She had a faraway look in her eyes.

"How will I cope without you?"

"Oh, you'll be just fine," she said.

"Australia will be lucky to have you. Which cities do you intend to visit?"I asked.

"Quite a few: we'll land in Perth and then travel to Adelaide, Melbourne, Canberra, Sydney, and Brisbane."

"Wow that sounds fantastic. You must have a party before you leave."

"Oh we will, definitely. You're at the top of the guest list." She smiled.

"Glad to hear it."

"In fact, you'll be the guest of honour."

"I like the sound of that."

She glanced at her watch. "Time we were making tracks. I'll just pop to the ladies' before we go."

"OK."

Time had flown this evening. I watched her make her way across the pub and enter the ladies' room. I'd miss her when she was away travelling. I'd grown close to her over the last year. I found her to be a logical, calming influence on me, while still understanding my fears about Glenn. She never once said I was being irrational or belittled my fear. She understood. My phone interrupted my thoughts and without thinking I answered it. It might be Rebecca.

"Hello?"

Silence.

My heartbeat quickened.

"Hello?" I repeated.

I could hear steady breathing. It felt almost mocking in its steadiness, whereas my breathing had accelerated to ragged gasps such was my fear. I was sick of the fear.

"Who is this?" I demanded, in a voice that sounded surprisingly stronger than I had expected. Nothing. Not a word. I couldn't hear anything except for the steady breathing.

"I know it's you, Glenn. You haven't fooled me, you know. I know it's you," I hissed down the phone.

Silence was the loud reply. I couldn't even hear breathing any more. The line went dead. He'd disconnected the call, the bastard. He was still out there. I put my head in my hands. Was this ever going to end?

"Frankie, are you ready to go?" Maria asked, as she returned from the ladies' room, car keys in her hand.

I looked up at her. I could see by her rapidly changing expression that she'd realised something was wrong. She dropped into the seat next to me.

"Whatever has happened? I was only in the ladies' five minutes."

"I received another silent call. I know it's him."

"No Caller ID again?"

"Probably, I didn't check who was calling before I answered. I thought it might be Rebecca and that she might need rescuing."

"Check now," she demanded.

"What's the point?" I knew I sounded defeated and, truth be told, I felt defeated. How much more of this could I take?

"Come on, Frankie. This isn't like you. Give me your phone, so I can check."

I handed it over.

She started to laugh as first she checked the identity of the last caller to my phone and then checked her own phone.

How could she laugh at a time like this? I was in bits, couldn't she see that?

"It was me," she said through her laughter.

"What?" Had she taken leave of her senses?

"I checked my text messages while I was in the ladies' room. Somehow I've called your mobile by mistake. I didn't even realise. She continued to giggle, but realising I wasn't yet seeing the funny side she put a hand on my shoulder. "I'm sorry, Frankie. I didn't mean to do it. It was an accident."

"It explains the fact that all I could hear was steady breathing, I suppose."

"I'm glad that was all you could hear. I checked my messages before I went to the loo, if you know what I mean." She raised her eyebrows as she finished talking.

Finally, I could see the lighter side of the situation.

"At least I was spared hearing you pee," I laughed.

She looked relieved that I was now laughing. "It was two pints worth of Coke; it went on for some time."

"It was less of a light shower and more of a downpour. Wouldn't you agree?" I asked.

"Niagara falls has nothing on me."

"You make me laugh, Maria."

"Good, come on, let's get you home."

We drove the mile or so home in silence. The radio was on. I was enjoying listening to some pop song I recognised but couldn't name either the song or the artist. Was I getting old? It hadn't been that long ago when I would have known every song and artist in the charts. Now I didn't have a clue.

Maria pulled up outside my house.

"Have you recovered?" she asked.

"Yes, I'm fine. I'm relieved it was you."

"Good. Is your mum babysitting?"

"Yes. Do you want to come in and say hello?" I offered.

"No, I'd better get back to Gav. He'll be missing me. How's your garden? Is she still working wonders with those green fingers of hers?"

"Yes, it looks lovely. I love that garden. Did I tell you about the spat I had with the neighbour recently?"

"No."

I explained briefly what had happened with Peggy and her predatory cat before hugging her goodnight.

"Speak to you soon. Say hi to Gav for me."

"I will. Take care."

I watched her drive off down the road before letting myself into my silent home. I glanced into the living room and could see my mum dozing in the chair. Popping upstairs, I looked in on Alex first and then Henry. They were both fast asleep. I stood on the landing for a few seconds and told myself to appreciate this moment. The three main people in my life were all here with me, safe and well.

The boys were growing up fast. I wasn't looking forward to the days that were fast approaching when they would be God knows where, until God knows what hour, with God knows who, doing God knows what. And Mum, well she was getting old. My mind shied away from thinking about my mum's age, and what I knew would inevitably come. I couldn't imagine my world without her in it. My mind simply wouldn't allow me to think about it. I took a deep breath and allowed myself to appreciate the moment. They were all here, and they were all safe.

Walking back downstairs to wake Mum, I heard my phone ping. What now?

It was Rebecca. I should have known. The message simply said:

*I think I'm in love.*

I raised my eyes to the ceiling. Hmm, in lust more like. Still I kept my thoughts to myself. I switched my phone off. I had had quite enough of it for one day. I shook my mum's arm gently.

"I wasn't asleep," she said. "I was just resting my eyes."

How many times had I heard that over the years?

"I know, Mum. It's time to go home. Are you up to it? Or do you want to share my bed?"

"I'll go home. You know your bed plays havoc with my back."

"OK, as long as you're sure."

She made her way out to the hallway and collected her things.

"Did you have a nice time?" she asked.

"Lovely thanks. I'll call you tomorrow."

She leant forward and kissed me on the cheek. "OK, bye."

"Bye, Mum."

I double locked the door behind her and climbed the stairs for the final time today. I was tired. I was hoping I'd have a nightmare-free night tonight. Ever the optimist, Frankie, I thought, as I walked into the bathroom and turned the light on.

# Chapter 15

The sound of the alarm clock came crashing into my dream like a freight train. I woke with a jolt and was disappointed to be awake.

Unusually, I had been in the middle of a nice dream rather than my usual nightmares. Damn, I was just getting to the best bit. Leo had been leaning in to give me a kiss, our first kiss. I closed my eyes, and was expecting to feel his lips on mine when instead I heard beep, beep.

Was it an omen? Did this mean we were doomed before we'd even begun? Oh come on, Frankie, where was my rational self? Superstitious mumbo jumbo, I said to myself sternly.

I pulled on my dressing gown and went down to the kitchen to get breakfast started. Tomorrow was Saturday, and I couldn't wait for a lie-in. I switched the kitchen light on and popped the kettle on for my usual cup of tea. I got the bowls out for the boys' cereal. I poured their favourite cereals into each bowl before shouting up the stairs.

The noise was more like a herd of wildebeest stampeding across the Serengeti during their annual migration than two boys merely getting out of bed. I shook my head; if they were this noisy now, what would it sound like when they were full-grown men? They were both descending the stairs at a rate of knots. I made sure I wasn't standing between them and their breakfast, or carnage could have ensued.

I made my cup of tea while listening to the clanking of metal spoons on porcelain bowls interspersed with the slurping of milk and the munching of Crunchy Nut Cornflakes. I turned to inspect the damage to, what had been only moments ago, my tidy kitchen. I was willing to bet there would be the usual dribbles of milk on the table around their bowls.

As predicted, each bowl was sitting in a puddle of milk. Soggy individual cornflakes had escaped both the confines of the bowl and the corresponding mouth and landed in a sticky mess on the table. It could be worse, I told myself. When they were toddlers, I would have been peeling dried cornflakes from the walls for weeks.

"Go and get ready for school. I'll tidy up AGAIN," I said, while bestowing a comic glare upon them.

They scraped their chairs back across the kitchen floor and shot from the room.

I could see light coming through the blinds, so I switched the light off and opened them. The morning light poured into the kitchen; it was going to be a nice day.

I glanced out of the window at the garden. It looked different. I couldn't make sense of it for a few moments. And then my brain allowed me to comprehend what my eyes saw: every flower, every shrub, and every branch of every tree lay on the ground. It was as if a combine harvester had swept through my garden in the night and devastated everything in its wake.

"What the . . . ?" I opened my mouth several times to say something only to close it again. I was at a loss for words. How could this have happened? Why had this happened?

Glenn, it had to be him. This was his way of proving he knew where I lived, but, why my garden?

I rushed out of the kitchen, down the hallway and headed straight for the front door. I swung it wide open. I looked it up and down. Unbeknown to me, I must have been holding my breath because now my lungs felt like a bursting balloon as the air rushed from them in relief. No graffiti; Glenn's preferred modus operandi of threat and intimidation.

"Mum, what's wrong?" a frightened little voice said from the upstairs landing.

I glanced up. Henry was standing on the top stair, half-dressed with a toothbrush in his hand.

"I heard you open the front door," he said by way of explanation.

"Nothing's wrong. I just thought I heard the postman knock, that's all. I'm expecting a package. But I was wrong. I must be hearing things."

"Alex did just drop something on his bedroom floor. Perhaps you heard that."

I nodded. "Yes, that must have been it," I lied.

He smiled and returned to the task in hand, or rather in his hand. He walked back into the bathroom to finish brushing his teeth.

I closed the front door. I didn't want to scare the Pant Bros unnecessarily. They had been through so much already. Returning to the kitchen I closed the blinds and turned the light back on. I didn't want them to get upset before school.

Looking down at my dressing gown and glancing at the clock, I realised I needed to get a wriggle on. Trying and failing to put the image of my ravaged garden to the back of my mind, I rushed upstairs.

While I was in the shower, I thought about what I was going to do next. I wanted to call DC Smithers. I still couldn't call him Andrew, not even in my thoughts. I still hadn't forgiven him for suggesting I needed counselling. Not that there was anything wrong with having or needing counselling. It was the fact that he didn't believe me.

Well, he'd have to believe me now, wouldn't he? I didn't go outside and wreck my own garden. Why would I? Hmm, he wouldn't think that, would he? I was aware of a voice outside the bathroom door.

"Mum, I'm leaving now," Alex called.

"OK, have a good day." That must mean it was 8.30 a.m. I needed to hurry, or Henry would be late for school. I eyed the bar of soap suspiciously, had I already washed myself? I had been so distracted by my thoughts that I didn't know if I had washed or not. Grabbing the soap I washed all over in double-quick time.

I noticed the boys used, damp towels lying in the customary heap on the bathroom floor as I located my own towel. I would berate them later.

"Come on, Mum. We're going to be late," Henry shouted up the stairs.

"Five minutes," I shouted back as I darted into my bedroom and put on the first thing that came to hand. Moments later, I was rushing down the stairs.

"Ready," I shouted. There was something of the role reversal in this situation, I thought ironically, as Henry stood there all ready for school tapping his imaginary watch with his finger.

"We'll be late," he said in his best mummy voice.

In spite of myself, I laughed.

"You're a cheeky devil. Let's go."I said, as I shrugged on my coat.

He chatted happily all the way to school, and I was content to let him. He kissed me goodbye and ran off into the playground as the bell sounded.

I hurried home to call DC Smithers.

*****

"Do you see what I mean?" I said sweeping my outstretched arm from one side of my decimated garden to the other.

"Hmm, yes I do."

He walked the full length of the garden inspecting the damage.

"It's Glenn. It has to be." I said, desperation creeping into my voice. Surely, he had to believe me this time.

He shook his head. "We've been over this, Frankie."

I really wanted to be snippy in that instant; demand that I was now Ms Wilson as far as he was concerned, but I caught myself before I uttered a word to that effect. Not liking what he was saying was no justification for churlishness.

He paused. "How did they enter the garden?"

I hadn't thought about that. My eyes went automatically to the six foot wrought iron side gate. It was open. Mum must have forgotten to lock the gate the last time she'd done some gardening.

"The gate is usually locked. My mum does a lot of the gardening, so she may have forgotten to lock up."

"Yes, it seems the obvious point of entry." He eyed the garden walls surrounding my property. "Otherwise, whoever did this would have had to access one of your neighbours' gardens first and then scale the wall. I doubt they would go to that much trouble. This feels more like a vindictive crime than a threatening one. If Glenn was alive, do you really think this would be his style?"

Begrudgingly, I had to admit he had a point. It had seemed odd to me that Glenn would choose to wreck my garden.

"Have you upset anyone lately, Frankie?"

"I don't think so," I said and could hear the defensiveness in my voice.

"I'm not suggesting you've done anything awful. It could be a minor incident that someone has taken offence to."

I thought for a moment. The only situation that came to mind was my interfering in David Shaw's relationship with Sarah Flattery. My sending that picture of David in an embrace with another woman to Sarah's father would most definitely have been upsetting for everyone involved. However, neither David, Sarah, nor her father had any way of knowing it was me that sent the photograph. Therefore, it was fairly safe to assume it wasn't them.

I shook my head at DC Smithers and said, "No, not that I'm aware of."

"Well, I'll report the incident. This kind of thing would normally be taken care of by your local Bobby. But seeing as I know your history, I didn't mind attending this time. However, in future, Frankie, it might be an idea to ring your local station first. They'll call me in if I'm needed."

So this was him washing his hands of me, was it? I didn't know whether to be annoyed or relieved. Annoyed because he couldn't be sure I wasn't at risk from Glenn Froom, and conversely relieved because he must be positive Glenn was dead. I wondered when I would believe Glenn was dead. That's easy, my psyche said, when you see a body.

"So, what's next?" I asked, already anticipating his answer.

"I'll let your local PCSOs know what's happened; they will make a few enquiries in the neighbourhood. They will find out if anyone saw anything, you know the kind of thing."

Yeah, I knew what he meant. They were going to do the bare minimum. This crime did not rate highly enough on their Richter scale.

"It's probably kids, Frankie."

"Hmm, maybe," I said, sounding unconvinced even to my own ears.

"We'll be in touch," were his parting words as he got into his BMW.

"I won't hold my breath," I muttered as I shut the door.

I walked through the house and back out to the garden. I stood and stared at the remnants of my once-beautiful garden. How was I going to tell Mum? She'd be devastated.

I heard a noise, and turned to see Peggy standing at the fence we shared inspecting my garden. I was shocked to see a smile on her face as she stared at the dead flowers and hacked shrubs and trees.

"You ought to be careful who you go upsetting," she said just loud enough for me to hear.

"Excuse me, Peggy. What did you say?"

"Me?" she said with a start as if she hadn't realised she had said the words aloud. "Oh, I didn't say anything. Come on Tibbles," she said to her cat, "it's time for your lunch."

It was as if I'd found the missing playing card in a pack; everything slotted into place in my mind. It had been Peggy. Only last night, I had been telling Maria about the little altercation we'd had in the garden. Why hadn't that sprung to mind earlier? It was so obviously her way of getting back at me for frightening that blasted cat of hers.

I was really rather shocked at how vindictive Peggy was. I didn't know whether to laugh or cry. I felt relieved by the realisation it was her and not Glenn. But then, my beautiful garden had been savaged by a nasty, vengeful octogenarian.

I was tempted to call DC Smithers and tell him who was responsible. Yes, I would do that. I strutted purposefully into the house.

I picked up my phone and paused to listen to the conflicting voices in my head before selecting DC Smithers' number. Go on, what are you waiting for? She shouldn't be allowed to get away with it. Hmm . . . she is an old lady. What if the shock of being questioned by the police brought on a heart attack? How would you feel then? But, shouldn't she face the consequences of wrecking your beautiful garden? What about all of your mum's hard work? Yes, poor Mum. She will be so upset. Yes, I'll call him. But would your mum want to punish a little old lady? Hmm . . .

"Oh all right. You win," I said aloud to no one in particular. I wouldn't ring the police. I'd let the PCSOs talk to her as part of their enquiries. If she confessed, well, then I'd be impressed by her honesty. If she didn't, I'd be disappointed in her lack of morality, but then leave it at that. Living with her conscience would be justice enough; if she had one.

I sat down on the kitchen stool and wondered if Glenn might actually be dead after all. Last night, I had been convinced the silent call in the pub had been Glenn; it had turned out to be a mistaken call from Maria while in the ladies' lavatory. Today, I had been convinced the desecration of my garden had been Glenn's handiwork; it turned out to be Peggy's. Perhaps everyone was right. I was being neurotic.

I spotted the box that contained the black silk scarf poking out from under a pile of unopened letters on the side. Rebecca must have put it there the day she brought me back from work. Maria's explanation made sense: it was probably just a present from a grateful client. For everyone's sake, I needed to get a grip on reality.

I'd even thought, fleetingly, that the garden may have been David Shaw's doing. That reminded me, I reached for my iPad. Switching it on, I located the list of websites I'd saved as my favourites. I touched the Portishead Times icon; it appeared instantaneously. I scanned the 'All Wedding Bells' section for the announcement of David Shaw and Sarah Flattery's wedding. There wasn't one. So far, so good, I thought. They didn't appear to be married . .

. yet. Hopefully, I had scuppered that plan. I wasn't proud of my tactics, but I had to do something.

The ring of my mobile interrupted my thoughts. I felt a knot of nervousness form in my stomach at the sound. Oh this was ridiculous, I thought. I was getting fed up with this. I felt a flash of irritation with myself, and I looked at the phone defiantly. I picked it up and could see it was Maria calling me. The knot disappeared immediately.

"Hello, Maria."

"Hi, you sound chirpy?"

"No need to sound so surprised. I am sometimes, you know."

"Oh, yes, of course you are." She hesitated as if trying to recall why she had rung. "I just wanted to let you know that you left your umbrella in my car last night."

"Did I? I must lose at least one umbrella a year. What is it about umbrellas that make them so forgettable?"

"Well, only if it isn't raining of course," she added.

"Yes, there is that. Just drop it off next time you're passing. Don't make a special journey on my account."

"OK. I just thought I'd let you know I had it. I didn't want you to think you'd lost it and go and buy another one."

"Thanks. I don't even recall having an umbrella last night. That's how absentminded I am lately."

She chuckled. "Well, you do have a lot on your mind."

"More than you think." And I proceeded to tell her all about this morning's events.

"Hmm, who do you think is responsible?" she asked when I'd finished speaking.

"I thought initially it might be Glenn." Before she could interrupt, as I thought she might, I went on, "But then I decided, and this is strictly between us, Peggy may be responsible."

"Funny you should say that, but after what you told me last night about your little spat with her, I thought the same thing."

"Yes, especially after what she's just said."

"Oh . . . , what's that?" she asked with obvious interest.

"She said that I ought to be careful who I go upsetting," I repeated.

"Hmm, sounds like an admission to me."

"That's what I thought. I don't think she realised that she had said it aloud. She is getting on."

"Not so old that she couldn't wreck your garden."

"True. Still it will sound weird, but I'm relieved it was her."

"And not Glenn?" Maria guessed correctly.

"Yes, after my mistakenly thinking the silent call last night was him and the garden today. I'm beginning to see that perhaps I'm being overly paranoid," I admitted.

"It's perfectly understandable, Frankie, in the circumstances."

"Thanks, Maria. I can always rely on you." There was a knock at the door. "I have to go. There's someone at the door. I'll call you soon."

"OK, bye," she said.

I opened the door. Mum was standing there. I hadn't been expecting her.

"This is a nice surprise," I said, my thoughts immediately turning to how upset she'd be when she saw the state of the garden.

"Is it?" she smiled. "Perhaps you could tell your face that. You don't exactly look overjoyed to see me."

"Oh, I am, Mum. Of course I am. Come on in."

Before she saw it for herself through the kitchen window, I thought it best to tell her about the garden.

"I don't know how to tell you this," I said.

Her face took on a stricken look. "That sounds serious. What's happened now?"

"It's your garden. Well, strictly speaking, it's my garden. But I know how much work you've put into it and how much you love it, so I consider it to be yours as well as mine."

"Frankie! Get to the point."

"Yes, of course. Someone vandalised the garden last night."

My mum's face blanched. "I don't understand. Why? How much damage is there?"

I shook my head. "There isn't a plant left standing. There isn't a flower that still has its petals or a tree that hasn't been hacked at."

"Who did it?" she asked, despite appearing to be afraid of my answer.

"I thought initially it was Glenn."

A huge sigh escaped her lips.

"But then I had second thoughts," I added.

Her eyebrows rose at my words.

"So you don't think it's Glenn?"

"No."

Her shoulders visibly sagged in relief. "Come on then; show me the damage."

"Brace yourself, it isn't pretty," I said as I led her through the kitchen and outside to the garden.

Her jaw dropped as she took in the scene of carnage before her. I saw a look of disbelief cross her face. It no longer bore any resemblance to the garden she'd spent hours maintaining over the last nine months. She stooped to pick up a flower that was lying forlornly on the grass; one amongst a sea of others lying side by side. They were strewn haphazardly where they fell. It was a carpet of colour.

"How did they get in?" she asked.

I pointed at the side gate. "It was left open."

She shook her head. "I locked that yesterday. I know I did."

"It was unlocked this morning, Mum." I was trying to be careful in how I said it. I didn't want her to think I blamed her for not locking the gate.

"Francesca, I specifically remember locking that gate yesterday. I may be old, but I'm not senile."

Wow, she must be seriously annoyed if she was calling me Francesca. "OK, I don't doubt you. But . . . ?"

She strutted over to the gate to inspect the lock for any signs of damage. There weren't any.

"I know I locked it," she said less stridently than she had the first time. Seeds of doubt appeared to be creeping in.

"Mum, I believe you," I said, and I meant it.

She'd been holding herself stiffly, as if ready to do battle, but upon hearing my words she relaxed a little.

"Have you reported it to the police?" she asked.

"Yes, I rang DC Smithers."

She winced. "Hmm, perhaps that wasn't the best idea after your last conversation."

"I'm inclined to agree, but when I rang him I thought Glenn was responsible."

She nodded her understanding. "So what happened to change your mind?"

I glanced across at Peggy's garden. "Come on in and have a cup of tea. I'll explain everything."

# Chapter 16

*Session three - Tom Ferris 10.00 a.m. - 11.00 a.m.*

I unlocked the office and plonked my briefcase on the table. I shrugged out of my coat and hung it up on the coat stand in the corner. I just had time to nip to the ladies' room before Tom arrived.

As I walked down the corridor, I noticed a single red carnation on the carpet. Had it fallen out of a man's buttonhole? It was so rare for someone to wear a flower in their buttonhole these days unless they were going to a wedding. I picked it up; walked into the first floor's communal kitchen, and placed it on the working surface. Hopefully, whoever had lost it would be reunited with it when they made themselves a cuppa at some point during the day.

The flower reminded me of my garden. When Mum popped round unexpectedly last Friday, I'd told her my suspicions. She'd agreed Peggy was the likely culprit. We discussed the possible impact of the event on the children. I agreed with Mum that a white lie was appropriate in the circumstances. I'm normally an advocate of complete honesty with children, but they had been through so much lately, and they were at no risk from Peggy.

During that Friday morning conversation we decided to tell the Pant Bros that we were remodelling the garden. This white lie depended upon our ability to tidy up the garden that day before they got home from school. Mum and I worked in the garden solidly from 10.00 a.m. until 3.00 p.m. with only a ten-minute break for lunch.

We were pleased with ourselves when we finally stood back to survey what we'd achieved. Our backs, however, were decidedly less proud. We were both in agony from so much physical exertion but needs must.

We cleared the flower beds and pruned the shrubs. The trees we couldn't do much about except for neaten the edges of the branches that had been snapped off. I had a small hacksaw, so I used it to cut the branches off close to the trunk. Hopefully, it would look as if a branch hadn't been there in the first place.

We did a good job because that afternoon when both boys were home from school they merely glanced out of the window and commented that we'd been working hard in the garden. Never one to miss an opportunity, Henry had even asked, now that we'd cleared the garden of all those flowers, if he could have a trampoline?

Tom was due any minute. I dried my hands with a paper towel and walked back to my room. Now I was confident both Tom and Susan knew where they were going; I'd let Theresa know she could send him straight up when he arrived.

I could hear Tom talking to someone in the hallway as he approached my office. He was still talking as he knocked on my door. Had he brought someone with him? His wife, perhaps.

"Come in," I invited.

He walked in with his phone to his ear and a harried expression on his face.

"Look, I've told you I have to go. I have an appointment."

I smiled and indicated the chair with my hand inviting him to take a seat.

He sat. He pointed at his phone with his free hand and silently mouthed the word 'sorry'. His face was flushed with what I assumed was embarrassment.

I nodded my understanding. The other participant in the conversation was persistent.

"Yes . . . with my counsellor. You know that I won't." He eyed me guiltily. "I promised, didn't I? I've got to go.

Bye." He didn't wait for their reply; he just cut them off. He sighed deeply. "I'm sorry about that, Frankie. I'm switching it off, so we aren't interrupted again."

I was curious about the call. What had he promised? Was it related to the counselling session? The guilty way in which he'd looked at me had felt as if he was promising not to say something during counselling. That was his right of course.

"That's OK. It sounded like a stressful call," I commented.

"Hmm, it was," he said.

There it was again: a guilty expression. But there was something else. He appeared to be having some kind of inner battle. It was a battle I'd seen people go through many times over the years: to tell your counsellor or not to tell your counsellor. I remained silent. I didn't want words to get in the way.

"It was my stepdad," he blurted out.

He appeared to have made the decision to tell me.

I nodded and waited, by way of a silent invitation, for him to continue.

"He knows I'm having counselling."

"You decided to tell him?"

"No," he said with meaning. "My wife—she told him."

He didn't appear pleased.

"Your wife told him?"

"Yes, she was trying to be helpful. My mum and my stepdad, Lenny, were visiting my wife, Jenny, and son, Jacob. Jenny had mentioned that I wasn't feeling myself. When my mum had become concerned, she'd said it was OK because I was having counselling."

"I have the feeling your mum and stepdad don't think it's a good idea," I guessed.

"You could say that. Lenny was the one who tried to call me and then texted me during last week's session. He and Mum were at my house at the time. Jenny had just told them about the sessions."

"He must have felt strongly about it to have tried to call you immediately."

He shrugged and sighed at the same time. "I've told him that I'm not going to talk about anything I shouldn't."

I wanted to know what he wasn't meant to tell me, but how much of that was the counsellor in me and how much was just plain curiosity. I only needed to know if it would help him understand the reasons for his anxiety. Unfortunately, I couldn't decide its relevance until I knew what it was. I thought it best not to probe at this specific moment as he may become guarded and suspicious. I decided to reassure rather than probe.

"What you tell me is entirely your decision."

He nodded and relaxed. "I know."

"But . . . you also know that whatever you tell me, within the limits I explained in the first session, is confidential."

"I remember; I mustn't tell you I'm going to commit an act of terrorism or stuff like that," he said glibly.

I regarded his attitude as evidence of his unlikeliness to commit such a crime rather than the forethought not to tell me.

"If I'm honest, I don't really know what he's worried about."

"You don't know what it is you shouldn't be talking about? Or you do know what you shouldn't be talking about, but you don't understand why you shouldn't be talking about it?"

"The latter," he confirmed.

So his stepdad's view and his view, of whatever it was, differed. I didn't know whether to pursue it or not. I'd let him decide where he wanted to go with this.

"If you don't want to discuss this further, we can look at your anxiety diary," I offered.

"Sure." And he pulled the folded piece of paper from his back pocket as he had last week. As he unfolded the paper, it appeared he wasn't ready to drop the subject entirely as he said, "He doesn't want me to talk about my childhood."

"OK, but you're not sure why he wouldn't want you to talk about it?"

"Exactly."

"How would you describe your childhood?"

He shrugged. "It was OK."

Hmm, his description didn't make sense of his stepdad's desire for him not to talk about it.

"When did your stepdad enter your life?" I asked.

"I was two years old. I don't remember my real dad. He died when I was six months old. Mum's always considered Lenny to be our saviour. At the time, she was a single mum and life was a struggle. We didn't have much money. When Lenny came along, we moved from the flat we lived in to a house. It had a garden. I hadn't had a garden before."

"That must have been nice," I commented.

His face was expressionless. I would have expected the memories to have invoked an emotion, either good or bad, but he appeared devoid of any feelings on the subject.

"I suppose," he responded.

"When you recall your childhood, how do you feel?"

He shook his head. "I don't feel anything." Changing the subject he went on, "Lenny is a successful business man. Lately, he's become heavily involved in local charity work. I think he's after some kind of knighthood or something from the Queen. You know what I mean: he wants his name to appear in the New Year's Honours list."

"He has aspirations."

"Oh yeah, he has always had aspirations. I don't want to talk about this any more," he said breaking eye contact with me and staring at the wall behind me.

"That's fine. Shall we look at your anxiety diary for last week?"

He nodded, and once again I had his attention. He spread the piece of paper on the table in front of me.

I could immediately see that last week he'd experienced fewer incidents of anxiety, which on the face of it was a good thing. In fact, there were only two incidents: one last Thursday in the middle of the night and one incident at the weekend.

"I've felt less stressed this week," he offered.

"Hmm, I can see that." I wouldn't have expected him to feel less stress yet. We'd barely scratched the surface of his reasons for the anxiety.

"Which incident do you want to talk about first?" I invited.

"I'll tell you about Saturday. Jenny had popped out to the shops. We needed some nappies. We agreed it was easier if we didn't all go. After our discussion about the meal last week, and how stressful it was when Jacob started crying in public, I decided to avoid the situation. Jacob was asleep; he wasn't due to wake up from his nap for a good hour, so I thought it would be OK."

"You thought, what would be OK?" I asked.

He sat forward in his chair, and placing his elbows on his knees he put his head in his hands. "I didn't think Jacob would wake up until Jenny got back," he muttered.

"Oh, I see."

"But he did wake up, and he started crying immediately."

"What do you think was the matter with him?"

"I don't know. I just wanted him to be quiet. As he cried, I could feel my stress levels rising," he confessed.

"I can remember when my children were babies. My stress levels rose when they started to cry, and I didn't know what was wrong." I commented.

As I spoke, his eyebrows rose as if he were surprised that I would get stressed by a crying baby.

"I don't think there is a parent anywhere who hasn't got stressed out, at one time or another, by their crying baby." I said attempting to normalise his reaction for him.

"Perhaps, but I don't think my stress levels are proportionate."

I nodded my understanding and pointing at his anxiety diary at the same time said, "It says here in the 'How did you try to cope?' section that you walked away." I was alarmed that he may have left Jacob alone in order to escape the crying.

He nodded, "Don't worry, I didn't walk out and leave him at home alone. I left him in his cot; he was safe there, and I left his room. I did shut his door because it muffled the sound. I'm not proud of myself," he said, putting his head in his hands.

"Still, as you said, he was safe and at no risk of harm. What happened next? Did he stop crying?"

"No, he cried for a full thirty minutes before Jenny came back."

"And how were your stress levels during those thirty minutes? Did they lessen by walking away?"

"No, it was hell. I felt guilty as well as stressed."

"So walking away doesn't appear to be the right coping strategy for you right now."

He shook his head and had the appearance of a defeated man.

"The other occasion of significant stress was Thursday night. What happened?"

He sighed, "Jenny insisted that if Jacob woke up in the night, it was my turn to see to him. He wakes up most nights; she's exhausted."

"I can imagine," I empathised.

"We had a bit of a row actually. She was accusing me of avoiding her and Jacob. It's not my fault I've had to work late a lot recently. We have a big order to complete," he said, with a note of insincerity in his voice.

"So you aren't avoiding spending time with your wife and child. It's just that you're required to work late recently to complete an order," I reflected.

"Yes," he said, but he avoided eye contact and plucked at an imaginary piece of fluff on his trousers. I strongly suspected he wasn't telling me the truth.

"What happened in the middle of the night?" I asked.

"Jacob woke up. He started to cry. I tried to console him. I really did," he stressed the last three words as if it were important I believe him.

"I believe you," I said.

"Jenny didn't believe me. I changed his nappy in case he was wet. He doesn't have a bottle in the night any more, so it wasn't that he was hungry. I cuddled him and still he cried. Eventually, Jenny stomped in and took him from me. The minute she cuddled him, he stopped crying. So, you see it was pointless my having got involved. I should have stayed out of the way like I've been doing all week. It would have been better for all three of us."

"You've been staying out of the way?" I repeated, mentally pouncing on his words.

"Uh . . . well I've been working late."

"You said 'stayed out of the way'," I persisted.

"Oh OK, I've been using work as an excuse. I mean . . . I have been at work. I wasn't lying. Well not about where I was. I kind of exaggerated my need to be there, though.

Oh look . . . I just figured it was better that I avoided home for a while."

"So your coping strategy was to avoid being at home altogether." I had suspected as much because the number of incidences of anxiety in his diary had reduced so drastically.

"Yes."

"How is that working out for you?" I asked gently. I suspected that while it may temporarily fix his anxiety issue, it may cause other problems in his relationship with his wife and son.

"Well, on the upside, you can see from my diary that I feel less anxious."

"And on the downside?" I questioned.

His eyes downcast he said, "It's causing problems between Jenny and me. We're rowing a lot. She's accusing me of avoiding her and Jacob. I think she's beginning to suspect I'm having an affair, which I'm not of course."

"Do you think avoiding your wife and son is the answer?"

"No, but I don't know what else to do. You're meant to be helping me."

He was feeling desperate. I chose to ignore the accusatory tone in his voice. My adopting any kind of defensive stance right now would be counterproductive. I needed to help him understand his feelings toward his son. This would enable us to find some kind of effective coping strategy: a strategy that didn't involve avoiding his family. I needed to understand what thoughts were triggering his anxiety before we could hope to find a strategy.

"Last week, I asked you to think about why you feel it is unacceptable for Jacob to cry. Have you been able to give it some thought?"

"Yes, I've thought about it. I just can't explain why I think it's unacceptable other than it is unacceptable."

"It's unacceptable to you, but it isn't to me," I countered.

He frowned. "Do you mean you think it's OK for babies to cry?" he asked, clearly confused by my comment.

"It's their only way of communication. They have to cry in order to let us know they need something; crying is fundamental to their survival."

"I hadn't thought of it like that. I know you're right, but it doesn't make it any more acceptable to me."

"You would have cried as a baby, and so would I. Obviously, neither of us can remember crying at such an early age, but can you recollect crying as a young child over something?"

He started to fidget in his chair.

"I'm starting to feel anxious, Frankie." He seemed surprised by his feelings as if it had taken him unawares.

"What were you thinking when you started to feel anxious?"

"I was trying to remember crying as a small child as you asked, and this overwhelming feeling of anxiety came over me. I don't like it. Make it stop."

He was starting to panic; his breathing had become shallow and rapid. His face was flush. His reaction to his own memories of crying as a child had triggered his anxiety as I surmised it might. I suspected something had happened in his childhood to make crying unacceptable to him, but what?

"Remember your breathing technique, Tom. Focus on your breathing and clear your mind. No more thoughts. Just empty your mind and remember to focus on your breathing."

He had his eyes closed. I could see he was breathing deeply and slowly. I watched as it calmed him. When he was sufficiently relaxed again, he opened his eyes.

"I'm OK now," he said.

"Good. We're coming to the end of the session. Before you go, do you think it might be time to explain to Jenny how you're feeling?"

His face took on a stubborn expression. "I don't want her to think badly of me."

"Would it be worse than her thinking you're having an affair?" I countered.

I watched as the stubborn expression was replaced by a defeated one.

"I see your point," he said.

"It's entirely up to you whether or not you talk to Jenny about how you feel when you're around Jacob. I can't guarantee she'll understand, but at least she'll know you aren't having an affair."

"Maybe. I'm not promising but maybe." He rose to his feet and switched his phone on. The phone immediately pinged several times. He glanced at his phone and then at me.

"Stepdad?" I guessed.

"Yep." He shrugged. "See you next week."

"I picked up his anxiety diary. Don't forget this. You'll need it. I'd like you to focus on trying to record your thoughts in the first moments of anxiety, if possible."

"I'll try."

"Great, see you next week."

# Chapter 17

***Session three - Susan Mackintosh 11.30 a.m. - 12.30 p.m.***

Susan knocked briefly before entering the room. I realised with a jolt that I was actually looking forward to seeing what she was wearing this week. Thinking about her outfit reminded me; I needed to plan what I was going to wear on Thursday for my date with Leo. I felt a flutter of nerves in my stomach at the thought. I couldn't think about that now. I banked down both my thoughts and feelings on the subject of my first date with PC Leo Acton and focused on Susan.

She was dressed much more conservatively today than she had been last week. She wore a figure-hugging navy-blue dress, sheer nude tights and navy-blue stiletto heels. In contrast, she wore a red tailored jacket, and a red clutch bag completed the outfit. Even though I couldn't identify the designer of the clothes, I knew instinctively she hadn't bought the items on the high street.

"Hello, Susan. How are you this week?" I asked.

"I think I should be asking you that question after what happened last week. How are you, Frankie?"

I'd naively hoped to avoid any reference to last week's fainting episode. I really should have known better.

"I'm fine, Susan. I need to thank you for your help. You were great."

"Oh, there's no need to thank me. I was actually pleased to be able to help," she said, her face lighting up with genuine pleasure. "Have you seen a doctor? Do you know why you fainted? You aren't pregnant, are you?" She fired each question at me in quick succession like bullets out of a machine gun.

"I appreciate your concern. I'm fine now. How has your week been?" I asked, bringing the focus of the session firmly back to her as I had intended.

Her face lost the glow of moments ago as she appeared to contemplate her week.

"I'm growing more and more convinced that Dickie is having an affair. Do you want to know why?" she asked, studying me closely.

I nodded.

"Well, as you know, I've been suspicious for a while, but I can't scrutinize his computer's search history because it's password-protected. So, I've been checking his pockets." She paused and looked me directly in the eye for a few seconds. I guessed she was searching for any signs of disapproval of her actions. She must have been satisfied there were none as she continued, "I found some receipts."

"What were the receipts for?" I asked.

"It's curious really. He bought expensive sports gear: a tracksuit and flashy trainers. He also bought an iPod and an iPad. I'm not sure why."

Susan's mention of the flashy trainers had reminded me of Alex's new expensive trainers; I still needed to have a word with Rob about them. I needed to park that thought for now. Refocusing on the here and now with Susan I asked, "Do you think this is further evidence of an affair?"

"Well, don't you? Dickie has never been sporty. He doesn't go to the gym. It just doesn't make any sense. I thought perhaps they were presents for the new person in his life."

I noticed she had said 'person' rather than woman in his life. Last week, she had said that Dickie had been looking at pictures of a young man. Did she think her husband was having an affair with a man?"

"He went out last Thursday," she continued.

"You mentioned he was planning to, and that it was out of character."

"Yes, I was tempted to follow him." She cast her eyes downward at the floor. "But, I just wasn't strong enough."

"Strong enough?" I probed.

She glanced up, briefly meeting my eyes before once again averting her gaze. In those briefest of moments, I had seen her fear of the situation.

"Please don't think me a coward, Frankie, but if I'd followed him and discovered what I suspect: his having an affair, then . . ." she visibly swallowed what I imagined to be a large lump of emotion stuck in her throat. "I would have to do something about it, and I don't feel strong enough to do that."

"You don't feel able to emotionally deal with the consequences of his having an affair," I reflected.

She nodded. "I can't go through this again," she said, her voice breaking with emotion.

I remained silent, giving her time to regain her composure. When I thought she was ready to continue, I said, "Last week, you told me about your relationship with Marcus."

"Yes, that's right. He was the first to cheat on me," she said, "but not the last." She laughed as if trying to make light of her words, but her eyes didn't agree. They wore a sad and hurt expression.

"We were examining which, if any, traits the men in your life shared. You'd identified that they were all rich and unfaithful."

"Yes, that's right. Those two attributes could definitely be applied to Lawrence. He was cheat number two," she said glibly. I met Lawrence when I was twenty and he was thirty-five. I know what you're thinking: that's quite an age difference." She paused and looked at me as if awaiting confirmation that was in fact what I was thinking.

I nodded my agreement. It was what I was thinking. There was no point in denying it.

A smug smile played around the edges of her lips. "Everyone thought the same. Lawrence owned a rival firm to Daddy's. At the time, Daddy was interested in merging their two companies. Lawrence wasn't so keen on the idea. Daddy had arranged a small party; you know the kind of thing—all the local bigwigs. He was trying to encourage Lawrence to go into partnership with him by demonstrating the kind of connections he had."

"Did it work?" I asked.

"No, Lawrence had influential connections of his own; he didn't need Daddy's. But at the party Lawrence paid me a lot of attention. It was flattering, especially after what had happened with Marcus. Daddy was annoyed, at first, because Lawrence only had eyes for me and wasn't talking to the influential people in the room. I can remember Daddy whispering in my ear at the bar, 'Why is he spending all night talking to you? Can't you go and talk to someone else?'

"I tried, Frankie, really I did," she said as her eyes filled with sadness as she recalled what her father had said to her. "But he was so persistent. Lawrence said I was the only person in the room he was interested in talking to."

"That's quite a compliment," I commented.

"Uh . . . yes, I suppose. But Daddy wasn't happy with me."

The fact that her father was unhappy with her seemed to overshadow any compliment Lawrence had given her.

"What happened next?" I asked.

She visibly brightened as she said, "Well, Daddy seemed to have a change of heart. I saw him coming over to us. I thought he was going to be really angry with me for not having done what he'd asked of me earlier."

"But, he wasn't?" I queried.

"No, he wasn't," she beamed. "He whispered in my ear, 'actually I've had a change of heart. It's a good thing he likes you. Be nice to him.' "

I frowned inwardly at her words but was careful not to frown outwardly. "What did you think he meant by that?" I asked.

"He meant exactly what he said. I was to be nice to him. I was just so relieved that Daddy was happy with me again. We had a few more drinks, and Lawrence suggested we go to a club. I can remember being quite surprised that a man of his age would be interested in clubbing. I mean, he was thirty-five."

She made it sound ancient. But then I suppose she was only twenty at the time.

"Of course, now I realise thirty-five isn't that old," she chuckled.

"Ditto," I agreed with feeling. I was thirty-five only last year. Not that I had had any inclination to go clubbing myself, but I liked to think I was still young enough to had I wanted to.

She smiled and continued with her recollection of events. "We stayed out until three o'clock in the morning. When he dropped me off at home, Daddy had still been awake in his study. He hadn't been too pleased to see me as I recall. I'd thought I'd got it wrong for the moment, and he hadn't wanted me to be nice to him. But then he said he hadn't expected to see me until later that morning."

"Why was that?" I asked.

She shrugged, "Oh, I don't know, maybe he wanted me to stay at the club with Lawrence until it closed. It stayed open until 6 a.m."

Her words were plausible, but they lacked conviction. I had a feeling she had decided to believe that was what he meant because the alternative was altogether too unpalatable for her.

"Anyway," she said pointedly, "Daddy encouraged me to ring Lawrence the next day. Like he said, it was the nineties; women didn't need to wait to be chased by men any more."

"So, your father is in favour of gender equality."

"God, no!" she reacted without thinking.

"Oh . . . ?" I was confused.

"Never mind," she said, making it obvious it wasn't something she was going to expand upon. "As I was saying, I phoned Lawrence; we went out and ended up living together. I was with him until I was twenty-five."

"How did your father feel about that?"

"Daddy was fine with it." She answered with a tone of voice that implied my question was a stupid one.

"But didn't you say they ran rival firms?" I asked, in an attempt to justify my previous question.

"They did when we met. But I told you Daddy wanted to merge."

"Yes, but you also said that Lawrence hadn't wanted to."

"Oh, I changed his mind. Daddy was very pleased with me when Lawrence came round to his way of thinking."

Hmm, I bet Daddy was, I thought.

"So, what went wrong?" I asked.

"You know what went wrong. He cheated on me . . . and with someone of his own age, no less. How mortifying. I did everything he wanted me to. I attended every business function looking immaculate; I was nice to prospective clients. I was the consummate hostess. I just don't understand why he'd prefer a middle-aged frump of a woman over me." She raised her hands to the sky as if to reinforce the fact that it made no sense.

"You've mentioned the social side of your life together, but I'm wondering what life was like for the two of you when you were at home, just the two of you."

"Oh fine. We had a cleaner who came in once a week. The flat was always clean, neat and tidy. So he couldn't have any complaints there," she huffed.

Hmm, I needed to be more specific in my questioning. "When you spent time together at home, what did you do?"

"Aside from the obvious?" she said matter-of-factly.

I naturally assumed she was referring to sex, but I needed to make sure.

"Do you mean aside from the physical side of your relationship?" I asked.

"Yes, Frankie, I do," and she smiled broadly. "That's another reason why I don't understand why he chose that frump over me. We had a great sex life. We were at it like rabbits."

"What other things did you do together?" I questioned.

"Well, we talked if that's what you're getting at. We regularly sat and discussed the business. He was actually impressed with how much I understood. I'm a keen observer you know," she said with meaning.

I decided to try another tack. "Would you say that you knew Lawrence well? Do you feel that you understood his personality?"

I watched as her eyes narrowed and her forehead puckered in confusion at my questions.

"What was there to know?" she questioned. "He was an astute businessman who was extremely ambitious. I knew how much he wanted the business to be worth by the time he was forty-five."

"Did he have a happy childhood?" I asked, trying to get a handle on whether she knew anything about Lawrence other than the superficial.

She grimaced, "How would I know? I wasn't there."

Her answer reinforced what I suspected. This relationship, like her first, appeared superficial.

Her words interrupted my ruminations as she continued, "Actually, that reminds me of something he said when he told me we were finished and I was to pack up my things and leave. He said something along the lines of, Linda is interested in me. She wants to understand me and share things with me." She shook her head. "I had no idea what he was talking about. Utter tosh! It was just an excuse as far as I was concerned. Do you think, perhaps, that was what he meant? That she was interested in his childhood?" She asked the question while seeming genuinely baffled.

"I can't be sure of what he meant. But based on what he said, he seems to be implying you didn't understand him. Discussing his childhood might have been one aspect of getting to know him. Do you think he may have meant that she listened to him?"

"I listened to him!" she yelled unexpectedly. "I did nothing but listen to him."

"What kinds of things did he say?" I asked.

"It was all about business. I don't recall anything else."

"Thinking about your relationship with Lawrence, is there anything, upon reflection, you would do differently?" I was hoping she'd think talking about something other than business might have been a good idea: to have got to know him on a deeper level.

"Yes," she said with certainty.

Great, I thought, she's given it some thought. I sat forward slightly, eager to know what she would have done differently.

"I would have made him marry me before I moved in with him. At least that way, I would have got a payoff when he cheated on me. As it was, I was entitled to nothing. I had to leave like a dog with its tail between its legs with only the clothes and presents he'd bought me over the five years we were together. I figured I was entitled to a lot more than that. So, I made sure I married the next one."

I sincerely hoped my mouth wasn't hanging open in shocked surprise at her answer. She'd caught me by surprise, and although I was accepting of her perspective on events; I didn't have to agree with it.

I decided to take a gamble, "I'm wondering if not understanding each other deeply enough might have been the root cause of the relationship breakdown."

"Not being able to keep it in his pants was the root cause of the relationship breakdown, Frankie," she said, glaring at me.

She was getting defensive, which meant she felt threatened by what I was saying, and that was counterproductive. I needed to back off and retreat to safer ground.

"You said that you married the next one," I stated in an attempt to change the subject.

"Ben. I married Ben. We were married for ten years. And, yes, I did know him well, Frankie, before you imply otherwise," she said, holding herself stiffly as if ready to do battle.

I raised my hands in surrender. "My intention is not to upset you. I merely want to help you explore your past relationships. In the hope that it will help you make informed decisions about your current relationship," I said gently.

She exhaled deeply and visibly relaxed. "I know you're trying to help. It's just that I can't see that it's anything I'm doing wrong other than picking the wrong men."

"I'm not implying that the breakdown of your relationships is anyone's fault. It's not about apportioning blame. It's about understanding your choices, and whether changing those choices might result in a different outcome."

She nodded and appeared to be actually considering what I had said.

"How did you meet Ben?" I asked.

"He worked for Daddy," she stated.

"So Marcus was the son of your father's friend, Lawrence was the owner of a rival firm to your father's who became a partner, and Ben worked for your father."

"Works," she corrected.

"I'm sorry?" I asked confused.

"Works," she repeated. "Ben still works for Daddy."

"Oh, I see. So your ex-husband still works for your father."

"Yes."

"I'm surprised he's chosen to stay at your father's company after having cheated on you."

"Ben offered to resign. But Daddy wouldn't hear of it. He insisted he stay. Well, as Daddy explained to me, Ben is the best accountant in the business. Where would he find someone else of that calibre? Business is business, Frankie." Her final words lacked conviction.

I felt she was repeating her father's words and attempting, I surmised, to convince not just me of their validity. I had been attempting to make the point that each of the men she had had failed relationships with to date had a connection to her father. I would revisit that point later. I was interested in how she felt about Ben still working at her father's firm.

"So, is that how you feel? That business is business. Are you OK with the fact that Ben still works for your father?"

She fidgeted in her seat and examined her nails. Her body language had already answered my question: she was uncomfortable with the situation.

"It was hard at first," she replied, and took a deep breath before continuing. "Especially as Lauren's bump was growing bigger every time I saw her."

I was confused. "I'm sorry, I've missed something. Who is Lauren?"

"Lauren is the woman Ben had an affair with. He left me for her because she was pregnant with his child." A single lonely tear trickled down her cheek as she spoke.

I handed her a tissue and gave her a few moments to recover as she dabbed at her eyes.

"So, why did you see Lauren?" I asked still perplexed.

"She's Daddy's secretary. She offered to leave too, but Daddy wouldn't hear of it."

Oh good heavens. So, not only had Daddy insisted on keeping Ben at the firm, but the woman he had cheated on his daughter with as well. This was unusual behaviour for a father.

"I can only imagine how hard that must have been for you," I empathised.

"Yes, especially as I can't have children of my own. I think that's why Ben left me for Lauren. We'd been trying to have a baby for a while but nothing was happening. The next thing I knew, he's leaving me for her, and she's having his baby." Tears were now flowing freely down Susan's cheeks.

I was speechless. Her father's lack of empathy for his own daughter was breathtaking; always assuming he knew his daughter couldn't have children of course.

"Did you tell your father how it made you feel to see Lauren's pregnancy progress?" I asked.

"I tried to broach the subject, but he was disapproving. He viewed it as my being overly emotional and not being objective. After all, the business has to come first."

"Do you believe that the business should come before your feelings?"

An uncertain look crossed her face. "I'm not sure. I've never really thought about it. Daddy knows best," she said.

I wasn't so sure about that, but she was.

It would seem that every man she'd had a relationship with was linked inextricably to her father. And yet, hadn't she said that she'd met Dickie in a bar? What's more she had described during our first session how they had 'talked for hours' and 'had a deep understanding of each other.' Based on what I now knew of her past relationships, I might question her interpretation of her current relationship.

"Susan, you said Dickie is a solicitor, and that you met in a bar. Is that correct?"

"Yes, he's Daddy's solicitor. We met at Daddy's Christmas party. He likes to throw a party for the employees at Christmas. He says it's good for morale."

She glanced at her watch and jumped up as if shocked by what she saw.

"I forgot to tell you, Frankie. I need to leave early today. I have a luncheon appointment; I mustn't be late. Daddy has a meeting with an important client, and he wants me to be there," she said smiling proudly.

Her father's approval was obviously very important to her. The appointment made sense of her outfit.

"I'll still pay you the full amount," she said, as if she felt I needed to be placated because of her early departure.

"It's a shame you need to leave early but needs must," I stated.

She gave a small sigh of relief and smiled; seemingly pleased by my acquiescence.

"I have to go," she paused to once again consult her watch and looking up wide-eyed with alarm said, ". . . NOW! Sorry, Frankie. I'll see you next week."

She rushed from the room with a cloud of perfume following in her wake.

# Chapter 18

Every item of clothing that I possessed was strewn across my bed. I was beginning to panic. No, scrub that, I WAS panicking.

"What am I going to wear tonight?" I said out loud to only the air that surrounded me.

I really should have sorted this out before today. What was I thinking? That was the problem: I hadn't been thinking about it. Every time I tried to think about my date, I had got nervous, so I stopped thinking about it. The result was that I now didn't know what I was going to wear.

Perhaps I should call Rebecca; she had lovely clothes. She was always bang on trend. Whereas I . . . , I contemplated the clothes piled haphazardly in front of me, I wasn't. My eyes settled on a particularly old blouse that I'd worn pre-children. Let me see, Alex was fourteen, so that made it at least fourteen years old. Hmm, funny, I would never have described myself as a hoarder . . . and yet . . .

I grabbed my mobile and rang Rebecca. It went straight to voicemail. I looked at the time. It was 3.10 p.m. on a Thursday afternoon. How stupid of me. She would be with a client. 3.10 p.m. Oh my God! Henry! I grabbed my boots and rammed them on my feet. I flew down the stairs and grabbed my coat and keys on the way out of the door. I marched down the road like a woman on a mission.

Huffing and puffing with the exertion of it all, I walked into Portishead Primary's playground with thirty seconds to spare. Upon reflection, I didn't know why I'd rushed so. Almost without fail, the children ended up leaving the classroom a good five minutes after the end of school bell had rung. I leaned against the school fence and attempted to moderate my breathing. I was unfit. I definitely needed to do more exercise. I had been telling myself that at least once a day for the last God knows how many years. So far, I'd not done a damn thing about it.

"Hello," said a lady to the left of me. She looked at her watch. "They're late," she stated.

"Yes," I smiled. "It's just as well; I was almost late myself today," I remarked.

"I know what that's like. Time can just runaway with you sometimes, can't it?"

"Yes," I smiled. I turned to look at her. She looked vaguely familiar. Since Henry had been at the school, a few of the mums had spoken to me briefly in the playground at pick-up time. Not that I could remember any of their names. Still, they seemed like a nice bunch, and this lady seemed to be too. The people of Portishead were a friendly lot.

"They're coming out now," she said, pointing at the children erupting from the open classroom doors.

"Oh yes. I always know if Henry's had a good or a bad day at school based on how quickly he leaves the classroom once the teacher has opened the door."

"Do tell. I'm curious now," she said.

"Well, if he's been naughty, he shoots out of the classroom and positively drags me from the premises before the teacher can speak to me. If he's had a good day, then he'll hang around chatting to his friends. He'll saunter over to me when he's finally ready to leave."

She laughed. "That makes sense. I'd say that was a typical kid."

"Yeah, and I'd agree."

A hand was suddenly in mine; tugging me away from the fence I was still leaning on.

"Come on, Mum. Let's go," Henry said with a sense of urgency.

My eyes met those of the lady I'd been talking to, and we both suppressed our amusement as she asked knowingly, "A bad day, Henry?"

He remained mute and tugged at my arm.

"Come on, Mum. Let's go," he repeated.

"OK, Henry. I heard you the first time. The lady asked you a question. Don't be rude," I berated him.

Eyes downcast he muttered, "Sorry." He looked up at the lady and said, "You could say that."

"Oh dear, well I'm sure it's nothing your mum can't sort out. If you let her," she offered kindly.

I smiled at her with gratitude. That was a nice thing to say. Hopefully, Henry would take note of her advice and let me help him. I glanced at Henry's face. He didn't look sure.

The lady put a hand on his shoulder and said, "Tell your mum. She will know what's best," she said with meaning.

Henry looked up, smiled and nodded. He took a deep breath and said, "I hit Charlie. But he hit me first," he said indignantly.

Here we go again, I thought. I smiled my thanks at the lady. She turned away and walked towards a group of Henry's classmates. An idea occurred to me: was she Charlie's mum? How ironic would that be? God, I hoped she wasn't.

"Let's go, Henry. You can explain it all to me on the way home."

His shoulders sagged with relief. "Yeah, let's get out of here, Mum."

We walked and talked. It had been a minor fracas between Charlie and Henry: the usual type of falling out between two ten-year-old boys. Charlie had insulted Henry's drawing of a robot, so Henry had insulted Charlie's drawing of a monster. It had descended into minor pushing and shoving. No black eyes were meted out by either offender. I hoped that if that lady did turn out to be Charlie's mum, she saw it as the minor incident I did. She seemed pretty level-headed and sensible from the little I saw of her.

The sound of my mobile phone ringing interrupted my thoughts. I checked to see who was calling. It was Rebecca. All thoughts of Henry's minor debacle at school left my head as my more pressing wardrobe drama once again pushed to the fore.

"Hi, Frankie, you called. Is anything wrong?" Rebecca asked with concern in her voice.

"I'm so glad you called back," I said, a sense of urgency in my voice.

"Whatever is wrong?"

"Wardrobe issues," I said, with a slight note of hysteria in my voice.

I heard her exhale heavily.

"Oh, is that all! I was worried there for a moment," she said with a hint of reproach in her voice.

"Sorry, but this is urgent! It's my first date, and I have nothing to wear. I've been through everything I own . . . TWICE . . . and believe me; I have nothing suitable to wear."

"It's funny. I've known you for years, and I never would have taken you for a drama queen. And yet . . . here you are doing a first-class impression of one."

She was openly laughing at me now.

"Umm, in the years you've known me, have you ever known me go out on a date?" I asked.

"No. I suppose these are unusual circumstances," she said with mock gravity.

"Uh yes, I'd say so. And let's not forget who encouraged me to go out with Leo. So the least that person could do is offer to lend her friend something decent to wear."

"You got me, girl. I'll be round in an hour with a selection of my best tops."

"That's all I ask," I said, with feeling.

I heard her laughing out loud as she disconnected the call.

"Mum, are you going out on a date?" Henry asked.

"Sort of, Henry. He's just a friend."

He frowned.

"What's wrong?" I asked.

"I don't want a new dad. Jayden, in my class, got a new dad. He says he's strict."

"You aren't getting a new dad. Your dad will always be your dad. I'm going out with a friend. You know him."

"I do? Who is he?"

"PC Acton."

"Oh, him, he's nice. I like him." He cheered up immediately; his worries were forgotten. "I might show him my drawing of the robot. See if he thinks it's rubbish like Charlie did."

"You may not get to see him this evening. But if you do, then I'm sure he'll love it," I said.

He nodded. "Yeah, then I can tell Charlie that a real-life policeman liked my drawing."

I grimaced. My son was obviously not ready to let this slight on his drawing abilities go quite yet. I put my key in the lock and let us both into the house. Henry dropped his bag where he stood and rushed into the kitchen.

"I'm starving. Can I have some biscuits, Mum?"

"Yes. Two."

He grabbed the biscuits from the biscuit barrel and sat down at the kitchen table. Before I had time to take my coat and boots off, he had turned the laptop on and was settling down to play for an hour before tea. His coat was on the chair behind him. His shoes had been kicked off and were under the kitchen table. I regarded the scene before me with dismay and sighed in defeat. The same thing happened every school day.

He looked up at me from the laptop screen. "I know, I know. I'll hang up my coat and put my shoes away when I've finished playing," he wheedled.

"Hmm and when do you propose to put away your school bag?" I asked as I pointed at the offending article currently acting as a trip hazard in the middle of the hallway.

He shot from his chair with lightning speed and grabbing his bag he shoved it toward the wall underneath the coat pegs. He gave me a 'are you happy now?' look as he settled back into his spot in front of the laptop. It was funny, but when he gave me one of those looks he always reminded me of his father. It was the type of look that never failed to make me feel like a nag, and I resented it because I wasn't a nag.

"What are you playing?" I asked, already knowing the answer.

"Minecraft," he said, already immersed in the game.

Trying to engage him in any further conversation was pointless. And besides, I needed to focus on what I was wearing tonight.

I heard the front door opening and assumed it was Alex.

"Have you had a good day, Alex?" I called from the kitchen.

"Yeah, Grams is here too," he called back.

She was early! I walked into the hallway, and sure enough, they were both there shrugging off their coats.

"Before you say anything, I know I'm early. But I figured this way I could cook the kids' tea, and you would have plenty of time to get ready," Mum offered.

"Mum, you're a mind-reader. I'm having a bit of a wardrobe crisis at the moment. Rebecca is on her way over with some of her tops for me to try on. So, actually, your arrival is a relief."

"You should have told me earlier. I could have brought over some of my tops for you to borrow," she said with a straight face.

Mum was great for her age, and all that, but I wasn't about to borrow a top from my septuagenarian mother.

"Umm . . . uh . . . that's kind of you, Mum. But I think Rebecca will probably have something I will like," I stuttered.

She burst out laughing. "Oh, Frankie, you should see your face. You thought I was being serious. I knew you wouldn't want to borrow anything of mine. I couldn't resist teasing you, though."

I noticed Alex was smirking as well.

"Oh, Mum, I wasn't sure if you were joking or not. I didn't want to offend you."

Mum and Alex walked into the kitchen giggling.

"I'll get on with the tea. You go and make yourself look beautiful. After all, you only have four and a half hours," she said, and I heard all three of them erupt into full-blown laughter.

"Oh you are so cheeky, Mum," I hollered as I walked up the stairs to my clothes-festooned room.

I sorted the piles of clothes into possible and impossible. Needless to say, as I stood back and perused my handiwork the impossible pile was significantly taller than the possible pile. I was starting to feel decidedly depressed.

I heard the doorbell ring. One of the boys answered the door shortly afterward. It was followed by the sound of someone coming up the stairs at speed. My bedroom door burst open. I could hardly see Rebecca because of the vast amount of clothes she was carrying.

"Oh my God! There was no need to bring your whole wardrobe," I commented.

"Darling," she said in a posh voice, "this is only a small proportion of my wardrobe. And besides, you said it was an emergency."

I giggled. "You're a lifesaver."

"I know. Now sit on the bed. I'll show you each top in turn; you can decide which ones you like best, and then you can try them on. Does that sound like a decent plan?" she asked.

"It does," I said.

I did as I was told and sat on the bed while Rebecca showed me each top. There were sparkly ones, colourful ones, see-through ones and tight-fitting ones to describe but a few. I finally settled on two tops. The first was black chiffon with beaded detail; the other was silky with bold, colourful flowers.

I put on my trusty black trousers. They were at least four years old, but still fitted like a glove, and looked as good as new. First, I tried on the black chiffon blouse. It looked sophisticated, but it drained my face of colour. I twirled in front of Rebecca.

"What do you think?" I asked.

"Nah! I'm not keen: too much black. You look positively funereal, darling!"

"Oh dear!" I unbuttoned and removed the blouse before slipping the silky top over my head. It had a slight 'A' line cut. It didn't have any sleeves, and it fell to just above my bottom. The flowers were varying shades of red and orange. They reminded me of my garden pre-Peggy.

"Well?" I asked Rebecca uncertainly.

"I love it! It really suits you. Actually, you look better in it than I do. I hate it when that happens," she said and jokingly pouted like a petulant child.

"Ha! I seriously doubt that. Do you think this is the one?" I asked, unusually uncertain of myself.

"I do, but don't take my word for it. Go and ask your mum. You know that she'll tell you if you look like a sack of potatoes."

"That's true!" I could always rely on my mum for the harsh, unfettered truth.

I walked downstairs with Rebecca, in front, leading the way.

"Wait here," she said, "I need to prepare the audience."

She left me in the hallway while she entered the kitchen and shut the door. I could hear muttering and kitchen drawers opening and closing. What on earth were they up to?

Finally, Rebecca called, "Come in."

I opened the door. Mum, Alex, and Henry were all sitting in a row at the kitchen table. They each had a piece of paper and a pen in front of them. I glanced at Rebecca in bewilderment.

"Now, I want you to score your daughter's or Mum's outfit, depending upon your relationship, out of ten."

I groaned. What was she doing?

"Could she turn around?" Henry asked Rebecca.

"Yes, judge. She can." Rebecca replied. "Frankie, do a twirl," she commanded.

I was feeling more and more self-conscious, but a part of me could see the amusing side of the situation. I dutifully twirled finishing with a curtsey.

"Judges, are you ready to score?" Rebecca asked.

"We are," my mum replied.

Each of them bowed their head over their individual piece of paper. Their free hand hid what they were writing with the other, so I couldn't see. When they'd finished, they put their pens down.

"Well?" Rebecca asked.

All three of them lifted their scores in the air and shouted, "Ten."

We all burst into a fit of the giggles.

When I eventually regained my composure, I asked, "Seriously, though, do I look OK?"

"You look fabulous, Frankie. It's nice to see you dressed up for a change," Mum replied.

"You look great, Mum," Alex said as he walked from the kitchen listening to music on an iPod.

"Thanks, Alex." I said. Hang on! He didn't own an iPod!

He was halfway up the stairs when I shouted, "Where did the iPod come from?"

He turned to look down at me, shrugged and said, "It was a present."

Rebecca called out from the kitchen, "Shall we have a sneaky glass of wine, before I leave, to get you in the mood for your date?"

"Stop calling it a date. It's freaking me out," I said, as I wandered back into the kitchen.

I'd deal with the iPod situation later. I couldn't believe Rob had bought him an iPod as well as those expensive trainers. I knew Alex was having a hard time lately, but buying him presents wasn't the answer. Rob was meant to have been having a chat with him, not buying him things to cheer him up. What about Henry? Rob wasn't buying him things. It wasn't fair.

Rebecca poured the wine and handed me the glass.

"You girls go into the living room while I get on with the cooking," Mum suggested.

"Good idea. I'll just pop upstairs and take this off. I don't want to spill anything on it before I go out."

Alex's bedroom door was closed again. When exactly did that start happening, I wondered. He always used to leave his bedroom door open; never bothered by my popping in and out to pick up dirty laundry or put ironed laundry away. But now . . . he objected every time I entered his room; asking me what I wanted as if I had to have a valid reason. Was it all part and parcel of being a teenager? I tried to recollect my fourteen-year-old self. Did I get stroppy every time my mum entered my room? I had to admit, I probably did.

I hesitated for a few moments outside his room and pressed my ear to his door. He was talking to someone, and he sounded happy. The same way he had last Thursday evening when I had been on my way out with Maria. When I had asked him, the next day, who he had been talking to he had said a new friend. He hadn't seemed keen on providing more detail. I was so happy he was finally making friends that I was happy to drop the subject.

I couldn't hear what was being said, but the tone of their voices was jolly and playful. I'd ask Alex about this new friend tomorrow. I'd try to get a little bit more information. Actually, I'd encourage Alex to invite him over, so I could check him out. Yes, that's what I'd do. Congratulating myself on my good idea, I walked into my bedroom. It was my turn to close my door, I thought, as I changed out of my first-date outfit.

# Chapter 19

As I waited for Leo to arrive, I realised I felt slightly intoxicated. I couldn't decide if that was a good or a bad thing. The first glass of wine I'd consumed with Rebecca had become a second glass of wine. She was a bad influence. Or perhaps, she knew I needed to have a drink to loosen up a little. I certainly felt a lot more relaxed than I had before the wine.

I'd hardly had time to worry about my date in the last few hours. After I'd changed out of my first-date outfit, I had rejoined Rebecca in the living room. She'd proceeded to regale me with what felt like a minute by minute account of her first, second and third date with Sam.

She'd had three dates with him in a week. He did seem remarkably keen on her. And even though I would have found it slightly off-putting, she seemed to be lapping it up. After her husband's betrayal and the losers she'd dated since, I could understand why.

I was happy that she appeared to have found someone who was potty about her. However, I was still concerned by the age difference between them, but she definitely wasn't. She'd explained that he'd dated girls his own age and had even been engaged, but that she'd broken it off. She'd gone off with another guy.

"So you see, Frankie, he knows how it feels to be betrayed."

I'd nodded. It also explained why he was happy to date an older woman. He may well have thought they were less likely to stray than women his own age. I'd kept that thought to myself. I knew Rebecca wouldn't have thanked me for voicing it. Although I was sure the idea had crossed her mind too.

"He's really easy to talk to, Frankie. We talk for hours. He's really in touch with his feelings. He's not afraid to cry," she'd said, clearly impressed.

Hmm, I wasn't. In fact, I was suspicious. Anything that felt too good to be true usually was in my experience. Wow, Frankie, when did you get so cynical? My silence hadn't appeared to bother her as she carried on talking about her new favourite subject.

"He's so fit, Frankie. You should see him in the buff," she'd swooned.

"Umm, no thanks," I'd muttered, feeling uncomfortable with the direction the conversation was going in. She was obviously sleeping with him. I hoped she was practising safe sex. Surely, that wasn't something I needed to worry about. No, I reassured myself, she wasn't some naive teenager.

"I'm only joking! I don't really want you to see him naked. He's all mine," she'd added with more than a hint of pride in her voice. "I can't quite believe he's with me. I mean he could have anyone. But he wants to be with me."

Despite my reservations, I'd said, "You deserve some happiness, Rebecca," and I meant it.

"I do, don't I?" she'd said with meaning. "And so do you."

I was brought acutely back to the present by a short, sharp rap on the door. My heart started beating a loud tattoo in my chest, and a vein on the side of my head that I never knew existed before this moment started to pulsate. It's not too late; you don't have to open the door. You could pretend to be out. My thoughts started to calm me until I heard my mum's voice in the hallway.

"Hello, Leo, nice to see you. I'll just call Frankie."

Damn and blast, Mum had answered the door. There was no escape now. I couldn't believe how nervous I felt. It was perfectly normal to feel this nervous on a first date,

I told myself. It had been years since I'd dated, I rationalised. I checked myself out, one last time, in my full-length mirror. I'd have to do.

"Frankie, your date is here," Mum called with much amusement in her voice.

I winced. She made it sound like I was going to the prom. She was enjoying this. I was already plotting my revenge. I descended the stairs carefully. The last thing I wanted to do was trip and land in a heap at the bottom. It also meant that I kept my eyes firmly on each stair in turn rather than look at Leo.

Once at the bottom of the stairs, I made much of finding my coat, so I could avoid eye contact for a few more seconds. I was facing the coat rack with my back to Leo reaching for my fitted black leather jacket; the one I reserved for nights out, when my peripheral vision spotted something black move on the wall to my left. My focus automatically shifted to its locale. I wasn't even aware of rational thought as my body reacted to what I saw. I screamed and jumped back grabbing Leo's arm.

"It's . . . it's . . . ," I said, like a mad woman who can't quite get her words out. I resorted to pointing wildly at the wall. "Get rid of it . . . , get rid of it . . . ," I squealed.

I glanced at my mum. She was looking at me like I'd taken leave of my senses until she looked at where I was pointing. As she spotted the offensively large arachnid, she gave a little yelp and jumped backwards. She grabbed Leo's only other available arm. So much for strong, independent women, I thought. We were both doing a great impression of helpless females right now. I realised that once I had chance to reflect on this situation, I may be rather embarrassed. But in this moment, right now, all I was feeling was terrified. I absolutely hated spiders.

"OK, ladies," Leo said in a reassuring, authoritative tone. "Just open the front door and then step back out of the way."

Mum was closest to the door, so she opened it wide and then shot around both Leo and myself and straight into the kitchen. I smiled apologetically and then followed suit.

"Let me know when it's gone," I said as I rushed from the hallway to the relative safety of the kitchen shutting the door firmly behind me.

Mum and I stood in the middle of the kitchen waiting. Seconds later, we heard the bang of the front door. We both visibly exhaled. The kitchen door creaked open slowly.

"Is it OK to come in?" Leo asked, poking his head around the door.

"Yes, yes, please do," I said. "Is it gone?"

"Yes," he said.

"What did you do?" I asked, suddenly realising I hadn't given him anything to deal with the situation. I usually provided my rescuer with a glass and piece of paper at least.

"I picked it up and placed it outside." He must have seen my look of fear as he said, "Don't worry. I placed it far enough away from the house so as not to encourage it to return."

"You picked it up with your bare hands?" I asked shuddering.

"Yes, do you think I could wash them before we go?" he asked.

I stepped aside immediately and pointed toward the kitchen sink. "Please go ahead."

There was no way I would be holding his hand during this date if he didn't wash them after handling that beast.

The first time I'd met him, a year or so ago, I'd thought he was significantly younger than he actually was. He had one of those plump-cheeked youthful faces. He'd told me one day that he was actually thirty-three. He was still younger than me but only by three years. I didn't have a problem with that and neither, it seemed, did he.

As he washed his hands, I studied his profile. He had a strong masculine jaw with just a hint of stubble. He'd shaven today, but my guess was this morning rather than for our date. He had a straight nose, neither large nor small; it was just the right size for his face. He had full rosy-red lips; I'd call them kissable lips. I noticed he had put gel on his short brown hair. I'd never noticed gel before, so he had definitely made an effort.

I glanced at what he was wearing. I had never seen him out of uniform before. He wore black jeans and a grey check shirt. The shirt hung loosely over the waistband of his jeans; he wore a grey tailored jacket on top. He looked stylish. I was surprised, but I didn't know why. I took a step toward him and could smell his aftershave. It was a fresh, clean scent. I wasn't sure, but I thought I smelt oranges and perhaps a hint of sandalwood. I liked it.

He turned, caught my eye and smiled. Holding up his wet hands, he asked, "Towel?"

I looked straight into his chocolate-brown eyes.

"Oh yes, of course," I said. I grabbed a clean tea towel and unceremoniously shoved it in his direction.

After drying his hands, he asked, "As the disaster has been averted, shall we go?"

"Yes. Sorry about the hysterics," I said.

"That's OK. You can't help being scared of spiders."

"I meant my mum's hysterics. She can be so embarrassing." I said straight-faced. I knew he didn't know how to react.

"Umm . . . well . . . ," he stammered.

"Ignore her," my mum said. "She's teasing you."

He glanced at me as if to check that was, in fact, the case. I smiled broadly.

"Mum's right. I am teasing you. I'm sorry for making a complete show of myself. Let's go before another eight-legged friend appears."

He exhaled deeply in what I imagined was relief. I gave Mum a peck on the cheek as I passed her.

"I'll see you later."

"Have a good time," she said, and followed us out to the hallway to shut and lock the front door behind us.

I climbed into the passenger seat of Leo's silver Volkswagen Golf GTI. I'd barely had time to do my seatbelt up when he'd sped away from the kerb. Hold on horsey, I thought. Was he a frustrated boy racer? We reached the bottom of my road in record time. His indicator was flashing to turn left, and while he waited for a gap in the traffic he said, "I thought we'd go into town and have a drink in a few pubs. Is that OK?"

He propelled the car round the corner at breakneck speed having spotted his opportunity to join the other traffic headed for the M5.

"Yes, sounds like a pl-a-a-a-a-n," I said. My voice rising as my body swung to the left.

"Sorry," he said, "I saw my chance, and I went for it."

Hmm, well, as long as all he was talking about was the traffic. We sped up the motorway in silence. I was beginning to regret my decision. He was usually so talkative. I couldn't remember our struggling to hold a conversation before.

"How's your day been?" I asked.

"Yeah, good!" he replied. "Well, actually it hasn't been good. It's been pretty rough. I had to attend a fatal road traffic accident today. It was a young girl. You never get used to it."

"No, I can imagine. You could have postponed tonight if you weren't feeling up to it. I'd have understood in the circumstances."

We'd left the M5 and joined the M32 motorway heading into Bristol. I could see the lights of the shops ahead of me. As we approached the traffic lights at the end of the M32, he braked heavily bringing the car to a stop at the lights.

Turning to me, he said, "No, I didn't want to postpone. I've been looking forward to taking you out." He coloured a little at his admission.

I was touched because I could see that he meant it. I glanced at the traffic lights. They were green. He'd stopped at a green light. I felt a giggle rise in my throat.

He could see my amusement but was momentarily bemused by it. I pointed at the lights and laughed out loud.

"I'm confused: where in the Highway Code does it say you should stop at a green light?" I asked.

I could see his panic as he fumbled to get the gearstick into first and pull away.

"That is so embarrassing," he said after a few seconds. "I was lucky that there were no cars behind me, or they would have been sounding their horns."

I was still giggling unashamedly. I couldn't stop for some reason.

He started to laugh too. We were both still giggling when he pulled into Trenchard Street car park.

We got out of the car and started to walk side by side towards the harbour side.

"Do you know, after the day I've had, which includes the whole spider and traffic light experience, I think I need someone to hold my hand to make me feel better."

I glanced sideways at him and could see the boyish grin covering his face and a playful glint in his eye.

I slid my hand into his. "Smooth, Leo Acton, very smooth."

He gripped my hand and gave it a little squeeze. "Smooth? Me? I just stopped at a green light."

I started to laugh again. "True." I gently tugged his arm. "Come on, let's get a drink."

We hurried past Bristol Cathedral and down a walk way to its side that led us on to Anchor road. There was a gap in the traffic, so instead of waiting at the pedestrian crossing Leo yanked my arm and said, "Quick, let's make a run for it."

"In these heels," I yelled as we ran laughing across the road.

"Umm, I think you just dislocated my shoulder blade," I said rubbing my shoulder with my free hand.

"Oh sorry, are you OK?" he asked suddenly sombre.

"Ha! Gotcha! You really are quite gullible. I'm fine, but shouldn't you be setting a good example?"

I'd watched the changing expressions flit across his face as I'd spoken: relief at my being unharmed by the unexpected exertion and then bewilderment at my question.

He shrugged. "What do you mean?"

"I'm sure it's an offence to jaywalk," I said, my tone heavy with meaning.

His lips twitched; the amusement was back in his eyes. "I won't tell, if you don't."

"My silence can be bought with a large glass of Prosecco," I offered.

"You're on."

We arrived at the harbour side and stood for a few seconds deciding which bar to frequent.

"Shall we go in the Slug and Lettuce?" I asked.

"Yes, for starters."

As we walked in, I was surprised at how lively it was for a Thursday night. While we were standing at the bar waiting to be served, I was reminded of my recent trip to Bournemouth. I recalled my conversation with Rebecca, and an image of a man's penis popped into my head. I started to giggle. Leo gave me a sideways glance while still trying to attract the attention of the bar staff.

"What's up?" he asked glancing at me briefly.

"I'll tell you in a minute when you've got the drinks. I want your opinion on something."

"I'm intrigued," he said. Having finally caught the barman's eye, he said, "A large glass of Prosecco and a pint of lager shandy, please." The barman hurried off and Leo said, "I'll only have one pint of lager shandy, and then I'll drink soft drinks."

"I trust you," I said, and I realised I actually did.

We found a vacant table in the window. Setting the drinks down, he said, "Well come on, spill the beans."

I was feeling playful and mischievous, so I decided to shock him. As he lifted his pint to his lips and took a large gulp, I said, "I was thinking about penises. That's why I was giggling." I beamed at him.

His eyes widened at my words. He started to cough and splutter. The brown liquid appeared to have gone down the wrong way. He was choking.

Oh dear! I had intended to shock him, but in an amusing way, not actually kill him.

"Are you OK?" I asked.

He was still coughing. His face had gone an ugly shade of puce.

"Do you want me to hit you on the back? It might help," I added.

He nodded at the same time as he continued to cough.

I took that to be a yes. I got out of my chair and walked around the back of him. I thumped his back forcefully a few times.

He turned to me and whispered, "That's enough."

I returned to my seat feeling like I'd played a small part in his recovery. The least I could do considering I'd played a large part in the initial emergency.

"Are you OK?" I asked.

He nodded. "I think I may still have a few ribs intact."

"Oh, I'm sorry! Did I hit you too hard?"

"Well, put it this way, the pain you inflicted on me took my mind off my choking, which coincidentally you were also responsible for. I wish I'd known how this date would go. I would have increased my life assurance before venturing out." He finished speaking and looked me in the eye with a serious expression on his face.

For once, I didn't know what to say. I couldn't tell if he was being serious or not. He certainly appeared to be serious. This may well be my first and last date with Leo.

"Gotcha!" he said as he burst out laughing. "You really are quite gullible," he retorted using my earlier words against me. "You'd better explain yourself, lady, because frankly I'm shocked you were thinking about penises. Not totally against it, of course," he said grinning like a schoolboy.

I relaxed. That was a relief. I was glad that he had a good sense of humour. I went on to explain the pictures Rebecca had shown me of the men from the online dating website.

"Is that the norm, these days?" I asked.

"Why are you asking me? Men don't send me pictures of their bits."

"Well, I thought, maybe . . ."

"I don't send women pictures of my . . . if that's what you mean. I don't use those online dating sites."

I raised my eyebrows. "Everyone seems to use them nowadays."

"Do you?" he asked.

"No," I retorted.

"Then why assume I do? I'll admit that I tried them a few years ago, but I didn't have any luck. I decided to wait and see if anyone came along the more traditional way." He looked at me meaningfully.

I found myself blushing.

He noticed my discomfort, and being the gentleman I was beginning to realise he was, he said, "Drink up. We'll go to another bar."

I grabbed my glass and drained what little contents remained. We got to our feet, and he offered me his hand. I took it, and we strode from the Slug and Lettuce pub on a mission to find our next venue.

We hadn't walked far when he was tugging me into a now familiar pub. It was Mizzi's. I wasn't sure if drinking in here would be a good idea. What if David Shaw was here? I didn't want to come face to face with him. I surveyed the pub's clientele as we walked in and over to the bar to order a drink.

"Are you OK?" Leo shouted above the loud music.

"Yes. I'm going to the ladies'." And just in case he couldn't hear me above the pop music blasting from the speaker directly above our heads, I pointed upstairs to further illustrate my point.

He nodded and sensibly avoided shouting by giving me the thumbs up.

I used the walk to the restrooms to look briefly at everyone I passed. I didn't see David Shaw, but that didn't mean that he wouldn't be coming in later.

I didn't linger in the restrooms. I quickly checked my make-up and reapplied my lipstick. I often wondered why we women did that. We reapplied a layer of lipstick before promptly putting a drink to our lips and leaving the aforementioned layer on the rim of the glass. Despite thinking it pointless, I went through the motions. As I retraced my steps, I scanned the bar for new faces.

We found a vacant table away from the speaker, but the music was still loud. Every word uttered was shouted. I calculated that I actually heard approximately one in every five words Leo was saying. I couldn't even lip read what he was saying because he was looking around the pub as he spoke. The words I did hear had the makings of an interesting, if somewhat unconventional, conversation.

"I . . . sleep . . . nervous . . . you?" he said.

"Excuse me?" I asked. Did he just say he was nervous about sleeping with me? Huh, that was presuming I was ever going to sleep with him. One date and he thought I was going to sleep with him, surely not. He hadn't given me the impression he was that type of guy.

He shook his head and pointed at the drinks. He raised his orange juice to his lips and drank half of it straight down.

He seemed to be indicating that we should finish our drinks. I was hoping it was because he wanted to go somewhere where we could actually hear each other; rather than straight home in the hopes he'd get a quickie. He'd be disappointed if it was the latter.

In hindsight, perhaps my choice of conversational topic had been a poor one. I had simply sought to lighten the mood and have a laugh with my talk of penises, but he may well have seen it as an invitation. Yes, it was up to me to make it clear to him that I was not sleeping with him on a first date.

I raised my wine glass to my lips and took a large gulp. As if on autopilot, I cast my eyes around the room. It was then that I spotted her sitting at the bar. She seemed to have entered the pub without my noticing her. It was the girl David Shaw had been with the night I had been here with Mum. The same girl I had taken a photograph of him kissing and sent to his fiancée's dad, Mike Flattery. David didn't seem to be with her . . . yet.

I picked up my wine glass and drained the glass in three large gulps. Leo looked impressed and eager to leave. Oh God, he probably thought my downing my drink with such speed indicated I was agreeable to his plan. He had no idea of the real reason I wanted to get out of here: I didn't want to see David Shaw. As soon as we had put some distance between us and this bar, I would have to be straight with him.

We both got to our feet and left the bar. I walked ahead of him at speed in the direction of the Horny Bridge.

"Hang on, slow down a bit. Where are you headed?" Leo asked, as he rushed to keep up with me.

"I'm heading for the Horny Bridge," I said. As soon as the words had left my lips, I wanted to snatch them back. What was wrong with me? First, I talk about penises and now horny bridges. No wonder the poor guy had got the wrong impression.

"OK," he said, clearly amused.

I was satisfied that we'd put enough distance between us and Mizzi's, so I stopped abruptly and turned to face Leo. "Look, I'm sorry if I've given you the wrong impression. I realise my talking about men's penises and horny bridges may have led you to believe you were on to a sure thing. But I can assure you that I will not be sleeping with you tonight. I'm just not that kind of girl."

I waited for his response. I hoped he wasn't the type of guy that got annoyed and accused women of leading them on. Well, if he was, then I had enough money to catch the bus back to Portishead, if necessary.

He was standing there with his mouth open. He seemed genuinely shocked by my impromptu speech. He started to shake his head and open and close his mouth as if he was unable to find the right words. Finally, he said, "What are you talking about?"

"You said you were nervous about sleeping with me."

"I said WHAT?" he asked. "WHEN?" he added as an afterthought.

"When we were in Mizzi's, you said you were nervous . . ."

He interrupted, "I heard you the first time. But you clearly didn't hear what I said the first time."

He was both smiling with amusement and shaking his head in disappointment all at the same time.

I was beginning to get the feeling I had made a mistake; one of epic proportions.

"What I actually said was, 'I didn't get much sleep last night. I was nervous about tonight. How about you?' "

I was rarely lost for words, but I found myself in just such a position. I stared at him, feeling immeasurably foolish and wanting the ground to open up and swallow me. I started to hop uncomfortably from one foot to the other. Partly due to my discomfort at the situation I found myself in, and partly due to the actual discomfort of the high-heeled shoes I was wearing.

"Umm . . . er . . . I'm so sorry. I completely misunderstood what you said," I apologised. I couldn't look him in the eye.

"Frankie, look at me," he demanded gently.

I tilted my head up and did as he asked.

"I've waited months for you to agree to go out with me. Why would I assume you would sleep with me on the first night? I like you. I mean, I really like you. I'm hoping this is the start of a relationship. I wasn't expecting a wham, bam, thank you ma'am."

"Aww, that is so nice. I feel so stupid. I'm really sorry," I said.

"Of course, if you happened to jump me on the way home, I wouldn't say no," he said, with a big cheesy grin on his face.

I knew he was joking and just trying to lighten the mood. I hit him playfully on the arm.

"You're safe tonight. Come on, stud. Let's go to another pub; one where I can hear what you're saying. I don't want any more misunderstandings tonight."

He held out his hand for me to take. "You can hold my hand. I won't eat you," he said, a mischievous glint in his eye.

I took his hand, and we walked into Lloyds bar. We walked upstairs and found a nice table for two. We sat there chatting happily for the next hour.

He looked at his watch, "It's time I took you home."

"Is it?" I was genuinely surprised. The time had flown this evening, which was a good sign.

"Yes, it's 11 p.m. I have to be at work early in the morning, and I don't want your mum telling me off for keeping you out too late."

I laughed. "She won't mind. She just wants me to be happy especially after . . . everything."

He nodded. "Yes, I can understand that. I purposely didn't talk about the events of last year because, for me, tonight is about getting to know you better."

"I appreciate that. I feel the same."

"Good, come on."

We walked back to the car hand in hand. Leo drove me home at a more reserved speed than he had on the way to town, thankfully. He pulled up outside my house. I suddenly felt nervous again. It would seem that it didn't matter whether you were sixteen or thirty-six: first-date jitters were first-date jitters. Would he kiss me? Should I kiss him?

I looked across at him sitting in the driver's seat. If he turned the engine off, then he definitely expected a kiss. If he didn't, then he was eager to get home and perhaps was not expecting a kiss. As I sat there debating this uncomfortable situation, he turned the engine off. I heard it die. The car shuddered slightly as the vibration of the engine ceased. My heart started to hammer loudly in my chest. I wondered if he could hear it. I hoped not.

"Frankie," he said staring straight ahead of him at the street before him. "Would you like to go out again?"

He appeared to be holding his breath. I realised he was nervous. It was so endearing that I forgot my own nerves as I reached across and touched the hand that was still gripping the steering wheel.

"I'd love to. I've had a great time," I said and added, "I hope you have."

He visibly exhaled, turned toward me and grabbed both my hands in his.

"I've had a great night despite, the spider, the traffic lights and you accusing me of being a sex pest."

I opened my mouth to argue that I hadn't called him a sex pest, and that it had all been a misunderstanding when he leaned forward in his seat and planted his lips firmly on mine. I was taken aback at first but only for an instant. His lips moved over mine, and I felt myself succumbing willingly to the kiss. As my lips parted, I felt his tongue move into my mouth exploring its warm depths.

I placed my arms around his neck and pulled him toward me. I could feel a heat start to build in me. The kiss quickly deepened as my tongue sought out his. I could feel his hand on my back. It seemed to be pulling me ever closer to him. I would have defied even air to have been able to find a space between us to fill in that moment. Suddenly, he pulled away and sat there facing me with a daft grin on his face.

"What?" I asked breathless from the kiss.

"I think that's what they call chemistry."

I smiled and nodded.

"I'd love to kiss you again. But if I do, you won't be getting out of this car in one piece." He stared at me meaningfully as if to reinforce his point.

"I hear you. Thank you for a great evening. Give me a call, and we'll arrange another date."

He pulled out his mobile phone.

"Who are you calling?" I asked bemused.

"You!"

Aww, that was so sweet. "I'm going now. Speak to you soon."

"Real soon," he added.

"Yep, now go home," I demanded.

"Yes, Ma'am," he said, and he saluted me as if he were a soldier and I his sergeant major.

He waited until I had unlocked my front door and walked in before he drove away. I closed the front door and stood with my back against it as I remembered our kiss. I liked PC Leo Acton. I liked him very much indeed.

I felt something other than the carpet under my left foot. Switching the hallway light on, I realised it was a large brown envelope; nothing was written on it, and it was unsealed. I reached inside and pulled out its contents. It took me a few moments to realise what I was looking at. It was a photograph. I was staring at a photograph of myself outside my house; the Pant Bros were in the background dressed in their school uniforms.

I felt my knees buckle beneath me. I sank in, what felt like, slow motion to the ground. My mouth felt dry; my head started to pound with fear. It was him; he'd taken the photograph. We certainly hadn't known we were having our photograph taken. I turned the photograph over looking for some kind of handwritten message but there was nothing. I turned the envelope upside down and shook it; there was nothing else in it. This was Glenn's way of telling me he knew where I lived, and he was watching me.

Mum, Rebecca, Maria and DC Smithers had almost succeeded in convincing me I was imagining it all, but now I had proof. DC Smithers would have to believe me now. I reached for my mobile phone to call him and then remembered what he'd said last time. I had to ring my local station. They'd call him in if necessary.

"Frankie, is that you? Why are you sitting on the floor?" My mum said walking into the hallway bleary-eyed. She looked as if she'd been dozing on the sofa.

"Yes, it's me." I managed to stand up, but felt as unstable on my feet as a newborn foal as I said, "Look at this," and without thinking shoved the photograph into her hand.

"I don't understand!" she said as she focused on the photograph.

"It was waiting for me on the mat, in an unmarked envelope, when I got home."

"But I didn't hear anyone put anything through the letterbox."

"You were probably asleep," I said sharply.

Mum visibly winced at my rebuke. I immediately felt ashamed of myself. I reached out a hand and put it on her shoulder.

"I'm sorry, Mum. I shouldn't take it out on you."

"It's OK. What do you think it means?" she asked.

"It's obvious. He's letting me know that he's watching me," I stated.

She sighed and stared at the ground. "You think it's Glenn."

"Who else could it be?"

"This time, I'm inclined to agree with you," she said.

"I'll call the local station like DC Smithers told me to."

"Stuff that!" said Mum.

I was shocked by the vehemence of her words.

"Call Andrew directly, or I will."

"Yes, Mum," and suddenly I was ten years old again and doing exactly as my mother told me to. All thoughts of Leo and our date vanished from my mind as I called DC Andrew Smithers.

# Chapter 20

"Who's touched the photograph?" DC Smithers asked while putting on plastic gloves. He took it from me carefully and held it by its edges.

"Oh, sorry, I should have thought about fingerprints. Only Mum and I have touched it."

He nodded, "I'm sure we already have both of your sets of fingerprints for elimination purposes."

"Yes, I'm sure you do. What happens next?"

"Well, I'll get SOCO to check the photograph for prints and see if they can get anything off of the envelope. Whoever sent it didn't write on it or seal it. That was clever on two counts: we can't use their handwriting to help identify them, and we can't use the DNA they may have left behind by licking the stamp or envelope. Not that it's easy to extract DNA from a licked stamp or envelope, I'm reliably informed, because it isn't. But something would have been better than nothing."

"Glenn's clever. We know that," I stated.

Andrew nodded and said, "You obviously think it's him."

"So do you. Or you wouldn't be here," I retorted.

"Hmm, all the evidence points to the fact that he's dead, Frankie. But I can't ignore the fact that this seems to be a blatant threat. What about those directors you helped jail earlier this year. They might hold a grudge."

I hadn't even considered them in all of this. Nah! I didn't think it was them.

"Do you think they may have hired someone to frighten me out of revenge?"I asked.

"I don't know. Maybe. I have to consider all of the possibilities. However, I will check Glenn Froom's bank accounts again and see if there has been any recent activity."

"He'd have a new identity by now. He's smart. He would know you were watching his accounts, and he wouldn't touch them."

"That's possible, Frankie. But if he'd intended on staging his death and creating a whole new identity, surely we would have found some kind of money trail? He didn't transfer any money out of his accounts or spend any unusual amounts before his death. Where did the money for this new life come from?"

"I don't know. Maybe he had an accomplice. He was having an affair with someone. Did you ever find out who she was?"

"We know that when he was meant to be working away during the two weeks preceding Verity's death he was only actually working from the Monday to the Wednesday. We can't account for his whereabouts on the Thursday and Friday of those weeks."

"You have nothing at all? Didn't he talk to his friends about another woman?" I asked.

"No. He was a private person."

"That's not all he was," I said with meaning.

"Look, Frankie, it's late," he said as he looked at his watch. "I'll get this photograph examined and look into Glenn's financials . . . again. If you notice anything unusual or . . . if anything else happens, give me a call."

"Is that it?" I asked incredulous. "A murderer is out there. He's gunning for me. And you say to let you know 'if anything unusual happens.' Newsflash, it just did," and I pointed at the photograph in his hand.

"This may or may not be related to Glenn. We have no way of knowing. There is no note, or anything that ties it to Glenn. Whom, I may add, we believe to be dead."

I raised my eyes to the heavens in desperation. "When will you believe he isn't? When I'm dead?"

He grimaced. "At this stage, there is no evidence to suggest that you are in mortal danger. I will call the local station. I'll ask that the beat officer patrols this street in particular."

"So, basically, I have to protect myself."

"No, that's what the police are for. If anything happens, then dial 999," he said trying to reassure me and failing miserably.

"Yep, sure," I said unable to keep the sarcasm from my voice. "Goodnight, DC Smithers. Thanks for coming." Or rather, thanks for nothing, I thought to myself.

"I'll be in touch," he said as he turned and walked out of the door.

"I won't hold my breath," I muttered. Or perhaps I should. It would save Glenn the trouble of finishing me off, I thought morosely.

I stared at the parked cars in my street. They didn't look occupied, but who knew which one Glenn might be lurking in. Watching and waiting for his opportunity to strike. I felt my chest constrict. I started to gasp for air at the thought. I closed the front door and locked and bolted it. I went into the living room where Mum lay dozing on the sofa. After what had happened, we'd agreed that she would stay the night.

She must have sensed my presence because her eyes opened slowly and she said, "Well?"

"I'll tell you in the morning. Go upstairs and get into my bed, Mum. We'll share tonight."

She rose slowly to her feet, her left hand gripping her right arm as she did so. She started to roll her right shoulder and winced.

"You're too old to be falling asleep on the sofa. Let's get you to bed."

I helped her up the stairs as she was half-asleep, and I tucked her into bed. It reminded me of the many times I'd fallen asleep downstairs in front of the television as a child and she had done the same for me. I tiptoed out of my bedroom and back downstairs. I set about checking every window lock and door was secure.

I peered into the understairs cupboard and found what I was looking for. Walking back into the living room, I opened the curtains just enough so that I could see the street outside. I'd picked up a blanket upstairs and wrapping it around me I settled on the sofa my mum had vacated only minutes before. It was still warm.

I glared at the silent street outside. I was gripping the baseball bat Rob had given me for protection after the shocking events of last year as if my life depended on it. When he came, I would be ready.

*****

A bright light shone through my closed eyelids. My face was bathed in warmth. Opening my eyes a crack I could see sunlight streaming through the living room window. I'd fallen asleep. It was a good job that I wasn't a night watchman. I would have failed in my duties miserably. I cast my eyes around the room; it was exactly as it had been last night. I moved gingerly. The sofa, although comfortable to sit on, wasn't the most comfortable of places to sleep.

As I stood up and stretched my aching muscles, I caught sight of my reflection in the mirror. I'd better change and fast. The boys would be coming downstairs for breakfast soon. If they saw me in last night's outfit, they'd think I'd been out all night. I needed to keep things as normal as I could for the Pant Bros. They'd been through enough already.

I made a bolt for the stairs and made it safely to my bedroom without discovery. Mum was fast asleep still.

Her head resting on the pillow and her hand pushed beneath it. She looked so relaxed and peaceful. I envied her.

Silently, I moved around the bedroom. Extricating myself from last night's attire, I placed the clothes in the washing basket. Note to self: check the washing instructions on Rebecca's top. I didn't want to ruin it after she had been so kind as to lend it to me.

I may as well have a shower and get ready for the day. I glanced at the bedside clock. It was 6:30 a.m. I had thirty minutes before the boys needed to get up for school. I needed the time to get my head together after the events of last night.

I opened the shower door as quietly as I could and closed it the same way. It was good to feel the hot water jets sting my skin. I grabbed the soap and began to work up a lather. Spreading the bubbles all over me, I set about the task of washing the fear of last night away. It was a shame, because I'd had such a lovely evening with Leo, but the implied threat of that photograph had wiped out all the joy I had felt with him.

I was sick of feeling helpless where Glenn was concerned. I felt as if I were the fly to his spider. I was helplessly hurtling toward his web; not even knowing it was there, ready to trap me.

I rested my head on the shower wall and let the water run in rivulets down my back. What could I do to help myself? Should I get a gun? Hmm, this was England, not America. I didn't even know where I'd get a gun and, in the unlikely event I managed to source one, I didn't know how to shoot. More importantly, I couldn't have a gun in the house with the Pant Bros. I had my baseball bat for protection. I would happily wield that if I needed to.

An idea popped into my head. I'd been watching a programme the other day, some kind of gadget show. The boys were more interested in it than I was. The presenter had been talking about finding a new use for your old smartphone. I had been intrigued as I liked to recycle things wherever possible and I had an old smartphone, or several, cluttering up my kitchen drawer.

Basically, you could turn your old smartphone into a surveillance camera. I couldn't remember how, off the top of my head, but I could google it after I'd dropped the Pant Bros off at school. Yes, that was what I'd do. I had a plan. It made me feel a little better; as if I had some small control over the situation. How much control I actually had over the situation was questionable. But for now, I was focused on what I could control rather than what I couldn't.

Bringing my long, hot shower to an abrupt end, I towel dried myself vigorously and got dressed with purpose. Just as I was leaving my bedroom as quietly as I could, my mum roused from her slumber.

"Frankie, is that you?" she asked, her head rising from the pillow in an attempt to see me.

"Yes, go back to sleep. I'll wake you in an hour. You don't need to get up yet."

"You OK?" she asked with half-open eyes.

"Yes," I said as convincingly as I could.

It worked because her head slumped back into the softness of the pillow and her eyes closed once again.

I woke the boys and asked them both to be quiet when getting out of bed. They usually leapt down the stairs in the morning like a pack of hungry lions having located their first kill of the day.

Alex walked into the kitchen wide-eyed and bushy-tailed. Henry followed rubbing the sleep from his eyes and appearing only semi-conscious. Alex was a morning person; Henry was not.

"Why have we got to be quiet, Mum?" Alex asked.

"Is there someone here?" Henry questioned.

"He didn't stay the night, did he?" Alex asked, and I could see the shock on both boys' faces at the thought.

I, too, was shocked that it had even crossed their minds.

"NO!" I blurted out with gusto. "It's Grams. It was late; she was tired, so I let her sleep in my bed."

Both boys looked visibly relieved.

"I'm going to drive you both to school today."

"Why?" Alex asked. "You don't normally."

I decided a little white lie was in order. "I had an email from the school. There was an attempted abduction of a young girl in Portishead recently. I just want to make sure you are both OK."

"Mum, I'm fourteen. I know not to talk to strangers. And if any guy tries to get me in his car, I'll kick him in the balls," he said matter-of-factly.

Henry giggled.

"Alex, language," I chastised.

"Sorry, Mum, but you get what I mean."

"Yes, I'm in no doubt of your meaning."

Henry giggled again.

"Henry, eat your breakfast."

"Yes, Mum," he said, attempting to school his features into a serious expression and failing miserably. He decided his best course of action, in the circumstances, was to look down into his bowl of cereal, so I couldn't see his grinning face.

"Can you just humour me for today?" I asked.

"Hmm, sure," Alex replied. "But I don't want you dropping me off in front of the school gates. Can you pull in round the corner so no one sees you?"

"Charming! Are you ashamed of me?" I asked.

"Nah! It's just . . . you know . . . it's not cool to have your mum drop you off."

He had avoided making eye contact as he spoke. I could see his internal battle playing out across his face. On the one hand, he didn't want to hurt my feelings. But on the other, he didn't want to be teased by his peers.

"It's OK. I understand. I was fourteen once you know. Still you're lucky," I pointed out.

"I am?" he queried.

"Yes! You have me for a mother; I have Grams. Need I say more?"

Both boys, knowing I was joking and were safe to do so without causing offence, laughed openly.

"What's that about Grams?" my mum asked as she wandered into the kitchen.

"I thought you were sleeping," I said.

"I couldn't get back to sleep, so I decided to get up. It's a good job too if I'm being talked about."

The Pant Bros and I looked at each other with conspiratorial grins spread across our faces.

"Come on, spill," said Mum.

"I was just saying what a great mum you are. You never embarrassed me once as a teenager," I said, not without a heavy dollop of irony in my voice. As I finished speaking, I pulled a face at the boys. They both started laughing.

"I don't know what you mean, I'm sure," said Mum, pretending to be affronted.

Both boys left the kitchen laughing on their way upstairs to get ready for school.

As they closed the kitchen door behind them, the mood changed rapidly from jovial to serious concern.

"Well? What is Andrew doing about the photograph?" asked Mum.

I explained what DC Andrew Smithers had said last night. Mum appeared to be as sceptical of the outcome of his investigation as I had been last night. I decided to tell her about my idea for using old smartphones as surveillance cameras.

She nodded. "Let's see what, if anything, Andrew's investigation turns up. The smartphone surveillance sounds like a good idea. Are you going to tell Rob about the photograph? I'd feel better if he stayed here for a while."

"I don't know, maybe. I haven't thought about it. I can't ask him to stay here. He's got Lucy and the twins now. It's not fair."

"Well, shall I stay here then?" she offered.

"No, Mum. I appreciate the offer, but I can't ask you to do that. Besides we just don't have the room. It will be all right," I said, but my words lacked conviction, and my mum knew it.

"Will this ever end?" she said and then caught herself. "I'm sorry, Frankie, that isn't helpful."

"It's OK, Mum. I know what you mean."

She nodded and walked from the room looking as defeated as I felt.

*****

I'd dropped Alex off first around the corner from the school, but in such a position as I could watch him walk through the school gates. Henry happily allowed me to pull right up to the school gates and give him a hug and a kiss in full view of everyone before alighting from the car.

I was vigilant while driving. I looked at every driver, every pedestrian. I was half expecting to see Glenn staring back at me with a mocking, murderous smile on his face.

I pulled up outside my house and let myself in. Mum had agreed to wait for me to return before she went home. I wanted to make sure that I had set up the surveillance camera before I left the house again. I didn't ever want to have to enter my house again not knowing whether Glenn was waiting for me or not.

As Mum heard my key in the door, she came to meet me in the hallway.

"Right then, I'll make a cup of tea, and you work out what you have to do to make those phones do what you want them to."

"It's a deal!" I said.

I strode purposefully into the kitchen. Within minutes, I'd located two old smartphones together with chargers in my kitchen drawer. Next, I switched on my iPad and typed into the Google search engine:

*How do I use a smartphone as a surveillance camera?*

Voilà! Pages of search results appeared. I can do this, I told myself. First things first, I needed to check that both phones could connect to the Wi-Fi. I switched each phone on and nothing happened. Their batteries were dead, which wasn't surprising, as they'd sat in the drawer unused for months.

I hurriedly connected them to their respective phone charger. And as soon as I was able, I attempted to access Wi-Fi. It was a success. Now I needed to decide where they were going to be located; as they needed to be connected to their chargers at all times. A mobile phone battery only had a limited lifespan. The last thing you wanted was your phone's battery dying just as someone broke into your home.

I needed to think sensibly and practically about where I was going to situate the phones aka surveillance cameras. I wanted both the front and back door covered. So that meant, I needed one in the hallway and one in the kitchen.

I plugged one of the phone chargers into the double socket in the kitchen. One socket was used for the kettle and the other was usually for the toaster. I'd move the toaster to the other working surface and put the surveillance camera in its place, next to the kettle. In that position it would be pointing directly at the back door and taking in pretty much the rest of the kitchen as well.

I walked into the hallway. The only available electrical socket was behind a small sideboard. I hadn't needed to use it until now. I pulled the sideboard away from the wall, just enough for me to plug the second charger in, and placed the phone between two photographs of the boys. It was pointing directly at the front door.

The phones' locations had been confirmed. All that remained was to download the application that would turn them into surveillance cameras onto each phone. According to the information on the website, I could monitor the surveillance footage remotely via my phone or iPad. I needed to decide which device I wanted to use. I decided my mobile phone would be best as I always had it with me.

I took a seat at the kitchen table and took a sip of tea.

"How's it going?" Mum asked with interest.

"OK, so far."

"Good. Not to put you under any pressure, but I'll stay until you have it working. It's for my own piece of mind."

I nodded. "I understand, Mum. Hopefully, it shouldn't take too long."

"I've got all day," she said, picking up her cup of tea and walking toward the living room. "I'll let you get on with it. I'll be watching TV if you need me."

I had to download the same application to my mobile phone and the soon to be repurposed phones. I downloaded the application to the old mobile phones first. By doing so, it generated a unique connection ID that I needed to use together with a username and password to access the video streamer monitor on my current mobile phone. I dutifully tapped in the ID together with the username and password. Two separate video streams appeared: one of my kitchen and one of my hallway.

I was actually looking at myself sitting at the kitchen table via my phone. What a surreal experience. Technology really was amazing.

I spent a good ten minutes reading about the application's capabilities. I learned that the cameras need not be recording all of the time or, in fact, record anything at all. If I simply wanted to see what was happening in real time, then I could.

Alternatively, it could be set up to only record or take a still photograph when it sensed motion, and then send an alert to my phone to notify me of it. It had sound capability; all I had to do was turn it on. It even had two-way talk, so I could talk into my phone and my voice would be relayed to whoever was in my house. The intention behind that idea appeared to be predominantly for pet owners. It was so the owner could berate an errant dog remotely rather than threaten a burglar.

If I wanted the cameras to record rather than just stream in real-time, then I needed to download whatever footage it stored on my repurposed phones to my computer on a regular basis. Otherwise, the phones would run out of storage space and be unable to record further footage. I couldn't let that happen because if, or should I say when, Glenn set foot in my home I wanted evidence; I needed evidence, then maybe everyone would believe me.

I selected the options on the application that I thought would serve me best: it was to be motion activated only and to send me an alert if and when that happened. I wanted it to record sound just in case Glenn spoke. It was another way of identifying that it was him.

I decided to have the surveillance cameras switched on whenever I wasn't at home and at night when we were all in bed. I'd sleep with my mobile phone by my bed, so if I didn't hear him break in, then at least my phone would alert me. I decided that I needed to do a few test runs to check it was working.

I shouted from the kitchen, "Mum, I think I've sorted it."

As she walked into the kitchen, she must have walked past the phone in the hallway. Ping went my mobile phone. I glanced at it.

"Yep, it works!" I said, sitting back in my chair with relief and no small measure of satisfaction.

# Chapter 21

***Session four - Tom Ferris 10.00 a.m. - 11.00 a.m.***

I'd arrived at the office for Tom's session earlier than usual. Since receiving the photograph last Thursday, I didn't like being in the house alone. It was more than that, I felt as if I were being watched. It wasn't a fanciful idea because the photograph proved someone had been watching me.

I stood up and glanced out of my office window, checking the parked cars for any occupants that could be Glenn. There was a cafe opposite, and I checked the face of each person sitting in the window. No, he wasn't one of them. But that didn't mean he hadn't been. I recollected the recent gifts: the flowers and the black silk scarf. The presents I had been convinced were from him and that everyone had been quick to reassure me were from a grateful client.

You could see reception from the window seats in the cafe. What if he'd sat in the cafe opposite and watched my reaction to the gifts? What if he had seen me faint at the sight of the scarf? I bet he'd have revelled in my distress. I shuddered as I felt an icy shiver go down my spine at the thought and turned away from the window.

I'd had my monthly supervision meeting with Rachel yesterday. She was worried about my fitness to practise at present. In all honesty, I was worried about my fitness to practise as well. But I had so few clients at the moment. I couldn't afford to turn away the two I had. It shouldn't be about the money, but I needed to eat and so did my children. I'd told myself that if after today's session I felt unable to continue, then I would refer Tom and Susan to Rebecca. I'd worry about the money later.

DC Smithers had done his best to help; he'd checked Glenn's bank accounts and there was still no sign of financial activity. He'd done everything he could, which included calling in a favour from the scenes of crime officers to rush through the fingerprint analysis of the photograph and envelope. There were no prints, other than mine and my mum's, as we'd expected. Glenn was too clever for what would have been such a basic error.

DC Smithers had promised to have a word with the local beat officer. He'd been true to his word: I'd noticed a patrol car driving past my house at least once a day over the past few days. It was a small comfort. Still I doubted they would continue to drive by indefinitely, and how useful was it really? If Glenn was watching, as I suspected he was, then he too saw the police car. He would simply wait until they had gone before striking.

I heard the knock on the door and jumped out of my skin with fright. It must be Tom.

"Come in," I said, sounding surprisingly calmer than I felt.

He opened the door wide and strode in, smiling briefly at me as he took a seat.

"I switched my phone off in the car park today," he said, with meaning.

"OK," I said, sensing I wasn't fully understanding the significance of his words.

"My stepdad keeps ringing . . . remember?"

Suddenly, I understood. "I do remember. Last week you weren't sure why he was so concerned about you talking to me about your childhood."

"Yeah . . . but . . . ," he stopped, and I could see from his expression that he was unsure whether or not to continue.

"Have you remembered something from your childhood?" I asked, guessing he may have.

"I'm not sure," he said with a troubled expression.

"Do you want to tell me about it?" I asked.

"I was in Jacob's room. He was asleep. I was standing there watching the way his chest rose and fell gently. I wondered what he was dreaming about. His blanket had wriggled down his body, probably from his moving around in his sleep, and I was tucking it in around him.

"All of a sudden I was aware of the sound of people arguing. The noise was coming from the living room. For a second, I couldn't work out who it could be. Then I realised it must be a programme Jenny was watching. At that moment, the nursery door opened and Jenny was standing in the doorway. The light from the hallway was behind her. In that split second I felt afraid, not just afraid, but terrified."

"Do you know what you were afraid of?" I asked.

He shook his head. "I think it may be linked to what happened next. I had a flash of memory. I could hear shouting; I think it was my mum and Lenny. I couldn't hear what they were shouting about, but I could hear my mum crying. I was scared, really scared. Then I could see Lenny, and he's standing in my bedroom doorway just as Jenny was with the light from the hallway behind him, and I felt frightened."

"What were you frightened of?"

"I don't know. Of what was going to happen next, I suppose."

"Can you remember what happened next?" I probed.

"I'm too scared to contemplate that, Frankie." His eyes beseeched me not to pursue the subject. He was silent for a minute or so. I let him remain with his thoughts uninterrupted. Finally, he said, "Still a good thing has come out of that situation."

"Oh?"

He continued, "Jenny saw how scared I looked. When we returned to the living room, she encouraged me to talk to her. I resisted at first, and she became angry. She basically said we couldn't go on like this and that if I didn't start opening up to her then . . . we were finished. I don't want to lose her, Frankie. I don't want to lose Jacob either. Faced with no choice, but to own up to my feelings, I ended up telling her about how I feel around Jacob. Particularly, the stress and anxiety I feel when he cries."

"That must have taken a great deal of courage."

"It did. I didn't know how she would react."

"How did she?"

He smiled. "She was great. She made me promise to tell her when the anxiety is building up, and we've agreed to avoid the most stressful situations for a while. So no family meals out until I feel I can cope with it."

"That sounds like a reasonable plan."

"We agreed that we need more time together as a couple. Jenny wants to ask Mum and Lenny to babysit." He made a face as if he wasn't comfortable with the idea.

"You don't think that's a good idea?"

"No, I don't. The flashback has unnerved me. If I combine that with Lenny's concern that I might talk to you about my childhood . . . I'm worried that . . ." He shook his head as if to dismiss his thoughts from it.

"Did you tell Jenny about the flashback?"

"No, I don't want to worry her. And besides, I don't really remember anything other than how I felt."

"Could you ask Jenny's parents to babysit instead? It would mean that you still get some quality time together, and you don't have to entrust Jacob to your mum and Lenny until you understand your feelings better."

He was staring off into the distance. I wasn't sure he was listening to me.

"Uh . . . yes. That's what we decided in the end. It feels good to have told Jenny how I'm feeling and why. I was afraid she'd think I was a bad dad, and I said that. But she didn't. She said it was important that I get to the bottom of why I was feeling this way."

"I agree with her. Last week, I asked you to focus on what you're thinking in the moment you start to feel really anxious around your son."

"Yes, I have tried. When he's crying, it's like a blinding panic. I just keep thinking, you have to be quiet, you have to be quiet. I feel frightened."

"His crying frightens you?"

"I feel frightened because he won't stop crying."

"Why? What might happen if he doesn't stop?" I asked and at the same time studied his expression. His eyes widened in fear; he started to wring his hands. He was looking at me but not seeing me. I wagered his thoughts were of somewhere other than here right now.

"He has to stop crying. He has to. He has to. I'll go mad if he doesn't. Good boys don't cry!" he blurted out. He was looking wildly around the room as if searching for the person who had uttered his words, as if the words had been uttered by someone else.

"Is that what you think? Good boys don't cry?" I probed.

He shrugged, "Umm . . . I have no idea where that came from. But, yes, I suppose I do."

"What happens to boys that cry, Tom?" I asked.

Fear flooded his eyes. He began to shake his head. "I don't . . . I don't know. Mum, I want my mum. Where is she?" His eyes desperately scanned the room.

The adult Tom knew he was in my office and that there was no likelihood of his mum being there. But something about my question had invoked the child in Tom, and Tom the child wanted his mum.

"She's not here, Tom," I said gently.

He was looking directly at me. I knew he'd heard my words, but there was a delay in his comprehension of their meaning. I watched his face and saw the moment my words finally made sense to him.

"I know that. I know she's not here." He laughed, but to my ears the sound was devoid of humour. He raked his hands through his hair. "Am I cracking up, Frankie?"

"No. I think you're beginning to remember events from your childhood that, for whatever reason, scared you at the time. It may be that those memories are linked to your feelings of anxiety around your son." He looked hopeful at my words. "Or, they may not."

My final words were uttered with the intention of not giving him false hope. I suspected his memories were associated to his current feelings of anxiety. But I couldn't be sure until we both understood what his memories were exactly.

He appeared to be experiencing repressed memories that were triggered by a set of circumstances resembling his original experience. Repressed memories are thought to be memories of a traumatic event that we bury deep down in our psyche because they frighten us too much to recall. It's an automatic psychological defence against emotional trauma and doesn't involve conscious intent. Sometimes these repressed memories can resurface spontaneously.

I was unwilling to give what Tom was experiencing a label. I wanted him to further explore his memories and feelings freely; to reach his own conclusions about what they meant.

If I explained to him that I believed he had experienced a repressed memory and that these types of memories are associated with a past traumatic event, then he may feel a victim in some way. This could have a number of side effects: unwilling to be a victim he could further unconsciously or consciously repress his memories further. Or, in his desire to remember, he could interpret what he had already remembered incorrectly.

I wanted Tom to recollect what had happened organically. The two of us could then piece together what it meant to him without any preconceptions.

Unwelcome thoughts of Glenn crept up into my mind and demanded attention. My eyes flicked involuntarily to the window. Was he out there staring up at my window hoping to catch a glimpse of me? To revel in the fear and distress he saw etched in every fibre of my being.

My thoughts had given rise to the now familiar feelings of panic starting to course through me. Without thinking, I plucked at the band around my wrist and silently recited my mantra in my head. He cannot hurt you any more; you are safe. Instead of its usual calming effect, it increased my alarm as I realised the words were now hollow. I didn't believe them.

Glenn could hurt me. The photograph proved he knew where I lived. I wasn't safe because of that fact. My heart was pounding so much it felt like it was trying to break my ribs in its efforts to escape my body.

"Frankie? Did you hear what I said?"

Tom's voice snapped me back into the here and now. Feelings of guilt slammed headlong into and fought with my feelings of fear. Guilt won, in this instance, as I realised I had been distracted by my own feelings.

"I'm sorry, Tom. I didn't hear what you said."

He frowned but more with concern than annoyance. "Are you OK?" he asked.

I let out an involuntary, heartfelt sigh. It shouldn't be about me; these sessions should never be about me. In the interests of being genuine, I had to admit how I felt, but I didn't need to go into detail.

"No, I'm not OK. But this session is about you and not me. I'm sorry I was distracted. It won't happen again," I said, and though it took herculean effort, I focused on Tom. "If you don't mind, could you repeat what you said?"

"Umm . . . yes sure . . . if you're positive that you're OK?"

I smiled and nodded.

"Well, I said . . ."

*****

"I'll walk you out, Tom, as I need to pick up today's post." I usually checked our mailbox in the morning on the way in, but I'd been distracted today.

"Sure," he said as he held the office door open for me.

I smiled and thanked him, genuinely pleased that he'd done that small thing for me.

We descended the stairs side by side. I turned to bid him farewell.

"I'll see you next week, Tom."

"Yes, see you then, Frankie."

I noticed an unfamiliar gentleman sitting in one of the chairs in reception. I assumed he was waiting to meet someone from one of the numerous offices in the building. Tom had his back to him, and I was facing him. Surprisingly he was staring straight at me with much interest as Tom said his goodbyes.

I didn't recognise the gentleman. Should I recognise him? I questioned my memory bank and came up blank. No, I definitely didn't recognise him. He got to his feet and approached Tom from behind. When he was within reach, he leaned forward and tapped Tom on the shoulder.

Tom shot six feet in the air. He evidently hadn't heard the man approach him. He spun around to meet the man's gaze.

"Lenny? What are you doing here?" he asked.

So this was Lenny. Not content with texting and calling Tom before, during, and after his counselling sessions, now he decided to turn up unannounced.

"I just thought I'd surprise you. I thought maybe I could buy you a coffee in the cafe opposite," Lenny said to Tom while staring at me.

"Uh . . . I've got stuff to do, Lenny. Sorry. Maybe next time," he muttered.

Lenny didn't seem particularly perturbed by the brush off. He hadn't taken his eyes off of me. It felt like I was being assessed, judged even.

"Who's this then?" he asked.

A question we all three of us knew to be pointless because Lenny knew exactly who I was. I remained mute. It wasn't my question to answer. If Tom wanted to let him know who I was, then that was entirely his decision.

"This is Frankie, my . . . ," he hesitated.

It was obvious that he didn't want to admit who I was.

Lenny filled in the blanks for himself, "Your counsellor," he stated with a distinctly chilly edge to his voice.

I remained mute and expressionless while waiting to take my cue from Tom. He wasn't comfortable with this situation, and neither was I.

"Bye, Tom," I said, seeking to cut the situation short. I turned away and walked toward our mailbox with purpose. As I turned the key in the lock, I tried to block out the two men standing behind me with their heads huddled closely together muttering furiously at one another.

I grabbed the two items of post and glanced briefly at them. I barely registered the fact that one was a flyer from a local takeaway and the other a brochure for retirement flats. God save me from junk mail. Had I known, I wouldn't have delayed my escape back to my office by the several minutes it had already cost me.

I relocked the mailbox and was turning around to retrace my steps back to my office when I was confronted by Lenny. He was standing, what felt like only a few inches from me, so close that I instinctively stepped backward. I winced with pain as I realised I'd backed into the corner of the square metal mailbox.

"Do you have children?" he asked, lowering his face to mine, so that he could look me directly in the eye.

Whether his intention was to intimidate me or not, I couldn't be certain. But I definitely felt intimidated. Tom put his hand on Lenny's shoulder in an attempt to pull him away, but Lenny shook it off. He was not to be distracted from his line of questioning so easily.

"Lenny, leave her alone. Come on," Tom said.

Lenny didn't move. It was obvious that he wasn't going to leave until I answered him.

"I do," I replied without further elaboration.

"Then you can understand how hard it is to bring them up. How hard it is to always get it right. Make sure you cherish them, Frankie, because one day they might not be there." As he spoke, his eyes bore into mine lending gravity to the situation that the words alone could not convey. What did he think Tom had told me? Was he trying to explain his behaviour during Tom's childhood?

This time, Tom had a firm grip on Lenny's arm. He pulled Lenny out of reception and into the car park. Lenny allowed himself to be manhandled out of the building but all the while kept looking back at me. I didn't know what he wanted from me. The encounter had left me feeling unsettled; even more unsettled than I had been feeling before.

I spotted the vending machine out of the corner of my eye. That's what I needed: sugar. Vast amounts of sugar to calm my nerves. I had some change in my pocket. Luckily, it was just enough money for the biggest, most highly calorific chocolate bar in the machine. I watched as the chocolate bar dropped into the delivery tray. I grabbed it and tore open its wrapper and stuffed a large gooey amount of it in my mouth. I glanced at the open lift door but rejected the idea of using it for one floor. Besides, I was consuming the best part of four hundred calories; I had better take the stairs.

I glanced at the coffee table as I entered my office. Damn, Tom had left his anxiety diary on the table. Oh never mind! I could return it to him next week. I'd actually wanted him to carry on completing it in the hopes it might unlock some more memories. I sank into my chair feeling unprofessional. I wasn't doing my job properly. This whole Glenn situation was messing up my life, in more ways than one. I glanced at today's text message from Leo:

*Are you sure you don't want me to stay at your house for a few days? On the sofa, of course.*

Sighing heavily, I text back.

*It's lovely of you to offer, but I can't ask you to do that.*

I hit send.

Leo had been great about the whole situation, but it wasn't how I had wanted our relationship to start. We'd had such a great first date; once we had got the misunderstanding out of the way. I'd wanted us to be a normal couple. I'd wanted our relationship to be carefree and fun for the first few months, at least. I hadn't wanted to be in fear for my life, and for him to feel that he needed to protect me every second of the day and night.

Ping. I glanced at his text:

*I don't mind. I want to.*

"Do you know what?" I said out loud to my phone, the coffee table, the empty chair opposite, and to the air in the room, "I'm sick of feeling like a victim. I'm sick of being afraid." I knew my voice was rising, but so was my anger and frustration at the situation I found myself in. "I'm sick of Glenn Froom and his affect on my life."

# Chapter 22

*Session four - Susan Mackintosh 11.30 a.m. - 12.30 p.m.*

As Susan walked in, she scanned the room as if expecting to see someone else there as well as me. Settling into the chair opposite, she asked, "Who's Glenn Froom?"

She'd caught me by surprise. I hadn't realised it was 11.30 a.m. already. She'd heard me ranting to myself. I wasn't painting a particularly professional image of myself today. I wasn't sure how to answer the question honestly without giving away details that I really didn't want to. My indecision must have shown on my face because she decided to take pity on me and not press me further.

"You know what, it doesn't matter. Dickie's definitely having an affair," she said, changing the subject with breakneck speed.

"You have proof?" I enquired.

"Well . . . not any hard evidence. But I did search his closet for the expensive trainers, iPod and iPad he bought recently and they're gone. In fact, I haven't seen the items since he bought them. That's suspicious. And I'll tell you what else is suspicious: he's started going out straight from the office. Last week, he went out three times straight from work. When he got home, he was exhausted. He's been going to bed earlier than usual. Now, why do you think that might be?" She raised her eyebrows expressively.

"Do you have a theory?" I asked, refusing to speculate on what her husband may or may not be up to.

"Well, it's obvious, isn't it? He's getting up to things with whomever he's seeing. Do I have to spell it out, Frankie? SEX. S-E-X." She paused between each letter for the maximum effect.

"If that's what you believe, then what happens next?"

Her whole body seemed to sag before me as if dragged down by the weight of the misery my question had inflicted. Even her eyes couldn't withstand the gravitational pull as they studied her shoes intently.

"I'm going to have to do something, aren't I?" she mumbled.

"There's always a choice. You don't have to do anything at all. You can choose to do nothing. But your husband's behaviour is so clearly affecting your happiness. If you do nothing, you may need to accept that you will continue to feel as you currently do."

Her head shot up. I could see in her eyes and hear in her voice a glimmer of hope as she said, "He might stop behaving this way."

I nodded. "He may, and if he does, can you forget your current suspicions?"

The glimmer of hope slowly faded from her eyes as she said, "No. It's hopeless. I have to tackle this, don't I?"

I sensed that she wanted me to collude with her. She wanted me to tell her that she didn't have to face this situation; that if she ignored it enough, it would all go away. But I wasn't going to collude with her like a friend might.

"I'm not going to tell you what to do. Only you can decide which course of action suits you best. I'm sensing that you want the whole situation to just go away."

She nodded vehemently.

"And yet, you've just acknowledged that if your husband stopped behaving the way he has recently and returned to normal, you still wouldn't be able to forget your suspicions."

"I might . . ."

"OK, but what if his behaviour doesn't change?"

"I can't stand it, Frankie. It's like I want to know and I don't, all at the same time."

"I can understand that."

"I'm going to have to be brave. There's no point in asking him. He won't admit it. I'm going to have to follow him."

"If you follow him and you discover, you are in fact right, he is having an affair. What then?"

"I kill him," she said matter-of-factly, her face not registering a single emotion.

"I'm going to assume you're joking," I said, even though she really didn't look like she was joking, but it was an expression almost everyone banded about when upset.

"You assume what you like."

"I meant practically speaking: living arrangements, finances et cetera."

"Surely, that's my business," she said, her demeanour suddenly haughty.

"It is. I'm not asking for details. I'm just trying to ensure that you've thought the consequences of your actions through. I want to make sure you are as emotionally and practically prepared for the fallout of your actions as possible."

Her demeanour visibly softened as she realised with every word I uttered that I was only thinking of her wellbeing, and not questioning her ability to cope.

"I'll have to go back to Daddy."

"Sorry?" I didn't understand what she meant.

"In answer to your question, how would I cope practically if he was having an affair? I'd have to move back in with Daddy."

"Oh I see."

"Of course, that would just be another thing Daddy could say I failed at."

I observed her as she spoke; her dejection was clear to see.

"What other things might he say you failed at?" I probed.

"Ha, everything!" she said flippantly and then thought better of it. "No, that was silly of me. Daddy loves me very much."

I couldn't decide if that last comment was intended to convince me or her.

"He does," she said, nodding all the while. "It's just; I can be a bit . . . what's the word? Interfering, yes, that's the word. I sometimes don't know when to keep my mouth shut. Take last week's meeting for instance. It was my reason for cutting short last week's session. Do you remember?" she asked, as her eyes met mine with the same question in them as her voice had just uttered.

I nodded and smiled.

"Well, Daddy had wanted me at the meeting. I really should have remembered to keep my mouth shut. I'm there to, how can I put it, look pretty and smile I suppose. 'Butter the old guys up' as Daddy would say."

Despite it being a clearly sexist, old-fashioned way of doing business, I was more surprised by her blind acceptance of her role in her father's business dealings. This was the twenty-first century, wasn't it?

"Are you happy with your role?" I asked.

She shrugged as if it were a ludicrous question, and one she had clearly never asked herself before.

"Why wouldn't I be?"

It wasn't my place to impose my feelings on the subject of women's equality upon her. If she was happy to be objectified by men, then that was entirely her right. I decided it would be best if I didn't answer her question.

Instead, I said, "You mentioned the fact that you should have kept your mouth shut during the meeting," my tone inviting her to expand on her previous comment.

"Yes, Daddy was furious with me."

"Oh?"

"Daddy was meeting with two important clients. There's a new contract in the pipeline, and it was what I call a 'keep them happy lunch'. You know the kind of thing: they can order what they want from the menu and drink the most expensive wine, and Daddy picks up the tab. It's what you might call a sweetener."

"I get the idea."

She nodded and continued, "I tend not to drink too much at these kinds of things. It wouldn't do to get drunk and embarrass Daddy, now would it?" she questioned, raising her eyebrows in expectation of a response.

I shook my head.

Satisfied she continued, "Daddy and the clients were talking shop throughout the lunch. As you can imagine, I have heard a lot of conversations about the business over the years. I listen; I'm interested, always have been."

"You aren't employed by your father?"

"No. He doesn't think it would suit me."

"What do you think?"

"Umm . . . I don't really think about it."

"Sorry, I interrupted you. Please go on," I invited.

"Well, it was silly of me really. I spoke without thinking. It was just that the clients were discussing an issue they had with the proposed future contract. They didn't want to commit to the full three-year deal upfront.

"I merely commented that it was actually more cost-effective for them to sign a three-year deal than a one-year deal. When they asked why, I simply explained that the price for the three-year deal was fixed at today's prices. So they were immune to cost of living and inflationary increases. However, if they wanted to sign year on year, then they risked the prices increasing each year."

"A salient point," I commented and watched the impact of my words on her as first her mouth opened in surprise then curved into a smile of pleasure.

"Do you think so?" she asked.

"I do. But more importantly, did your father's clients?"

"They commented that a one-year contract would allow them to shop around for a better deal from our competitors. To which I pointed out that we prided ourselves on our competitiveness on price. We won't be beaten on price. I also suggested that the lengthy process of procurement and contract negotiation was expensive and time-consuming for everyone involved.

"By shopping around each year for a new supplier, they would be incurring the associated costs three times during the three-year period rather than once. In the end, they would spend more than they would save."

I was impressed. Susan clearly had a head for business.

"It sounds as if you made some excellent points."

"I thought so," she said.

"What happened?" I asked.

"They said they needed to think about it. Once they'd left, Daddy was furious with me. He told me I had no right to open my mouth, and that if he lost the contract because of me he'd . . ." She stopped and wiped a stray tear from her eye. She was clearly upset.

"He'd what?"

"Oh, I don't know. He didn't finish the sentence. He got up and stormed out of the restaurant."

"Out of interest, did your father explain how he was going to handle the situation had you not said what you did?"

"No, he didn't. He hasn't spoken to me since."

"He hasn't spoken to you in a week?"

"That's right. It's not the first time; I'm sure it won't be the last," she said in such a way as to indicate she was resigned to her fate.

"Do you think your behaviour at the meeting warranted your father's reaction?" I asked.

"Um . . . uh . . . I've never really considered that before. I'm used to the way he is with me, I guess."

"The way he is with you? Is he that way with anyone else?"

"No, he's only that way with me. Well, I've never seen him that way with anyone else. Whenever I disappoint him, he stops talking to me. I sometimes wonder if he was like that with my mother," she mused aloud.

This was the first time she'd mentioned her mother.

"Have you asked her?" I ventured.

Her eyes widened at the question as if it were absurd. "I can't. My mother left us when I was a little girl. She hasn't contacted me since. I barely remember her."

I felt for her. It must have been tough growing up without her mother around. Some of what I was feeling must have shown on my face because she started to shake her head at me.

"Don't feel sorry for me, Frankie. I had Daddy. He was really all I ever needed. I'm lucky to have him."

"And he's lucky to have you," I said.

"Hmm, I'm not so sure about that. You see, my mother left because of me."

"Children often blame themselves when their parents split up, but it isn't their fault. They're just children," I countered.

"I understand what you mean, but she really did leave because of me. Daddy told me that she left because she couldn't handle being a mother. She wasn't maternal and wanted to be free of me."

I studied her face as she spoke. She could have been telling me about the weather, or what she'd watched on television last night such was her air of normality. She was completely accepting of what her father had told her. She didn't appear to be hurt by it. And yet, how could anyone fail to be hurt by their mother's rejection at such a young age?

"When Daddy's angry with me, he says I remind him of her."

I could see that the thought of her father's displeasure clearly upset her as the tears were back in her eyes.

"I have a picture of her. Would you like to see it?" she offered, at the same time as reaching for her handbag.

The fact that she carried a picture of her mother would suggest she had some feelings for her.

"I'd love to," I said, sitting forward in my chair in anticipation.

She reached into her bag and pulled out an old photograph from her purse that she passed across to me.

An attractive young lady smiled back at me. She was approximately twenty-five years old and wore a tight-fitting, bright orange top with big yellow flowers on it. Her auburn hair had a centre parting and was so long that it reached down past her shoulders and beyond the bottom of the photograph. Her twinkly green eyes were further enhanced by a mass of jade green eye shadow that seemed to extend from her eyelid all the way up to her eyebrow in one solid block. This photograph had to have been taken in the seventies. I couldn't remember such a clash of colours considered cool in any other decade.

Thoughts of the conversation I'd had with Maria about the photograph I'd received from Glenn filled my mind. She'd called me on Friday evening wanting to hear all the juicy gossip about my date with Leo. But instead of a humorous recount of the night's antics, what she'd actually got was a sobbing wreck on the end of the phone.

Poor Maria, she hadn't known how to react initially. I was incoherent. At first, she'd assumed I was crying because the date had been a disaster. It took me a full five minutes to articulate that the date had been good, but that Glenn had sent me a photograph of myself and the children taken outside of my house. Once she understood the situation, she had been her usual calming influence.

"You can't be sure it's from Glenn."

"Who else could it be?" I'd demanded.

"I'm not sure. Have you upset anyone lately? Hang on, what about the old lady next door? Didn't she wreck your garden over a dispute regarding her cat?" she recalled.

"I hadn't considered that it might be Peggy. But why would Peggy take a photograph of the three of us and post it through the door? That doesn't make any sense. No, it has to be Glenn. It's his way of warning me that he knows where I live, and he's watching me."

"Maybe, or maybe not. What are the police doing about it?" she asked, concerned for my and the Pant Bros' welfare.

"Huh . . . what can they do? DC Smithers checked Glenn's finances again and . . ."

"Did they find any activity?" Maria asked interrupting what I'd been about to say, her voice rising with anxiety for my welfare.

"No. But like I said to them, he could have a new identity by now."

"Hmm, true," she said and sounded as perturbed at the idea as I was.

"You're a good friend, Maria. I'm sorry to have blubbed down the phone at you," I apologised.

"Oh that's perfectly OK. What are friends for! I feel bad that I'll be thousands of miles away soon, but still I'll only be a phone call away. You haven't forgotten the leaving party?"

"No," I sighed. "I haven't forgotten the party. I'll be there. I wish you weren't going. What am I going to do without you?"

"You won't survive," she said and chuckled.

"Exactly! I won't!"

"Frankie, can I have it back please?" Susan asked, her voice cutting through my thoughts.

I was brought sharply back to the present. Susan was sitting forward in her chair with her arm outstretched and her hand open expectantly.

"Yes, of course." I handed the photograph of her mother back to her. I watched as she restored it safely to its previous home within her purse. "You look like your mother," I said, recalling I'd been struck by the resemblance.

"Oh don't say that. Daddy doesn't like it when people say that."

"Do you think you look like your mother?" I persisted.

"Yes, I do," she said, guilt etched into her face. Her need to be honest appeared stronger, in this moment, than her need to please her father.

"You feel guilty about admitting that?"

She nodded. "I never admit that I think I look like her in front of Daddy. I don't want to upset him. He dislikes her so. I don't want to remind him of her in case . . ." She left the sentence unfinished.

I watched as she bit the corner of her bottom lip. She was clearly agitated.

"In case . . . ?" I persevered.

She took a deep breath, "In case he decides to dislike me too."

"Even though you may resemble your mother, you're his daughter, not his ex-wife. It's a different relationship entirely."

"I know. But he blames me."

"Blames you for what?"

"For my mother leaving."

"Has he actually said that?" I asked.

"Yes, on many occasions. No matter how hard I try, I can't seem to . . ." Once again, she stopped mid-sentence. She made much of consulting her watch.

I realised that I'd been so distracted by my own life today and its complications that for the first time since meeting her I hadn't taken note of what she was wearing. I hadn't even noticed the bubble of pungent perfume surrounding her.

She looked her usual immaculate self. I sniffed the air and registered the fact that it was the same perfume she had worn for the last three weeks.

"Frankie, this isn't like you," she said, surprise mingled with mild rebuke in her tone.

"What isn't?" I asked.

"We've gone over the hour," she said, pointing at her watch.

My eyes shot to my own watch. I couldn't believe it. We had indeed exceeded the hour by five minutes no less.

"I'm so sorry to have kept you," I offered.

"Oh, it isn't a problem. I'm just surprised, that's all. You're usually so punctual. Are you sure you're OK? You don't seem your usual self."

"I'm fine, really. I'd better let you go," I said as I got to my feet.

"See you next week."

"Yes," I said sounding surer than I felt.

I watched Susan close the office door behind her before flopping back into my seat.

After my performance today, I needed to seriously consider recommending Tom and Susan see Rebecca from now on. I'd call Rebecca first and check whether she could fit them in, before I mooted the subject with them.

I fumbled in my bag for my mobile phone. I had a missed call. My heart fluttered momentarily with dread until I realised the missed call was from ASF Technologies' CEO, Michael Graham. I hadn't heard from him in a while. Not since he rang to say he'd recommended me to a friend of his, Richard Sullivan. He'd left a voicemail. I was curious.

"Hi, Frankie, it's Michael Graham." From just those few words, I noted that he didn't sound his usual confident self. "Um . . . uh . . . do you think you could call me back please, as soon as possible? It's about Richard. Richard Sullivan. Call me back."

Well that was a curious message. Why did he want to talk to me about Richard Sullivan? I'd only known Richard in a professional capacity, so I couldn't discuss him with Michael. It would have to be a one-sided conversation. I'd call him later.

# Chapter 23

"Oh damn," I said out loud and to no one in particular. After Susan left, I checked my diary. I had a dentist's appointment at 3.20 p.m. today. What on earth had possessed me to book it at that time? I couldn't pick Alex and Henry up from school and still make it to my appointment. I'd been dropping them off and picking them up from school since last Friday.

Alex was being decidedly sullen about this turn in events. He didn't like having his independence curtailed. I had decided not to tell the Pant Bros about the photograph. Instead, I made the attempted child abduction in the area my reason for hiking up their personal security detail. If they knew about the photograph, they'd be frightened and concerned for my welfare. I'd rather they thought I was being an overprotective mother. I would take Alex's moody silences and dirty looks over fear and concern for me any day of the week.

I knew the dentist would charge me ten pounds for a missed appointment if I didn't show up. It wasn't a huge amount of money; still I didn't want to have to pay it if I didn't have to. I knew Mum couldn't help me out. She'd told me she was shopping with a friend in Bath today. All right for some, I thought. I would have to take a chance on Rob. He worked from home on Tuesdays, so he may be able to nip out and get them, fingers crossed.

Rob's phone went straight to voicemail. Not a good sign. Oh well, here goes nothing.

"Rob, it's Frankie. I need a favour. I'd forgotten I have a dentist's appointment at 3.20 p.m. today. It means that I can't pick up the boys and get to the appointment. I was wondering if you might be able to pick them up. If you can't, I'll have to miss the appointment. Oh and while I think of it, I want to talk to you about the presents you've been buying Alex lately."

I glanced at my watch. It was 1.00 p.m. I'd give him until 2.30 p.m. to reply. If he hadn't, then I'd assume he couldn't pick them up and cancel the appointment. I decided that I may as well go home for a couple of hours. There was nothing left for me to do in the office.

After today's sessions, I'd decided it was best if Tom and Susan saw another counsellor. Rebecca's line had been engaged when I called her twenty minutes ago to ask if she could take on my clients. I'd call her again later. I wanted to be able to offer them an alternative counsellor when I called them to say I wouldn't be seeing them any more.

The question Rob asked me after I'd told him about the photograph popped into my head: 'Do you think it's time you thought about another profession?' He'd questioned my choice of profession on numerous occasions over the years, usually in anger, and each time I'd bristled and argued in favour of counselling. There was something different about this time. He wasn't angry; he hadn't raised his voice. It was quite the contrary: he was calm, rational and worried for both my and the Pant Bros' welfare. They were his children too.

I could see the situation from Rob's point of view. What had happened to me last year had impacted upon the boys. Not only had they had to move home, schools and go through the emotional upheaval that entailed, but they'd almost lost me to a murderous maniac. I wasn't even sure Alex was coping with the aftermath of it. Come to think of it, I wasn't sure I was. I conceded that it might be time to consider whether I should continue counselling people.

Rob believed this latest threat to my safety was linked to one of my clients, either past or present. He wasn't as convinced as I was that Glenn was responsible. He was concerned about what the picture meant. He'd asked me what the police were doing about it. I'd explained what DC Smithers had done, and how he'd drawn a blank on the financial checks he'd had carried out on Glenn Froom.

Rob had wholeheartedly agreed with me that the boys should be dropped off and picked up from school. I'd explained my do-it-yourself surveillance equipment inside the house; he had been impressed. When I'd explained that I had the baseball bat he'd given to me by the side of the bed, he'd offered to get me another to keep by the front door. I'd surprised myself by accepting his offer. He'd dropped the additional bat off on Sunday. I hid it behind the coats in the hallway, so that the Pant Bros wouldn't notice and start questioning me about its arrival.

I looked at my watch. It was 1.10 p.m. Only ten minutes since the last time I'd checked. I had hoped it would be later. I was avoiding going home, and I knew it. I tapped the surveillance app on my phone. I could see both the hallway of my house and the kitchen as I'd expected. I hadn't received any alerts. So that meant no one had activated the cameras by entering the house. I was safe to go home.

I walked over to the office window and scanned the car park. I was particularly interested in anyone sitting in their car. Nope. No one. Satisfied, I scrutinised the faces of every cafe patron I could see from my current vantage point; there was no one I recognised. I turned to gather my things and lock up for the day.

I found myself checking the backseat of my car before getting in. I'd seen too many movies where the heroine's driving along, with not a care in the world, and some psychopathic killer pops up from the back seat with a long jagged knife in his or her hand. I shuddered. Frankie, you really aren't helping yourself here.

I got in my car and immediately locked the doors. It wouldn't do for Glenn to suddenly appear from nowhere and get in my car while I waited at traffic lights or was stationary at a junction. I sounded paranoid to my own ears, but still, the doors remained locked.

I glanced at every pedestrian I passed on the way home as well as every driver going in the opposite direction. I was looking for Glenn. As I pulled up outside my home, I reached for my phone. Rob had sent me a text message. I'd read it once I got in the house. One final look at the surveillance camera footage reassured me that I was safe to enter my home.

I visually checked the vicinity before I got out of the car. I had my house keys at the ready. After quickly letting myself in, I immediately locked the door behind me. I walked through the hallway to the kitchen switching off the mobile phones aka surveillance cameras as I went. I'd switch them on again when I left for the dentist's surgery.

Switching the kettle on for a calming cuppa; I read Rob's message:

*I can pick them up. I'll drop them back to your house around 6.00 p.m.*

That was great. Why hadn't he commented on the presents? Oh never mind. I'd tackle him about it when he dropped the Pant Bros off later.

While I waited for the kettle to boil, I walked over to the back door and tried the door handle. Yep, it was locked as it should be. Every fibre of my mind and body were on high alert and had been since last Thursday night. I was exhausted in every possible sense of the word.

I didn't know how much more of this I could take. One half of me was ready to fight, and willing Glenn to appear and get it over with. The other half of me was hiding: crouched in a dark corner with my fingers in my ears, and my head buried in my knees, never wanting to be found.

I made the tea and sat at the breakfast bar. I couldn't relax enough to do anything other than stare out of the window. I knew what I was doing. I was watching and waiting for him to appear.

Eventually, the seconds, minutes and then hours passed. Finally, it was time for me to escape my house and go to the dentist's. I hauled myself to my feet, which were suddenly leaden. Careful to remember to switch the surveillance cameras back on, I checked the back door one final time and made for the living room. I stood and stared out of the window for a few minutes. There was no one around. I left the house as swiftly as I had entered it and got into my car.

I heard the familiar ping of a text message. It was from Rob.

*BTW what presents? I haven't bought Alex any presents.*

I was confused by his response. Or, perhaps, he was confused by my comment. Maybe he didn't think of the trainers and iPod as presents. Well, what else would you call them? I decided to be specific:

*The expensive trainers and iPod you bought him.*

He responded almost immediately:

*I didn't buy them.*

I was confused. If he didn't buy them, then who did? My brain just didn't have the spare capacity to think about this right now. I had to get to my appointment, but we would definitely all be discussing this later.

*****

I was sitting in the dentist's chair, a long-handled mirror stuffed into my wide-open mouth together with what felt like the fingers of both of the dentist's hands, when I heard my mobile phone ringing.

It would have to wait. By the time the dentist extricated his hands and implements from my mouth, I warranted it would have stopped ringing anyway. Sure enough, it stopped but then immediately started again.

"Do you need to get that, Ms Wilson?" the dentist asked.

I nodded because verbalising my response wasn't an option.

The dentist withdrew his hands, implements and himself to the other side of the room to update my dental records while I grabbed my phone from my handbag.

"Sorry about this," I gabbled to his back. It was Rob calling. "What?" I snapped. "I'm at the dentist's."

"He's not here," he said. I'd never heard Rob's voice contain such fear. "I've turned up to pick him up, and he's not here."

My heart immediately felt the impact of the situation. It crashed into my rib cage with every supercharged beat. The sound of each beat filling my ears. A myriad of thoughts whirled around in my head; each crashing into the other in my brain's attempt to make sense of what Rob had just said.

Alex wasn't at school. Could he simply have walked home on his own? No, I'd told him not to. He'd been told to wait at school to be picked up. Was he being held up by a teacher? Or was there a more sinister explanation? Had Alex been taken? As soon as I allowed the idea to penetrate my consciousness, I made the connection between Alex's unexplained absence from school and the recent presents he'd received. The presents I'd thought were from Rob, but that I'd just learned weren't. Could Glenn have given them to Alex? No, surely not. Well he couldn't have given them to him in person because Alex knew what Glenn looked like. He'd seen his picture on the news and in newspapers.

Had Glenn somehow befriended my son? If so, how? Then it hit me: Alex's closed bedroom door of late. The conversations I could hear through the door. Glenn had befriended him online. He must have been pretending to be someone else, probably a boy of Alex's age. Alex knew about Internet safety; he knew not to chat to strangers. But Glenn was clever. Somehow, he'd got close enough to Alex to enable him to snatch him from school.

How could I have been so blind? Unfortunately, I could answer my question with little soul-searching. Because I've become so self-obsessed, that's how.

For the last year everything had been about me and my obsession with Glenn. I hadn't taken enough interest in my children, and what they were up to. I hadn't kept them safe. I'd noticed the warning signs, but I hadn't asked enough questions. I had allowed my concerns for my own welfare to get in the way of taking care of my children. What kind of a mother was I? I didn't want to answer the question. I already knew.

I could hear Rob speaking, but I wasn't processing what he was saying. Finally, I found my voice.

"What was that you said?" I asked surprised at how normal my voice sounded.

"I said you haven't forgotten that he was meant to be going to a friend's house for tea or something similar?" he asked, sounding hopeful that there could be some innocent explanation for our son's absence.

Alex hadn't visited a friend's house for tea in years. He was fourteen. They hung out; they didn't have tea. Rob was seriously out of touch, I thought.

"No, Alex wouldn't go to a friend's for tea. And besides, as far as I'm aware, he still hasn't made any real friends at that school yet."

"I'm not talking about Alex. He's here with me. It's Henry. Henry's not here."

"H-E-N-R-Y," I repeated in disbelief, "not there? I thought you had meant Alex." It simply didn't make any sense. "Have you spoken to the teacher? Perhaps he's hiding in the toilets. He might be, if he's been particularly naughty today."

"I've spoken to the teacher. She said she let him out with the others."

I didn't understand, "Didn't you see him come out of his classroom?"

"That's the thing; I was a few minutes late arriving to pick him up."

I could hear the guilt in his voice, and my only thought was that if anything had happened to Henry, I would kill Rob. I'd put my hands around his throat and throttle him. It was hardly fair of me considering it was my doing that a murderous maniac had entered our lives. But I wasn't feeling fair and balanced in this moment.

"So you didn't see him come out?" I asked, aware that my words were loaded with accusation.

"No, but I went to his classroom. The teacher said he'd left. She had assumed he'd left with you."

"Well he didn't!" I said, my voice rising to such an alarming level that the dentist turned around and stared at me with concern. "Check the toilets, Rob. Now!" I commanded.

"I am. I am. Wait a second."

I could hear him breathing heavily as I pictured him running across the playground to the toilets. I sat on the edge of the dentist's chair while I waited what felt like hours, but in reality was only seconds, for his reply.

The dentist cleared his throat as if to get my attention. I glanced in his direction.

"Everything all right?" he asked.

"No, I'm going to have to leave." I jumped to my feet and grabbed my bag. All the while keeping my phone glued to my ear. I grabbed the door handle and yanked the door open. I was in the street in seconds.

"He's not in the toilets, Frankie. Where is he? Where is he?"

Rob was losing it. I could hear it in his voice. Rather than join him in his panic, something about his loss of control insisted that I not do the same. Suddenly, my thinking was calm and rational.

"Right, speak to the teacher and ask that everyone still in the school search every classroom. Are there any parents still in the playground?"

"Umm . . . uh . . . a few," he responded.

"Go and talk to them. Tell them you're Henry's dad, and ask if they saw him come out of the classroom at home time. Ask their children too," I added as an afterthought.

Rob was silent.

"NOW, Rob!" I barked, "you need to do it now, before they leave."

My words seemed to jolt him into action.

"I'm on it," he said.

"I'm on my way. I'll be there in less than five minutes."

I sprinted to my car and was pulling up outside the school in no time at all. I ran into the playground looking wildly around me for Henry's smiling face, to no avail. I hurtled toward his classroom. Rob saw me coming and opened the door for me.

"Well?" I asked the question but already knew the answer. It was obvious from the grave expression on each of their faces.

Henry's teacher, Miss Hancock, stood next to Alex with her hand on his shoulder. I could only assume that she was attempting to comfort him. I zeroed in on Alex's face; I was searching for signs of distress. He was biting his lip and was close to tears. It was unlike him to openly show emotion especially in public.

Something in my mind shied away from his fear and concern. I couldn't worry about him right now. I had to focus on finding Henry and to do that I had to remain calm.

"We've searched the whole building. He isn't here," Rob said, shaking his head in defeat.

"Did you speak to any parents?" I asked, pushing past my mounting desperation.

"There were only a few left, but they said they didn't remember seeing him."

A name popped into my mind: Max.

"Miss Hancock," I said.

"Uh . . . yes?" she stuttered.

Her concern was evident as I watched her bite the side of her lip. She appeared incapable of standing still as I observed her hop from one foot to the other.

"Could Henry have left with, his new friend, Max?" I asked.

Miss Hancock's expression changed from worried to bemused. "Max?" she asked.

I was getting impatient. It was a simple question, or so I had thought. I knew my impatience was reflected in my tone as I said, "Yes, Max!"

She shook her head. "I'm sorry, but I don't have a Max in this class."

I frowned. "Well, is there a Max in any of the other classes? He's new to the school, so perhaps you don't know him."

"We haven't had any new children join the school recently. But if you wait a moment, I'll check with Mr Jones, the head teacher." She rushed from the room.

"Henry, where are you?" I said out loud as if he could hear me. I wanted him to spring out from some hiding place and shout, 'here I am' as if he were simply playing a game of hide and seek. Oh please, let it be some silly schoolboy prank. Please!

Miss Hancock returned to the classroom accompanied by Mr Jones.

He spoke first, "Ms Wilson, this is an unfortunate situation. Hopefully, it's just some sort of misunderstanding. Miss Hancock tells me you want to know about a boy called Max. Is that correct?"

"Yes," I said.

"I'm afraid that we don't have a boy in the school called Max. We haven't had any new children transfer from another school in the last six months."

An idea suddenly occurred to me. "What about a little girl called Max? Maybe Max is short for Maxine."

Both teachers shook their heads.

"Frankie, who is Max?" Rob asked.

"Henry's been playing with him online a lot lately. I was sure that he'd said he was a new boy at school." But now I wasn't so sure. Had he told me that? Or had I assumed it? Did I actually ask him who Max was? Oh God, I'd been so distracted lately. I thought that I had my children's online safety all worked out. I thought that I was tech savvy. I was supposed to be a responsible parent; one who only allowed my youngest son to play online in the kitchen because I could keep an eye on what he was doing and who he was doing it with. Only I'd failed to do just that.

"Well he isn't," Rob said, stating the obvious.

"Could Max be one of those men who pretend to be a kid, so he can . . ." Alex paused, unable to put his fears into words. Instead he continued, "Do you think he might have something to do with Henry's disappearance?" Alex visibly shuddered as he uttered the words. "Do you think that, whoever this Max is, he's taken Henry?" Alex asked.

"Whoa, hang on, Alex, that's quite a leap. Just because we don't know who Max is, at present, it doesn't mean Max is an adult and that Henry's been abducted by him. There still could be an innocent explanation," Rob said.

Rob's words were both logical and sensible. But after having scanned the faces surrounding me, I could tell that no one believed them, including me.

Alex's words had brought the photograph sharply back into focus in my mind. It had been of all three of us. I had been in the forefront of the photograph and Alex and Henry in the background. I'd assumed the main threat was to my wellbeing, but what if Glenn had decided to get to me through my children? What if Glenn had been masquerading as Max online? Suddenly, I was convinced that Glenn had befriended Henry and had now taken him.

"Glenn!" I said, as I stared straight into Rob's eyes. I saw the exact moment that he comprehended the full meaning of my single word explanation for the situation we found ourselves in.

"I'm calling the police," Rob said.

Up to now Rob had argued Glenn was dead, but he wasn't willing to bet his son's safety on it, and for that I was grateful.

"Hello, I'd like to report a missing child. My son has gone missing from school. He's ten years old," he said to the emergency call handler. There was a pause as he listened to whatever was being said at the other end and then he responded with, "No, this is out of character. He has never runaway before. He is around five feet tall, slim with brown hair . . ."

I listened as Rob proceeded to give a description of our son to whoever was on the other end of the phone. Was this really happening? This kind of thing happened to other people. Didn't it?

"Frankie, they need a current picture of Henry that they can circulate to all the police patrols in the area. Have you got one on your phone?" Rob asked while the call handler waited patiently on the other end of the line.

I scrabbled for my phone and proceeded to swipe through each of the photographs I'd stored on it until I came across a recent photograph of Henry. He was beaming at the camera with not a care in the world. Tears stung my eyes as I said, "Yes, I have one. It was only taken a month or so ago. Where do I send it?"

"Hang on. I'll find out," he said returning his attention to the call handler.

Henry had only been missing for thirty minutes, and yet it felt like days. If his absence already felt like an eternity, what would it feel like if he was actually missing for days? I rejected that thought. I didn't just reject it; I grabbed it and threw it kicking and screaming out of my consciousness. For if I allowed it to fester, I feared I'd lose my mind. And if that happened, what help would I be to Henry then?

# Chapter 24

The call handler confirmed receipt of Henry's photograph and assured us it would be distributed to all officers immediately. I couldn't stand there waiting for the police to arrive for a moment longer. I had to do something. I set about searching the school, properly. I marched around yanking open every classroom door and peering under every desk. I checked each cupboard in turn and examined its contents in the hopes that Henry would leap out from behind a pile of books and yell, 'surprise'. He didn't. I inspected the staff room and the office. He wasn't there.

Rob came to find me, "The call handler suggested that someone check he hasn't wandered home on his own."

My spirits momentarily rallied as I imagined him standing at the front door waiting for me to arrive home to let him in. He'd never walked home from school on his own before, and it wasn't something we'd arranged. But perhaps a sudden need for independence had exerted itself. God, I hoped so.

"I thought that I'd go and check while you wait for the police to arrive. Is that OK with you?" he asked.

"Yes, yes. You go. Ring me the moment you get there," I said.

"Of course," he said. He paused momentarily to put a comforting hand on my shoulder.

I squeezed my eyes shut as the emotion of what was happening threatened to overwhelm me. If that happened, I knew I would be useless to Henry. I would be a screaming, blubbering wreck.

Putting my hand over Rob's fleetingly I said, "I know you mean well, but I'm just about holding it together. Please don't try to comfort me, or I might shatter into a million pieces."

He nodded and said nothing as he walked away from me and toward his car.

"Mum, should I go with Dad?" Alex asked looking as helpless as I felt.

"Yes, good idea. Go and catch him up."

Alex sped off in his dad's direction.

I could see Miss Hancock and Mr Jones in Henry's classroom. They were sitting on the children's desks; neither saying a word but both looking extremely worried. The concern that I could see in their faces only served to panic me further. I turned away. Grabbing my phone from my handbag I sent a text to all my contacts:

*Urgent—Have you seen Henry in the last thirty minutes? Please let me know immediately.*

My mobile started to ring. It was Mum calling. I wanted to speak to her and I didn't, all at the same time. I didn't want to have to manage her feelings as well as my own. I didn't want to hear the panic in her voice. But I couldn't let her sit and wonder what was going on either. That would be too cruel of me.

"Mum."

"Frankie, what's going on? Why do you want to know if I've seen Henry in the last thirty minutes? Is he missing?" she asked, her voice rising with alarm.

I took a deep breath and steeled myself to say the words aloud, "Yes, Henry is missing." I heard my mum gasp. "Rob arrived at the school to collect him, and he wasn't there. Miss Hancock remembers him leaving the classroom at home time, but she didn't see who he left with. We've searched the school grounds. He isn't here. The police are on their way . . ." I let my words trail off. I didn't want to say anything else. I didn't want to voice my fears to Mum.

"Is there anything I can do?" she asked with desperation in her voice.

"No . . . actually," a thought had occurred to me, "can you come over and be with Alex. It would help if I knew he was being looked after. Then Rob and I can focus on finding Henry."

"Of course! It might take me a little while to get there because I'm in Bath, but I'm on my way."

Oh damn, I'd forgotten she was having a shopping day with her friend. I was ruining it.

"Oh, Mum, I'm sorry. I forgot it's your day out."

"Don't worry about that. This is far more important than some silly shopping. I'm on my way," and she hung up.

The phone immediately rang again.

"Is everything OK?" Maria asked.

"No, Henry's missing," I said, choosing to get straight to the point.

"Oh my God! Is there anything I can do?"

"Not at the moment. The police are on their way."

"I'm coming over," she insisted.

"But aren't you at work?" I asked.

"I've got the day off. I won't get in the way, I promise. I can help look for him. I'll be there in twenty minutes," she said, and before I could respond, she'd hung up.

She was a good friend. I'd miss her when she left for Australia.

"The police have arrived, Ms Wilson," said Miss Hancock hovering in the doorway of the office. She stood to one side to reveal two policemen standing directly behind her.

"Ms Wilson?" the taller of the two asked.

"Yes."

"I'm PC Brownley. I need to ask you some questions."

*****

I glanced at my watch for the hundredth time since Rob had called me to let me know Henry was missing. It was 4.30 p.m. Henry had been missing precisely seventy-five minutes, and I felt as if I'd aged seventy-five years. I was standing in my living room peering out at the street while PC Brownley spoke to Rob. He didn't look much older than Alex. What was it they said about getting older? You know you're getting old when the policemen start looking younger. Yes, that was it. Well I wasn't that old; I was only thirty-six.

Rob had called me while I was still at the school and confirmed that Henry wasn't at home. At that moment, my flicker of hope that Henry might have walked home alone had been extinguished.

PC Brownley had informed us that they had every available officer scouring the local streets and parks looking for Henry. He'd asked me if I could think of anywhere Henry might go after school—a favourite place. There was nowhere I could think of specifically. He'd asked me to contact everyone that knew Henry in the hopes they may have seen him. I informed him I'd already text everyone I knew and had been checking my phone for responses every five minutes since. So far, no one had seen him.

I understood why he was asking me these questions, but I needed him to understand that it was my belief that my son had been taken by Glenn Froom. I'd suggested that he let DC Smithers know my son was missing and who I thought had taken him, but he appeared to be unsure of the merits of such a suggestion. So I had called DC Smithers myself. Unfortunately, my call had gone straight to voicemail. I had left a message asking him to call me back urgently.

I became aware of PC Brownley asking Rob if he could think of anywhere Henry might go. The question angered me. Henry hadn't run off! He'd been taken. When was he going to get that into his head?

Maria's car was pulling up outside. All of a sudden, I felt a massive urge to get out of the house. I shouldn't be standing here doing nothing. I should be out there searching for Henry.

Before Maria had even managed to fully emerge from her car, I was standing beside her. She reached for me and enveloped me in a big hug. I was holding on to her for dear life. I wanted to scream and shout, but I didn't. I pulled back from her and simply said, "Thanks for coming."

"Don't be silly. What are friends for! So, what's happening? Do you need me to . . ." she said before being interrupted.

"What's going on? Why is there a police car here?" Peggy asked.

I hadn't noticed her approaching us.

"Henry's gone missing, Peggy. I don't suppose you've seen him?" I said, my heart jumping in my chest at the slim possibility that she had.

She shook her head. "No, I haven't seen him. Oh dear! My Harold went missing once." She frowned and patted my hand as if to offer comfort. "I can remember how it feels."

Harold must be her son, I thought. He must have been found because he visited her occasionally. I took some comfort from that, but then I'd warrant he hadn't been taken by a murderer.

"Is Harold your son?" I asked.

She nodded. "He was missing for three hours. They were the longest hours of my life."

I empathised with her. I just wanted it all to end. I wanted Henry back. Would I wake up in a minute? Please let this be a bad dream.

"What happened?" Maria asked.

"Oh," she chuckled, "he'd gone to the park with his friends. He knew he wasn't allowed, but he'd decided to ignore me and do it anyway. I lathered him when he got home. He didn't do that again, I can tell you."

She had a stonelike expression on her face. In that moment, I was more than prepared to believe she had 'lathered' her son as she put it. Perhaps that was why he didn't visit as often as she would like.

"Anyway, I'll let you get on with the search for him. If I see him, I'll let you know," she said already turning away toward her house.

"Thanks, Peggy," I said to her retreating back.

She stopped halfway up her path as if something had just occurred to her. Half-turning she gave Maria an odd look and said, "It's good to see you two have sorted out your differences. You need your friends at times like these," and she shuffled back into her house and shut the door.

"What on earth did she mean by that?" I asked Maria.

She shrugged her shoulders and then she lifted her left hand to her ear and proceeded to rotate her index finger. "Mad old bat! As I was saying, before we were interrupted, do you need me to drive around looking for him?"

"That would be great, thanks, but . . ."

"But, what?" she questioned.

"I think Glenn has taken him."

"I thought you might," she said.

"Frankie," Rob called from the front door, "PC Brownley wants to talk to you again."

"Talk, that's all that policeman has done so far. Meanwhile, Henry is out there with HIM," I said, my temper flaring.

"I know what you think has happened, but I'm hoping there's a far less sinister explanation. To that end, I'm going to drive around the High Street and the Lake Grounds to see if I can find him. OK!" Maria stated firmly.

"OK!"

"Frankie?" Rob called impatiently.

"Yep, I'm coming."

I had my phone in my hand. At present, my phone and I were inseparable. I was living in the hopes that someone would ring or text with some news of Henry at any moment. My phone pinged. I couldn't resist checking my text messages before seeing what PC Brownley wanted. It was a text from Rebecca:

*What's up? Not too serious, I hope. Let me know. Do you need me to come over*?

A seemingly wild thought popped into my head while reading her text: Rebecca's new boyfriend, Sam. What did I actually know about him? Could Sam actually be Glenn? The more I considered it, the less of a wild thought it became.

I hadn't seen a picture of Sam. Rebecca had wanted to show me his picture on the dating website, but he'd already removed it. She'd thought it was because he was serious about her, but what if he didn't want me seeing it?

Rebecca had re-entered my life after the terrifying events of last year. So I wasn't sure that she would recall what Glenn looked like from the news coverage. Besides, if he was living close by, he must have altered his appearance in some way. Or else someone would have identified him by now. He could have targeted her specifically because she was my friend and business partner. The way she'd described his behaviour toward her had sounded too good to be true.

I was aware that there was a small part of my brain that remained rational and sensible and was appalled by my current reasoning. My current thoughts were completely paranoid, I realised. Why would he get close to Rebecca? To what end? He didn't need Rebecca in order to snatch Henry. Hmm, yes, my rational side was beginning to win the argument. Glenn wouldn't need to masquerade as Sam. I shook my head violently in an attempt to clear it. Get a grip, Frankie, this isn't helping.

I walked into the house. PC Brownley was sitting on the sofa waiting for me.

"We have checked the school video surveillance footage, and although we could identify Henry leaving his classroom; we couldn't see who he left the school with."

"Why couldn't you see who Henry left the school with?" I asked.

"It would seem that the camera that is usually trained upon the school gate has been repositioned, so that it now surveils a corner of the playground instead. The head teacher seemed to think it may have been unintentionally repositioned as a result of having been struck by a stray football or two."

Hmm, a plausible explanation, but I was inclined to believe a more sinister one.

"Or perhaps, someone, aka Glenn Froom, repositioned the camera in advance, so he wouldn't be seen taking my son," I stated.

"Ah . . . yes . . . Glenn Froom. I managed to have a word with DC Smithers." He paused, and I got the distinct impression he was thinking about how he should phrase his next comment.

"Just say it," I demanded.

He looked me straight in the eye and said, "Everything would suggest that Glenn Froom is dead." He rushed on before I could react. "We are currently searching for Henry and have every reason to believe he will be found safe and well. However, I do need to inform you that the more time that elapses without him being found would suggest the distinct possibility of foul-play."

I shuddered at the thought.

He continued. "We're in the process of posting Henry's image on various social media outlets in the hopes that a member of the public has seen him and can help us find him."

I nodded.

"Can I ask, Ms Wilson, is there anyone apart from Glenn Froom that might wish you or your family harm?"

I gave it a few moments thought. "Um, not that I can think of," I said, shaking my head.

"I understand you were involved in uncovering a kidnap and attempted fraud last year."

"Uh, yes, that's right. What are you getting at?" I asked. But before he could respond, I added, "Oh I see. You think it might be revenge. But all three of them are currently in prison," I stated. I watched his face as I spoke. He lifted an eyebrow. I knew that I was jumping to conclusions, but I really didn't care. "Do you think that they could have arranged for someone to grab Henry? Is that what you're implying?"

"Whoa, I'm not implying anything, Ms Wilson. DC Smithers filled me in on what happened to you last year. If you don't mind me saying, it was some heavy-duty stuff."

"Yes, it was a difficult time," I confirmed.

"You can say that again," Rob said with meaning.

I could hear the anger and frustration in his voice, but more than that I could hear his fear. He was frightened for Henry, and so was I.

"Give the question some more thought. If you think of anything, let me know," PC Brownley said before walking away to respond to a message coming over his radio.

"I'm going to drive around looking for him, Frankie. I can't just sit here and do nothing. I'm going out of my mind," Rob said.

"Good idea, I'll do the same," I said, at the same time as locating my car keys.

"One of you needs to stay here in case Henry returns," PC Brownley advised breaking off from the conversation he was having on his radio.

He'd clearly been listening to our conversation at the same time. It suddenly occurred to me that he might suspect us in our son's disappearance.

"Oh, yes, of course," I agreed and put my car keys back on the sideboard.

"I'll take Alex with me. Two pairs of eyes are better than one," Rob said.

"Yeah, that's a good idea. I'll stay here. If there's any news, then call me straight away," I demanded.

"Of course, the same goes for you."

I nodded. As if by magic, Alex emerged from his bedroom and flew down the stairs. He had his hand on the front door latch ready to go.

"Come on, Dad," he insisted. "We're wasting time." He was hopping from one foot to the other in his impatience to be doing something to find Henry. I knew how he felt.

"Let's go," Rob said, and they were both out of the door in a flash.

I wandered into the kitchen. My eyes settled on the laptop. Max. I hadn't told PC Brownley about Max. How could I have been so stupid?

"PC Brownley," I hollered, unnecessarily as it turned out because he was right behind me. "I need to tell you about someone Henry has been playing online with recently. He's called Max and . . ."

I explained that I had thought Max was a new boy at school, and how he had turned out not to be. I also explained that it was why I suspected Glenn had taken Henry.

"Do you think Glenn was masquerading as Max to win your son's confidence?" he asked.

"Yes. I do."

"Hmm, well there could be an innocent explanation," he surmised. "However, in the circumstances it's best if we try to find out Max's identity. We'll need to examine your laptop."

"Of course, take it."

"Does your son have email? Social media accounts?"

"No, he's too young. I'm careful about what I let him do," I said, and then decided to revise my last statement. "I thought that I was careful about what I let him do."

"It's not easy to keep them one hundred percent safe online these days," he said.

I appreciated his response, but it didn't make me feel any less of a failure as a mother right now.

*****

Henry had been missing for three hours or one hundred and eighty minutes to be more precise. I'd endured ten thousand eight hundred seconds of the types of feelings every parent dreads from the moment their child comes into the world. The types of feelings you instinctively know are possible when they're born, and fight tooth and nail to avoid by protecting them with every fibre of your being. I'd failed; I'd let Henry down. I hadn't kept him safe. This was my fault. I'd brought this madman into our life.

The darkest thoughts were insinuating themselves into my consciousness. They crept up on me. Before I realised it, they were crowding my mind. Each one louder than the other in their fight to be heard: Henry will be frightened.

He'll be crying. Oh God, is Henry hurt? What if he's in pain? What if he's in agony? The loudest thought fighting for supremacy and successfully muscling to the forefront: what if he's dead?

I couldn't take much more of this. I felt as if I were losing my mind. I had to regain control of my emotions. Somehow I had to stay rational. I had to block these thoughts; I had to.

I retreated to the bathroom. I closed and locked the door. I sat on the side of the bath gently rocking backwards and forwards. My hands wrapped around my waist. Somewhere, in the depths of my mind, I knew I was attempting to self-soothe.

I glanced at the bathroom mirror opposite. It took me a few moments to focus. I didn't recognise the woman staring back at me. This woman was clearly overwrought. Didn't she know that she needed to get a grip if she was to prove of any use to her son? Didn't she know that? I watched with detached interest as her mouth opened wide. To all intents and purposes she was screaming, but there was no sound. Over and over again her mouth opened wide, pausing only briefly to breathe. Her face showed the anguish that accompanied a scream but not a sound came from her mouth. Visibly exhausted, the woman eventually stilled. Calm descended.

My image came sharply into focus. I was looking at myself in the mirror. It was me! The woman that I'd been watching emotionally disintegrate in front of my eyes had been me. How was that possible? Somehow I recognised that my subconscious had erected a defensive wall in my mind. I instinctively knew that it had been erected to keep my sanity intact, and it was refusing to let in any thought that I couldn't cope with. I'd stopped feeling anything and that was welcome right now. I'd make tea. Yes, that was what I'd do. I'd make everyone a cup of tea. I left the bathroom and headed for the kitchen.

I moved around the kitchen with purpose. The kettle was boiling, and the cups were on the side with a teabag in each. It would probably be more cost-effective if I used a teapot. I had one somewhere. I started to fumble around in my kitchen cupboards.

"Frankie, what are you doing?" Mum asked.

"Huh?" I asked turning to look at her. She was sitting on a kitchen stool. She'd arrived an hour or so ago. I'd thought that I'd find her presence reassuring, but I didn't. Her being here just reminded me of my failings as a mother. She'd never allowed this to happen to me or my sisters. She was a great mum. I was . . .

"What are you searching for?" Mum persevered.

"A teapot," I said, as if it were the most natural thing in the world at this precise moment.

"A teapot?" Mum repeated, staring at me as if I were unhinged.

"Uh-huh." I muttered as I concentrated on the job in hand.

"I'll help you look," she said, appearing at my side. She put her hand on my shoulder. I glanced at her. I could see the concern written all over her face. She was worried about Henry, but she was also worried about me. I could see it.

"Don't worry about me, Mum," I said, suddenly irritated by her concern.

"I can't help it, Frankie. I don't know what to do for the best. I'm aware that I don't always get it right."

Something about her words bothered me. Someone had said something similar recently. Who? And what exactly had they said? I had a feeling it could be significant.

"Frankie, did you hear me?" Mum asked.

"Shh! I'm thinking," I snapped.

She winced. I knew that I'd hurt her feelings. Normally that would have shamed me, but today was different. Today my son was missing, and I didn't care about a few hurt feelings. I needed to think. I needed to find him.

I could hear the words: 'how hard it is to get it right. Make sure you cherish them, Frankie, because one day they might not be there.' Lenny had said that, Tom's stepdad. Had he been threatening me? Had I got it wrong? Perhaps Glenn hadn't taken Henry. Lenny really didn't want Tom talking to me about his childhood.

What was it Tom remembered? He described Lenny standing in his bedroom doorway and his associated feelings of terror. Could it be sexual abuse? If he'd abused Tom when he was younger, he certainly wouldn't want him talking about it. Tom had said that Lenny had political aspirations. A scandal would wreck his chance of a job in public office, and likely see him end up in prison to boot.

But why take Henry? Perhaps he thought Tom had already told me of the abuse, and he was attempting to frighten me into keeping silent. Didn't he know that as a counsellor I wouldn't report or openly discuss historical abuse? No, it didn't make sense.

Perhaps he'd targeted Henry simply because he had a predilection for young boys. The thought sickened me to the pit of my stomach. If that was the case, what had he already done to him? My stomach flipped; I knew I was going to be sick. The room started to spin. I reached out for the kitchen work surface to stop me from falling.

I was vaguely aware of the doorbell ringing. Someone else would have to answer it. I didn't trust my legs not to buckle from underneath me. I could hear Rob and Alex talking in the hallway.

"We couldn't find him, Mum," Alex said, as he walked into the kitchen. Rob trailing forlornly behind him.

I wasn't able to let go of the work surface for fear of falling to the ground in a heap. I edged along slowly until I was standing over my stainless steel kitchen sink. I peered down the plughole and waited for the non-existent contents of my stomach to make an appearance.

"Are you going to be sick?" Mum asked.

I nodded.

I heard the doorbell ring a second time. I lifted my head from the sink for the few moments it took to see Maria walk into the kitchen and shake her head in defeat. I lowered my head once again and felt the acidic bile rise in my throat and blaze a burning trail to freedom.

I needed to talk to PC Brownley. I needed to tell him what I suspected about Lenny. I knew I was professionally bound by client counsellor confidentiality, but my maternal responsibilities took precedence. At this moment, I'd say and do anything to get my son back safe and sound.

I grabbed some sheets of kitchen towel and wiped my mouth. I was vaguely aware that Rob had gone to answer the door. The doorbell must have rung again while I was being sick, which would explain why I hadn't heard it. Rob was making an odd sound in the hallway. Was he laughing? I strained to identify the sound. No, he was crying. Oh God! Oh no! He wasn't . . . dead? Every muscle in my body was trembling with fear as the kitchen door opened.

Rob was standing there in the doorway. Instead of the grief I expected to see on his face, there was joy. Tears were streaming down his face, but they weren't unhappy tears. He was smiling. It didn't make any sense until he stepped aside to reveal Henry, looking none the worse for wear, standing behind him.

# Chapter 25

The relief was so immense and all-consuming that I felt the dam of emotion I'd been holding back break through my defences. My body shook with uncontrollable sobs. Tears streamed down my face as I covered the distance between us with Olympian-like speed. My arms outstretched, I enveloped Henry in a bone-crushing hug. I was holding on for dear life, and I was never letting go again. And I mean never.

"Mum . . . , Mum . . . ," Henry said, while wriggling within my embrace, "I can't breathe."

"Oh sorry," I said, immediately easing my vice-like grip. "Let me look at you. Are you OK? Where have you been?" I questioned, my voice rising with emotion.

Henry appeared baffled by my question. "You know where I was!" he said.

He was so sure of himself that I stood there gawping at him. My mind was working overtime. Had I forgotten something? Had he told me where he was going? I was vaguely aware of the fact my mouth was opening and closing without my uttering a sound. It crossed my mind fleetingly that I must resemble a goldfish. Usually I would have found it an amusing observation, but at present I did not. I shook my head in denial. No, I really didn't know where he had been.

His initial adamant expression was slipping. Henry began to look unsure.

"But . . . ," he said frowning.

PC Brownley had entered the room and was listening intently.

"Hello, you must be the Henry I've been hearing so much about," he said as he stepped forward to stand beside me.

Henry was visibly shocked by the presence of a policeman.

"Why are you here?" he stuttered.

"Your mum and dad called me. They didn't know where you were. So can you tell us where you've been and who with?" he asked, his tone friendly.

The tension in the room was palpable. It was as if everyone had taken a deep breath in anticipation, and we were all holding it for fear of what Henry might say.

"I'm not in trouble, am I?" he said unsure. He was looking around the room at everyone and appearing to register the gravity of the situation. Tears were starting to well up in his eyes.

"No, of course not," I said, attempting to reassure him.

He didn't look convinced but was able to continue. "I was with Mum's friend," he said, as if it were the most natural thing in the world and really didn't understand why everyone was so upset.

My gaze flew to Maria. She stared back in shocked surprise.

"He wasn't with me," she said, alarm in her voice.

"No," Henry agreed. "I wasn't with Maria."

Maria's shoulders sagged in relief at his words.

"Rebecca?" I asked. Not quite able to believe that she would take my son and not tell me.

"No," Henry said. "I don't know her name. But you know her, Mum."

"I do?"

"Yes, you talk to her in the playground."

"Is she one of the other mums?" I asked.

He nodded.

"Whose mum?" I questioned.

"Max's mum," he replied.

I looked from Rob to PC Brownley. We knew there wasn't a Max at Henry's school.

"Henry, is Max in your class?" I probed.

He shook his head. "No, silly."

"Then why would his mum be in the playground?" I asked.

The question made him frown. He was unsure of himself once again.

"Hmm, I don't know, but she was. She said she was taking me to meet Max, and that he couldn't wait to talk to me about Minecraft."

"How do you know Max?" I questioned.

"I play Minecraft with him," he stated as if it were obvious, and I was some kind of simpleton for asking the question.

"I know that. But if Max doesn't go to your school, then where did you meet him?"

He knew what I was getting at, and he bowed his head.

"I don't know him. I met him online," he mumbled.

"But you know our rule: you are only allowed to play games with people online that you actually know in the real world," I said shaking my head. I wasn't entirely able to believe that he'd been speaking to a stranger online, under my very nose.

"Uh-huh!" he said his eyes never once meeting mine. "But . . . , I was bored. None of my friends were online. Max started to talk to me and . . ."

"When did you start talking to Max?" I asked.

"At Dad's when you were away with Rebecca."

I glanced at Rob. His whole demeanour screamed guilt. He was staring straight ahead. I suspected his youngest son's words had left him unwilling to make eye contact with me for fear of my reaction. In reality, I was only too pleased to have him share my feelings of parental failure. I recalled sensing Henry was keeping something from me the day I'd picked him up from school after my weekend away. I had meant to follow up on it, but I hadn't. It made sense now.

"You knew talking to Max was against the rules. Didn't you?" I asked careful not to sound as angry as I felt with both him and myself.

"I told you about him. I didn't lie! I didn't!"

"You said that he was a new friend, Henry. You didn't say that you'd met him online."

He hung his head in shame. "I wanted to play with him. He was fun."

"Did you get to meet Max, today?" I questioned.

He shook his head clearly disappointed. "No, he wasn't there. His mum forgot that he had football practice after school."

"So what have you been doing for the past three hours?" PC Brownley interjected.

"She said it seemed a waste not to do something fun, so she took me to McDonald's while we waited for football practice to finish. She bought me a Big Mac and fries. Oh and she let me have a chocolate milkshake," he said.

He was clearly excited about the fact that he'd had the type of food I wouldn't usually allow.

"Then what happened?" PC Brownley continued to question.

"Well, we went to pick him up from practice, but he wasn't there. She checked her phone and said that he'd texted her. Max wanted me to know that he'd gone to a friend's house and that he was sorry; he'd talk to me about Minecraft another time. She took me to the cinema to cheer me up, and then she dropped me off here."

"Did you have to tell her where you lived? Or did she already know?" PC Brownley asked.

"She already knew. I thought Mum had told her," he said frowning.

"Why would you think that?" I asked bemused.

"Because she said that she'd texted you and let you know."

"She didn't text me, Henry. I don't know who this woman is," I stated.

"Yes, you do. I've seen you talking to her."

"What? When?" I asked flabbergasted.

"You were talking to her a week or so ago in the playground. She asked me if I'd had a bad day. I didn't answer her because I'm not meant to talk to strangers, but you told me to answer her and not to be rude. So I did. You'd been talking to her before I came out of school. I saw you from the classroom window."

Oh my God! I remembered. I had told him off for not answering her. I could see Henry's point. We spend so much time telling our children not to speak to strangers only then to berate them if they don't reply to an adult who's spoken to them in our company. It was confusing for them. I'd given him permission to trust her by my insistence he talk to her. In his head, she was no longer a stranger. Moreover, my chatting to her had made him think we were friends. This was my fault.

My mobile phone was ringing. I could see from the caller ID it was Michael Graham. He'd called earlier. I was meant to call him back. He'd have to wait. The ringing seemed to be going on forever. I wanted it to stop. I pressed what I thought was the disconnect button, but it was immediately obvious that wasn't the case when I heard Michael's voice.

"Frankie? Oh thank goodness I've got hold of you," he said.

"Michael, I'm sorry, but this really isn't a good time right now. Can I call you back?" I said while checking my finger was hovering over the disconnect button this time.

"Umm . . . I'd rather you didn't. You need to hear this. I think you might be in danger."

His last words had my attention.

"What on earth do you mean? Hang on a minute. I'll just move into another room. There's a lot going on here at the moment." Lowering my phone to my side, I addressed everyone in the room as I walked to the kitchen door. "I need to take this call, but I'll be as quick I can."

"I'll carry on talking to Henry," PC Brownley said.

I shut the kitchen door behind me and walked into the living room.

"OK, Michael, what do you mean?"

"Well . . . ," he said, suddenly sounding hesitant. "I may have it all wrong, but I'm worried. So . . . , I thought, rather than say nothing and then something happen to you, well . . . , it's best if I voice my concerns."

"Please, Michael, can you tell me what you're worried about? I have a situation that I'm in the middle of."

I heard him take a deep breath, and I knew that he was ready to tell me.

"It's about Richard Sullivan."

"What about him?" Michael knew that Richard had been a client of mine as he'd recommended him to me.

"Well, I'm worried about him. After he finished the counselling sessions with you, he seemed like the old Richard again. He was a lot happier."

"That's good, isn't it?" I questioned, wondering when he was going to get to the point.

"Yes, but a little too good. Oh dear, I'm not making much sense, am I! Basically, Richard went home after his final counselling session with you and asked Abigail for a divorce."

"Oh!" I said. I hadn't expected that. I was certain that we hadn't discussed that particular course of action. I had thought that he was going to seek marriage guidance. Still, his actions were ultimately his decision.

"You sound surprised?"

"You know I can't comment, Michael."

"Yes, I know. It's just that Richard said you had made him see what he had to do next. He implied that you had encouraged him in the course of action. It was certainly how Abigail saw it anyway."

It sounded as if there had been a misunderstanding between Richard and me. I could remember Richard saying he knew what he had to do next during our final session; I had taken that to mean get help for his ailing marriage, not divorce her.

"You've received counselling from me, Michael. Do you think I would encourage a client to end their marriage?" I asked.

"No, I don't. But Abigail did."

"Well, that's unfortunate, but what . . ."

"Frankie, you don't understand."

No, I didn't. And to be honest, at this moment in time, I didn't care a great deal either. Henry was in the other room, and I needed to be with him. It took every ounce of my self-control not to just end the call.

"Then please explain, Michael," I said tersely.

"Abigail has been calling me since Richard asked for a divorce. At first, I thought it was just the ramblings of an emotional woman. You know the kind of thing. But, she rang me last night, and she'd been drinking. She was saying some odd things. To cut a long story short, I think she's going to do something to you."

"Me? Why? Is it because she thinks I encouraged Richard to leave her?"

"Yes, and because she thinks he's having an affair with you."

"WHAT?" I said, the word coming out as a screech.

"She told me last night that when Richard asked for a divorce she became suspicious. She didn't believe the reasons Richard gave her for wanting a divorce. She started following him." He paused. "I have to ask, Frankie, have you recently received a big bouquet of flowers delivered to the office?"

"Yes, how do you know about that?"

"When Abigail was following Richard, she saw him deliver the flowers by hand to your building. She waited in the car park and watched to see who picked them up. It didn't take her long to work out you were Richard's counsellor."

The flowers had been from Richard. I should have known. He had wanted to give me that beautiful watch as a thank you, and I had refused to accept it. Clearly he hadn't been satisfied with my refusing his gift.

"She was rambling on about other gifts. She wasn't specific."

The silk scarf came to mind. It hadn't been a veiled threat from Glenn. It had been a thank-you present from Richard.

"When she admitted to waiting for you to leave the office and following you, I started to worry about your safety, Frankie. She knows where you live. She even said that she'd let you know she was watching. I didn't know what she meant by it."

"Oh my God! I know what she meant. I received a photograph last week. It was a picture of me and the boys taken outside my house. I thought . . . , I thought it was Glenn."

"Oh, Frankie, I'm so sorry. You must have been terrified."

"I was. I am," I revised. "What do you think she's going to do?"

"Well, she said she wanted you to feel the same level of loss as she has," he said.

The living room door was ajar, and Maria's head suddenly appeared through the gap.

"Wait a second, Michael."

When Maria was sure she had my attention, she said, "Sorry to interrupt, but I need to go. I thought I'd let your next door neighbour know Henry's back safe and sound on my way out."

"Great. That saves me a job." I smiled my thanks at her.

She turned to leave.

"Maria . . ." I called.

"Yes?" she said turning to look at me once again.

"Thanks for your support today. You've been great."

"Aw, shucks, it was nothing. I'll call you tomorrow to see how you're doing."

"Michael, I'm back," I said as I watched Maria walk down the path and wander toward Peggy's.

"As I was saying, she wants you to feel the same level of loss as she has."

"Oh my God! It all makes sense now," I gasped.

"What does?"

"Henry was taken today. He was taken from school by a lady."

I could hear his deep intake of breath as I spoke.

"Oh no!"

"It's OK. He returned unharmed about ten minutes ago." I was quick to reassure him.

"What a relief! Do you think Abigail could be responsible?" he asked.

"Well, don't you? I think it's a fair assumption based on what you've just told me."

"Yes, I think you could well be right. I'm so relieved she didn't hurt him in any way."

"Can you text me the contact details you have for Abigail? I'm going to pass them on to the police."

"Yes, of course. I'll do that straight away. I'm so sorry, Frankie."

"Why are you sorry? You've helped enormously," I said.

"I recommended Richard see you. If I hadn't . . ."

"You couldn't have foreseen this outcome, Michael. No one could have."

"Hmm, maybe. I'll send you those contact details right away."

When I had been chatting to the lady in the playground, I had thought she was vaguely familiar. And now I knew why. Richard had shown me a picture of Abigail. But he'd commented that she looked different now because she'd had cosmetic surgery. I must have seen her resemblance to the photograph. I was now sure the lady had been Abigail Sullivan.

Michael had said that Abigail had admitted to following me from my office. She would have seen me picking up Henry from school, and that was how she knew which school playground to be standing in. She'd struck up a conversation with me knowing I'd assume she was just another mum waiting for her child. Henry had seen us talking and assumed we knew each other. My insisting he answer her question and not be rude had played into her hands.

Abigail had spoken to me and then Henry with the sole intention of establishing trust with him. It meant that when she put her plan into action he would believe her when she said I already knew of the plan to meet Max. By that time, she knew the lure of meeting Max would be too great for Henry to resist.

My phone pinged. Michael had done as he promised. I rushed into the kitchen.

"I know who took Henry," I announced.

# Chapter 26

Henry was safely tucked up in bed and fast asleep. I stood in his bedroom doorway watching him breathe. I did this from time to time. I would alternate between Alex's and Henry's room. I would often use the time to marvel at how quickly they'd grown. They weren't my little babies any more. I was grateful that they were still young enough to be tucked up in bed, safe and sound. One day, they'd be all grown up and out partying. When that happened, I seriously doubted I'd ever sleep again.

Today had been the worst day of my life. Well, more specifically, the worst three hours of my life. I'd thought Glenn trying to kill me had been the worst thing I would ever experience. But not knowing where Henry was and if he was dead or alive had been worse. I gripped the doorframe to steady myself as I felt what little energy I had left leave my body. I was both physically and mentally exhausted.

I felt a hand on my shoulder. Rob wasn't keen on leaving us alone tonight because the police hadn't yet been able to locate Abigail Sullivan. After my call with Michael Graham, I'd repeated to PC Brownley and everyone else in the kitchen what Michael had said to me. I went on to express my suspicions that Abigail Sullivan was responsible for the recent photograph and Henry's abduction.

I'd given PC Brownley Abigail's contact details. He'd wasted no time in letting his colleagues know. His colleagues had visited her address immediately, but she hadn't been there. So far, she hadn't returned to the address and wasn't answering her mobile phone. The last thing I'd been told was that they had contacted Richard. He had a key to the house, and he was meeting them at the property to let them in.

"Come and sit down and have something to eat. You look dreadful," Rob said.

"Thanks!" I said indignantly.

"Oh you know what I mean. It's been a harrowing day for everyone except Henry it would seem. Who, despite being the person we were all worried about, has actually managed to enjoy himself."

The irony of the situation wasn't lost on either of us.

"Still, I'd rather it was us that had been traumatised by the events of the day than him," I said.

"Don't you think it odd that this Abigail woman went to the lengths she did to abduct Henry only to treat him to McDonald's and the cinema? Of course, I'm relieved she didn't hurt him or terrorise him," he added.

"Yes, I've been thinking about that. Her intention was to terrorise me and only me, thankfully. Michael said she had wanted me to feel the same loss as she had by the breakup of her marriage, which she held me responsible for. In her mind, the sheer fact Henry was missing would put me through the kind of hell she felt I deserved. Luckily, although she is clearly mentally unbalanced at present, she isn't so disturbed as to want to hurt an innocent child."

"Thank God. Come on. Your food's ready."

"Hang on, Rob. I've been meaning to ask you, did Alex talk to you about his feelings during my weekend away?"

He sighed as if defeated and said, "I tried to broach the subject of how he's been feeling since you moved, and the impact of the whole Glenn incident on him, but he clammed up. He said he was fine and walked away from me. He didn't need to say, and that's the end of the subject because the physical distance he put between us said it all."

I felt as defeated regarding Alex's feelings as Rob looked right now.

"Well, you tried. But we need to get to the bottom of who gave him the trainers and the iPod, and who he has been speaking to online recently. Especially after what's just happened to Henry."

"I agree."

I followed him downstairs and into the kitchen where I could see scrambled eggs on toast waiting for me. Mum was busy making a cup of tea.

"Thanks, Mum," I said as I sat down and tucked into the food.

"Oh, it isn't much, but it will keep you going."

"I'll just make this tea, and then I'll be on my way," she said.

"OK," I said. I had little energy for anything other than to eat, drink and crawl into bed.

"I'm going to stay here tonight," Rob said. "I'm not prepared to leave you and the boys until the police inform us that Abigail has been arrested. That is, unless Leo objects?"

I frowned into my plate of food at his final words. Alex must have told him about my date with Leo. I didn't have the energy, right now, to deal with whatever feelings Rob might have on the subject.

"That's fine, Rob. I'll get you the spare duvet and a pillow. I warn you the sofa isn't any softer than the last time you slept on it."

He grimaced. "My back isn't any younger, either. Still I'm not leaving you three on your own tonight."

I'd successfully sidestepped the subject of Leo. It seemed Rob was happy to let me, for now. No doubt the subject would rear its head again in the near future. Leo had called me an hour ago. He was on night shift so had been asleep when I sent out the SOS text message about Henry. He'd only just read it and rang me immediately. It felt good to know that he cared.

As the scrambled eggs and toast hit my empty stomach, I started to feel better. I sipped at the steaming hot tea Mum had put before me. Hmm, I was beginning to feel human again. My mobile phone rang and all three of us jumped. I grabbed it and answered.

"Yes."

"Ms Wilson, it's PC Brownley. I'm ringing to let you know my colleagues gained entry to the Sullivan's house. Mrs Sullivan had left a note . . ."

"Oh God," I gasped. "She hasn't killed herself," I said, immediately jumping to my own conclusions.

"No, it wasn't a suicide note, far from it. She's packed her things and hopped on a plane. She made it clear that she doesn't plan on returning to the UK."

"What next?" I asked.

"Well, we'll try to find her, but . . . ," he hesitated.

"Yes, I know. I shouldn't hold my breath."

"I didn't say that, Ms Wilson."

"No, I know you didn't officer. I'm just connecting the dots. I suppose her having fled the country offers some reassurance. It means that I might be able to get some sleep tonight."

"One other thing, we've questioned Richard Sullivan. He wasn't aware of his wife's movements. They've been separated for the last month or so. He had no idea what she was planning. However, he did know that she suspected him of having an affair.

"It would seem she became suspicious when he asked for a divorce. He moved out of the marital home but didn't have time to stop all of his mail being delivered to the address. She had opened his credit card statement and was questioning him about some flowers and an iPod he'd bought."

"I suspect the flowers were sent to me," I interrupted. "They were sent anonymously at the time. Michael

Graham told me today that they had been from Richard. They had been intended as a thank-you present. Hang on . . . did you say iPod?"

He hesitated as if checking his notes. "Yes, that's right."

"Was there any mention of an expensive pair of trainers?"

"Yes, she was also suspicious of his purchasing trainers. Apparently he never wears trainers. He admitted to us that he had purchased the items as gifts."

"I bet I know who for. My eldest son has recently acquired some new trainers and an iPod. I had thought my ex-husband was overindulging him as he's had a hard time at school lately, but I found out today the gifts weren't from him. Now, I suspect they were from Richard."

"OK, we'll question him further and let you know."

If my suspicions turned out to be correct and the trainers and iPod had been from Richard, then why hadn't Alex said anything? He knew better than to take gifts from strangers. I would be having a serious conversation with that young man in the morning. And I still wanted to know who he was talking to online when his bedroom door was closed.

"Have you had chance to examine our laptop yet? I'm fairly sure Abigail was pretending to be Max online and using the alias to talk to Henry."

"We've started to look at it, but we haven't had time to examine the correspondence between your son and Max yet. But we will."

"What I'd like to understand, is how she knew Henry played Minecraft? And how she identified which player he was?"

"Well . . . we suspect she knew your son liked and played Minecraft from your Facebook account."

"What? I'm careful. I have the right privacy settings on my Facebook account. No one other than my friends can see my pictures and posts," I said.

"Yes, but unfortunately everyone can see your profile picture," he paused, allowing the information to sink in.

"Oh!" I had nothing else to say. Once again, I thought I'd been smart and tech savvy, and I hadn't. My profile picture was of myself with Alex and Henry. Henry was wearing a Minecraft t-shirt.

"But . . . how did she know which player was Henry?"

"Your son's Minecraft login ID is HenryWilson."

I couldn't believe that he had used his own name as a login ID. The login IDs I had seen were made-up, crazy names like 'boy warrior' so that the player remained anonymous. I'd assumed Henry's would be the same. Why hadn't I checked the login ID he'd created? What kind of a mother was I? I thought I had their online safety covered. How wrong could a person be? I felt deflated by my own naïveté.

"We'll be in touch, Ms Wilson."

"Uh-huh," I muttered. I had nothing else to say. I wanted this day to be over. As I placed my mobile phone down on the table, I looked into both Mum and Rob's expectant faces. They wanted to know what had been said. I didn't want to have to explain the further damning evidence that had come to light in the case against my fitness to practice as a mother.

"I can't sleep," Alex said, walking bleary-eyed into the room before I could say anything about the phone conversation.

"That's not surprising. Do you want anything? A drink? Or something to eat?" I asked.

"Nah!" he said as he leaned against the kitchen work surface.

Deciding I couldn't wait until the morning to question him about the trainers and iPod I asked, "Alex, about those trainers. Where did you get them?"

"Dad gave them to me," he said.

I studied his face as he spoke and had to admit that either he was telling the truth, or my son was the best liar I had ever seen. I sincerely hoped it was the former because the prospect of him being the latter sent shivers down my spine.

I glanced at Rob; he was standing open-mouthed, gawping at Alex. Before he said anything, I asked, "Did your dad actually hand you the trainers?"

"Well, no. You see, the weekend you were away with Rebecca, and Henry and I stayed at Dad's we were supposed to go shopping for a new kit. Dad forgot to take me. When he dropped me off at school on the Monday morning, he said he'd sort it out and drop the kit off that afternoon."

I glanced at Rob. He studiously avoided my gaze.

Alex continued, "When I got to school, my tutor handed me my PE Kit. Apparently a year seven found it on the field and handed it in. When I got home from school and found the trainers left on the front doorstep, I realised Dad must have dropped them off. They were so cool that I didn't want to tell you both I'd found my kit in case Dad took them back to the shop. Sorry," he muttered, his eyes trained firmly on the floor.

"If I'm honest, I completely forgot about your PE kit," Rob admitted. "I didn't buy the trainers, Alex."

Alex's head shot up, "Then, who did?" he asked.

"I suspect Richard Sullivan left them as a gift. What about the new iPod?" I asked.

"Who's Richard Sullivan?" Alex asked.

"I can't go into details. What about the new iPod?" I repeated.

Alex's eyes returned to the floor as he mumbled, "Hmm, well, it might have been left outside the front door." His eyes sought mine as he said, "There was no label on the box, Mum, honest. I didn't know where it had come from or who it was intended for."

"It didn't occur to you to tell me about it so I could try and find its rightful owner?" I asked.

"I really wanted an iPod," he said by way of explanation.

"Oh, that's all right then. My son wants an iPod and one appears, as if by magic, on his front doorstep and that entitles him to keep it, does it?" I said, aware that my tone was dripping sarcasm.

"Erm, no, I'm sorry, Mum."

"I suspect the iPod was another gift from Richard Sullivan. The police are trying to confirm my suspicions. In the meantime, get the trainers and iPod. You won't be keeping either."

Alex looked crestfallen but acquiescent as he sloped out of the kitchen in search of the unsanctioned gifts.

When he'd left, and I was satisfied that he was out of earshot, I said, "Rob, so he doesn't miss out, shall we club together and get him an iPod? He really should have told us about the gift, but after everything he's been through lately I think he deserves a treat."

Rob smiled, "Yes, good idea. It might make me feel less guilty about forgetting to get him a new PE kit, even though he didn't need it in the end."

"Good, we're agreed," I nodded.

I watched as Rob's expression clouded as a disturbing thought seemed to occur to him.

"How did Richard know what size trainer to get Alex?" he asked.

"Yeah, good point," my mum agreed.

"Hmm," I said. A vague memory popped into my head. "I seem to recall a brief conversation we had about shoes after a session one day. He was complaining about how his new shoes were rubbing. He said how surprised he was that a size eight shoe could vary in fit so much across shoe suppliers. I happened to comment that his shoe size was the same as Alex's."

Both Mum and Rob nodded their understanding just as Alex walked back in, head bowed. He held his arms outstretched and dropped the trainers and iPod on the side. He turned to leave.

"One more thing, who have you been talking to online lately? I've noticed you've been closing your bedroom door when you've been speaking to him. In view of what's just happened to your brother. I need to know," I said.

"I'd rather not say," Alex said, his cheeks colouring.

"Why?" I questioned, immediately suspicious.

"I just don't want to, that's all."

"No, I need to know who you're talking to. I insist, Alex!" I said.

"So do I," Rob said, backing me up.

Alex, the picture of despair as he accepted his fate said, "OK."

I braced myself. What next?

"Her name's Charlotte. She's in my year. We . . . like each other," he mumbled.

His whole face had turned scarlet with embarrassment at having to admit to his parents that he was talking to a girl. I wanted to laugh out loud with relief. But didn't, for fear my son's humiliation would be complete.

Rob was smirking. I knew he, too, was on the verge of laughter. He turned away and made much of washing up his cup. Only I noticed his shoulders shaking with his contained mirth.

"Oh, I see. Well that's nice. You could invite her over for tea, or something, if you like," I offered.

He rolled his eyes. "That is so last century, Mum. I'll swerve that if you don't mind. I feel tired now. I'm going to catch some Z's."

I blinked and he was gone; such was his need to escape the situation. When Rob, Mum and I heard the telltale sound of Alex's bedroom door closing behind him, we erupted into mid-volume laughter. After all, we didn't want him to think we were laughing at him.

# Chapter 27

***Session five - Tom Ferris 10.00 a.m. - 11.00 a.m.***

I could see an ambulance parked directly outside of the main entrance of Marina Offices as I drove into the car park; its back doors wide open. A lady was being attended to by a paramedic. Oh dear, someone wasn't having a good day today, I thought. I hope it isn't anything too serious. I was reminded of Peggy. Poor old Peggy! OK, so she was a difficult, sometimes abrasive, old lady, but I didn't wish her any harm. It had been with real sadness that I'd learned from her son that she'd had a fall.

It had been last Wednesday evening when I'd seen the flashing blue lights outside the living room window. I'd got up to look at what was going on and realised the ambulance had pulled up outside next door. Instinctively I'd gone outside to see what was happening. I could see a man outside frantically waving the ambulance men inside. I was about to go back inside, having decided I was being voyeuristic, when they brought Peggy out on a stretcher. Her pallor was deathly. She resembled a tiny frail bird.

Without thinking, I'd asked the man who'd ushered the ambulance men inside, "Whatever has happened?"

"I'm not sure. I rang Mum several times today. When she failed to answer, I came over. I found her unconscious in the hallway." He was visibly shaken by his discovery.

"Oh dear, I'm so sorry," I said. He must be her son, I thought. I couldn't remember his name.

"Thank you. If you don't mind, I need to go with Mum," he said edging away from me and toward the ambulance.

"Oh, yes, of course. Don't let me keep you. I hope Peggy is going to be OK."

"Me too," he said as he jumped into the back of the ambulance and the doors closed behind him. I hadn't heard any news about Peggy since. But she hadn't returned home yet, so I was assuming she was still in the hospital. I was hoping to have a word with her son the next time he visited to feed her cat.

"Good morning, Theresa," I said as I passed reception.

"Morning, Frankie," she chirruped.

I took the stairs and arrived at my office in moments. Plonking my briefcase on the coffee table, I slipped my jacket off and hung it up. I had a few minutes before Tom arrived for his last session. We'd originally contracted for six sessions, but I'd called both him and Susan last week to discuss my suitability to continue as their counsellor in view of my current personal circumstances. I didn't go into detail, but I offered them Rebecca as an alternative counsellor. I'd checked with Rebecca, and she could accommodate them.

When I'd spoken to Rebecca, she'd been keen to talk about Sam. She'd told me how enthusiastic he was to meet me. She'd suggested that she call me again later that evening when she was with him, so that all three of us could agree on a suitable date and time to meet.

I recalled the excitement in her voice when she'd rang me that evening as agreed.

"Frankie, I've spoken to Sam, and he says that he can make next Tuesday evening. Is that OK with you?" she asked.

"Yes, that's fine."

"Great! I can't wait! I've got some exciting news for you."

"Oh? That sounds intriguing. Do tell!" I invited.

"Nah! Sam wants us both to be there to tell you! Don't you, Hun!" she said, her last words directed at Sam. I couldn't hear his reply.

"How exciting! I can't wait," I said.

"Do you want to speak to her, Sam?" I heard Rebecca ask him.

"Sorry, Frankie, Sam has just gone to the bar to get another drink. He said that he looks forward to meeting you on Tuesday. We'll get to your house for 7 p.m. Does that give you enough time to get ready?"

"That gives me plenty of time. I look forward to seeing you both then," I replied.

I felt a tingle of nervousness as I recalled the conversation. I was meeting Sam for the first time tonight. I felt apprehensive. Swallowing down my feelings on the subject, I recalled how neither Tom nor Susan was keen on the idea of changing counsellor. I wasn't too surprised. When given a choice, most people preferred to stay with the counsellor they'd built a trusting relationship with and already shared so much with. It was more likely that they'd elect to stop counselling altogether than start again with another counsellor, which would be a shame as they were both making progress.

Tom had been the first to inform me that he'd come along for one final session, provided that I was agreeable. He wanted to talk to me about an illuminating conversation he'd had with Lenny after our last session. I'd been intrigued, so I'd agreed.

Susan had refused point-blank to entertain the idea of another counsellor. She wasn't 'going through all that again with another counsellor. It was only two more weeks,' she had wheedled. She had assured me that she understood I had my own 'stuff' going on at the moment. If that meant she didn't always have my full attention, she was fine with it. So I'd agreed to see her for the next two weeks.

A tap on the door interrupted my revelry. "Come in," I invited.

"Hi, Frankie," Tom said as he walked in.

He looked different: lighter somehow, as if the weight of the world was no longer upon his shoulders.

"You look different, Tom," I observed.

He smiled. "I feel different."

"Do you want to tell me about it?" I asked.

He nodded. "But first, I want to apologise for what happened with Lenny last week in reception. He was out of order, and I told him so. He asked me to pass on his apologies."

"Apology accepted, or should I say apologies accepted," I said smiling my reassurance.

He sighed. "Good. I'll let Lenny know you're cool with it. He'll be relieved." He paused before continuing, "After we left last week, I was furious with Lenny. I was so angry with the way he'd treated you that I confronted him. I demanded to know why he didn't want me to talk to you. I needed to know what it was he was so scared I'd tell you. I told him about my recent flashback, and how I'd felt. How scared I had been when he'd been standing in the doorway. I asked him . . . ," he hesitated. "I asked him why he thought I had been so scared."

"That was brave of you!" I commented.

He gave me an appreciative smile for my understanding of the situation. "The flashback had made me suspect that he'd abused me in some way as a child."

I nodded.

"I suspect that you thought the same," he said.

"It was a possibility. I wanted to wait and see if your memory unlocked any further memories that would give you a clearer idea of what happened before drawing any conclusions."

Tom continued eager to tell me what Lenny had said, "What he said next surprised me."

I was intrigued. "Oh?"

He sat forward. His face was animated as he went on, "He broke down in tears. At first, I understood his tears to be an admission of his guilt. I was convinced more than ever that he'd done something to me that he was ashamed of, but I still had no recollection of it. I was concerned that his admitting to the abuse might trigger a memory that I really didn't want to recollect."

"I can understand that."

"Can you? It felt cowardly at the time."

"I think it's perfectly natural not to want to confront something you know will cause you emotional pain. Take physical pain for example, you know a flame will burn you, so you don't touch it. Why then would you want to hear something you suspect will hurt you emotionally. Every instinct invites you to avoid it."

"It makes sense when you say it like that. A kind of self-preservation," he said.

"Yes, that's how I see it, although, sometimes it is necessary to face those things we know will hurt us emotionally in order to heal and move past them. If we don't, we risk being stuck in a constant state of emotional limbo."

"Yes, I can see that. Anyway, I didn't shy away from the situation despite my instincts telling me that I should. I repeated my question: why did he think I'd been scared? It was then that he dropped the proverbial bombshell."

I leaned forward in my chair braced for what I was about to hear.

"He said, 'I know what she was doing was wrong, but she was ill. You have to understand that she wasn't herself.' Well as you can imagine, I was dumbfounded. Whatever did he mean? So I asked him to explain.

"Lenny explained that he'd known my mum when my dad was alive. He and my dad had been friends. When my dad died, Lenny lost contact with my mum. He happened across her one day when she was out shopping. He said that he took one look at us and knew something was wrong.

"Lenny described Mum as chatty and gregarious when Dad was alive, but the woman he saw in front of him was listless. The light he had once seen burn so brightly in her eyes had been extinguished.

"He turned his attention to me in my pushchair. He described me as looking uncared for. He explained that I wasn't just a bit dirty, as a toddler might look if they've been playing in the garden, but that I was filthy: my face, my hands, my clothes. But what bothered him the most was my silence. He spoke to me and tried to engage with me, but he said my light, like my mother's, had been extinguished."

"Did he think your mother might be depressed following the loss of your dad?" I surmised.

"Yes, he did. He described how, for both her sake and mine, he felt compelled to try and help her. He asked her if there was anything he could do, but she said she was fine. He didn't believe her and he decided to follow her back to her flat, so he would know where we lived.

"He described how he waited outside not knowing what to do. He wanted to help. But if she refused it, then what more could he do? It was then that he heard me crying, and crying, and crying. He kept expecting my mother to comfort me, but he said she didn't. Not knowing what to do, he left. But my cries kept reverberating in his head. He couldn't shake the feeling that I wasn't being cared for as I should be.

"He returned to the flat the next evening and heard my cries again. He couldn't stand it any longer, so he knocked on the door. My mum answered and didn't want to let him in. But when he'd insisted, she'd stood aside.

"The flat was filthy and uncared for. He could smell dirty nappies. The rubbish bag was overflowing in the kitchen. The television's volume was at its maximum; he suspected it was because she was attempting to drown out the sound of my crying.

"Lenny and Mum argued. He threatened to call social services. Mum demanded that he leave. Rather than do as she asked, he made for my bedroom. He described how he wrenched open my bedroom door, and found me standing up in my cot with tear-stained cheeks, a heavily soiled nappy and wet, dirty bedclothes surrounding me."

The final scene he described seemed to correlate to his recent flashback, and I wondered if he'd made the connection yet. Lenny had been there to protect him, not abuse him as he had suspected.

"Do you think Lenny's description of events may explain your flashback?" I asked.

"Yes, most definitely! Lenny went on to explain that my mother pushed him to one side, but instead of picking me up to comfort me she just kept saying the same things to me over and over again. He went to great lengths to explain that her behaviour was because she was clinically depressed. I think the things she said to me makes sense of my anxiety around my son's crying."

"Oh really, please do go on," I invited, eager to understand.

"Lenny described how my mother kept saying 'big boys shouldn't cry' and that 'I had to be quiet.' 'I had to be quiet, or she would go mad.' "

I sat back in my chair. "Yes, that would seem to explain the root cause of your anxiety around your son's crying."

"I can't tell you how good it feels to realise I'm not going mad."

"I can imagine," I empathised. I thought that I was going mad on a regular basis where Glenn Froom was concerned, so I could most definitely relate to Tom in this instance.

"Have you spoken to your mother about this?" I asked.

"I have. It wasn't easy. You see, my memories of my mum are all positive. She's a great mum. She has always been there for me. However, when Lenny described what he'd witnessed all those years ago, I believed him. Lenny called Mum immediately and warned her that he had told me.

"We both went to see her. She was distraught. She explained that Dad's death had left her bereft. She was young, bereaved, and she had a small baby to take care of. She wasn't really aware of it at the time, until Lenny showed up, but she'd sunk into a clinical depression. He had insisted she see a doctor and get help. In return, he wouldn't report her to social services.

"Mum described how Lenny had dropped by every day to make sure I was being taken care of. Slowly, Mum got better. Her relationship with Lenny developed into a romantic one. She didn't think that I remembered anything as I had been so young, and certainly didn't realise that I'd been affected by it.

"It was only when Jenny told her that I was having counselling and described how I behaved around Jacob that she suspected I'd been impacted by her behaviour toward me in the early years. As you can imagine, she feels incredibly guilty."

"Yes, I can understand that. Having heard what your mum has had to say, how do you feel toward her?"

"She's my mum. Nothing has changed for me. I love her and always will. She only neglected me as a baby because she was ill. She would never have let me suffer if she'd been well. However, I do shudder at the thought of what might have happened if Lenny hadn't come along when he did."

"Yes, thank goodness for Lenny," I commented. I never imagined I would be saying that a few weeks ago. "Lenny was so keen that you shouldn't talk to me about all of this. How does he feel about you being here today?" I asked.

Tom grimaced.

"He still isn't happy?" I guessed.

Tom relaxed back into his chair, "Oh he's fine with it now."

"It's just that you grimaced when I asked the question. I assumed . . ."

"You assumed that he still wasn't happy with my seeing you. No. I grimaced because your question reminded me of the accusation I flung at him when we argued last week. I accused him of not wanting me to talk to you because he was scared of whatever I might remember becoming common knowledge. I screamed at him that now he was a public figure he had his precious reputation to consider, and that he couldn't afford a scandal." He winced as he finished recounting his words.

"And that wasn't the case?" I asked.

"No, it was not the case. He explained that he was worried my talking to you would trigger memories of my mum's neglect. He didn't want me to hate my mum. He was also worried about how my finding out might impact upon my mum's mental health. However, now it's all out in the open, and he can see that it hasn't affected my feelings for my mum; he's relieved. I can tell you, I felt pretty crappy about the things I said to him, and the things I thought he may have been capable of."

I nodded. "The things you said and thought were understandable based on his recent behaviour and your limited memories of your infancy. You took the memory, and you filled in the blanks with what you thought may have happened.

"I could have discussed your memories with you and helped you fill in the blanks. But that would have been unintentional collusion on my part. Everything you felt and remembered led you to feel abused by Lenny. In turn, that led me to feel you had been abused by Lenny.

"We were wrong. Fortunately you were able to fill in the blanks of that memory with fact in a short timescale. Some people aren't so lucky."

"I'm relieved to be able to make sense of my feelings. Whereas before it felt completely illogical to be so anxious around my son and to be so perturbed by his crying; now it makes perfect sense. I'm still anxious around him, but I feel like I can do something about it now. Does that make sense?"

"Yes, it makes perfect sense. Now you understand where your feelings stem from, you feel able to move on and actually tackle them. I realise this is our last session, but I would encourage you to seek counselling with another counsellor."

He'd been shaking his head while I spoke, and I knew from his reaction that he wasn't willing to entertain the idea.

"I'm going to suggest that you consider graded exposure therapy," I persisted.

"What's that when it's at home?" he asked with obvious bewilderment.

"It sounds grand, but it really isn't. Graded exposure therapy is used in Cognitive behavioural therapy. It means to gradually expose yourself to that which causes you great anxiety. If, for example, you were frightened of spiders and wanted to stop being afraid, I would suggest you started to overcome the fear by looking at pictures of spiders. Perhaps learn a little about spiders, and build up gradually to eventually holding a spider."

He shuddered. "I'm glad I'm not here about my fear of spiders."

I laughed, "Me too. I don't like them either."

"What do you suggest that I do about my anxiety around Jacob?"

"Pardon the pun, but I suggest you take baby steps."

He chuckled, "Oh very good, Frankie, I like it."

"I would suggest you make a cry checklist. To put it simply it's a list of reasons a baby cries: hungry, wet, tired, et cetera. You can use it each time Jacob cries to remind you that you aren't powerless. He's crying for a reason, and it's your job to identify that reason."

Tom was nodding. "Yeah that makes sense."

"Have a conversation with your wife, Jenny, and have a plan. Perhaps, initially, you agree to shadow her when she's with Jacob."

"What . . . like you'd shadow someone at work?" he asked.

"Yes. That's exactly what I mean. Watch how she deals with Jacob. How she soothes him and interacts with him. Just as importantly, watch as she too may get het up when she can't soothe him. She may well need your support at times."

He raised his eyebrows. "You think so?"

"I do! Believe me when I say that everyone at one time or another has felt out of their depth as a new parent."

"That had never occurred to me. I mean it never occurred to me that other people may struggle with parenting. It felt as if everyone else was a natural, and I was an epic fail."

"Things are rarely as they appear. Not every parent is a natural. More people struggle than you think."

"Then what?" he asked.

"Huh?" I wasn't sure what he was asking me.

"What do I do after I've shadowed her for a while?"

"Oh, yes, well then you put what you've learned into practice. I suggest Jenny is there at first to offer advice and support. Then gradually she's in the next room while you deal with Jacob. Until, eventually, you feel confident enough to look after him on your own."

"I can't imagine that ever happening," he said.

"You'd be surprised by what can be achieved. I have faith in you."

"Thank you. That means a lot."

I glanced at the clock on the wall behind him.

"I'd like to spend the last ten minutes of the session recapping on the last five weeks. Specifically, how far you feel you've come and more importantly where you're headed," I said.

# Chapter 28

*Session five - Susan Mackintosh 11.30 a.m. - 12.30 p.m.*

I had a few minutes to spare before Susan's session, so I got up out of my chair and stretched my whole body rather like a cat might. As if on autopilot, I headed for the window and stared out. I scanned the car park and the cafe opposite. No, I couldn't see him. I realised with a jolt that I had moved on from consciously looking for Glenn everywhere I went to subconsciously looking for him. It had become a kind of weird muscle memory. Only I wasn't riding a bike or typing on a keyboard; I was looking for Glenn.

I had to acknowledge, in light of recent events, I may have been wrong about Glenn Froom. Perhaps everyone had been right. Perhaps he was dead. Richard was responsible for the gifts. Abigail was responsible for the photograph and taking Henry. All of the things I had, at the time, attributed to Glenn. I had been wrong. I'd been wrong a lot lately. If only they could find his body . . . , then I could be sure. I would find peace in the knowledge that he was actually dead. I knew that finding him was unlikely after so much time. Still, I could hope.

Turning away from the window, I returned to my seat just in time to hear Susan knock on the door.

"Come in," I said.

I watched her as she walked in, took off her jacket and made herself comfortable in the chair. She crossed her legs and regarded me expectantly.

"How are you, today?" I asked.

"I'm good," she replied.

I observed an unusual lack of tension in her shoulders and lightness to her voice. She appeared to be relaxed; more relaxed than I'd ever seen her.

"Thank you for agreeing to see me for the final two sessions. Can you understand my reasons for not wanting to see a new counsellor?"

"Of course I can. I hope you understand why I felt the need to give you the option of changing counsellor."

"Yes. I understand. You're human too. We all have stuff that gets in the way from time to time."

"Thanks for being so understanding. Changing the subject, I can't help but notice how relaxed you look."

She smiled. "I managed to gather my courage sufficiently to follow Dickie last week. I sat outside of his office in my car. I was careful to park a little ways down the street so as not to be noticed by him or his partners when they were leaving for the day. I have to say that I felt sick at the thought of what I might discover as a result of my subterfuge."

"That's understandable in view of your suspicions."

"Yes, well I soon discovered that, wherever he was going, he was going on foot and not driving. He walked straight past his car parked in his allocated space. I had to act quickly, so I jumped out of my car and followed him on foot. I prayed the whole time that he didn't look behind him. I don't know what I would have said if he'd seen me. Anyway, I followed him for a good ten minutes before I lost sight of him. I couldn't understand where he'd gone. I'd only looked away for a second. I carried on walking in the direction I'd seen him take in the hopes that I'd spot him." She paused.

"And did you? Spot him? I mean."

"Yes, I spotted him down a side street. I waited a while before following as there was no one else around. By the time I'd rounded the corner, he was nowhere to be seen. I concluded that he must have gone into one of the buildings on the street I was now standing in.

"The street was a mix of shops, bars, and restaurants with residential flats above. My first thought was that he'd disappeared into one of the flats. But if he had, I'd never be able to guess which one.

"As I walked down the street, I found myself standing outside of a glass-fronted gym. You know the type: people sitting on exercise bikes or running on treadmills, in full view of passersby, sweating profusely with an air of superiority over those of us who aren't."

"I know the type of gym you're referring to," I said.

"Something caught my eye, it may have initially been the six pack on the guy I could see lifting weights," and she raised her eyebrows meaningfully as she spoke. "But it was soon his face that had my full attention. You see, I recognised him. It was the guy that I had seen Dickie looking at online."

"The same guy whose name began with an 'S'?" I asked.

"Yes, that's right. As I was watching him pump iron, out of the corner of my eye, I saw Dickie walk into the gym. I knew that I had to find a different vantage point from which to spy on him. I was sticking out like a sore thumb just stood there on the pavement.

"I decided to walk into the gym. I asked the receptionist if I might have a little look around on the pretext that I was considering joining. She explained that she was too busy to show me around herself, but that I was free to wander around on my own if I liked. Well, that was perfect.

"I found a small cafe area where you could sit and watch the people exercising in the gym. And that is exactly what I did. I sat and watched as Dickie and the muscle-bound hunk exercised together."

"Didn't you say that Dickie wasn't keen on visiting the gym?" I questioned.

"As far as I was aware, he wasn't. No one could be more surprised than me to be watching my husband workout. They exercised for an hour, and then they left together. I followed them at a discreet distance and watched them get into Dickie's car back at the office.

"I drove home and waited for Dickie to return. I didn't have to wait too long. When he walked in, I decided to tackle him head on. I told him that I'd followed him because I thought he was having an affair. And if he was having an affair with the guy at the gym, then he needed to tell me."

"How did he react?"

"Well he was stunned at first. Then he started to laugh. It wasn't the reaction I had expected. When he managed to stop laughing, he explained that Simon, the guy whose name began with an 'S', is his personal trainer. He met him a few weeks ago for an assessment, and now he trains at the gym three times a week. He dropped him off at his home after the gym session as a favour because Simon's wife needed to use their car."

"That Thursday evening, a few weeks ago, when Dickie was going out and you weren't sure where, was he meeting Simon?"

"Yes, that was his initial assessment."

"So can I assume that when you saw a picture of Simon on Dickie's computer he was researching personal trainers?" I asked.

"Yes."

"You said that he got aggressive with you when you questioned him about it. Why do you suppose he felt the need for secrecy?"

"That's precisely what I asked him. I explained how his behaviour had led me to believe he was having an affair. He seemed genuinely shocked. Men . . . they can be so stupid, can't they? What possible alternative conclusion could I reach based on his behaviour of late? Anyway, his explanation surprised me." She lowered her gaze and studied her shoes intently. I sensed her mood shift from relaxed to pensive.

"In what way did it surprise you?" I probed.

Her eyes flitted from her shoes to my face and back again. I could see that she was uncomfortable with the direction our dialogue was taking. She remained silent, and so did I. I let the silence exert its own pressure. Finally, I heard her sigh, and I knew she was about to tell me.

"You know I can't have children, right?"

"Yes," I said.

"Well . . . I didn't exactly tell Dickie." Her eyes met mine for a fraction of a second before she looked away.

"Your husband doesn't know that you can't have children?"

"No. Well he didn't. He does now because I've told him." She gave a heartfelt sigh before continuing, "Now you know. I'm a terrible person." She was staring firmly at her feet. Her shoulders sagged. She appeared to have aged in front of my eyes.

"I'm not judging you. I'm sure you had your reasons for not telling him."

"I wanted him to love me," she said, her eyes pleading with mine for understanding. "It was as simple as that. I sensed that he had emotionally distanced himself from me recently. I secretly figured it was because I hadn't been able to get pregnant. I know how desperate he is to be a dad." I saw the shame she felt in her eyes before she glanced away.

I recalled our first session. When I'd asked her if she could think of any reasons other than an affair for her husband's recent emotional distance, even though she had said no, I had been sure she was hiding something. I'd been right.

"I imagined that he'd become frustrated with the fact I wasn't pregnant and was seeking a more fertile quarry, much as my previous husband had."

"Why didn't you tell him that you couldn't have children?" I asked.

"I didn't tell him at the beginning of the relationship because I didn't want to say anything that might put him off me. I hoped that I'd be enough for him and his desire for children would lessen as time went by. After all, we're neither of us in the first flush of youth. But it seemed I was wrong; his need seemed to intensify with the passing of time, not diminish. I found myself in this situation; where I'd left it so long that if I told him, I thought he'd leave me."

"But you thought that he was having an affair and was going to leave you anyway?"

"Yes, but if he had been having an affair and left me for her, then he would be the bad guy in that situation. If I admitted that I hadn't been honest about my fertility and he left me as a result, then I would be the bad guy or bad woman as it happens. I don't want anyone to think badly of me."

"You said earlier that you've told him about your infertility. Now that he knows the truth, has he left you?"

She shook her head. "No. He's surprised me in a good way. You see, he'd assumed that my not getting pregnant was his fault. He's a little older than me, and he has what most people would describe as middle-age spread. He's been researching male fertility. He didn't want me to find out and that's why he's been holed up in his study with the door closed. His research led him to believe that he could improve his fertility by losing weight and getting fitter."

"Let me guess, that's why he bought the expensive trainers," I chipped in.

She nodded. "And he bought the iPod, so he had something to listen to when he was exercising. The reason I couldn't find it at home is because he keeps it in his locker at the gym."

"What about the iPad?" I asked.

"He bought the iPad because he realised his secretive computer activity at home was causing rows. He reasoned that if he had an iPad, he could keep it at work and surf the net in his lunch time. That way, I wouldn't know what he was looking at and when."

"That makes sense. So from what you've said he's done all this to improve his fertility. Why didn't he tell you?"

"That's the funny thing . . . No, it's not funny actually. It's sad. He didn't tell me because he was embarrassed. He felt that if he admitted his suspicions about his infertility, it would make him less of a man in my eyes. My finally admitting that I was the one with the fertility problems was actually a relief to him."

"So what's next?"

"Well Dickie wants us to investigate fertility treatment together. I haven't taken any form of contraception for years. Up until now, I've just accepted that I've never been able to get pregnant. I'd decided it was probably for the best that I didn't have a child."

"You've never consulted a doctor about your infertility?"

"No, I figured it was for the best. After all, Daddy says children ruin relationships. I caused Mummy to leave him."

I wondered how long it would take before Daddy's influence would re-emerge in proceedings.

"Up until now, you've chosen not to seek a medical solution to your infertility because your father feels children ruin relationships. Is that correct?"

"Yes."

"How many families do you know where the mother and father are still married?"

"I don't know, lots, why?"

"Humour me. How many?"

"Too many to count—maybe twenty."

"And how many of those parents would you say are still happily married?"

She thought for a while and said, "I would say sixty percent."

"Sixty percent of the couples you know with children are happily married."

"Yes, that's what I said."

"So, it is possible."

"What is?"

"To have children and remain happily married."

"Oh, I see what you mean. Well of course it is."

"And yet you appeared to wholeheartedly believe your father when he said that children ruin marriages?"

"Not children. Me. I ruined his marriage."

"You single-handedly ruined his marriage. How old were you when your mum left?"

"Three years old."

"If I were to tell you that at the age of three I was responsible for the breakup of my parents' marriage, what would you say to me in response?"

"Well that's ridiculous. You were so young. How could it possibly be your fault?"

I sat there in silence and let her words pervade the air around us and sink into her consciousness.

"Hmm, I see what you mean. But I feel as if it's my fault."

"Perhaps because you've always been told it's your fault."

"Daddy loves me. He does." She frowned at me as if sensing my disapproval of her father's behaviour.

"I'm sure he does. Tell me, how do you feel when you're around your father?"

"Umm, that's a strange question. He's my dad!"

"Yes, he's your dad. Let me ask the question in a different way. When was the last time you saw your dad?"

"Yesterday, as it happens."

"Can you remember how you felt when you were with him?"

"Hmm! I felt nervous at first, then happy, really happy."

"OK, why nervous at first?"

"Well he hasn't been speaking to me."

"I remember."

"He summoned me to his office. I wasn't sure why. I thought perhaps he'd lost the contract, and he was going to be really angry with me."

"If he had been angry with you, what do you think is the worst thing that could happen to you as a result?"

"I don't like it when he's angry with me."

"No one likes their parents being angry with them, but what is the worst outcome?"

"Well, he might never speak to me again. He might never want to see me again."

"Do you really believe that? Or, might it be that he gets angry, and in time he gets over it and everything gets back to normal?"

"Perhaps, but I don't feel confident enough to chance it."

"Have you always felt this way?"

"Yes."

"In previous sessions, I asked if you could identify any common traits in the men you've had relationships with. We've identified that they were all rich and unfaithful."

"Yes, that's right. Although, Dickie appears to be only guilty of one of those traits," she smiled.

"Yes, thankfully, but I see another common trait. Do you?"

She shook her head.

"Daddy," I said careful to use her word for her father.

"What do you mean?"

"The men in your life have all, in the first instance, had some kind of relationship with your father: a friend's son, a business rival, and employees."

"So? What's strange about that?"

"Be honest with me, why did you date each of these men?"

"I liked them."

"Was there any other reason?"

She shrugged.

"It seems to me that on each occasion it has suited your father that you date them."

"Oh yes, of course," she said, as if it were the most normal thing in the world.

"It seems to me that your desire to please your father and win his approval overshadows all else in your life. Would you agree?"

She remained silent for a few minutes giving my question some thought.

"I haven't really ever considered it before. Don't get me wrong, I know I want to please Daddy, but I've never considered to what lengths I go to do so."

"Has it worked?"

"Excuse me?"

"Your attempts to please your father, have they worked?"

Her shoulders slumped, and she shook her head.

"At what point, do you think that you may need to give up?"

"I hadn't really considered that it was an option."

"I'll give you some time to consider it. If you want to, we can talk about it next week."

She nodded.

"You were telling me about how you felt nervous yesterday when you saw your father and then happy," I said encouraging her to continue.

"Yes," she visibly brightened. "I was happy because he informed me that the company I told you about last week had signed the three-year deal. He said that I was off the hook."

"Off the hook?" I questioned.

"Yes, I was so relieved that I hadn't messed up."

"On the contrary, I think that you sealed the deal. Hadn't they tried to secure a one-year deal? It was you that convinced them to go with the three-year deal.

She blushed. "Well, yes, I suppose I did."

"There's no suppose about it. Was your father grateful?"

She laughed and shook her head, "No."

"Do you think it would be unfair of you to expect some thanks in this situation?"

"No," she said for the first time appearing indignant. "I don't think it would. I have a lot to think about."

"Hmm," I agreed.

# Chapter 29

I inspected myself in my full-length mirror. I'd do. I couldn't believe that I was nervous about how I looked. What did it matter? I was meeting Sam for the first time. It was natural to want to look your best, I told myself. I shook my head. Was I for real?

The boys were at their dad's. Mum was out with her friend tonight, so she wouldn't be popping in unexpectedly. Leo was on duty tonight, so he couldn't be here to meet Sam. Not that I would have invited him anyway. We weren't at that stage in our relationship yet. Still, things were going well with Leo. I smiled as I recalled a recent conversation. He cared about me; of that, I was sure.

I just had time to pop downstairs and check for the umpteenth time that everything was ready for my guests. Rebecca had text me ten minutes ago to let me know they were on their way. I walked through the hallway mentally ticking things off of my checklist as I went. I surveiled the kitchen and ticked it off before walking into the living room. I glanced out of the living room window and pulled the curtains. That was the last thing on my list checked off. I was as ready as I ever would be.

I heard the car pull up outside. I took a deep breath and waited for the expected knock on the door. When the knock came, it was a confident knock. Some might say jaunty; a rat-a-tat-tat as opposed to a bang on the door. Sam must be doing the knocking, I surmised. Even his knock exuded confidence. Pasting a smile on my face, I opened the front door wide.

Rebecca was standing on the doorstep with a smile that matched my own. She looked fantastic in a black trouser suit with red clutch bag and red stilettos. I was struck by her lipstick. It was the same shade of red as her bag and shoes. She was standing in front of Sam obscuring my view of him.

"Rebecca," I said as I moved forward to embrace her, "lovely to see you. Please do come in."

"And you, Frankie," she said in my ear as we embraced. Pulling away from me and turning toward the man standing behind her she said, "Let me introduce, Sam."

I turned to face him with a fixed smile and my hand extended. As my hand connected with his, so too did my eyes. It was as if I'd just touched a live wire. The shock started at the tips of my fingers, ran up my arm and through my body. My heart felt like it might explode in my chest.

He was grinning at me. He was evidently enjoying himself. I could see the revelry in his eyes at my discomfort. He spoke first.

"It's nice to meet you, Frankie. I've been looking forward to it for so long," he said, his every word oozing sincerity.

"Frankie, is it OK if I put the bottle of champagne we brought in the fridge? It's best served chilled, and we wanted to make a toast later. We have some great news," she said and smiled conspiratorially at Sam.

"Uh . . . yeah of course," I muttered.

I watched as she sashayed into the kitchen and turned my attention back to her boyfriend. He was still holding my hand in his. No, holding was too gentle a word. He was gripping my hand with intent, and he leaned in toward me to whisper in my ear.

"Now there's a good girl. I knew that you wouldn't let me down. We don't want to upset Rebecca now, do we? In front of her, I'm Sam. Is that clear? It will be our little secret."

He smiled, and it sent shivers down my spine. He was standing so close to me that I found the smell of his aftershave overwhelming. I wondered if I might throw up. In my heart of hearts, I'd suspected this day might come. We had unfinished business. I was staring into the face of a murderer—David Shaw.

"Why would I want to keep your true identity from one of my best friends?" I hissed.

"You wouldn't want to hurt her, now would you? She's been through enough at the hands of unscrupulous men, wouldn't you say?"

"I would, which is precisely why I should tell her that you rank most highly among them."

He grabbed his chest in mock dismay. "Frankie, I'm wounded that you have such a low opinion of me."

I glowered at him. But before I could reply, Rebecca called from the kitchen. "Are you two coming into the kitchen any time soon? We have an announcement to make, remember?"

David aka Sam smiled smugly. "Ah, yes . . . our news. I can't wait for you to hear our news, Frankie. Really, I can't wait. Please do lead the way."

I was trembling with a mixture of trepidation and anger. I knew he was a dangerous man. I wanted to know what he had planned. I would play it his way for now, but only because he was right about my desire to protect Rebecca from any further hurt.

Rebecca had found the glasses and had already poured the champagne.

"I decided that I couldn't wait," she said with her glass in hand. She gestured to the remaining glasses on the table. "Sam, come and stand beside me."

"Of course, darling, we should do this together." He picked up his glass and walked over to join her.

God, he was a snake; a slithering, cold-blooded reptile. Actually I was being unjust to snakes. He was a . . . Words failed me.

"Frankie, we'd like you to be the first to know that we're . . . ," Rebecca said pausing dramatically.

She appeared to be milking this moment for all she was worth. David was perfectly still never taking his eyes from mine. I sensed that he wanted to savour my reaction to their news; he wanted to drink it in.

"Oh come on, Rebecca, please do tell me," I said a tad sharply.

She frowned, and realising how it must look I attempted to soften the impact of my words with a smile.

"Sorry, Hun, I'm just impatient that's all. I didn't mean to steal your thunder. You carry on in your own time," I said.

She chuckled. "Oh it's OK. It's just that I've been waiting a long time to be able to say this. I'm pregnant, Frankie," she blurted out.

I felt as if I'd been hit in the solar plexus with a baseball bat. I felt completely winded. I couldn't breathe. I hadn't expected that! Not that! I looked from Rebecca to David. Rebecca was smiling and touching her stomach lovingly, and David . . . David was watching my reaction with abject glee. To Rebecca he would look as if he was overjoyed about the news of the baby, but I knew that his joy stemmed from my reaction.

Dragging my eyes away from his smug face, I glanced at Rebecca. Her hand was no longer on her stomach but covering her mouth. She looked as if she might be sick at any moment. I sprung into action.

"Are you going to be sick?" I asked moving toward her with lightning speed.

She nodded.

"Quick, get to the sink," I instructed as I gripped her shoulders and propelled her around to face it.

She dutifully bent over the stainless steel bowl. Her hands either side to steady herself.

David stood behind her rubbing her back. He appeared to be the consummate partner except for the fact that I could see the disgusted expression on his face. He clearly wasn't comfortable with the idea of vomit.

"Do you know what; I think I'll use your bathroom, Frankie, if that's OK with you? I need to sit down. I'm not sure if I'm going to be sick or not. If I'm up there, I can sit on the bath with my head over the sink."

"Eww, too much information," David said with a grimace.

Careful David, or should I say Sam, your halo is slipping, I thought.

Rebecca raised her eyebrows in surprise. Noticing her reaction he swiftly recovered his facade.

"Sorry, darling. It's just that I'm not good with sick." He gave a little laugh as if that should be a sufficient enough explanation for him to be forgiven.

"Who is?" Rebecca commented as she made her way to the door.

"Do you need any help?" I asked.

She waved her hand dismissively as she left the kitchen and made her way upstairs.

As soon as I was sure that she was out of earshot, I asked, "Why? Why are you doing this?"

"Oh come on, Frankie. You know exactly why I'm doing this. I have to say, you have only yourself to blame."

He knew. He knew that I'd been behind the photograph of him and that girl in Mizzi's. But how did he know? I was torn. I didn't know whether to admit that I knew what he was talking about or deny everything. I made my decision: deny everything.

I shook my head. "No, I have no idea why you appear to have specifically targeted my friend in order to get at me. Please do explain."

"Tut-tut! You're normally so honest, Frankie. What has happened to you over the last year to change you? Oh wait, I know the answer to that one. It's a shame Glenn didn't finish you off as he so clearly intended. If he had, I wouldn't have to exact my revenge."

"Revenge for WHAT?" I demanded.

He ignored my outburst and continued. "I had a good thing going for a while. But then you knew that, didn't you?" He glared at me expectantly.

I remained expressionless.

He appeared to be unphased by my lack of cooperation. "Have it your way. I was engaged to a lovely young thing. Daddy was as rich as Croesus, which is just the way I like them. There was a family firm that I was destined to have an executive role in once we were married. Sarah was set to inherit everything when Mummy and Daddy shuffled off this mortal coil, which I calculated to be in around five years or so."

"Were they both ill?" I asked.

"No," he said.

"Elderly?"

"Not particularly."

"Then, why . . . ?"

He smiled at my confusion. Then it dawned on me that he had intended to kill them as he had his first wife.

"Enough of this! What I want to know is how you found out about Sarah and me?"

I shrugged, "I don't know what you're talking about."

"Was it that article in the local paper? I didn't want the publicity, but Sarah couldn't help herself. She was in love with me. She said that she wanted to tell the whole world about us. Besides, it was good publicity for the family firm. That's what I like about her: she has a good head for business. I digress. Did you read the article? Is that how you found out?"

I remained mute.

"Hmm, well I think that's how you found out. You couldn't leave it alone. You had to interfere. Why did you have to do that? Huh?"

Why did he think? Murdering bastard! Still I said nothing. I watched his frustration building.

"It doesn't matter. You don't need to tell me. I know that you learned of my relationship with Sarah; that you felt compelled to do something about it."

I raised my eyebrows. How could he know that? I wasn't going to give him the satisfaction of asking. I waited. I knew that his ego would compel him to tell me. I didn't have to wait long.

"You're not being any fun, Frankie. I know it was you that sent the compromising photograph of me and Lydia to Sarah's dad. You would have been pleased with his reaction. He was furious. He wouldn't believe me when I said I'd been set up, and that the photograph had been staged. He wasn't prepared to accept that some random girl had come up to me and surprised me with a kiss. No. He wasn't buying my brand of bullshit because it happens to be the same type of bullshit he's been telling his wife for years; he wants better for his daughter." He started to belly laugh. He found it genuinely amusing.

The guy was seriously unhinged, I thought.

"He showed the photograph to Sarah. I had seriously underestimated her. I'd assumed that she would believe me where her father hadn't, but no. It turns out that she'd watched her mother fall for her dad's lies over the years and had vowed not to be the same kind of sap. She broke it off with me that instant. It's funny, but it was the first time that I actually felt the stirrings of something genuine for her. It was an odd feeling."

I bet that it felt odd. I didn't think David Shaw was capable of feeling anything for anyone else but himself. He paused and waited for me to comment. I saw the slightest hint of disappointment cross his face when he realised I wouldn't be. I was pleased not to be giving him the reaction he wanted.

"Don't you want to know why I'm so sure that it was you who was responsible for both taking the incriminating photograph and sending it to Daddy dearest?" he asked, a slight frown marring his good looks.

It bothered me that nature had bestowed such a good-looking face upon such an evil human being. It was as if nature had assisted him in his manipulation of people. Ideally, everyone should have the looks to match their intentions: the better the intentions, the better looking they are. Surely, a purely evil person, who had the looks to match, might be encouraged to change their ways if their outward appearance were like a signpost of their intent. Still, I knew that wasn't the reality, and it never would be.

"Frankie, are you listening to me?" he hissed.

My inattention was rattling him. My reaction clearly wasn't what he had expected or desired.

"Yes, I'm listening," I answered.

"Good. Well when Sarah's dad threw the photograph at me, I knew straight away that it had been taken at Mizzi's. The fact that it was Mizzi's, and not some other random bar, was good news. Do you want to know why?"

He clearly hadn't learned yet that I wasn't going to give him the responses he wanted.

"OK, well I'm going to tell you anyway. I'm a surveillance specialist, Frankie."

Here we go again, I thought. He was exaggerating his role within ASF Technologies. He organised the installation of surveillance cameras and house alarms. That did not make him a 'surveillance specialist'.

"I oversaw the installation of the surveillance cameras at Mizzi's. They have an annual maintenance contract with us. I simply paid them a visit shortly after my debacle with Sarah and her dad on the pretence of a regular maintenance check. Once I was left alone in the office by a pretty, but I have to say gullible, bar manager, I was able to scroll through the surveillance footage of the night in question. Imagine my surprise when I spotted you, Frankie, mobile phone in hand." He had a self-satisfied grin on his face as he finished speaking.

I imagined that he was mentally patting himself on the back right now for how clever he'd been. I put my hands up in mock surrender. "You got me. How did you find me? How did you even know Rebecca and I were friends?" I asked.

The grin on his face spread still further with each question I asked. He was enjoying himself enormously.

"Oh that was easy! I asked around at work if anyone knew where you were working now. I referred to you as 'the one that Glenn Froom tried to kill' if they couldn't recall who you were initially."

I shuddered at his callousness.

"I was getting nowhere until one day I struck gold. Someone knew that you'd become friends with Maria Simpton, Verity Froom's supervisor. They suggested that I have a word with her if I wanted to locate you. So, that's what I did. I paid Maria a visit while at work. I explained that you'd been my counsellor. I wanted to get in touch with you to resume our sessions because I was still struggling after the death of my wife. She told me that you rented a room in Marina Offices in Portishead. After that, it was easy. I hadn't decided, at that stage, what form my revenge would take. I parked in the Marina Office's car park, and I watched your comings and goings."

I had been right. I knew that someone was watching me. I just hadn't realised it was David Shaw. I had assumed it was Glenn Froom.

"I hadn't been watching you for long when I saw you leaving with another lady."

"Rebecca?"

"Yes, Rebecca. I followed her and saw her enter a local cafe. I followed her in and stood behind her in the queue as she waited to pay for her coffee. I watched over her shoulder as phone in hand she scrolled through pictures of men on an online dating website. I took note of her preferred dating website, and I started to hatch a plan."

"But why go after my friend? Why not target me?" I asked bewildered.

"You're a caring soul, Frankie. Somehow I thought that you'd be more concerned about keeping the people you care about safe than yourself. So here is the deal: you back off, stop interfering in my relationships and forget you ever met me, and I walk out of Rebecca's life. She never sees me again. You insist upon meddling in my life, and I make Rebecca's life a misery. I'll go after custody of the baby. I'll say that she's unfit to be a mother. I'll say whatever I have to, to get the child and ruin her career."

"But that isn't true. She'll make a great mum," I reacted.

"Who cares about what's true? I'll wreck her reputation and take the one thing that I know she's longed for her whole life away from her. Now, do you want to be responsible for that? All you have to do is say that you'll leave me alone and your friend gets to keep her baby. I have to say that my ultimate revenge is in knowing that you'll see a mini-me running around the place every day. He or she will be a permanent reminder of me."

God, he made me sick. He had it all worked out. I needed to get out of the room. I needed to get away from him, if only for a few minutes.

"I'm going to check on Rebecca. I'll be back in a moment," I muttered. I had a desperate need to breathe in some air that he wasn't sharing.

"Of course," he said his solicitous self once again.

I rushed from the kitchen and up the stairs. I knocked on the bathroom door.

"Are you all right?" I asked from the other side of the closed door.

Rebecca opened the door. Her eyes were puffy, and her nose was red; it was safe to assume that she'd been crying.

"I'm fine," she said.

"Pregnant? I didn't expect you to say that. Are you?" I asked.

She shook her head. "No, of course I'm not. But I needed your reaction to be convincing, or he would have noticed something was off. You were expecting me to say that we were getting married."

I exhaled deeply in relief. "Thank God. I thought for a moment that you were actually pregnant."

"No, but he thinks that I am. Go get him, Frankie, and make it good," she said, a tear rolling down her face.

I squeezed her hand in a vain attempt to offer some modicum of comfort. Then I turned on my heels and braced myself for what was to come.

"How is she?" he asked as I re-entered the kitchen.

"Not so good, poor thing. She's going to hug the porcelain for a little while longer."

Once again, a look of distaste crossed his face.

"You don't like the idea of someone being sick, do you?" I asked.

"No, but as Rebecca said, who does?"

"True. But you've seen more than your fair share of vomit, haven't you?" I probed.

He stiffened. "What do you mean?"

"Well, your mum and dad liked a drink or two, didn't they? And that's putting it mildly."

"I don't know what you're talking about," he said.

"No? David James Shaw, born to George Edward Shaw and Margaret Jane Spiller, was a quiet child. He didn't say much. He lived in a council flat on an estate in Hillfields. His parents drank—a lot. Some of the neighbours felt sorry for the lad. They would take him in and feed him. There was never any food in the cupboards at home." I paused. I'd watched his face slowly drain of colour with every word that I uttered about his childhood. He was now the colour of pale alabaster.

"That's not true," he mumbled before adding, "How do you know?"

"Make up your mind, David. Either, it's not true, or it is true and you want me to explain how I know. Which is it?"

"It's not true. I had a nice childhood with nice middle-class parents."

I laughed out loud. "Do you honestly believe the crap you make up?" I demanded.

His jaw dropped, and there was an incredulous look in his eyes.

"Wh-a-t?" he spluttered.

"You heard me. You are full of crap. You sat there in front of me for an hour's counselling session each week for six weeks, and you lied about everything."

"Not everything," he smirked, clearly happier to be talking about the counselling than his childhood.

"You lied about everything. You implied that you're in a position of power within ASF Technologies. You aren't."

"I am," he insisted.

"You aren't! You're a minion! You're a nothing; a nobody! The day you were late for a session you claimed you were at some big meeting; you had to 'make sure the project was on track'. That was rubbish! Your supervisor sent you to deliver an urgent package to an important customer. You're the team gofer, nothing more and nothing less."

"That's not true!" he spat out in a fit of apoplexy.

"Oh, but it is. You've never been worth anything. You've always secretly known. So you make things up to make yourself appear to be more successful than you really are. If people knew the real you, they wouldn't like you, would they? It's far better this way."

His face, once the colour of alabaster, was now scarlet. His initial shock at my having details of his childhood had turned into rage at my insults.

"You'd better shut up, Frankie. You know what I'm capable of." His hands were clenched into fists. He took a menacing step toward me.

My brain registered the threat; the possible danger I was in, but I wouldn't allow it to show on my face. Instead I said, "Huh . . . ," my voice dripping with disdain. "You aren't capable of anything but lies. Did you think it made you more interesting to imply that you killed your wife? It made you more dangerous and sexy, perhaps?

"I know that you didn't kill your wife. That would take guts, and you're nothing but a snivelling little coward. I bet when your dad got drunk and hit your mum, you hid under your bed. I bet that you did nothing but cry."

"That's not true!" He put his hands over his ears. "It's not true! I fought back! I did! But he was bigger than me. I couldn't stop him. Not that Mum thanked me for it, stupid bitch! She was more interested in where her next drink was coming from."

"More lies," I goaded. "You never fought back just like you never hurt your wife. Her death was an accident. Why don't you admit it?"

"I did! I did fight back! And I did kill my wife!" he shouted.

"I don't believe you," I sneered.

"I did! I planned it meticulously. Why do you think that the police never caught the hit and run driver? I stole the car the day before it happened and left it in a local car park. I was careful; I made sure that I paid for twenty-four hour parking. I didn't want to get to the car only to realise it had been clamped. I identified which streets in town had no surveillance cameras, and I made sure that she was there when I needed her to be. I nipped out of work, hit her and returned, without anyone knowing I'd left."

He was grinning. Smugness exuded from his every pore.

"So you see, I do have 'guts'," he said with pride in his voice.

"Hmm, perhaps you do. I'll admit that it takes guts to admit to me that you killed your wife. You do realise that THIS conversation isn't covered by client counsellor confidentiality?"

"I'm not worried about that. It would be your word against mine. Besides, don't forget I have the baby as leverage. Imagine how poor Rebecca would feel if Sam was arrested for murder. You wouldn't want to upset Rebecca so much that she might lose the baby, would you?"

"Oh, yes . . . the baby," I said as if I'd somehow forgotten the figurative ace up his sleeve.

"There is no baby," Rebecca interrupted.

I hadn't heard her open the kitchen door. She was standing in the doorway completely motionless as if rooted to the spot by what she'd heard.

David spun around to face her. "What? I don't understand. You said . . . ?"

"Surprise, surprise, I lied!" she said.

"Why?" he asked, his expression that of bewilderment.

I couldn't believe it, he actually sounded hurt by her betrayal.

"I've been deceived by more convincing liars than you. You thought the fact that I've been cheated on and deceived by men over the years made me a soft target. You were wrong!

"I learned a lot from my husband's cheating ways. I learned to question everything a man says and does. And you didn't add up. Oh I wanted to believe that you were for real, but the voice in my head kept on demanding that I not fall for it again. You mentioned Frankie once too often. I was suspicious. I rang her and asked her to take a look at a picture I had of you."

"But . . . ?" David said. He looked shocked.

"Oh, and that was another thing. You kept avoiding having your picture taken. Why? I managed to take a sneaky picture of you last week. I have to admit that I was surprised when Frankie told me your real name. She didn't go into details of your shared history. But suffice it to say, she warned me that you may be looking for revenge against her.

"I took it upon myself, once armed with your real name, to find out a little bit about your history. I employed the same private investigator to find out the basics about you as I had to get evidence of my ex-husband's affairs. Once armed with your childhood address, I paid the neighbourhood a visit.

"Betty, your old neighbour, sends her love by the way. As for the non-existent baby, well, you'd been mentioning wanting a baby from the moment I met you. I figured that the baby was a part of whatever revenge you had planned for Frankie. So I simply gave you what you seemed to want so much. From what I just overheard, I was right."

"It doesn't matter. I'll just disappear and reinvent myself somewhere else," he said calmly.

I could see the sweat of unease forming on his forehead. We had him rattled.

"No," I said, "you won't."

"Who's going to stop me? You two?" he scoffed.

I smiled. "You called yourself a 'surveillance expert' earlier."

"Yes, that's right," he said his chest puffed out with self-importance.

"Yes, I am too. Well that may be stretching the truth a little. I've recently learned how to make use of old mobile phones that you have lying around. Did you know that you can download an application and turn them into surveillance cameras?"

"Of course I did."

I watched his face closely while I waited for him to realise what I meant by my seemingly innocent words. It took a few seconds and then his eyes started to scan the kitchen.

"Where is it?" he demanded before his gaze located the mobile phone on the side by the kettle. He made to grab it.

"Don't bother wasting your time trying to destroy the phone. The whole thing has already been backed up to my iCloud."

His face wore a murderous expression. I wagered that he was assessing the likelihood of his getting away with committing two further murders. He took a determined step toward me. I stepped backwards.

"Before you make things worse by hurting us, you should know that PC Acton has been sitting outside of my house the whole time watching events unfold as they occur," I stated.

"I don't believe you. You're bluffing," he sneered.

As if on cue, there was a loud knock on the door.

"Open up, police!" PC Acton shouted.

David was sweating profusely now. He didn't need to voice his thoughts; his expression said it all. He was calculating his chances of escape.

"Attempts to escape are futile, David. The game's up," I said, as Rebecca walked to the front door and let Leo in.

David appeared to agree with me. I watched as he reigned in his emotions. Calm descended upon him. A broad smile dominated his face as he turned to PC Acton. The manipulative, charming David Shaw was back in play. His demeanour leading me to believe that he thought he could charm his way out of it all. He still believed that he was cleverer than everyone else, and probably always would, despite there being weighty evidence to the contrary.

"Officer," he said, "there appears to have been a misunderstanding."

"Sir, if you could accompany me to the station, I'm sure we can sort things out."

Leo was playing along with him—for now. I guessed that he wanted to get him out of my house without a struggle.

"Of course, I have nothing to hide," he said.

As Leo led him from the house, he glanced back at me with a triumphant glint in his eye. He honestly thought that he was going to talk his way out of this.

# Chapter 30

The sound of the front door closing behind Leo and David as they left my house was the catalyst for my mind and body to feel the full effects of what I'd been through for the last twenty minutes. I stared at my watch. Had it only been twenty minutes? It felt like hours.

Every limb in my body started to shake uncontrollably. If Henry were here, he'd call me Mr Spaghetti Man. I felt incredibly hot. Perspiration erupted from my every pore. The light in the kitchen danced in front of my eyes. I started to feel sick.

"Sit down, Frankie. You look dreadful. It's not surprising after what you've just been through," Rebecca said manhandling me into a chair. "You need a cup of sweet tea. Yes, that's what you need."

Yuck, I could think of nothing worse. I hated sugar in my tea. My distaste at the thought must have shown on my face because Rebecca asked, "Don't you like sweet tea?"

I shook my head.

She opened my fridge and rummaged through its contents. She pulled out two chocolate bars and said, "One for you and one for me. The sugar will help."

I grabbed the chocolate bar and took a hefty bite. Neither of us said anything as we munched our way through the chocolate. Sure enough, the shaking started to subside, and so did the sick feeling in the pit of my stomach.

"How are you doing?" I asked Rebecca. I was aware of the fact that despite her brave words in front of David this latest betrayal must have hit her hard.

"I'm OK," she said, her voice cracking with emotion. I could see tears forming in her eyes.

"Let it out, Rebecca," I begged. She knew, as well as I did, that it wasn't a good thing to bottle up your emotions.

I watched as her face crumpled, and a sound emanated from her that could only be compared to that of a wounded animal. She started to rock back and forth. Her arms wrapped tightly around her as sobs wracked her whole body. I couldn't help but feel responsible for the pain she was feeling. David had targeted her because of me.

When she'd called me last week to talk about Sam, she'd been hesitant in her suspicions. She explained she had a niggling suspicion that something wasn't quite right about him.

The first flush of euphoria about meeting such a seemingly perfect guy was wearing off. She started to notice that he dropped my name into the conversation a lot. At first, she thought he simply wanted to know more about her friends. But then it went beyond a casual interest: he talked about wanting to meet me. He was so keen to meet me, too keen. Rebecca told me that she didn't understand his motivations but something felt off.

She went on to explain his reticence to have his picture taken, which added to her suspicions. She managed to take a sneaky photograph of him when he wasn't looking.

"I know it's daft, but I'm going to send you the photograph on the off chance that you recognise him," she said.

I could tell by her tone of voice that she wasn't proud of herself.

She sent me the photograph. The minute that I saw him, I knew who he was. I told her his real name. The shock in her voice as she repeated his real name back to me was both palpable and heart-breaking. Life could be so unfair; after her disastrous marriage, she deserved a good guy in her life, not David Shaw.

Client counsellor confidentiality dictated that I couldn't tell her about his wife, and what I believed he'd done. But, I did encourage her to google him. Once she'd read the newspaper articles about his wife's death and the announcement of his subsequent engagement, she put two and two together promptly.

Rebecca explained that at first she was thrilled that he wanted a baby as much as she did. She'd told him of her previous failed attempts at pregnancy. How she'd accepted that she would never have a baby, but he insisted that it wasn't too late. 'What did the experts know?' he said, his arrogance shining through.

She was only too happy to go along with the idea. However, once she knew his real name and his chequered background, she realised that he had an ulterior motive for dating her and wanting a child with her. She guessed that it was linked to me. What she didn't know was why.

The conclusion I quickly reached and shared with her without going into detail was that I must have been successful in scuppering his wedding plans. He was coming after me because somehow he knew that fact.

It was then that we'd hatched a plan. She would give him exactly what he wanted. She'd arranged for the three of us to get together.

I had to admit Rebecca had been immensely strong to be able to act as if nothing had changed where he was concerned. When this whole situation was less raw, I would suggest she consider a new career in acting because she was extremely convincing.

Rebecca had led me to believe that when the three of us met she would announce they were getting married. I didn't expect her to pull the pregnancy card out of her hat.

I was genuinely shocked at her announcement. And that was her intention.

As she said when she was feigning nausea in the bathroom, she needed my reaction to be convincing. She clearly didn't think that I was as good an actress as she was, and she was probably right. Together we lulled David into a false sense of security. He'd believed that he had complete control over the situation. That everything was going according to his plan. I'd blindsided him when I'd referred to his childhood.

Rebecca's sobs had subsided. She blew her nose and wiped her eyes. I marvelled at the fact that she still looked great. She didn't have make-up streaking down her face or panda eyes as I would have in her place. I didn't voice my thoughts as to do so would be indelicate of me. Instead I asked, "Are you going to be OK?"

She shrugged, "Eventually, I'm sure that I shall be. But if I as much as look at another online dating website, you have permission to shoot me."

"You've got a deal. I'm so sorry this happened."

"It's not your fault, Frankie. I'm trying to look on the bright side: at least a murderer has been caught. His poor wife will get some justice and another woman won't meet the same fate at his hands." She shuddered.

"Thanks for being so understanding. I don't know if I'd feel the same in your shoes."

"Oh, who are you kidding, you know you would."

I smiled. "I don't know if what we did tonight will convict him of his wife's murder. But at least the police now know he's guilty, and they can set about finding the hard evidence to prove it."

"Did you know that he'd murdered his wife?" Rebecca asked. "Is that why you meddled in his engagement? You guessed that she might end up in the same predicament."

"I didn't know for certain, but I was fairly sure that he'd killed his wife. I felt compelled to act. I couldn't tell Sarah Flattery the truth. I couldn't compromise client counsellor confidentiality and even if I had, she may not have believed me.

"I had to find another way. I knew that he was a womaniser. I suspected that it wouldn't be difficult to get evidence of his philandering ways, and I was right.

"When I sent the photographic evidence of his infidelity, I hadn't expected him to find out that it had come from me. You know the rest."

She nodded. "What did you plan to do? Try and scupper every future relationship he had?"

"I know that it sounds crazy and impractical. I don't know what I would have done in the long term. Thankfully, I now don't have to worry about that. I wasn't keeping a conscious track of him when I happened across the picture of him and Sarah Flattery announcing their engagement in the newspaper. But once I'd seen it, I had to do something."

"I understand." She rose to her feet. "Do you think that the police would mind if I went home?"

"No, I doubt it. I'm sure that they'll want to question you, but Leo has your contact details. He'll call you when they are ready to talk to you."

She nodded and as her shoulders slumped I was struck by how thoroughly defeated she appeared.

I crossed the room and threw my arms around her. "You were fantastic this evening."

She hugged me back briefly and said, "I need to go and lie down. I'll speak to you tomorrow."

"Yes, of course."

I watched her walk to her car and drive off. Returning to the kitchen I realised she hadn't asked what the exact nature of David's intended revenge had been. Perhaps she had already guessed. Perhaps she knew that she just wasn't strong enough to hear any more tonight. Who could blame her? Not I.

My phone pinged, and I picked it up to check my messages. I had a message from Leo:

*You were great tonight. I'll let you know the outcome of the interview. Remind me never to cross you. Leo x*

I chuckled at his last comment. He'd watched tonight's events unfold from the comfort of his car parked outside. He must be referring to my taunting David with his insecurities: pushing him emotionally to the brink, so his narcissistic tendencies felt compelled to defend his ego.

The only way that David could defend himself against my cruel taunts was to admit that he was guilty of killing his wife. I found it interesting that it wasn't enough for his ego to be secure in its own knowledge that what I was saying was untrue. After all, he was intelligent enough to know that it didn't matter what I thought of him. The most important thing for him should have been to get away with murder.

Under normal circumstances, I think that David would have remained rational and silent. But my using his childhood to wrong foot him had returned him emotionally to a stage in his life where he wasn't secure and confident—far from it. I was banking on the fact that all those old feelings of inadequacy would come flooding back, and his need to prove himself would come to the fore. Luckily for me, I had been right.

I had used my skills as a counsellor, not to help him, as I would have normally, but to emotionally cripple him. I wasn't proud of that fact, but I had to do what I could to stop him from hurting someone else.

Once I had discovered Sam's true identity, and Rebecca had set up tonight's meeting, I had called Leo. He had come over for a coffee, and I'd explained the situation to him leaving out the part about my suspicions that David had murdered his wife. As far as Leo was concerned, we had a guy using a false identity whose intentions were unknown and questionable.

The good part about dating a policeman was that he agreed to my little charade. I'd explained my DIY home surveillance and given him my phone, so he could watch the action unfold. We'd agreed that I'd let him know Rebecca and Sam aka David were about to arrive by closing the living room curtains.

I couldn't begin to imagine Leo's reaction to what he heard David Shaw say this evening. Still, I'd deal with the fallout from that later. The important thing was that he was now being officially investigated for his wife's murder.

The David Shaw chapter in my life was about to be concluded, and I was immensely relieved. If only the Glenn Froom chapter could end too.

Was Glenn dead? Almost every action that I'd assumed Glenn had been responsible for lately could be attributed to Richard and Abigail Sullivan. Was it time for me to finally accept what everyone else had been saying for months: Glenn Froom was dead!

Hmm, I stood up and stared out of my kitchen window at the pitch black beyond. Suddenly, the ring of my mobile phone pierced the silence enveloping me. The unexpected sound startled me and I leapt three feet up in the air. My heart thumping, I checked the caller ID.

"Hi, Maria, I have a lot to tell you. Yes, I'm still coming to your leaving party. I wouldn't miss it for the world." I sat on the closest chair available and resigned myself to a lengthy chat.

# Chapter 31

*Session six - Susan Mackintosh 11.30 a.m. - 12.30 p.m.*

It was 11.30 a.m. precisely. Susan wasn't here yet. She was usually so punctual. I wondered if she'd decided not to come to our final session. Oh well, perhaps she didn't like saying goodbye, and this was her way of avoiding it. I wasn't fond of goodbyes, either. Especially the last goodbye one had to make when someone died.

I'd gone to a funeral only yesterday: Peggy's funeral. I still had the order of service in my handbag. I rummaged around in my bag and pulled it out. It had not fared well it would seem. It had a crease in it as a result of having to fend for itself amongst the varied contents of my bag. I attempted to smooth the crease away; when it refused to budge, I felt a pang of guilt. I should have taken better care of it. It was as if my treatment of it was a reflection of my feelings for Peggy. I felt as if I had let the old lady down in some way.

I don't know why, but I hadn't expected Peggy to die from her fall. It was silly of me really because she was an old lady. Perhaps it was her feisty disposition that blinded me to the fact that she was old and vulnerable to all that age brought with it. She had seemed so strong and robust that her death just hadn't seemed likely.

As I had intended, I'd managed to catch up with Harold, Peggy's son, last week when he popped in to feed the cat. For that afternoon only, I had turned into a curtain-twitcher; frequently checking to see if he'd parked his car outside Peggy's.

Finally, after the umpteenth time of checking, I saw his car. I rushed outside and knocked on Peggy's door. I wasn't prepared for the obvious signs of grief displayed upon his face. He couldn't even muster a friendly smile as he answered the door. His whole demeanour stopped me in my tracks. I knew the answer to my question before I even asked it.

Harold informed me that Peggy had died that morning. I felt as if each word that he uttered punched me in the gut. I found myself uttering the usual trite platitudes. The shock I felt at the news rendered me incapable of finding anything remotely thoughtful or original to say. It didn't matter, however, because I suspected that Harold was so deeply immersed in his own grief that he didn't hear a word I said. He said that he would let me know about the funeral arrangements. True to his word, he had popped a note through my door a few days later.

When I'd told Maria about what had happened, she'd insisted on coming to the funeral with me. As she had supported me at Verity's funeral, so she did at Peggy's. It was good of her to be there for me. Especially as her and Gav's trip to Australia was in less than a week's time, and their leaving party was scheduled for this coming Saturday. I imagined that she had a hundred and one things to organise before she left. I was going to miss her while she was away.

I'd managed to have a more meaningful conversation with Harold at the funeral than I had when he'd told me the sad news of his mother's death.

Harold was a nice man, and despite Peggy's protestations to the contrary he seemed to have taken good care of her. He told me that he'd called her twice a day, every day, and visited her once a week. He was distraught about the fact that she had fallen down the stairs and led there alone for some hours before he found her. He explained that the fall must have happened sometime after his second call of the day. He only realised something was wrong when she didn't answer his call the following day.

It saddened me greatly to think of Peggy lying there in her hallway unable to move, and my being only the thickness of a wall away, unaware of her plight. She may have been a vindictive old girl, my garden could lay testament to that, but had I known that she needed me then I would happily have helped her.

Peggy never regained consciousness after her fall, and Harold spoke of his regret at not being able to tell her that he loved her one final time. It brought tears to my eyes, and my thoughts turned to my own mum. I didn't know how I would ever cope without her. It was then that Harold said something curious. He thanked me for calling the hospital each day to check on his mother's progress. I was about to tell him that I hadn't; that it must be someone else, when some fellow mourners interrupted our conversation to extend their condolences. I hadn't got a chance to set him straight, but I would when I saw him next.

"Frankie, I'm so sorry I'm late," Susan said as she came bursting through the door.

"Oh, that's quite all right," I said.

"No, it's not. I don't like to be late," she said, a frown marring her perfectly made-up features.

"I forgive you."

She smiled, clearly relieved. However, it wasn't long before the frown had returned as she said, "I've been thinking about what you said last week."

"Oh? Which part in particular?"

"The part about the lengths I'd go to in order to please Daddy." She paused deep in thought.

"Would you like to share your thoughts with me?" I invited.

She nodded. "I think you may be right. It hadn't occurred to me before, but the more I think about it the more I realise everything I do is to please Daddy. The reason I was late today was because . . . this is going to sound so stupid for a woman of my age." She put her head in her hands in embarrassment.

"I can assure you that I won't think anything you say is stupid," I said, attempting to reassure her.

"Really?" she asked.

"Really!"

"OK, so as I said, I've realised everything I do is to please Daddy. Everything! And that includes what I wear. He likes women to look like women: to be well-groomed and immaculate at all times. I was late because I decided that for the first time I was going to wear what I wanted to wear, and I realised that I didn't know what that was. I told you it would sound stupid."

I shook my head. "It doesn't sound stupid. It sounds as if you don't know where your father's influence over you ends and your free will begins."

"Yes! That's it," she said suddenly sitting forward in her chair.

"How did you come to your decision on what to wear today?"

She touched her jeans self-consciously. "Do you think I look OK?"

"Do you think that you look OK?" I asked pointedly.

She didn't look sure, but she nodded nevertheless.

"Your opinion is the one that matters. But for what it's worth, I think that you look great."

She beamed, clearly happy to have my seal of approval. Her self-confidence would grow in time.

"So tell me, why jeans?" I asked referring to my original question.

She shrugged, "I decided to go with comfort. Jeans are comfortable. I realised that although I like wearing all the designer clothes I have I rarely feel comfortable in them. I enjoy the fact that they're expensive, and I like to look good. What woman doesn't? But I don't want to wear them all of the time. Today, I felt like being comfortable."

"So, what do you think your father's opinion would be of what you are wearing today?"

Once again, she appeared unsure of herself as she said, "He wouldn't like it."

"He wouldn't like what you're wearing. So what's the worst thing that could happen?" I enquired.

"What do you mean?"

"Imagine that your father is here now. What's his reaction to your outfit?"

"Oh he'll make an unpleasant comment about how I should really make an effort, and that he won't be seen anywhere with me until I've changed."

"So the worst thing that could happen is to earn your father's displeasure?"

"Yes."

"So when you do exactly as your father wishes, he is happy and approving of you?"

"No."

"So let me get this straight. You do everything that you can to please him, and yet he still isn't pleased. Is that right?"

"Yes."

"I think that you know where I'm going with this."

"Why not just please myself as I'm never going to get his approval?"

"I can't comment on whether you will or won't get your father's approval. But what I can see is that you have given your father power over your happiness. What he thinks of you has supremacy over what you think of yourself. You will never have control over your own life and happiness as long as you place more worth in his opinion than your own."

"How do I change that?" she asked looking like someone who was clearly overwhelmed by the size of the task ahead.

"Slowly, but you're already doing it. Today, it seems is the first step. You chose to wear jeans knowing that your father wouldn't approve. You put what you wanted before what your father wanted. Well done."

"Thank you. I've also given some thought to Dickie's suggestion that we seek fertility advice."

I nodded and waited for her to continue.

"I'm not sure I want to."

"OK. Do you want to tell me what's fuelling your indecision?"

"I'm not sure I want children. It's not because I think having a child will ruin my relationship. It's because I simply don't want to have a child. I don't think that I ever really have."

"Lots of women make the decision not to have children," I stated.

"Yeah, I know, but if I tell Dickie how I feel, it may mean the end of our marriage."

"It may. But what's the alternative? You don't tell him. You go along with the fertility advice followed by fertility treatment, and then what? Your best case scenario: it fails. You're relieved, but Dickie is devastated. Your worst case scenario: it works and you have a baby that you don't want."

"No . . . I can't put myself through that. I can't put Dickie through that. I'm going to have to tell him, aren't I?"

"That's your decision."

"I'm going to tell him. If it means we split up, then at least it will be the first relationship I've had that hasn't ended because of my partner's infidelity."

"What do you want out of life, Susan?" I asked.

"Hmm, I'm not entirely sure, but I know that I like business. Funnily enough, do you remember Daddy's business deal? The one I interfered in."

"The one that you successfully negotiated," I reworded.

"Yes, that's the one. Well the bosses from the other company were impressed with me. Clive Smithson, he's the managing director of the company," she offered by way of explanation, "called me and well . . . I guess he offered me a job."

"What are you going to do?" I asked, immediately feeling excited for her.

"Daddy will be furious when he finds out."

"Do you want to take the job?" I persevered.

"It sounds great, Frankie," she said and for the first time today her eyes lit up with excitement.

"I think that you know what you want out of life. It's just a case of being brave enough to grab it," I said deciding to take a gamble on whether or not I'd understood the situation correctly.

She nodded. "I think you're right."

"Of course, taking the job may well have repercussions on both your relationship with your father and your husband."

"Yes, I know. I need to give it a lot of thought, but I haven't felt this excited about anything since . . . well ever. I really want to give it a go."

"It sounds as if you may be at risk of pleasing yourself rather than others," I said with a glimmer of humour.

She laughed.

*****

We were coming to the end of our final session.

"I can see now that I chose the men that I did to please Daddy," Susan said.

"Can you see how choosing those men for the reason you did meant that you had a hand in the outcome of the relationship?" I was being tough, and I knew it. But this was our last session, and I wanted her to understand the part she'd played in the downfall of her relationships. So she would realise that she had some control over the outcomes in the future.

She prickled at my words. She sat upright in her chair and squared her shoulders as if ready to do battle.

"I'm not implying that you deserved their infidelity. What I'm saying is that you chose those men for the wrong reasons. As a result, the odds of your relationships succeeding were always, in my opinion, stacked against you," I said.

I watched the fight in her gradually dissipate as she took a few moments to process my words. Until, finally, she relaxed once again into her chair.

"If I'm honest, I'm not sure I really loved any of them. You're right; my whole life seems to have revolved around gaining Daddy's approval."

"Can I ask, have any of the men in your life known the real you?"

She frowned, "What do you mean?"

"As I've listened to you describe your various relationships over the weeks, I couldn't help but draw comparisons with your relationship with your father. What I mean is that you've tried to be the person you think your partners want you to be in order to make them love you. No one can keep up that kind of facade forever. Don't you find it exhausting?"

"Hmm," she shrugged, "I suppose I do, but I don't know how else to be."

"Well, how about being yourself first and foremost."

"But what if no one likes that version of me?"

"Do you want to know what I say to that?" and without waiting for her reply I said, "I say to hell with them. I don't know how many billions of people there are on this planet, but I'm not prepared to believe that there isn't one person who isn't going to like you for you. I'm willing to bet that if you let them know the real you, there will be many people only too pleased to get to know you."

"Hmm, perhaps," she said still not sounding particularly convinced. "Can I ask you a question? And I want an honest answer," she cautioned.

"Of course."

"What do you think of the colour of my hair?" she asked at the same time as touching her hair self-consciously.

I hadn't been expecting the change in direction that the conversation had taken. I was taken aback. "Um . . . it's auburn. Auburn is a nice colour."

"My natural hair colour is brown. I haven't had brown hair since I was seventeen. I think it's time to go back to my natural hair colour."

I was beaming both on the inside and the outside. Susan may not realise it yet, but this was the exact moment when she learned to be herself and to please herself.

Susan's hair colour had been a symbol of her need to please her current partner since the age of seventeen. Her first boyfriend had liked blondes, her current husband red heads. She had reinvented herself to please each new partner, and in pleasing them she had ultimately attempted to please her father.

The simple act of choosing her own hair colour meant that she was no longer pleasing anyone but herself. It was the first step in what I imagined was a long road, but she was going to take it nevertheless.

I surreptitiously glanced at the clock on the wall behind her. Her time was up.

"We've reached the end of our final session," I stated.

"Indeed. Thank you, Frankie. I came here looking for a substitute friend: someone I could pour my troubles out to but without being judged. I had no idea what I had let myself in for." She tempered her final words with a laugh.

"I hope that it's been a worthwhile experience."

"It has. I think it's time I got to know myself."

I smiled.

As she reached the door, she turned and looked over her shoulder at me. "I want you to know that you're a brave lady. I admire you."

"Thank you, but why?" I asked puzzled.

"Glenn Froom."

Just hearing his name set off the familiar chain reaction in my body. I reached for the arm of the chair to anchor myself.

"I don't understand," I stuttered.

"When I heard you mention his name, a couple of weeks ago, it sounded familiar.  I couldn't remember why, so I decided to google him. I discovered that he killed his wife and then he tried to kill you."

What was there to say? I simply nodded in response.

"That's why when you rang me to suggest I see another counsellor, I decided to stick with you: partly because I didn't want to start over with another counsellor, but also because I understood why you were sometimes distracted. If I'm honest, I think you're amazingly together considering what happened to you."

Her sincerity shone through her words.

"Thank you for your understanding," I said.

"You're welcome," she beamed as she turned and left for the final time.

I hadn't expected that. She'd completely unnerved me by mentioning Glenn's name. Damn that man to hell. When was he going to stop affecting my life? When you stop letting him, my inner voice replied.

I gathered up my things and locked the office door. As I wandered down to reception, my mind was full of the events of last year. Verity's face kept entering my mind's focus. I waved goodbye to Theresa without thinking and stepped out into the afternoon sunshine. It was good to feel some warmth on my face. Without thinking, I raised my face to meet the sun's rays and closed my eyes.

"Watch out!" a man shouted from nearby. The urgency in his voice was palpable.

As my eyes flew open, I felt someone's arm wrap tightly around my waste. Suddenly, I was being propelled backward through the air. My feet had left the safety of the ground. My arms were flailing around futilely, it would seem, as all I could grab was air. Although I sought the stability of the ground, it was a shock when my body finally found it. My bones jarred as they hit the pavement, and I felt a great weight land upon me.

"Are you OK?" asked the man on top of me as he extricated himself from the heap that was us.

I wasn't sure whether I could answer that question. I'd never been winded before, but I suspected that I had been now. I attempted to nod.

I was aware of the sound of a car being driven at speed from the car park. I glanced at the exit just in time to see a car wheelspin away toward Portishead High Street.

"That bloody idiot was driving straight at you. I had to do something. I play rugby," he said by way of explanation.

So I'd been rugby tackled, by a rugby player. No wonder I felt as if I'd been hit by a truck. Still it could have been worse: I could've been hit by that car.

"Are you OK?" he repeated his previous question. "Shall I call for an ambulance?"

I shook my head. "Just give me a few moments," I croaked. My ribs hurt like hell. But, hopefully, it was just bruising.

"Frankie, are you OK?" Theresa asked as she came rushing out of reception. "Whatever has happened?"

I looked pointedly at the guy who'd saved me. He, quite rightly, took it as his cue to explain.

"Oh my God," Theresa said, after hearing what rugby guy had to say. "Let's get you inside."

"No, I'm fine. Just help me up, and I'll be on my way."

"Are you sure?" They both said at the same time.

"Yes. Thank you for saving me," I said to the rugby tackling man-mountain standing before me.

"Oh, that's OK. I just hope I didn't hurt you too much."

I shook my head. "I'll be fine. Did you see who was driving the car?"

"I didn't get a good look, but I'm sure it was a man."

"OK, thanks."

I hobbled to my car. I'd been right all along. He was alive. It had to be Glenn. He'd tried to knock me down once before. He was trying again. I was sure of it. There was no point in reporting this to DC Smithers. He'd made it clear that he thought Glenn was dead. I'd call Leo. I'd tell him what happened, and if he thought I should report it officially, then I would.

I attempted to put my car key in the ignition; a simple task that I had performed many times before, but this time it seemed to be beyond me. Thankfully, my fifth attempt was successful, where the first, second, third and fourth hadn't been, and in the nick of time because I was on the verge of tears. I had managed it; I had turned the engine on. I was reassured by the gentle ticking over of the engine. It was time to go home.

# Chapter 32

"Leo, it's me," I said.

"Where are you?"

"I'm at home. Are you on duty?" I asked.

"Yes, but I finish in an hour. I could pop over straight from work, if you like? Are you OK? You sound a little . . ." he hesitated, and I could tell he was searching for the right word in an attempt to be tactful.

I took pity on him and interjected, "No, I'm not OK. I want to talk to you about something. If you could come over when you're finished, that would be great."

"OK. I'll see you soon."

He'd already ended the call before I could reply.

I sat at the kitchen table nervously twisting a tea towel in my hands. My anxiety was making my stomach do somersaults. It was Glenn. I was sure of it. He was finally going to finish what he'd started. When I'd turned in to my street, less than fifteen minutes ago, I'd half expected him to be inside the house waiting for me. I still had my DIY surveillance system in place, so I'd checked the coast was clear before I entered the house.

My mobile phone rang. Automatically I checked to see who was calling. No Caller ID. I recoiled from the phone. If I answered the phone, it would bring him into my house. I couldn't allow his voice or even the sound of his breathing to contaminate my home. The thought of answering the phone made me feel physically sick. Stop ringing! Please make the phone stop ringing! I pushed the phone away but couldn't take my eyes away from the caller display screen.

"Shut up!" I screamed at it.

It instantly stopped ringing. A coincidence I knew. Or was it? I'd been surveilled in my own home before. What if . . . ? I jumped to my feet wildly scanning the kitchen for places that could hide a pinhole camera. The smoke detector caught my eye. Why not? It had been done before.

I grabbed a chair, dragged it over, and climbed up onto it. I twisted off the cover. Nothing. Damn. Where else could it be? From my vantage point, on top of the chair, I scrutinised the contents of my kitchen.

Hmm, where could it be? I spotted the kitchen clock on the wall. That would be a perfect place for a hidden camera. I jumped down from the chair and strode over to the clock. In my haste to extract it from its nail on the wall, I didn't grip it properly. It fell from my hand and dropped to the floor with a smash. Shards of plastic casing and glass covered the floor. Picking up the clock face and battery housing, I inspected them both carefully. No, nothing.

My mobile phone started to ring again. No Caller ID. Every nerve ending in my body was jangling. I put my hands to my ears in an effort to block out the sound. I had to put some distance between me and the phone before I lost all self-control. I stumbled toward the kitchen door and snatched at its handle. The door flew open in one fluid motion.

As I entered the hallway, I could see someone was at the front door. Blinding panic assaulted my every sense. I felt the vomit rise in my throat. My eyes sought out the door chain. I'd remembered to lock the door when I came in, and I'd secured the chain. It was some small comfort.

It was Glenn. I knew it. But what was he doing? He was bending down. I could see his outline through the translucent glass in the door. Was he daubing graffiti? Let's face it that was his modus operandi. Or worse still, and my stomach somersaulted as the thought occurred to me, was he trying to pick the lock? I needed my baseball bat. The only problem being that it was by the coat rack, which meant getting closer to the front door.

My instinct was screaming at the top of its voice that I should not take one step closer to that murdering bastard. But I needed that bat. I took a tentative step toward it. He was still bending down, I noticed.

I was willing my feet to take another step when the shrill sound of the house phone pierced the air around me, and destroyed the modicum of self-control that I still possessed. I screamed and jumped three feet in the air.

My eyes shot to the figure at the door. He had stood up. He'd heard me. The phone continued to ring, and I made a split-second decision to dash for the bat. I grabbed the handle and held the bat high. I was ready. I'd crack his skull open if I had to.

I heard the rattle of the letterbox being opened. What was he doing? Suddenly, it occurred to me that if he couldn't get in, he was going to force me out. What if he had petrol? What if he was going to pour it through the letterbox and follow it with a lit match? That was it. He was going to set fire to my house with me in it. Either way, he won: I either came out to escape the flames and he killed me, or I stayed here and died anyway. I stepped backwards into the coats on the coat rack. I was both metaphorically and literally backed into a corner.

Glenn was putting something through the letterbox. I shut my eyes tight. I was waiting to hear the telltale sound of liquid splashing onto my hallway carpet; for the smell of the fumes to assault my senses.

I could hear a voice. It was a familiar male voice. Who and where was it coming from? I was momentarily disorientated. The voice wasn't coming from outside. It was coming from inside my home. I gripped my bat as hard as I could. He sounded as if he were in the hallway with me. I peeked out from behind the coats. No, there wasn't anyone there. But I could still hear his voice.

"Could you give me a call back please, Frankie. I'm on a new number. It's . . ."

My terror-stricken mind struggled to make sense of the words. The answer machine; he was speaking to the answer machine. Whoever had just called the house phone was leaving a message.

My attention flew back to Glenn at the front door. I stared down at the doormat. Was it soaked with some kind of flammable liquid? I couldn't smell any kind of accelerant. Instead there was a folded piece of paper lying there. Perhaps he'd decided to leave me a threatening note this time: extend the psychological torture he was putting me through.

I peered through the translucent glass in the door. I couldn't see him. Had he left? Or was he hiding? Ready to pounce when I opened the door. With shaking hands, I picked up the piece of paper and attempted to prepare myself for what it might contain.

Unfolding the note, I tried to focus on the words and make sense of them, but my brain was refusing to cooperate. There was a picture. It was of a shop. A shop? My fear-fogged brain immediately began to clear as it became obvious that I was looking at a picture of my local takeaway. I was holding an advertising flyer for a Chinese chip shop. The guy at my door must have been delivering them around the neighbourhood.

I rushed to the answer machine. Now my brain was able to function properly, I realised that the voice I'd heard on the answer machine was DC Smithers'. I played the message. He didn't say much; he wanted me to call him back. With trembling fingers, I managed to jot down the number. It would seem that I hadn't yet physically recovered from, what appeared to all intents and purposes to be, a self-induced scare.

My fingers fumbled over the numbers on my phone's keypad. It would be a miracle if I'd managed to call the right number.

"DC Smithers? It's Frankie Wilson. You called me."

"Frankie, I'm glad you called me back. I've been trying to get hold of you for most of the day."

"Oh?"

"Yes, I've tried your mobile multiple times and your home phone number. I decided that it was probably best just to leave a message for you to call me back."

"Do you have a new mobile phone number?"

"Yes."

All of a sudden, I realised what had happened. I had his old mobile phone number stored in my phone, but I didn't have his new number. That was obviously why his multiple attempts to call me today had appeared on my phone as having no caller ID.

"I'm calling about Glenn Froom," he continued. "We've found him."

I felt my legs buckle from underneath me as the meaning of his words infiltrated my brain. I sank to the ground while still gripping the phone.

"Oh thank God! You've found him. Do you believe me now? He's been stalking me. Only this morning, he tried to run me down again. You must have only just picked him up. Where was he? How did you catch him?"

"Frankie . . . ," he attempted to interject.

"Oh, I'm so relieved," I rambled on. "I thought he was here, at my home, a few minutes ago, but I was wrong. I made a mistake, but I haven't been wrong about the other times. You'll see that now. Once you question him, you'll see that."

I wasn't letting DC Smithers get a word in edgeways, and I knew it. But I was so damn relieved to know that they had him at last.

"Frankie!" he said, louder this time.

"Yes?"

"I don't appear to have made myself clear."

"Oh? You mean that you've found him, but you don't have him in custody. Is that what you're saying? I'm still in danger."

I felt the familiar stirrings of fear start to take a hold of me. I looked behind me as I was expecting Glenn to be standing there. His usual one step ahead of the police once again.

I heard DC Smithers sigh heavily into the phone.

"In hindsight, perhaps, I should have visited you in person. I might have been able to make my point more succinctly."

What the hell was the man talking about? I wanted to scream down the phone that he should get the hell on with whatever he wasn't explaining very well. But I didn't. What I actually said was, "Please do explain."

"OK, but please do me a favour; don't speak until I say you can. OK?"

"OK." I clamped my mouth shut in a determined effort to hear him out and waited.

"Glenn Froom has been found. More to the point, his body has been found. Well, part of his body has been found. But, in my opinion, it is the most important part: his skull. Before you interrupt me, Frankie, with questions such as, how do we know that it's his skull et cetera? We're sure because the skull was found a while ago. We've identified him through his dental records. I didn't want to call you until I was absolutely sure it was Glenn Froom. Now . . . you can speak if you wish."

I found myself unable to speak. I was struggling to make sense of what he'd just said.

"Umm . . . ," was all I managed.

"You might be wondering why just the skull was found?" DC Smithers anticipated. "Well, I'm reliably informed that when a human being decomposes in the sea it's not unusual for the head as well as the hands and feet to separate from the body."

"Do you think that he's been in the sea this whole time?" I asked.

"Yes, we do. We believe that he drowned on the day that he entered the sea over a year ago."

"Who found him?"

"We were lucky. He could have stayed on the bottom of the sea floor forever undetected."

I shuddered at the thought.

"A local dive school were taking some students out into the Bristol Channel. They usually dive in the same spot but decided to change it up a little this particular day and went further out. One of the instructors dove down to the sea bed, and he spotted a skull. He called us. The rest is history as they say."

"I can't believe it," I said.

"You can," he said gently, "and you need to."

"But I was so sure that he was still out there. And that he was stalking me."

"I know you were. It isn't surprising after everything he put you through. But, now you know that he's dead. He's really dead, Frankie."

The emotion finally hit me. I couldn't hold back the sob in my voice.

Uncomfortable with my obvious distress DC Smithers said, "OK, I have to go. Is there anyone who can come and be with you?"

"Oh, yes, yes," I rushed to reassure him. "Don't worry about me. I'll be fine."

"Good, well I'll be going."

"Oh, DC Smithers . . ."

"Yes?"

"Thank you for everything."

"No need to thank me, Frankie. Just doing my job." He hung up.

I sat back on my haunches in the hallway staring at the baseball bat. Only moments ago, I was prepared to batter some innocent guy who put a flyer through my door because I thought he was Glenn Froom. Thank God I hadn't felt brave and opened the door wielding the bat. I'd have been arrested.

All those times over the last year or so when I'd believed that I'd seen him. The silent calls that I'd attributed to him. Every single bad thing that had happened to me over the last twelve months I had firmly believed was down to Glenn Froom. I'd been proven wrong about the gifts and Henry's abduction, but still I'd believed he was out there. Watching and waiting to finish the job that he'd started. I was wrong!

"I was wrong!" I shouted out loud. "Glenn Froom is dead! He's dead!"

"Frankie, are you OK?" shouted Leo from outside my front door.

Getting up from my knees, I rushed to unlock the door and flung it wide.

"He's dead!" I shouted.

"Who is? Are you OK? What's happened?"

I could see him scanning the hallway behind me for evidence of some kind of fracas. He was ever the policeman.

"He's dead!" I repeated. "Glenn Froom is dead. DC Smithers just called to give me the news. He's been dead this whole time."

"Oh, Frankie, I don't know what to say. You have to be so . . . happy doesn't seem to be an appropriate word in view of the fact someone has died, but . . ."

"I never thought that I'd say this about someone's death, but I'm bloody ecstatic, Leo," and with arms outstretched I launched myself at him.

He readily followed my lead and wrapped his arms around me. I was content to stand there in his strong, comforting embrace. For the first time in a long time, I felt safe, completely safe.

After what seemed like an age, he pulled away from me and looking down into my face he said, "Was that what you called me about earlier?"

I'd forgotten about that. The hit and run business had paled into insignificance now that I knew Glenn couldn't have been behind the wheel.

"No, it was about something else, but it doesn't seem so important now."

"Let me be the judge of that. I'll make you a cuppa, and you can tell me all about it."

"Shouldn't I be making the cuppa seeing as it's my house?"

"Well, if you're offering?"

I tapped him playfully on the arm. "Men!" I commented, and I set about making two cups of comforting tea.

Setting his cup before him, I explained this morning's events while he drank his tea.

"What do you want me to do?" he asked.

"Well, when I thought Glenn was driving, I wanted you to identify the car. But now I'm going to assume it was just an inattentive driver."

"It sounds like dangerous driving to me. Did you get the name and number of the guy who saved you? He may have seen the number plate."

"No, sorry, I didn't think. I was too shaken up."

"That's OK. I'll swing by your building tomorrow and see if the incident was caught on the security cameras. If it was, then I may be able to get a number plate."

I nodded. "Thanks. You're right. He was driving dangerously."

"He?"

"The guy who saved me said it was a man driving, which is why I jumped to the conclusion that it was Glenn."

"Why didn't you ring the police?"

"Because they already think I'm crazy. I decided to wait and talk to you about it."

"Because I don't think you're crazy?" he joked, grinning from ear to ear.

"Oh, very funny, you're a real joker."

"I like to think so. Now shut up and come here."

"Oh you're getting all alpha male on me now, are you?" I asked playfully.

He grabbed me and pulled me to him. "You bet ya!" he said as he planted his lips firmly on mine.

I wound my arms around his neck and allowed myself to melt into the embrace.

# Chapter 33

I'd bought something new to wear to Maria's party tonight. But now, standing in front of the mirror, I wasn't so sure. The new top looked OK but it was clashing with my flowery knickers and stripy socks. Hmm, it wasn't a particularly attractive look. Hopefully, I'd look better once I'd completed the ensemble with my new skinny fit grey jeans and boots. No time like the present. I pulled on my jeans having to tug more than I had in the shop to get them over my hips.

Had I put weight on? I giggled at the ludicrousness of the thought. I'd only bought them this morning. I knew that muffin I'd had at lunchtime was a mistake. What was it they said, 'a moment on the lips a lifetime on the hips'? Well something like that I was sure. I managed to do up the button on the waistband. Hmm, breathing may be a problem this evening.

Luckily my top ended below the waistband of the jeans so, if necessary, I could undo the button on my jeans without anyone noticing. I eyed the way the denim hugged my thighs, and decided that I was in no danger of my trousers falling down. In fact, I may need someone to peel them off of me later. I thought of Leo, and my cheeks burned. He was working tonight, so he couldn't come to the party.

I opened my bedroom door and yelled for Henry.

"What, Mum?" he yelled back from the bowels of the kitchen.

"I think that I may need your help."

I heard him come bounding up the stairs, taking two at a time.

"Yep?" he asked without the slightest hint of breathlessness I noted enviously.

"Now don't laugh. But I may need your help getting these jeans off."

He started to giggle.

"I said don't laugh."

He giggled even more.

"I'll lie on the bed and get them down over my hips, and then you pull them over my ankles. OK?"

"OK, I'm ready," he said planting each leg in turn down firmly on the ground rather like a sumo wrestler preparing to fight.

I lay down and wriggled and tugged. "OK, your turn. Pull!" I commanded.

Henry dutifully pulled at the material. He managed to negotiate the material free of first one ankle and then the next. Both of my legs started to tingle as the blood was once again able to flow freely.

Suddenly, loud music filled the air. It was coming from Alex's bedroom. The song was Gangnam Style. Henry started to dance around the room; looking as if he were riding a horse one minute and attempting to lasso the imaginary four-legged animal the next.

"Come on, Mum," he said encouraging me to join in.

We were both soon dancing around my room. I had to admit that he was much better at it than I was.

When the song ended, he began to laugh hysterically.

"What? What is it?" I asked.

"It's less gangnam style and more knicker style," he said pointing at my trouserless legs.

It took a moment for me to understand what he meant. Then, as I saw the humorous side of the situation, I dissolved into giggles. I had to admit that it felt good to laugh. I watched the laughter crease Henry's face. I'd been watching him closely since the Abigail incident, for any signs that it had affected him adversely. I'd seen none.

Oddly, it was quite the opposite: he seemed to revel in the attention that it brought him.

Henry happily regaled the other children in his school with the story of his kidnapping. In fact the teachers had asked me to curtail his storytelling as some of the children were having nightmares. When I asked him what he was telling them to inspire nightmares, he did admit that he may have embellished his story somewhat in the interests of excitement. I was sure that he was going to be an actor when he grew up. He definitely had a flair for the dramatic. Still, I was relieved that he seemed unaffected by the experience.

Alex, however, was a different character altogether. At first, he had seemed more affected by his brother's kidnap than Henry was. Alex understood that the outcome could have been very different for Henry and that was what was haunting him: what might have been. Still, at least I had been able to tell him that Glenn was dead. We no longer had that shadow looming over us.

It wasn't until I saw the relief cross Alex's face at the news of Glenn's death that I fully appreciated the burden Alex had been carrying around for the last year. His stature had visibly risen as if upon hearing the words a vast weight had been lifted from his shoulders. I had felt guilty at the sight. I was aware on some level of his worry and fear, but I hadn't realised just how much it had affected him. I'd been too wrapped up with how it had impacted upon me.

"Mum, you're frowning? What's up?" Henry asked, immediately subdued.

"Nothing," I smiled once again. "I was wondering when Grams was going to get here."

As if on cue, the doorbell rang.

"I'll let her in," he said running from the room.

I could hear her familiar voice as she came in and took her coat off.

"Mum, I'll be down in a minute. I want to call Rebecca," I shouted from my bedroom.

"OK, love," she hollered back.

"Mum," Alex said, his head popping out from behind his bedroom door.

"Yep?"

"Erm, umm," he said as his cheeks reddened significantly.

Hmm, this didn't look promising, I thought.

"Well, I was wondering . . ." he stalled.

"Just spit it out, Alex."

"Can Charlotte come round tonight?" he blurted out.

Charlotte was the girl that he'd admitted to talking to online when I'd suspected he was being duped into talking to Glenn. He hadn't mentioned her since that day. But I knew they were still friends because I regularly heard him talking to her online. After what had happened, I had insisted that if his computer was to remain in his room then the door stayed open, which was why I was sure that he was speaking to her. His asking if she could come round was progress, but it had caught me off guard as I suspected it was designed to do.

"You know that I'm going out tonight."

"Oh, are you?" he said feigning surprise monumentally badly.

"You could learn a thing or two from your brother in the art of acting."

"Uh?" he said.

"So, let me guess. You think that it is better to have your girlfriend round for the first time while your mum is out and Grams is babysitting. Is that right? Perhaps you're right. I'm sure that Grams won't tell Charlotte any embarrassing stories about her grandson's childhood. I'm sure that you can trust her not to embarrass you," I said, my words loaded with irony.

He blanched. "Uh, hmm, I get your point. Tonight's not a good idea."

"I tell you what. Invite her round tomorrow afternoon. I promise that there will be no fuss. It'll just be me and Henry here. I don't mind if she's in your room with you, but the door will stay open. Is that clear?"

"Oh, Mum!" he said reddening. "We're only going to be playing music and watching YouTube. We aren't going to be doing anything else."

"I know and that's why the door stays open, so I can make sure of it."

"You are so embarrassing," he muttered as he closed the door.

"Have we got a deal?" I shouted through the door.

"Yeah!" he shouted back.

"Good, and open your door."

I heard him huff and then open the door a crack.

Pushing it wide open, I smiled at him. "Now that wasn't too difficult, was it?"

He rolled his eyes at me.

"Mum, do you think that you could make sure you're fully clothed when Charlotte comes round tomorrow?" he asked, a cheeky grin on his face.

"Huh?" I was confused by the question. Then I remembered my state of semi-undress.

I chuckled as I walked back into my bedroom. I grabbed my old pair of jeans and put them on. Now, time to ring Rebecca.

"Hi, how are you?" I asked as she answered the phone.

"Hi, Frankie. Yeah, I'm OK."

She didn't sound OK.

"Now tell me the truth, not the polite version," I encouraged.

"I should have known better than to try to fake it with you," she admitted.

"Yep, you should."

She sighed deeply. "I'm still struggling with the whole Sam thing, David thing."

"It's not surprising. I feel guilty because if it hadn't been for me this wouldn't have happened to you."

"It's not your fault."

"We'll agree to disagree on that one. I don't want this call to be about you making me feel better. I've called to see how you are."

"I'm feeling crap! There you are. Now I've said it."

"What are you going to do about it?" I challenged.

"Sit, mope and drink copious amounts of mind-numbing alcohol. That's what I'm going to do about it."

"I can understand your reasons, but how about you come to Maria's party and drink copious amounts of mind-numbing alcohol there instead?"

"She hasn't invited me."

"There will be lots of people there. She won't mind one extra."

"I appreciate the thought, but I'm not in the mood. Is there any news on the case against David?"

I hesitated.

"Just tell me, Frankie, I want to know," she insisted.

"Well, this is just between us because Leo has told me unofficially."

"Are you seriously talking to me about confidentiality?" she asked.

"I know that I can trust you. I need you to know that the information is not in the public domain, so you don't inadvertently repeat it," I explained.

"I'm sorry. I understand."

"They are about to charge him with his wife's murder. They presented the Criminal Prosecution Service (CPS) with the evidence they've gathered. The CPS think there is enough to charge him."

"That is good news. What evidence do they have?"

"Are you sure that you want to hear this?"

"Oh for God's sake just tell me."

"OK. There was a girlfriend. He met her when he was still married. They used to meet at Mizzi's. She was the girl in the photograph that I sent to his fiancée's father.

"It wasn't hard for the police to track her down. She still frequents Mizzi's on a regular basis. They caught up with her there one night and invited her into the station for a chat. She wasn't willing to talk about David at first. Not even when the police suggested that she could be considered an accessory to murder."

"You're joking?"

"No. She's quite a tough lady apparently."

"So, what happened?"

"Well, Leo had an idea. He dropped the other women in David's life into the conversation. She had thought that she was the only one since his wife died. She had no idea about Sarah Flattery or you. She turned on him and told them everything. As we know, he's a narcissist and, as such, his ego demands that at least one person admires his greatness. He had told her everything. She knew the plan inside and out, and she is willing to testify against him. Combine that with what we recorded that night and the CPS think they'll get a conviction."

"That's good."

"Yes, it is. Are you going to be all right? I wish that you would reconsider coming to this party. I'll text you the details in case you change your mind."

"Don't hold your breath. I'll see you soon. I promise."

"Make sure you do, or I'll come round and drag you out kicking and screaming."

She chuckled and put the phone down.

I felt so guilty that she had got caught up in all of this. She'd had such a hard time with men, and to add insult to injury David Shaw entered her life. I needed to get drunk. I had two more hours before I needed to be at Maria's. I'd stick to drinking cups of tea until then.

I wandered downstairs and into the kitchen.

"Hello, Mum. How are you?"

# Chapter 34

Damn, I'd just driven past Maria's house. It had taken me longer than I'd expected to find it. In all the time I'd known her, I'd never once visited her home. She'd either come over to my house, or we'd met in pubs and restaurants. I was going to meet Gav for the first time. I was looking forward to it. I glanced in my rear-view mirror and noticed at least three or four cars behind me. I wasn't going to be able to turn around. I'd have to drive around the block.

Maria had invited me to stay overnight, so I didn't have to worry about getting a taxi home later. I felt like a teenager on a sleepover at my friend's house. Mum had waved me off earlier, much the same way as she had when I was fifteen, with a stark warning to behave myself. We'd both chuckled at that. It was nice to see my mum looking happy and relaxed again. She was as relieved as I was that Glenn's body, well skull to be specific, had finally been found. It was the end of months of worry and fear for both of us.

I spied the bottle of champagne on the front passenger seat. I'd put it in one of those fancy bottle bags and attached a shiny silver bow. I knew Maria loved champagne, and it was my goodbye gift to them both. I was going to miss her, I thought sadly. She'd been a good friend when I'd needed one most. I hadn't had chance to speak to her in the last few days. I wanted to tell her the news about Glenn, but I wasn't sure there'd be an opportunity tonight. She'd told me that she'd invited sixty people to their party, so it was going to be busy. As she was the hostess, I didn't imagine that I'd get to see much of her. I'd tell her in the morning over breakfast. That way, she could leave for Australia knowing that I was safe.

She kept saying that I was the guest of honour at her party and as such she wanted me there before everyone else arrived. She'd said that she had some kind of surprise for me. It was her leaving party, and yet she was thinking of me.

I spotted her house in the distance and managed to pull on to her drive this time. I climbed out of the car and grabbed my overnight bag and the present. I checked that I hadn't left anything on the seats to invite the attention of passing thieves, and satisfied that I hadn't, I locked the car.

I admired her house as I walked to the front door. It was a modern semi-detached house with hanging baskets on either side of the front door. I rang the bell and waited.

"Hi, Frankie, come on in," she invited as she stepped aside to let me pass.

"Hi, Maria, you have a lovely home," I said as I inspected her hallway. "In fact, it puts mine to shame."

"Thank you and nonsense. You have a lovely home too."

"OK, enough of these polite pleasantries. Where's Gav? I've been looking forward to meeting him."

"He's just popped out to get more booze. He decided that I hadn't bought enough."

"Men!" I said.

"Exactly, I thought that I had more than enough, but you know what they're like. They don't want to be embarrassed in front of their friends by running out of beer."

I lifted my overnight bag, "Is there anywhere I can put this?" I asked.

"Yes, sure, I'll show you to your room for the evening. Follow me," she invited.

She walked ahead of me up the stairs and turned left at the top. "This is the spare room. This will be your room for the night. Sorry about all the boxes."

"That's fine. I quite understand. How is the packing going?"

"We're nearly finished. I just have the final few things to pack: the everyday necessities. You know what it's like."

I nodded. "Yep, the kettle and things like that."

"I knew that you'd understand. You can put your bag on the bed. Right then, shall we get this party started?" she asked, while raising an imaginary glass to her lips.

"Yes, great! When is everyone else due to arrive?"

"Let's see," she said while checking her watch. "It's seven now. I put eight-thirty on the invitations. So we have plenty of time."

"I'll be drunk before the first guests arrive if I start drinking now," I warned.

"You'll be fine. Follow me to the kitchen; I'll get you a drink. Prosecco?"

"Hmm, yes please," I said as we left my bedroom for the night and retraced our steps. I was still carrying the champagne. I'd give her the present when Gav arrived. After all, it was a gift for both of them. Once in the hallway, she opened the first door on the right.

"This is the kitchen," Maria announced, rather like an enthusiastic estate agent might to a prospective buyer.

"Very nice," I said as I took in the modern units and the stainless steel appliances.

I watched as she poured the wine into two glasses.

"Actually, there's something I want to tell you, but I didn't think I'd get the chance," I said.

"Hold that thought," she said. "Let's go into the lounge. There's something I want to show you as you're the guest of honour."

"Oh, what have you done?" I laughed. "Tonight is about you and Gav, not me."

"You're wrong," she said, "it's most definitely about you." She passed me my drink. "I'll lead the way."

She opened the lounge door and stood aside, so I could walk in before her.

I was struck by how dark the room was with the exception of some candles in the far corner.

"Are you having a disco? Where's the glitter ball?" I joked.

"No, it isn't a disco," she said. Something about her tone of voice instantly made me feel uneasy.

I turned to face her, but she'd closed the lounge door behind her. It meant that I could see where she was standing, but I couldn't see the expression on her face.

"What was it that you wanted to show me?" I asked.

"Over there in the corner of the room," she instructed.

"OK." I took a step forwards, but it was hard to see. She must have blackout curtains because they weren't letting a scrap of light into the room. Most people had blackout curtains in their bedroom not in their lounge. I shuffled forward cautiously.

"Ow!" I yelled as my shin made contact with the corner of what I assumed was her coffee table.

"You might want to watch out for the coffee table," she said.

"Oh you don't say," I said, and laughed as I hobbled my way across the room.

There were four red pillar candles on a table. They were surrounding a photograph. I could see that the photograph was of a man, but I couldn't see what he looked like. What was this? Some sort of shrine? Why did Maria particularly want me to see it?

"Um, I'm a little confused, Maria," I confessed.

"Take a closer look at the photograph, Frankie. Things may become clearer."

The earlier feeling of unease returned. I was beginning to feel that something was wrong. I leaned over to see the person in the photograph. He was smiling at the camera looking every inch a charming, self-assured young man. I recoiled from his image without thinking.

"You do recognise him then?" she asked.

"Yes. Is this some kind of sick joke?" I asked.

"No. Who is it? I want to hear you say it."

"It's Glenn. Glenn Froom."

"Yes, that's right, my Glenn Froom."

I shook my head in denial. "No, what are you talking about?"

"Glenn Andrew Vincent Froom," she said by way of explanation.

"Glenn Andrew Vincent," I repeated slowly.

"Yes, otherwise known as Gav," she said.

My heart began to race as I made sense of what she was saying.

"Your Gav?" I stuttered.

"Yes. I must say, Frankie, you aren't usually this slow at understanding."

"No . . . , well, uh."

"Would it help if I explained?" she asked.

"Yes," I managed to mutter. Then a thought occurred to me and I said, "Wait, you showed me a picture of Gav when I first met you. It wasn't Glenn."

"No, it was a picture of my brother and me. I knew that you would never actually meet him, so it was easy to pretend that he was my boyfriend. I knew that if you thought you knew what my boyfriend looked like, it would put you at your ease. And I was right. Just look at how you were with Rebecca's Sam. You thought that Glenn was masquerading as Sam."

"I wasn't completely wrong about him. Sam turned out to be David Shaw."

"True. But you must admit that you are prone to paranoia where Glenn is concerned."

Is she for real? What the hell is going on? I was aware that I was just standing there staring at her.

"No need to answer," she continued. "I was going to explain. I knew Glenn as Gav. It had been his nickname during his school days. We'd agreed that I should call him it, so that if his name should ever slip out of mouth inadvertently, no one would be suspicious."

"You were having an affair," I guessed.

"Yes. Verity was a member of my team as you know. We had to be careful. I could talk about my boyfriend, Gav, and no one knew that I was really talking about Glenn. It's clever, isn't it?"

"Inspired," I replied.

"Are you being sarcastic?" she asked.

I was taken aback by the menace in her tone. Did she mean to do me harm? My instincts screamed that extreme caution was required.

"No," I answered.

"Good. As I was saying, we were having an affair. He'd tell that stupid, weak bitch that he was working away, and he'd meet me in a hotel somewhere."

So it was Maria that he'd been with when Verity thought he was away on business. He'd admitted that he was seeing another woman on the day he'd tried to kill me. I hadn't imagined that it was Maria. She'd been Verity's supervisor. She had worked with her every day. Glenn must have been referring to Maria when he had described his other woman to me as 'a good girl' who 'understood the situation'. Then it hit me.

"It was you that told him Verity had stood up to you at work. That she was still going to counselling even though he'd told her not to."

"Yes, he had a right to know," she said as if her actions were completely justified.

"I'd thought perhaps Verity felt pressured by you at work simply because you hadn't appreciated her workload, but now I see that you were putting undue pressure on her because you were jealous of her. You were, weren't you?"

"Jealous of HER?" she exploded. "Don't be ridiculous! She was pathetic!" she spat. "It was easy to bully her."

Then it occurred to me that was how Glenn had known to look under Verity's trays on her desk, and why he had found the women's refuge card: Maria had told him where to look.

"It was you!" I said, shaking my head in disbelief.

"What was?" she asked.

"You told Glenn where Verity hid things that she didn't want him to see."

"Yes, he had a right to know that she was hiding things from him."

"Did you know, at the time, what she was hiding?" I asked, already suspecting that she hadn't.

"No."

I started to laugh at the extreme irony of the situation.

"Why are you laughing?" she demanded.

"Well, you now know that it was a card for a women's refuge, right?"

"Yes."

"If you had left well alone, she would have left him. And who knows, the two of you could have lived happily ever after. Instead . . ."

"No," she said talking over me, "I know the press said that she was trying to leave him, but they were wrong and so are you. He killed her because she would never have let him leave. She was never going to leave him. She clung to him; holding on to their loveless marriage. It was pathetic to watch."

"No, Maria, that's not how it was. He told me himself that he killed her because he found a card I'd given her for a women's refuge. He said that no one left him. He wouldn't allow it."

"Stop lying!" she screamed while taking a step toward me and raising her hand as if she might strike me.

Instinctively, I covered my head with my arms to protect myself. She seemed to think better of it and lowered her hand again.

"He loved me. He was going to leave her. He rang me that morning: the morning Verity died. He asked me how I felt about going to Australia. We were running away together. We ARE running away together," she corrected.

"But he committed suicide," I interjected.

She started laughing hysterically. "No, that was a ruse. You were all meant to believe that he'd killed himself, but we'd arranged to meet in Australia once everything died down. He was going first; I'd follow a few months later."

"And yet, here you are, still here over a year later," I stated. I was incredulous at her continued blind faith in a plan hatched by a deranged murderer.

"I've been waiting for him to get in touch," she said, her loyalty to the man undeniable.

"So, does your imminent trip to Australia mean that he finally has?" I asked. I was confused. Glenn was dead. Wasn't he?

I watched as she started to bite her lower lip and suddenly appear flustered.

"I've decided to go and find him. It can't be too difficult," she said.

"No, it can't be too difficult," I agreed, "because Australia isn't a big country or anything," I added sarcastically. She was seriously deluded.

The pain exploded in my cheek before I'd even realised that she'd hit me. I took a step backwards and lost my footing. I fell backwards, dropping the bottle bag that contained the champagne, and landed on the floor. My hand flew to my cheek instinctively. It felt like it was on fire. Pains were shooting through my jaw.

"Agh, what the hell are you doing?" I demanded.

"Shut your mouth, you stupid little bitch. Do you understand?"

"Yes," I said as I struggled to my feet. I felt a little dizzy, so I reached out my hand in the hopes that I'd find a piece of furniture that I could lean on to steady myself. Needless to say, I'd never seen this side of her before. I wondered whether I should tell her Glenn was dead or not. Perhaps not yet. Instead I asked, "So, the suicide note and his clothes et cetera were just to make the police think that he had killed himself, so they'd stop searching for him?"

"Yes. He's an excellent swimmer. He knew that he would have to get into the water and swim to the beach in order to avoid detection. He told me that he'd put some clothes in a waterproof bag and buried them in the sand between some rocks at Uphill Beach in Weston-Super-Mare. He'd studied a map and knew it was approximately a mile from his entrance into the water to his exit. He assured me that he regularly swam at least a mile at his local swimming baths. He was sure that he could do it."

She actually sounded proud of his swimming prowess. I couldn't believe what I was hearing. "OK, let's assume that he manages to swim a mile in the freezing Bristol Channel. He changes his clothes and makes good his escape. Then what? How did he think that he'd get away with it? The police checked his bank accounts. He didn't make any unusual cash withdrawals either in the weeks leading up to his disappearance or after."

She grinned. "But they didn't check my bank account. Did they?"

"You gave him the money to escape?"

"Yes, of course. I'd have given him anything he asked for."

"Have you given him any money since that day?"

"No. But I didn't need to. He told me that he was going to use part of the money I gave him to get a fake passport. He knew a guy who could supply him with one."

"So you assumed that he'd got himself a new identity and flown to Australia?"

"Yes."

"Then why hasn't he contacted you?" I asked.

She raised her hand once again as if to strike me.

"No, please. I'm not trying to upset you. The question must have crossed your mind, surely?"

I appeared to have appeased her because she lowered her hand.

"I have considered the question many times. Do you want to know what conclusion I've reached?"

"Yes, of course." Perhaps I wouldn't have to tell her that he was dead. Perhaps she had secretly reached that conclusion and this trip to Australia was just . . .

She interrupted my thoughts as she said, "I think that he's angry with me for not finishing what he started."

Oh, I hadn't expected that.

"What exactly are you meant to finish?" I asked.

"You, I'm meant to finish you," she said as calmly as one might talk about the weather.

I took a step backwards. "What?"

"Don't you see? When I kill you and fly to Australia, he will know just how much I love him. I will have proved myself to him. I had thought originally that he wanted me to terrorise you. I thought that would be enough, but now I see it isn't. He won't contact me until you're dead."

Holy crap, this woman is insane. How the hell had I missed that? Call myself a counsellor. If I got out of this alive, which I was beginning to doubt, I wasn't going to counsel anyone ever again. How the hell was I going to talk myself out of this?

"You terrorised me?"I asked.

She started to laugh. "Of course I terrorised you. It was so easy. Do you want to know when it started?"

"Was it the day that we met in the church? Let me guess, you befriended me on purpose. You knew exactly who I was, and you targeted me."

I remembered how upset I'd been at seeing Verity's scarf that day. The scarf Maria had said Verity had bought and had been so excited about. A theory started to formulate in my mind.

"Did you tell Glenn about Verity's shopping trip? Did you tell him about her excitement at buying the purple scarf?" I didn't wait for her to reply as I already knew the answer. "That's why he offered to take her shopping the day she died. He knew that she'd be so excited at the prospect. Perhaps, she even thought that he might be mellowing. And the whole time he was revelling in the fact that he was going to throw her from a multi-storey car park."

Maria laughed. It was a chilling sound.

"Of course I told him," she said. "Don't you get it? I told him everything I could about that spineless, plain little nothing."

I shuddered at the ferocity of her words. "I suppose you brought Verity's scarf to the church that day on purpose. You intended that I should see it; that it would have the effect on me that it did," I added.

"I did, and you're right that was precisely why I brought it that day. I never intended to give it to Verity's parents. Why would I? I didn't want to offer them any comfort. After all, if they hadn't spawned that silly cow none of this would have happened. My sole intention was to watch the terror in your eyes at the sight of the scarf. I knew that Glenn had planned to kill you with her scarf, so I guessed what seeing one of her scarves would do to you. But that wasn't when it started."

"But I didn't know you before that," I stated.

"No, you didn't. But I knew you. 'I WARNED YOU BITCH!' " she said with meaning.

I gasped. "The graffiti on my front door that day Glenn tried to kill me. It was you!"

I'd wondered at the time how Glenn could have daubed graffiti on my front door and rang my doorbell one minute and been standing in my kitchen the next. It made sense that he'd had an accomplice. Woah! The woman I'd seen walking away down the street shortly after I'd discovered the graffiti; it had been her. Oh my God!

My eyes had grown accustomed to the darkness in the room, and I could see her facial expression as she clearly revelled in my shock. A smug smile played at the edges of her lips.

"Yes, it was me."

"But why help him? You're not a murderer!"

Her smile grew broader at my words.

"After he'd killed Verity that day, he called me as I said."

I interrupted her. "The police found Glenn's mobile phone that day with the rest of his belongings. They didn't find a trace of any calls that he'd made that morning."

"He had a separate pay-as-you-go phone that he used to call me. It was our secret. He told me that he would throw it in the sea and that the police would never find it. He was protecting me you see."

"How thoughtful of him," I muttered under my breath not wishing to incite her fury further.

"He suggested that we go to Australia," she continued. "He said that he had to leave now. I was to fly out later. He needed cash, and he needed it immediately. I guessed that something bad had happened. I assured him that whatever he'd done it wouldn't change how I felt about him."

Oh please, pass me a sick bag. What kind of a fool was she? No, scrub that. She wasn't a fool; she was something much more dangerous—she was a deranged worshipper.

"He came to my house and then drove me to my bank where I withdrew all of my savings. I handed him the cash, and he explained how he'd told Verity about us. How she'd refused to accept it. She told him that she would never allow him to leave her. She would make his life a misery. So you see, he had to do it—for us, so we could be together. Do you understand?"

I nodded, appearing to play along with her version of events.

"But why come after me?" I asked. "Why not just get on a plane and escape?"

"I asked him that when he said that he needed to drop by your house. He said that it had been you that had convinced Verity to stay committed to the marriage. It had been you that had encouraged her to become strong-willed and insist that they keep trying to make it work."

If only she knew that nothing could be further than the truth. As she spoke, I could see the hatred that she felt for me in her eyes.

She continued, "So, it was your fault that he had to kill her. He felt that you deserved the same fate for meddling in other people's lives."

She had clearly accepted his twisted, evil logic that I should die. What's more, she was prepared to see his plan through because she'd convinced herself that it was the only way to get him to contact her.

"And you agreed with him?" I asked.

"Yes! I was only too happy to do as he asked. I painted the graffiti on the door and rang the bell, and then I walked away as he had told me to do."

I shuddered at the matter-of-factness of her words. It was as if she considered her actions to be perfectly acceptable in the circumstances.

"But his plan didn't work. I didn't die," I said, aware that I was stating the obvious.

"I know. I decided that while I waited for Glenn to make contact, I'd get to know you. I'd make you pay in another way. I was confident that he'd approve. It didn't take me long to realise that the best way to exact my revenge was to exploit your belief that Glenn was still alive. I would make you think that Glenn was stalking you."

"How clever of you," I commented.

"Thank you. I thought so.  At first, I left the occasional silent answer machine message, untraceable of course. I knew that you'd think it was Glenn calling."

"Congratulations! I did think it was Glenn calling. But no one else would believe me."

"I know. Genius, wasn't it? Everyone thought that you were going crazy except for your good pal, Maria."

What a first-class bitch, I thought.

She continued, "After you'd received the mysterious bunch of flowers, I decided that it was too good an opportunity to be missed. I have to say, I did rather enjoy your reaction to the black silk scarf that I sent to your office.

"Did you like the accompanying note?" she said, and proceeded to recite what she'd typewritten word for word. " 'Thank you for everything. How can I repay you?' To the world it would seem like the innocent words of a grateful client, but I knew that you'd see the veiled threat contained within them. I watched as you turned ashen and then fainted. I enjoyed the spectacle."

I had come to believe that Richard had sent me the scarf as well as the flowers. But come to think of it, he hadn't actually admitted to that particular gift. How had Maria known about the flowers? I couldn't recall ever having told her about them.

"Let me guess, you're wondering how I knew about the flowers?"

I nodded.

"Well, I happened to pop into your office block to see you the day you received them. You'd already left for the day. Theresa really was exceptionally chatty. She couldn't wait to tell me all about the mysterious bouquet of flowers you'd received."

That made sense; in view of the fact that I suspected Theresa had told Rebecca the same thing. Rebecca had known about the bouquet during our weekend away and had questioned me about it. What had she said? Ah, yes, 'a little dickybird' had told her. A Theresa-shaped dickybird I'd warrant.

Maria had said that she'd seen me faint in reception on the day I'd received the scarf, but I couldn't recall seeing her.

"You saw me faint. Where were you?" I asked.

"I was sitting in my car. I'd parked directly in front of reception. I had the perfect view of the scene that unfolded."

"Wasn't that risky? What if I'd seen you?"

"So what if you had? I would have merely invented a reason for coming to see you. Perhaps, I was there to take you for a cup of tea to cheer you up. You wouldn't have suspected me, Frankie. Let's face it; you've never suspected me of anything."

Hmm, she was right. I had been completely blind where she was concerned.

"Do you know what I enjoyed the most?" she said with obvious glee.

"What?" I asked, feeling sick to the pit of my stomach.

"The way that I could send you to the edge of hysteria one minute and then pull you back from the brink the next by convincing you that there was a plausible explanation for what you'd experienced."

"I don't understand," I said, feeling a mixture of confusion and complete horror as a result of her admission.

"No, of course you don't. Let me enlighten you. When we were in the pub recently, you received a silent call while I was in the ladies' room. Do you remember how you lost your shit for a few moments as you kept asking who it was and no one spoke?"

"It was you. You admitted it at the time," I stated.

"Yes, but I said that I'd inadvertently called you without realising. Remember?"

"Hmm, so you're saying . . . ?"

"I'm saying that I called you on purpose you dumb bitch. I was sitting there smiling the whole time. Lapping up the fear that I heard building in your voice. I thought it was pure genius to admit I'd called you and that it had all been a mistake. Poor Frankie! Did you think that you were going mad?

"Oh and I almost forgot that night you were away with Rebecca in Bournemouth. Those stupid rambling text messages that you sent me about some guy that you'd met. Well I couldn't have that. You don't get to be happy; not when you've wrecked my life. I knew that if I called you over and over again on your mobile, it would freak you out. It was a shame that you appeared to be too drunk to answer.

"Still, I knew that you'd be unnerved when you saw how many missed calls you'd received from an unknown caller. And then, finally, the next day you answered the phone. I wasn't disappointed by the abject fear I heard in your voice. I couldn't resist following up the silent call with a text message. I imagined you jumping out of your skin in fright as your phone pinged to signal the arrival of a text message. Was I right?" she asked, eager to have her suspicions confirmed.

"Yes. But I don't understand. Why didn't my phone recognise that it was you calling me that night? Why were the calls displayed as having come from an unknown caller?"

"I have a separate pay-as-you-go phone for just such an occasion, Frankie."

It would seem that she'd thought of everything.

"Rebecca thought that the calls had been made by the guy I had met the night before. So did I, eventually," I continued.

She nodded knowingly. "Excellent! That was exactly what I had intended. I knew the minute I read your text telling me that you'd given some random guy your telephone number that I could turn it to my advantage. Luckily, on this occasion, Rebecca unwittingly did my job for me.

"Of course, I didn't anticipate the whole Abigail situation. It was remiss of me because I know what an interfering bitch you are. It makes sense that you would have incurred someone else's wrath. I admire Abigail. But the timing of the photograph and kidnap incident was unfortunate. The photograph was a credible threat, and one that I knew the police would take seriously. I couldn't afford for them to start poking around. I even wondered if Glenn had decided to come back to finish you off himself."

"At the time, you tried to convince me that Peggy may have sent the photograph," I recalled.

"Of course I did. If it was from Glenn, then I didn't want him discovered."

I remembered her keen interest when I'd mentioned that the police had checked Glenn's accounts for any recent activity. I'd assumed it was out of concern for me, but now I knew otherwise. She'd wanted to know if her precious Glenn was back in the country. I recalled how alarmed she'd sounded when I'd told her that I'd suggested to the police that Glenn had a different identity now. She hadn't been concerned for me but that somehow the police would discover his identity. After all, she believed that he was living under an assumed identity. She didn't know that he was dead.

She was breathtakingly manipulative. Still I could take some small comfort in the fact that she wasn't a murderer; despite her recently proclaimed intent to kill me. It was one thing to talk about murder but quite another to see it through.

"Maria, I can understand why you've done these things to me. Really, I can. But, killing me? You're not a murderer. Do you really think you're capable of taking a life?"

"Oh spare me your counselling mumbo jumbo. Don't think that crap will work on me. I don't THINK I can take a life. I KNOW I can."

"What do you mean?" I asked, my fear increasing with her every word.

"I've already taken a life. I had to. I wasn't ready for you to find out, you see. I wasn't ready for you to know that it was me."

"Who have you killed?"

"Peggy."

"But she fell down the stairs. It was an accident."

"No, I pushed her down the stairs."

My hands flew automatically to my mouth to stifle the scream that I felt rising from within.

"But why?" I gasped unable to comprehend her possible reason.

"She'd seen me. It was her comment to us on the day Henry went missing that made it obvious she'd seen me."

I was confused. What was she talking about? What had Peggy said? Something about her being glad we'd 'sorted out our differences' and needing 'your friends at times like these'. I had dismissed her words as nothing more than an old lady getting us confused with someone else. Had I been wrong?

"I volunteered to go and tell her that Henry had been found. Do you remember?" she asked.

"I do. I watched you walk next door from my living room window." I couldn't recall what I had been doing at the time. Then I remembered that I'd been talking to Michael Graham.

"Well, when I got there, I asked her if she'd seen me that night. She admitted that she had. She thought that you knew it was me and had forgiven me. I asked her to show me which upstairs window she'd seen me from. She was happy to oblige me. The silly old dear had no idea of the danger she was in. Well, not until she felt my hand in the small of her back as she stood at the top of the stairs. She turned to look at me in shock. I could see from the expression in her eyes that she knew what was coming next."

I could hear her words, but somehow I couldn't make sense of them. It was all so unreal.

"I don't understand. What night are you talking about?" I questioned.

"Oh, for pity's sake, I'm referring to the night your garden was decimated. I did it! You were so happy and excited that night as we sat in the pub, and you told me how you were going out on a date with Leo. You even blushed. Have you got any idea how angry that made me feel? Do you? You were the reason why I couldn't be with my true love. I couldn't allow you to be happy.

"The silent call in the bar wasn't enough for me. Sure it had unnerved you, but I wanted more: I wanted to eviscerate your happiness. When you told me about the contretemps with Peggy, I saw an opportunity to destroy your precious garden and eventually point the finger of suspicion at her. I knew how much you loved your garden. You were always going on about how beautiful it was. How relaxed it made you feel to stand and gaze at your flowers and the birds. I knew, initially, that you'd instinctively think it was Glenn's handiwork and then eventually Peggy's, never once suspecting the real culprit."

"You!" I stated. I remembered her appearing to be put out when I told her about my date with Leo, but I'd assumed that it was because I had discussed it with Rebecca and not her. I hadn't suspected the real reason.

"Yes. I have to say, I was rather disappointed when I rang you the next morning and you were so upbeat. I had expected you to be a nervous, sobbing wreck."

I remembered the call. "You said that you were ringing because I'd left my umbrella in the car. Come to think of it, I don't recall you ever returning it."

"I didn't return it because there was no umbrella. I needed an excuse to call you that morning. I wanted to hear the terror I'd inflicted in your voice, but you'd already decided it was Peggy. I'd anticipated that I'd have to convince you of Peggy's guilt, but you'd already arrived at that conclusion on your own."

"That same morning Mum was adamant that she'd locked the garden gate, but it was open. I assumed that she'd left it unlocked. But now, I'm not so sure."

She was grinning like a Cheshire cat as she said, "I know where you keep the spare key for the gate. You keep it in the cutlery drawer. I noticed it when I was making a cup of tea at your house when you first moved in. I knew that it may come in handy one day, and I was right. You didn't even check that it was still there after what happened. You were happy to accept that your mum had forgotten to lock it despite her protestations to the contrary."

She was right. I was guilty as charged.

"I put the key back where it belonged on the day that Henry went missing. Oh and by the way, when you thought that I was being a great friend and searching for your bastard son, I was actually at home revelling in your distress.

"However, once it became obvious from the old dear's comment that she'd seen me that night, I had to silence her. I couldn't risk her telling you that it had been me. I wanted to be the one to tell you. I wanted it to be a surprise."

"Oh, you've succeeded. I'm well and truly surprised," I said feeling both surprised and repulsed in equal measure.

She chuckled.

"She didn't die that night. You took quite a risk. What if she had regained consciousness and told everyone that you pushed her?" I questioned.

"I know. It was a dilemma: did I finish her off and risk a murder investigation? Or did I hope that such a frail old lady wouldn't last the night lying injured on the cold hallway floor?"

I shuddered at the complete lack of feeling in her words. She was talking about taking Peggy's life as if it were nothing, as if she were nothing.

"But she did survive the night. She was tougher than you thought," I challenged.

"Yes, she was," she conceded.

A thought occurred to me. Harold had assumed it was me who had called the hospital everyday asking after Peggy. I now knew who it was. "It was you who rang the hospital every day to check on Peggy's condition. What if they'd told you that she'd regained consciousness? What then?"

"I would have had to execute my plan before I was ready."

"Kill me, you mean?"

"Yes."

"I'm curious. Why wait? Why today?"

"It's our anniversary. Three years today. Killing you will be my anniversary present to him."

"How do you propose to get away with it? Won't your guests start arriving soon?"

"Oh, Frankie, you really are so gullible. There is no party. There never was. The only invite issued was yours. I'll be leaving for the airport," she paused to check her watch, "in thirty minutes' time. You've told everyone that you're staying the night, so no one will miss you until . . . shall we say ten o'clock tomorrow morning? By that time, I'll be well on my way to Australia."

I'd told Mum not to expect me back until midday, at the earliest. I wasn't going to tell Maria that.

"But everyone knows that I'm here. This is the first place they'll look. As soon as they find me, they'll know it was you."

"You think that I don't know that? It's what I want. I want my face emblazoned across every news channel together with what I did."

"Why?"

"Then he'll know. Glenn will know that I finished what he started, and he'll know that I'm on my way to meet him. He'll come and find me."

"But the police will work out that you've left the country. They'll be waiting for your plane to land in Australia."

"No, they won't. She produced a passport from her pocket. The day that Glenn left he gave me the details of a guy that I could contact for a fake passport. And violà!" She waved it around in the air proudly. "Say hello to Lindsey Baker. I have a fetching blonde wig upstairs that I need to put on before I leave."

"You really have thought of everything," I commented.

"I'm smarter than you. That's for sure," she scoffed.

I couldn't take it any longer. This mad bitch thought that she was just going to kill me and walk away. I was sick of being afraid. I'd been afraid of Glenn for so long, and now I knew he was dead. But she didn't. No one was coming to save me this time. I was on my own. No matter what happened, I was going down fighting.

"Are you really smarter than me? I know something about Glenn that you don't," I goaded.

Her rage was sudden and volcanic as her hand flew out. I felt her talon-like nails cut through the soft skin on my cheek. Something wet was trickling down my face. I had to fight every instinct in my body not to retaliate in kind. Not yet, Frankie, not yet, I told myself.

"What?" she spat. "There is nothing that you can tell me about Glenn that I don't already know—NOTHING!"

Now it was my turn to have the upper hand. "Oh, but there is."

"Huh, go on then," she said, her tone of voice inviting me to do my worst.

"Glenn is . . . ," I paused for maximum effect and then hit her with it, "DEAD!"

She snorted, "Don't you listen, you thick bitch. I already told you that it was a ruse to escape."

"They found his skull in the sea," I said. Ignoring her outburst, I pressed on. "I found out earlier this week, but I hadn't had chance to tell you the good news. That's what I wanted to tell you earlier, before you led me in here."

"You're lying! He's alive. I'd know if he was dead. We have a connection: a deep bond. I'd know, I'd know," she screamed at me.

"He's dead!" I shouted at the top of my voice seeking to drive my point home with sheer decibels.

"Stop saying that. It's not him."

"It is. They compared the teeth in the skull with his dental records. They're sure. He died the day that he jumped into the sea. He wasn't as good a swimmer as he thought he was," I said.

I saw her raise her hand as if to strike me again, but this time I was ready for her. My clenched fist shot out first and connected with her jaw. Oh Christ! That hurt, I thought as pain shot through my hand. I hoped it hurt her more than it had me. She reeled backward and fell awkwardly to the floor. I'd caught her off guard. She clearly hadn't expected me to defend myself.

Seeing my chance to make a break for the lounge door I seized it. I recollected the coffee table's central position in the room and was careful to avoid it. I had the door in my sights when I felt a great weight descend upon me from above. Jesus, she must have used that very same coffee table to launch herself at me. The weight of her was crushing, and I crashed to the ground with her on top of me.

I was face down on the carpet. Her weight kept me pinned there. She shifted slightly, so that she was putting more weight on my upper body. It was hard to breathe. I could move my arms and hands but only along the surface of the carpet. I couldn't raise them.

"Aargh!" I screamed as she pulled my head backwards. She had clumps of my hair in her hands; it felt as if she was attempting to rip it out from the root. I wriggled and writhed in my attempts to free myself. It felt as if I needed the strength of a bucking bronco to unseat her rather than the strength of a Shetland pony that I was currently displaying. How was I going to get out of this? I wondered.

"Do you want to know how I intend to kill you?"

I could feel her hot breath against my ear; her face only millimetres from mine. I could barely breathe let alone talk. I banged my hand on the floor like a wrestler in the ring when they want their opponent to show them mercy. She lifted her weight off of me just enough so that I could speak.

"How?" I choked.

"With this of course! Oh, don't worry! You don't need to see it. You'll recognise what it is the moment it touches your skin."

I could feel silk wrap around my throat. Oh no! Not again!

"You see, I knew that you'd recognise the feeling. When I said that I'd finish what Glenn started, I meant it."

She pulled the scarf tight. I was powerless to fight it. She once again put her full weight on my back as she pulled my head back with the force of her stranglehold on my neck.

Suddenly, the sound of the doorbell filled the air. It must have caught Maria by surprise because she eased her grip on the scarf and lifted her weight from me. Rather like doing a press up, I put my arms out to each side and pushed up with all my might. It caught her off guard; she toppled to the right side of me. This was my chance, and I jumped to my feet.

"Help me!" I screamed in the hopes that the person at the front door would hear my cries. My hand grabbed the lounge door handle. Precious seconds passed as I tried in vain to open the door.

I could hear her laughing as I struggled. Why wouldn't it open? I kept turning the handle, first one way and then the other; it wouldn't open. I could feel the silk scarf dangling from my neck, and I ripped it off as if it were on fire. I never wanted to feel silk on my skin ever again.

"It's locked. You can't escape this room, Frankie."

She must have locked the door as we entered. I needed a weapon. It was the only way that I was going to get out of here alive. She was once again on her feet, and she was walking toward me. I couldn't let her overpower me again. I edged slowly away from the door. Suddenly, she threw herself at me. I dodged away from her. She managed to seize my arm. With my free arm, I lashed out wildly. My fingers brushed her face. I calculated that all I had to do was move my fingers up a few centimetres and bingo. I drove my fingers into the soft flesh of her eye socket.

She yelped much like a wounded animal and let go of my arm. If I could get to the windows, I could pull back the blackout curtains. At least then I'd have some light. Maybe I could break the window or at least make some noise to attract some attention.

I made a dash for the window. She must have realised what I was thinking because she intercepted me as I reached for the curtain. She pushed me with all her might and I fell awkwardly to the floor. As I reached out to push myself up, I felt it: the bottle bag I'd brought earlier complete with champagne bottle. I reached inside and grabbed the neck of the bottle.

I tucked it under my body. As she leant over me and grabbed my other arm to pull me to my feet, I swung the champagne bottle in a wide arc. It hit the side of her head with a thud. I watched as the force threw her sideways.

I sprung to my feet as adrenaline coursed through my veins. I could see that she was out cold. If she so much as moved, I was ready to hit her again. Where was that key? I put my hand in her trouser pocket, and I felt the hard metal of a key. I pulled it out and ran to the door. My hand was shaking so much that I had trouble getting the key in the lock, but somehow I managed it. As I flung the door wide open, the light from the hallway temporarily blinded me. I stumbled toward the front door and wrenched it open.

A lady was standing there with her back to me. As she started to turn toward me, she said, "It's about time too. I've been waiting ages out here. Show me where the party is." Her smile wavered and her words dried up as she took in my appearance.

"Am I glad to see you," I mumbled as I realised it was Rebecca. "Call the police. I think I may have killed Maria."

# Epilogue

"Are you sure about this?" Leo asked me for the umpteenth time since we'd arrived at the restaurant.

"How many times do I have to say it?" I said gently so as not to hurt his feelings but at the same time trying to make mine clear, so he didn't ask me again.

"OK, OK," he said raising his hands in mock surrender.

"I talked it over with my supervisor, Rachel, today. She didn't like it either, but she respected my decision," I said pointedly.

"I hear you. I won't say another word on the subject."

"Good."

Leo was referring to the fact that I'd decided to give up counselling people. Both Leo, Rachel, and everyone else in my world with the exception of Rob thought it was a bad idea. Rob had never supported my career choice in the first place, so he was the only one relieved by my decision. Well, the only one besides me of course. I was relieved.

Over the last eighteen months, two innocent people had died and my family and I had lived in a perpetual state of fear because of what I did for a living. I'd heard all of the rational arguments against Verity's and Peggy's deaths being my fault, but still I felt responsible. I doubted that would ever change.

"How's Rebecca?" Leo asked.

She was another casualty of my career choice; another burden of guilt that I was carrying.

I nodded. "She's doing OK. She still swears that she's off of men, but I've caught her eyeing up the guy who works in the office opposite on more than one occasion. So I would say that it's just a matter of time."

"That's good."

"Yes. How's Maria?"

He stiffened. I knew how he felt about her after what she'd done to me and what she had wanted to do to me.

"She's undergoing a psychiatric assessment. As you know, she didn't get bail because she's been judged to be a danger to the public."

"Particularly, this member of the public," I said pointing at myself.

"Yes." He dropped his gaze and pretended to study the beer mat on the table.

I reached out and covering his hand with mine I squeezed gently. "I'm OK."

His eyes met mine, and I could see the worry and fear he was feeling.

"I can't get it out of my mind. I keep seeing your bruised and battered face as I arrived at Maria's house."

Leo had arrived at Maria's house seconds after I'd answered the door to Rebecca. He had been shocked to see me. He had followed up on the car that had tried to knock me down at the office earlier that week. He'd managed to identify the registration plate of the car by watching the footage from the surveillance camera that covered Marina Office's car park.

Leo had traced the ownership of the car; it belonged to a Toby Simpton. When he'd visited Toby at his home address earlier that day, Toby had told him that he'd lent the car to his sister on the day in question. His sister was Maria Simpton. At the time, Leo hadn't made the connection between Maria Simpton and my friend Maria. He had just arrived at Maria Simpton's address when he found me holding on to Rebecca all bloody and bruised. It was quite a shock, especially as I proceeded to tell him that I thought I may have killed Maria with a champagne bottle.

Luckily, I'd only knocked Maria out. I hadn't killed her. However, the impact of the champagne bottle had caused her brain to swell. She'd had to stay in hospital for a while but the doctors confirmed that it didn't appear to have caused any long-term brain damage.

When Maria was eventually questioned about the car incident, she had admitted to being the driver that day. So much for the witness thinking it was a male driver. Just goes to show how witnesses can get it so wrong. Maria denied trying to kill me on that occasion. She had just wanted to scare me. It was all part of her campaign of terror aimed at destroying me little by little. She admitted that her intention was always to kill me on her and Glenn's anniversary.

"Well the cuts and bruises have healed nicely," I said sounding more confident than I felt. The outward scars of my ordeal had healed, but I wasn't so sure about the internal ones. I had a feeling that I would carry those for quite some time to come.

"Yes, you're as beautiful as ever."

"Oh please! You're such a charmer! Are you ready?"

He gulped, grabbed my hand and gave it a squeeze. "As I'll ever be."

"It'll be fine. They'll accept you; I'm sure of it."

It was the first time that Leo was officially meeting the Pant Bros as my boyfriend. We were going bowling.

"I hope so. Oh, and by the way, there's something you need to know about me. I haven't been entirely honest with you."

My heart sank. A sense of dread enveloped me. There was only so much one person could take. Please someone give me a break. What next? Was he about to tell me that he was a mass murderer? I stared at him, waiting for the inevitable.

He opened his mouth to speak, his mouth stretching into a broad grin. "You remember our first date?"

"Yes," I said.

"Well . . . I have to confess to hating spiders as much as you do. How I picked that spider up and took it outside, I will never know. Please don't ever ask me to do it again."

A few moments passed as I digested his words and then a bubble of laughter rose to the surface and escaped my open mouth. Followed by another and then another. Well I never! Thankfully, his confession was one that I could live with.

Facebook: www.facebook.com/KBrittBadman/
Twitter: @KBrittBadman
Email: kbrittbadman@gmail.com

Printed in Great Britain
by Amazon